I0583568

The Underland Tarot

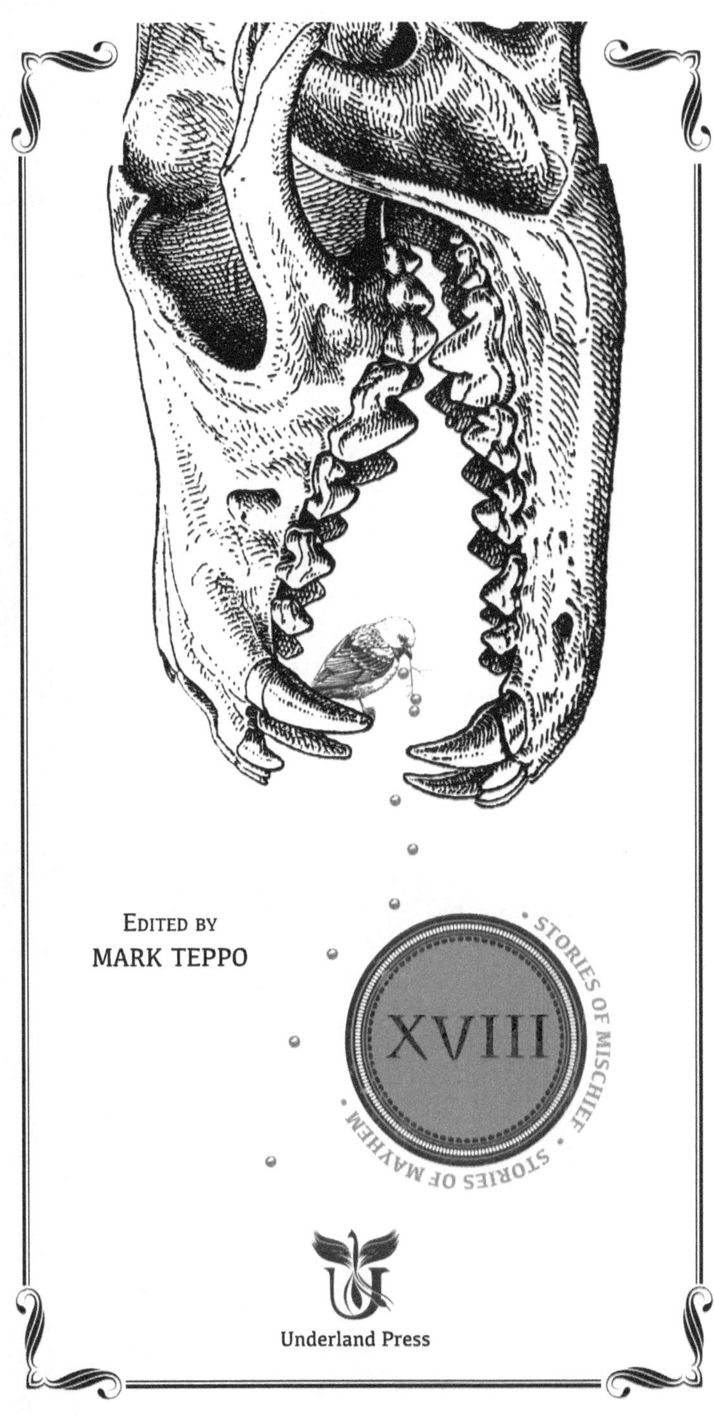

EDITED BY
MARK TEPPO

Underland Press

This book is published by Underland Press, which is part of Firebird Creative, LLC (Clackamas, OR).

One is the path of mercy; the other path is darker.

Edited by Mark Teppo
Book Design and Layout by Firebird Creative.

This Underland Press trade edition: March 2020.
It has an ISBN of 978-1-63023-067-8.

Underland Press
www.underlandpress.com

Contents

To H, who waits for us at the crossing.

The Collective

~ Erica Sage

Nobody tells you that grief has teeth.

She picked up her phone again and swiped through his social media accounts. She stared at the artwork. The devil, a landscape, an owl, a serpent. He'd been commissioned the summer right before it all fell apart, when he started shooting up again.

Nobody tells you that grief gnaws and chews, leaving you hollow and howling.

She put down the phone and pushed the heel of her hands against her closed eyes and breathed and breathed until her sorrow stilled. And then she eyed his ashes sitting at the table with her. A jar of her brother.

Rachel took another sip of wine.

She should've had her dad pick them up, but she tried to spare him.

Now she had a mason jar of her brother, and the contents clanked at the lid of the jar, like a rock collection. Because it was never just ashes. It was bone in there. And maybe teeth. Bone and teeth.

Nobody tells you that ashes are not just ashes.

She unscrewed the ring around the lid and popped off the top of the jar, and there was what remained of her brother. Gray ash and small white chips of bone.

Rachel took another sip of wine. Then she dipped her finger in the glass. She licked away the red drip of her merlot, and poked her wet finger in and out of the mason jar. She stared at the fine dust. There was no difference between her brother and Mount St. Helens. Destruction and ash. If only it were just that, and not so much beauty.

She wiped the ash across her forehead. Up her cheek. The other. Then both again. She was a savage. A wild thing christened. She was a grief goddess. Later, she would wake up in the morning, head aching from wine, eyes swollen by sobs, and she would see those ancient sacred markings, and she would not be embarrassed.

She licked her finger again and dipped it in the jar. This time, when she brought the ashes out, she opened her mouth and dabbed her finger to her tongue. Her brother's ashes tasted like nothing. Or maybe like the time she fell off her bike, splayed out on the dirt, the dust of her clumsiness clouding up around her and into her mouth. Her brother's body was dust. He promised to be so much more.

Rachel peered into the jar. She knew the density of this mess. She and her brother and father had dumped some of her mother's ashes into the creek only a few years before. She'd liked to say "spread," but that was just what people said when they didn't know what happened when a body burned or they wanted to spare you the reality, which is this. Our dead bodies are dense. Or maybe our bones and cells are just loyal. They don't want to spread or soar or fly on a light breeze. They want to spill, dump, fall into one pile. Stick together. Her brother and Rachel had used a broken branch to urge their mother's ashes downstream. They would not budge.

Nobody tells you about the stubborn dead.

Rachel stuck her finger into the jar and stirred, felt the pebbly bone. With her thumb and forefinger, she picked out a piece. Her brother's bone. Maybe it was his femur or his tibia or his phalange or his skull. Maybe a small piece just below his eye socket. Here in her palm. White, fibrous. Burned bright and broken. It was the size of a small rock of heroin, not even enough for a hit.

She put the bone in her mouth. She swallowed him like a pill. Like a cure for the forever without him that spilled out in front of her.

She left the last of her wine in her glass. She didn't drink like her brother had. She crawled into bed, his ashes on her skin, his bone in her belly.

The next morning, Rachel showered, the light everywhere too piercing for her grief. She made coffee, a futile attempt to clear her brain. Maybe if she drank more coffee than creamer.

She drove to her father's.

"You look like hell," he said when she let herself in. He sipped coffee at the table with this crossword book open in front of him.

"Just purgatory."

"As if the eternal present is any better."

She walked to the back bedroom, the gift bag with the mason jar tucked under her arm. Her mother was in a small jelly jar, wrapped in a plastic grocery bag, in the top drawer of the dresser. Some of her was in a creek bed by her childhood home, most of her was in the National Cemetery, but they'd saved some to spread/dump in the ocean. That's where she'd meant to be the day she died. Planning a retirement. Finding a cottage.

Rachel folded the gift bag down and set it next to the grocery bag.

She had not been back to work since her brother had died the week before. She'd been allowed to work from home, but she'd gotten very little done.

She sat before her laptop and pad of paper, like she'd done with the ashes the day before. She'd already finished half a bottle of wine since returning home from her father's, and it was not even the end of a work day yet.

She fingered a pencil. *Tap, tap, tap* on the blank paper, and so it went. So it would go, as it had all week. Nothing getting done. She'd stare at a wall, stare at the table, stare at the empty paper before her, and then minutes would pass. A whole afternoon would pass.

Like every other day, she slipped inside her own head without knowing where or when she'd gone. If she were a reader, she wouldn't remember the paragraph or the chapter she'd just read. But, as she wasn't one to read, she just wouldn't remember the numbers changing on the clock on her screen. And so it went.

But then, as it was, she came back. Her brain woke up, not quite startled, but fully aware again. Only this time, she found she had done something on her pad of paper. Not her job, but a drawing. She'd drawn a face. Not her own, not any countenance she recognized, but clearly a human face. Beautiful, shadowed. Ribbons in her hair, small pearls, eyes that twinkled alive. She had drawn something. Rachel was not an artist, and she did not draw. She had no creative bone in her body.

But here was something.

She flipped to the next page. She stared at the blank space. She rested the pencil on the paper a beat, then decided: a man with a top hat. She sketched a shape. She used no lines to guarantee symmetry. Didn't know lines. She shadowed. Cheeks, jaw. Ears right where they should be. And those eyes. She could draw an eye that had life. And there it was. Exactly the form she saw in her mind.

She folded back the paper. She drew a hand. Next, a cat. And then a fruit bowl. A chair by a fireplace. A barn in a field of wheat. She spent all day drawing anything she saw, anything she thought of. Anything. She was out of paper. She was out of wine.

She wiped her finger at the bottom of the wine glass and licked the red off her skin. She held her fingertip between her teeth, then bit down hard. And then harder. It hurt, but somewhere far away.

You need all fingers to draw, her brother said, but did not say.

Rachel jerked her hand from her mouth.

Try a dog.

"I can draw," she said. "Like you, Josh. Exactly like you." She flipped through the pictures on her desk. She held them up to her own eyes. Her brother complimented each one.

Try a dog.

She drew a dog. It was a fairly simple sketch.

Draw an apple tree.

She did.

Draw Jesus.

She didn't dare. For so many reasons.

Draw the field where we picked blackberries that eventually became pie.

So she did that. It took a bit more time, but Josh watched and waited. He said nothing. He busied himself inside her head, setting up a space for himself.

"You promised you wouldn't overdose," she said while she shadowed behind the sticker bushes, while he moved a large something from one side of her mind to the other side.

I messed up, he said. He clicked on a lamp and stretched out his legs.

Rachel felt the sob at her belly button. It was going to gnaw through her chest.

And then she asked him to tell her exactly how it had happened. Where he got the heroin, where he died. How long he lay there before his body was found. What it felt like. And he told her every-thing, though not all of it made sense, as it would not for someone who had not died before. And then they told stories. About that one time. About all the times. At some point, she fell asleep with her brother somewhere near her. Like in the womb. Like when they had bunkbeds. Like that year when she returned home from college.

Her brother gave her permission to call the man who had attempted years before to commission his artwork. Louis Moelle. When she asked her brother who exactly this man was, Josh laughed at her. *Don't you read the Internet?* He was so rich. So famous. Only the most talented artist and designer. Her brother didn't, however, need to teach her how to pronounce the artist's name properly. Rachel knew a bit of French just then. Her brother had taken three years in high school, after all.

She and Moelle met at a coffee shop near a gallery soon after, enough time for her to put together a portfolio of sorts.

The man leafed through her samples. "So much your brother's style."

"We were twins," Rachel said.

"Yes, I suppose a bit of him will always be inside you."

She did not have to wait to tell her brother that she would be paid to do a painting. And Joshua remained with her while she painted. He didn't have to tell her how to do it. He didn't have to tell her it was beautiful. She had a creative bone in her body.

When Louis Moelle called again, he wanted something more complex. He invited her to join an art collective, just on a singular project, though her involvement could become something more long-term. The project was called The Parade, and it was the 5th annual event in which they invited visual artists to submit a piece on a theme. Writers joined the night of, doing some kind of impromptu poetry that complemented the visual pieces. There would be sculp-tures and paintings.

"I can write poetry too," she said.

He appeared dubious. "Your brother could not."

"It runs in my family. My mom—"

The man held up his hand. Of course she would be a featured artist, and of course she could join on the writing bit too. The fanfare would be directed toward her painting, and she could have a bit of fun with the poetry.

Rachel listened intently that night while her brother lectured her on Moelle's contemporary masterpieces and who bought what and in what gallery she could see them and what artists he'd promoted.

After he left her, tucking himself in somewhere, turning out a light somewhere, Rachel opened a bottle of wine. She thought of poems. She tried to write one, not believing she actually could, but she wanted to try her own hand at it first. She opened her sketch book and wrote something about city streets. The result would make a mediocre children's book. She finished the bottle of wine, opened a second. She drew a set of teeth. She shadowed them, stained with age. She wrote a bad poem, exhausting all words that rhymed with gnash, before she twisted the cork back into the bottle of merlot.

Up early the next morning, she paid another visit to her father. When he had gone outside to get the mail, she went to the back bedroom and found the plastic grocery bag. She unscrewed the lid on the jelly jar and fingered the dust till she found a smallish bit of bone. She dropped it into her pocket and closed everything up before her father returned to the kitchen.

That night, she took the bit of her mother's bone and swallowed it with the leftover wine.

She took out a pencil and pad of paper. She knew a poem would come. Her mother was never published. She never tried, but her words were immaculate. Her sentences—her sentences!—were beautiful. Internal rhyme and whimsical images. In fact, this is why she knew her mother loved her brother more than her. They shared this ability to—

I absolutely did not love your brother more than you, her mother stated.

Rachel had assumed, of course, she'd come, just as her brother had.

And here she was.

The last time she'd seen her mother, she lay on the floor, mouth fallen open and fingertips turning blue. So fast. She was gone and cold and so far away and so not at all her mom so fast. And now she wasn't gone.

I'm here. I'm here.

And she was. And Rachel felt relief, and Rachel felt something else.

Rachel, what did you do? Joshua marched over too quickly, leaned against something. Her mind titled.

"Stop doing that," she said.

There is like barely any room in here for my stuff, and now Mom?

"Josh."

Joshua, there is plenty of space if you would just, her mom struggled against a heavy something, *move this over here. I can be right,* she pushed, *here.*

I put that there for a reason.

"Mom."

Her brain went silent.

"Joshua, it's Mom."

I've been dead for months. This is not the first time I've seen Mom, Rachel.

And did she just hear a snicker, or perceive an exchanged glance? An inside joke inside her head?

"Can you just let Mom and I have a moment?"

Where am I supposed to go?

"How am I supposed to know?"

He was gone.

I'm right here, honey.

And she was. And she was. And she was.

And Rachel longed to touch her faraway hands.

The next morning, her coffee black and thick and perfect (cream sounded far too rich, she was pleased to note) and her pencil and paper ready, Rachel wrote and she wrote and she wrote. Beautiful things. Tiny bits of poetry. Short stories.

"Did you ever write a novel?" she asked her mom.

I just didn't have the time.
"Well, I'm going to."
It's not like I didn't have the talent.
"I'll write it for you then."

Rachel wrote and she painted. Days upon days. There were times when she felt a block of sorts, but she'd always create something if she sat down and kept at it. She didn't need to ask her mother or brother for ideas or for lessons.

The night before The Parade, her painting complete and perfect, her brother asked what she'd named it.

"'Every Taste in the Forest,'" she said.

Too long.

"Well, I like it."

Rachel, it's too long. And kind of mundane. Don't be so literal.

"I can name it what I want." She lit a cigarette. Exhaled. "It's my painting."

Her brother knocked something over. He claimed breaking the thing was an accident.

She'd invited her brother and mother to The Parade, and they both came, though Rachel demanded they sit still and remain quiet. Joshua had been giving her the silent treatment anyway, but she couldn't have them rearranging their belongings unexpectedly.

The painting was received well, and later—in response to the praise of her writing—she'd applied for and was awarded a small grant for an Indie Writers retreat. A full month. She would have to quit her job.

Her employer understood what trauma did. They said they'd hold her job for her. A leave of absence.

Rachel let them, although she didn't intend to be back.

Her father thought she'd lost her mind, giving up her career, a career she'd earned in degrees and the debt that goes with them.

But she was an artist now. A painter and a writer.

○

Moelle came to her again, this time not to commission her work. Instead, he wanted her to participate more fully in the collective. He wanted her to meet some people, talk to some people. He invited her to a garden soiree. Cocktails. Fine clothes. Would she join him. The man had ideas for her. Things he could see her doing. Projects for the rest of her days, if she liked.

She was flattered. She assumed her mother and brother would be too, though she'd have to wait to tell them. They'd been bickering, so they hadn't heard Moelle's invitation.

Her father stayed mostly quiet on her accomplishments and direction. He didn't attend her social events, her poetry reading, her author visit to the library, the museum that featured her first piece, the coffee shop where she sold prints of her paintings.

And of course she was not earning much money, as her father pointed out regularly. Yes, she'd sold some work, but it wasn't what she had been earning. Not even close. And she wanted to keep writing and painting. She loved what she was able to produce. She loved how (mostly) pleased her mother and brother were.

At the soiree, Louis Moelle urged her to invest her energies in the collective's projects. "The Parade is one event. Imagine partnering with designers and filmmakers. Imagine touring with like-minded artists. Imagine a movement."

Rachel didn't know any filmmakers.

The man sighed. "You have gifts. True, beautiful, raw talent."

"I'm not sure I can afford not to work."

"Art is about the soul. It is not about money." The man waved over a server with another tray of cocktails. "Sometimes you get lucky, and sometimes you are born into it."

"And if you are neither?" Rachel asked, unsure if he was talking about art or money.

"Invest right."

The waiter arrived and bent low to offer the cocktails. Moelle reached for a glass, and Rachel watched his fingers, the bones under his skin moving like the felt hammers inside a piano.

Rachel could try her hand at investing. She asked the waiter, "Do you serve wine here?"

○

"How was that party of yours?" her father asked the next morning when she arrived.

Rachel told him about the conversation with Moelle, about his offer to join the collective, about art not being about money.

"Something only a rich person could say."

"He suggested investing and talked about branding. You know, like Aunt Sherry used to do. Like with my art and writing, I could—"

"You look hung over."

"Okay, never even mind what I'm trying to talk to you about," Rachel snapped.

Yes, she *had* been drinking more. And she *did* know that her brother started with alcohol before the Oxy and Xanax and the heroin. Of course she knew.

And now she had her brother in her head. *Faites attention,* he'd said, every time she'd pour another glass. And with their mother nodding (somehow Rachel knew this) next to him. As if her mother even understood French.

"And you're smoking."

Rachel ignored him.

"You had a problem with your mom smoking, but you have no problem doing it yourself now."

She, in fact, wanted a cigarette right then. "Where are Aunt Sherry's ashes?"

"What do you need those for?"

"Well, at some point, we need to bury these people. They can't just sit in a dresser drawer."

"Jesus Christ, Rachel." He leaned back in his chair and crossed his arms over his chest. He stared at Rachel, and she waited him out. "Aunt Sherry wasn't cremated. She's buried."

Rachel bought a shovel, a crowbar, and a mallet from the hardware store on her way home. She also stopped and bought two bottles of wine and a pack of cigarettes.

Aunt Sherry, her dad had told her, was buried in the same cemetery as Jimi Hendrix.

"I knew she had a marker there, but I thought we always kept some ashes," she'd said.

"Why are you so interested in her all the sudden?"

"I miss her." This was as true as the reason she would never tell him.

"It's been over twenty years," her father said.

"It's never long enough." Nobody tells you that grief is teeth, lasting long after the body's gone.

Rachel had already drunk a bottle of wine before she parked her car.

It took hours to dig deep enough.

It took less to break open the coffin.

It took another half a bottle of wine for her to actually open it.

And when she did, mallet in hand, she realized twenty years was most certainly not long enough.

She hadn't planned on needing a blade of some kind. She had only planned to open the casket and use the mallet. Now, she traded that tool for the crowbar. At least it had some sharp edges.

At the gala, Rachel wore a long gown. Too expensive and probably a little too loose. She'd lost weight this past year as her back had started hurting more. The hunching with the writing and the painting. Not much helped with the pain anymore. It was constant, so she dealt with it as was customary these days, with prescriptions being written so sparingly.

She'd worn the dress anyway, despite the fact her mother and brother liked a different one. She'd told them to just stay home then. They were not coming to the gala.

Her brother slammed a door somewhere, and her mother watered the indoor plants she'd potted despite the fact her brother hated them. *It's like a jungle in here,* he'd said. *They're going to take over.*

Rachel had wanted to look stunning in her dress. The artwork looked stunning. Her debut novel, featured tonight, her eighth or ninth signing event—at her own studio!—looked stunning. That cover art. She'd designed it herself.

She shifted about the room, smiling. She knew people were talking about her weight. It didn't matter. She also knew they were talking about how hard she'd worked, how savvy she'd been. How talented she was. How magnanimous to invest in the collective so generously, securing a future not just for herself but for those younger artists, attempting to gain footing, attempting to make a mark. *No,* she'd told each of them, *I did not inherit my aunt's money. It runs in the family,* she'd said.

She stepped outside into the night air, her clutch in hand, and walked down to the corner. Light laughter drifted from the studio. She only had two more signings planned. Maybe she'd do a tour.

She lit a cigarette.

Rachel.

Rachel rolled her eyes and ignored her aunt.

I saw you speaking with Moelle tonight.

"He wants to meet next week." She took a drag on her cigarette. "An activism through art thing."

When you shook his hand, you held it awfully long.

Rachel waited.

Your thumb on his. The way you pressed. Your thumb on his knuckle, it was . . .

Rachel took a sharp drag on her cigarette.

. . . measuring. His bones.

She exhaled. "He has nice hands. He's an artist."

Indeed, he is an artist.

"I can hear what you're insinuating." Rachel pressed her lips together and shook her head. Then, "I would not do anything to Moelle."

Her aunt stood up and moved across the room. *Need I remind you of what you did to me.*

"You were already dead. I would never *kill* anyone."

Well, he is *an amazing artist, far greater than your brother.*

"Yes, but *I* am an artist, and a writer, and I can brand myself. I didn't just come from it. I wasn't just born into it."

You are not born into *gifts of the soul. They are born* unto *you.*

"Whatever. I have these talents now."

You most certainly do.

Rachel tossed her cigarette onto the ground. "I can't believe you thought I'd do something like that." She turned toward the studio door. "He's not even family."

She

~ Gerri Leen

I was born in this laboratory. I'm a creature of steel and flame and wet cotton. I woke to pain, and she was there.

She looks at me like I should know who she is.

I don't.

I try. I remember nothing. How could I? I was born hours ago, and yet she sits and stares at me, asking me questions I can't answer.

I say I was born and yet to be born is to be a child. I'm not a child. I don't think as a child, or so she says. I don't remember how children think, or speak, or play—play? Do I remember play?

No. She showed me a book, with pictures of children playing. With a doll. A doll with red hair and dressed in green velvet.

But . . . the children in the books were playing with blocks.

"Do I have a doll?"

"It's all right," she says, smiling in a way I don't understand, her hand warm on mine.

Hand—how do I know this word? How do I know how it should feel—cold or warm, soft or hard?

Why does her hand feel so good on mine? Why do I think it should be other places on my body?

"Are you my mother?" The children in the book had a mother.

She laughs. "Oh, heavens, no. I'm not that much older than you. Come see." She leads me down to a looking glass that hangs at the far end of the laboratory. She says I'm beautiful, and I take her word for it. We don't look alike, she with her little glasses and pulled back dark hair. My hair is blonde and wavy and hangs wild around my shoulders. My eyes are green while hers are brown.

Chocolate. I reach out to her reflection and touch her eyes reflected in the glass. "What is chocolate?"

She smiles. "Your favorite."

"My favorite what?"

Her smile dies. "I'll get you some. Soon."

"So it's something you . . . eat?"

"Or drink. You like to drink it."

I nod, but I don't remember drinking it. I only remember water, just hours ago, when I woke screaming, my flesh on fire, and she was there, wrapping me in cool, wet cotton, letting me sip water from a cup, murmuring that I was back.

Where did I go? Would one not have to leave to come back?

"I'm thirsty," I whisper, and I hear an echo of that in my mind—have I said that before? I begin to cough and look down at my hand in alarm.

It's fine. Just a hand. Not covered in . . . red.

"Why was it red?"

She makes a face that somehow I know means she doesn't want to speak of this.

"It was red."

She turns us away from the mirror. "Let's get you some water."

I think I hear her add, "My darling," so I ask, "Am I?"

She turns.

"Your darling?" The words are familiar, like her hand, like the expectation of blood—yes, red is blood. Blood on my hand, on the handkerchiefs, on the bedclothes. "Oh."

She pushes me into a chair, hurries to the pitcher, and pours more water. The sound is so familiar. I close my eyes and feel the soft touch of bedclothes, hear her gentle murmurs as she soothes me.

"You've done this before."

"Yes." She holds the glass for me, and that, too, is familiar. "Always," she whispers. "I will always do this for you."

I wake in a bed this time. She's sitting in a chair by the window, gazing out and the sunshine lights up her hair, giving it a red tinge.

Like the doll. Why do I remember a doll?

She put me to bed in this room last night. Tucked me in and kissed me on the forehead. "Sleep well, my dearest," she said, and then she handed me a glass of water.

Water that tasted strange. But strange in a way that I know.

"You drugged me." I struggle to sit up, and she's at my side in an instant.

"Only because you were fighting sleep, and your body desperately needed to rest. You've been through a lot."

I frown. What could I have possibly been through? I was just born. I look around the room and see a doll sitting on a low dresser. "That—the doll."

She brings it to me. "Do you like it?"

"It's mine." I say this and I know it, somewhere, in the deepest part of me, even though it makes no sense.

She smiles. "Miranda. That's her name."

I touch the doll's red hair and trail my finger along its porcelain cheek. Then I look at her and ask, "What's my name?"

"Isabelle." She says it with such . . . emotion. Heavy and dark, but her eyes are so soft.

"What's your name?"

"Mary." She takes the doll from me. "Let's put this back where it's safe."

"Is it not safe with me?"

"Of course it is," she says gently, but when she puts the doll down, I see that one of its legs flops strangely. She has to fiddle with it to make it sit as it had been. "There, safe as houses."

That saying. She's said it before. I look down, at these butter-cream-colored sheets, at the coverlet in cornflower blue. The bed is made of some dark wood—ebony, I think, but I have no idea how I know that.

"Let's get you dressed for breakfast. It's a big day today. Your first whole day."

I slip out of bed and let her help me with the complicated clothing. She names each piece as she slips it on me: stockings, drawers, chemise, the corset—how uncomfortable this thing is, and she says she is lacing it loosely—then the bustle, the camisole, and petticoat until, finally, a skirt and bodice. She kneels and puts small boots on my feet, brown to match the ivory and brown pattern of my skirt.

"There. Aren't you a sight for sore eyes?"

I touch her cheek beneath her glasses and check to see if her eyes are indeed sore. They don't appear so, the deep brown—chocolate, yes, that is how I cannot help but think of them—seem happy as far as I can tell, and she laughs.

"I've made all your favorites for breakfast, Isabelle."

"How do you know them?"

"I know everything, dearest." She takes my hands in hers, bends down, and kisses them and my body tingles as I seem to remember her lips other places. "I've memorized every detail."

I don't ask how this can be, even though her knowledge seems strange when I myself am not sure of my favorites. I don't ask because she won't give me a straight answer—I know this, if nothing else.

I find her in the laboratory after breakfast. She left me to wander the house, and it's huge and somewhat dark. There are no pictures anywhere—no photographs, I mean. There are plenty of paintings scattered around the walls of this place.

Then I wondered how I know what a photograph is. I can picture one, a hazy image of Mary and me, taken...when? Is this a memory I have concocted?

She's sitting at a steel table, a white cat lying stretched out before her.

"Is he ill?" I hurry over and feel a pang as I look at him.

"He is." She doesn't stop me from touching the creature, and he sniffs my hand, then rubs his cheek against it.

"What a sweet animal." He lets out a small cry and I lean down. "What is it?" He licks me, his scratchy tongue making me laugh, and I say, "Snow, stop it."

How do I know his name?

I look up at Mary, and she closes her eyes for a moment. "Snow's sick, Isabelle."

"What's wrong with him?"

"He's dying." She pets him gently. "I can fix him. You can help me."

"But he's dying." Dying is dying. Isn't it?

"I can fix it. Now, will you help me?" She's agitated in a way I've not seen before so I murmur, "Of course."

She picks the cat up, carrying him to a different steel table—the one that I first awoke on. "Hold him while I give him something to calm him."

I pet the cat as he purrs, and I can hear the catch in his breath as he cuddles into me. She motions for me to lay him down and I do, holding him while she injects him with a large needle.

He cries but then goes still, his eyes half lidded.

"Snow," Mary says, "I do this for so many reasons, my loyal friend." She reaches under the table, brings up straps that she lays over him, tightening them above his shoulders and hindquarters.

She nods to the next table and hands me a bottle. A roll of cotton lies on the table. "Soak the cotton in this. It is diluted carbolic acid. We will need to cool him once this is done—and relieve his pain."

I put the cotton in a small bowl and pour the liquid over it. The smell is familiar: it was what she wrapped around me when I woke to fiery pain.

"Move back, Isabelle."

I step to the other side of the table and watch as a clear glass covering, like the top of a cake dish, goes over Snow. Mary walks to the wall, pulls down some large switches, and sparks begin to fly inside the glass container.

Snow screams; he moves but not much—clearly whatever she's given him prevents him from getting up, but not from making it known that he's in pain.

I close my eyes, suddenly assailed by the memory. Fire through my whole body. And the pins-and-needles feeling of a limb gone to sleep—only all over, and so many times worse. Pain and pain and pain and then . . . this. This whimpering silence.

"Snow," I say and my voice comes out as a sob. "Let me help him."

She flips the switches back, the sparks die down, and the clear box lifts off the poor creature. He's moaning, a low, horrible sound.

I think I remember that sound. Did I make that sound?

I grab the bowl, pull out the soaked cotton, and lay it over him, winding it around his body when he ceases to struggle, when he lays his head back, and the horrible keening stops. "My dearest boy," I murmur as I work. "All will be well."

I look up and see that Mary is watching me with a look so gentle and full of . . . of what? Is that love?

Is what I feel for Snow love?

Can I feel love? I'm new to this world. I know things I should not, yet I don't know other things, such as why her smile makes me feel safe. Why the touch of her hands as she comes to help me and the feeling of her breath on my hair moves me so.

She grasps my shoulder for a moment, then goes and gets a strange contraption that fits into her ears, with a small bell-like thing hanging down from the other end.

"It's a stethoscope." She takes it off and puts it on me, the ear bits sinking slightly in, and she holds the bell against my chest.

I laugh at the sound.

"That's your heart."

She touches my cheek, and I hear my heartbeat become louder and faster. I swallow hard, take the earpieces out, and hand her the thing. She puts it on again and listens to multiple parts of Snow's body, then begins removing the cotton. "Too little of this carbolic acid treatment and he feels the pain. Too much and it will cause him more. It's a balancing act, getting it just right."

She picks the cat up and carries him upstairs, and I follow her. She gestures with her chin to a chaise. "Sit. You can hold him. He'll like that."

I recline in the chaise and hold my hands out. She gives him to me gently, then once we are settled, covers us both with a light blanket. "Rest, my darlings."

"What is love, Mary?" I gaze up at her, and I imagine my heart begins to beat harder again as she leans down and puts her lips against mine, a soft touch, a short one, too.

"This, my dear. This is love." She touches Snow on the forehead, rubbing on the bridge of his nose, and I hear him purr. "He's happy to be back with us."

Back. We all seem to come back. "You said I was back."

"I did say that, Isabelle. You and Snow. Life is very good indeed."

We're outside, having a picnic. Snow romps around us, chasing birds and stalking squirrels. We laugh as he fails to catch anything, and he tears around us, finally collapsing on the blanket, his chest heaving.

"He's the best company," Mary says, and I smile and pet our white terror.

He licks my hand, then rolls and looks at Mary, as if to say, "You, too."

We both laugh and share a look—a look of pure affection, I think. I know that I don't know this woman well, but deep inside me, I feel so much regard for her. Love, I suppose. She has taken such care of me, her tenderness so dear.

"I love you," I say into the silence, and her expression changes to one of pure joy.

"I love you, too, Isabelle. I always have. I always will."

I pull her to me, and we kiss over our cat, who rolls and kneads my leg as if to say, "I'm still here."

When we pull away, she grins at me. "That was nice." She strokes my face, the feeling bringing up more of the warm feelings. "And I didn't have to make the first move. I very much like that."

I laugh. "I am a wanton woman, clearly."

"You are free and innocent, dearest. You've never been wanton. It is one of the things I love most about you. You love only me."

I frown, and for a moment her look changes to one of wariness and she swallows visibly. "Have I known anyone else?" I ask. Other than the servants who come and go, changing frequently since none of them seem to meet Mary's exacting expectations, we see no one. "Why do we not entertain?"

"Am I not enough for you?" Her tone is light, but her expression isn't.

"I'm just curious. How can you know how I behave—how I am? If I've only just been born?"

She seems to relax. "Character is always apparent."

I pet the cat. "Did you know how he would be when you picked him out?"

"I did." There is something off in her eyes although her smile is real. "He was the sweetest of the litter. And look at him now. So dear."

"Yes. He is." I offer him some chicken from my plate, and he gobbles it up.

"You've eaten so little of your food, Isabelle."

"I'm not hungry." I drink some of the wine she poured us, but it goes down the wrong way, and I begin to cough. A cough that doesn't seem to want to stop.

She watches me with an almost hopeless expression. "It will pass. It will pass." She sounds as if she is trying to convince herself as much as me.

I finally stop coughing and sit, not moving, afraid to set off the fit again.

She reaches out and touches my hand. "I will make you a syrup of honey and whiskey. It is good for coughs."

"So is laudanum." I don't know why I've said this—I'm not sure I even known what laudanum is.

She sighs. "Yes, laudanum's good. But perhaps a bit strong? You just swallowed the wrong way. You don't feel chilled or feverish, do you?"

"No." I smile at her.

"Are you fatigued?"

I laugh. "With you? Never."

She shoos the cat from between us, and he takes off after a bird he has no chance of catching. Then she eases me down and seems to be waiting to see if I'll cough again.

"I'm fine."

She slowly begins to touch my body. "Is it all right if I do this?"

The feeling is new—but also familiar, the touches the ones I've remembered since my birth. I can feel a slow fire building. "That fever you mentioned....?" I smile.

She laughs. "This one is of an entirely different origin." And then she kisses me, while she continues to run her hands up and down, to the most amazing effect.

My skirt and petticoat are soon up, and I am very noisy as we lie on our blanket. "My," I say, enjoying the trembling ennui that has overcome me. I turn my head to look at her and she's smiling. "Shall I return the flavor?"

"It would be the ladylike thing to do."

I laugh, sure that it would probably not be, but I do it anyway. She's even noisier than I was.

"Darling, are you coming down for dinner?" Mary has found me in my dressing gown, lying on the fainting couch and sipping water. "Are you all right?"

"I had another coughing fit. Perhaps you should make me some of your remedy."

She comes over, settles her hand on my forehead, and frowns. "You're so warm."

"I'm also tired."

Snow comes in, mewling for his dinner, no doubt, but he jumps up on the couch with me and crawls up my legs to my chest to nose me.

"Yes, my love," I say as I stroke his soft fur—does it feel a bit oily? "You'll make me feel all better."

Mary smiles. "I'll bring the food in here. We'll enjoy a little tête-à-tête in our bedroom."

My bedroom has become our bedroom. Ever since the picnic, when she showed me how love could be when it was acted upon, how good we could make each other feel. "Yes, that would be lovely."

She turns, and Snow deserts me for the possibility of dinner. I notice he's moving more slowly and seems to be limping. "Mary?"

She turns back.

"Snow—something's wrong with him."

"He probably jumped down from one of the china cabinets again. You know how intrepid he is. It's his misfortune that the concept of finessing the landing eludes him more often than not."

I laugh. She's right, of course.

Mary and I lie in bed, and I stare over at the doll, Miranda—why did I name her that? But, how could I have named her? She's Mary's doll no matter how much I might delude myself that she is mine.

Mary follows my gaze and smiles, slipping from my embrace and getting up to fetch Miranda, to bring her to me. I take her as Mary gets back into bed. She cuddles against me and I kiss her forehead, then turn back to the doll.

"She's so beautiful." I realize her leg moves strangely because it's been broken. "What happened?"

"She fell." There's something in Mary's voice that makes me think there's more to this story.

"Fell?"

"Yes. The maid. Clumsy girl. I let her go, of course."

"You let all of them go. No one stays around here for long."

"I have high expectations for how they'll keep this house. They never seem to share those expectations. I prefer to try again than live with a poor outcome."

I laugh and put the doll between us. "If I had a daughter, I'd name her Miranda."

Mary's look is haunted, but before I can ask why, I begin to cough. She helps me up, and I reach for the handkerchiefs I keep by the bed. Then she gets up and hurries to her room, coming back with laudanum. "Here. This will make it better."

I take the syrup reluctantly. It does make the cough better but leaves me so enervated that all I do is doze. "We should call a doctor."

"I am a doctor, my darling. This is best." She rubs my back as I continue to cough, but the fit calms, as it always seems to with this medicine. "Rest. Lie close to me. I'll look after you. I will always look after you."

I lie in bed, sipping the cup of hot chocolate Mary has brought me. Snow lies on the coverlet, his eyes only half focused, his breathing as labored as mine has become.

"He's sick again," I say, and she nods. "Your procedure didn't heal him."

"It did. For a time." She reaches over to pet him, and he presses his head against her hand. "I love him so. I know you don't remember, but he was ours—we got him from a farmer who had a basket of kittens on his wagon. *We* picked Snow out, not just I. He was the sweetest of the litter. He loved us both so much."

I frown. I have no idea what she's talking about. "When did we do this?"

"He's nine now. We got him when he was but a few months old."

"Nine years? We have been together that long—but how? I was...I don't remember."

"I know." She pets Snow, and he rolls over slowly, clearly not an easy movement for him, but he seems to want to let her rub his belly. "I'll fix him again. Each time he lasts a little longer."

"But he's only been with us for a few months since you fixed him the first time."

"Not the first time. And when I started working on him he only lasted days." She meets my eyes. "He seems to remember less and less each time about this place. Has to explore every nook and cranny to learn the smells again. But his essence—his sweetness— that never changes. And he always loves me—us. No matter how much he forgets."

"How many times have you fixed him?"

She looks away, seems to swallow hard, and then says, "Eighty nine."

I do not doubt her. She has a mind for such details. I meet her eyes and see a sadness in hers, but also an openness that isn't usually there.

I realize she's not hiding anything anymore, and a chill runs through me.

I put the cup back onto the saucer. "And me? You've done it to me, haven't you? That's why I woke up—was born—on that slab."

She nods.

"Why?" I start to cough again, the racking hurting my sides, and I cough something up into my hand.

Blood. It's blood. Just like I first expected to see.

"You have consumption, my darling. You're dying. You're always dying. But each time I get you back, it lasts a little longer."

Just like Snow. "And do I forget more each time?"

"You do." She reaches over and grasps my hand firmly in hers. "But you always love me. Always. No matter how much you forget. Next time you may forget how you think my eyes look like choco- late. Or how much you love that doll. But you never forget me. Not at your essence. We're destined to be together."

I'm not sure what to say. I gaze down at Snow, then let my eyes go to Miranda, sitting so still, so perfect—except for that leg. Never leaving this room, posed and pretty and...a prisoner.

"Mary, you love me. You said so."

"I do love you. I would do anything for you." She lets go of my hand and pets Snow again. "I'll fix him one last time, and he'll be here when you next wake up. But he's the problem, every time. Because I cannot resist bringing him back as many times as he needs it. But I have to resist because he's what tips you off. Makes you question. Makes the days you have between the current waking and the next full of doubt." She leans down, her lips lying on his forehead, and he pushes up into her. "I'll let him go after this last healing, so that I can keep you."

"Me? How much of me is going to be left when you get done? I've lost so much already." I stare at the doll. "Did she really fall?"

"No. You broke her. Early on. When you had almost all your memories and you figured out what I was doing. You were angry with me—compared yourself to her—and threw her across the room. It was lucky that she wasn't more damaged." She studies the doll, biting gently into her lower lip. "I probably need to get rid of her, too."

"Mary. I won't let you do this. I'll leave. You can't bring me back if you can't find me." I start to get up, but the room begins to spin.

"You said that last time, my darling. And the time before that. And the time before that. Once you even managed to get to the stables, but you'd forgotten how to saddle your horse. I caught you before you could leave."

"I'm your prisoner?"

"You're my love."

I stare at her. Her expression hasn't changed, and it's so full of love for me that I reach out to her. "If you love me, then don't do this. It's not what's best for me."

"But it is what's best for us." She looks down, her hand still on poor Snow. "And for me."

I feel a terribly lethargy come over me—the chocolate, she has drugged my chocolate—and I see her expression change to one of utmost sorrow. "Let me go," I whisper.

"I'm sorry, Isabelle. But I can't."

I feel her hand on my cheek, her lips pushing lightly on mine, the same kiss as our first one—how many first kisses have we had?

And then the world goes black.

I was born in this laboratory. I am a creature of steel and flame and wet cotton. I woke to pain, and she was there.

She looks at me like I should know who she is.

I don't.

SP World

~ Lorraine Schein

Under a blank, emptied sky that had stopped filling with snow, the red lights of the giant Ferris wheel glowed like blood and long icicles hung like frozen tears from its swaying cars.

The fair was only open in winter.

How did she know that?

It's cold up here, A. thought. Looking down from her car at the wheel's top, she saw people swarming like bees in a hive, going from one hopeless ride to another.

But why was she here?

That man down there, the roller coaster operator, looked familiar. *He's a handsome man, with big hands*, she thought. *I miss his hands. He wouldn't leave her for me. I am not blonde or English. He wouldn't replace her with me.*

And who was she? A. had slept in her bed and lived in her house and all she remembered was how she wouldn't let A. be with him . . .

The wind blew A.'s brown hair into her face. A child . . . and where was her child?

She did remember when she first got here.

"Welcome to SP World, dear," the official Park Greeter had said.

A. wondered what the initials stood for.

"What brings you here, dear? Pills, gas, drunk driving? Poetry, perhaps?" the Park Greeter said with a practiced smile.

She wore a gray uniform with the SP World logo, a yellow hive embroidered on the pocket.

"Have you read the requirements for an admission ticket?" The woman pointed to the sign over the entrance to the grounds.

ENTRANCE REQUIREMENT:
At Least 2 Attempts And A Note From A Doctor
Saying You Should Be Under Careful Observation.

"I'm not sure I qualify . . ." A. said. "I don't even know how I got here."

"No matter, sweetie. If you are here, it must be for a reason. Go, enjoy yourself!" She gave A. a ticket, then pushed her toward the ticket booth, where a clerk in a cap and brown shirt like a Nazi uniform punched a bee-shaped hole in a ticket and handed it to her.

On one side of the fair was a row of stalls. A large wooden arrow pointed to them. It said THE 10-IN-1 SIDESHOW. It looked less crowded, so A. started there.

The first freak show stall had a banner proclaiming:

SEE THE DISQUIETING MUSES!
JUST ARRIVED FROM THEIR EUROPEAN TOUR!

Here were two dressmaker's dummies, standing in front of a painted backdrop that showed a red fortress in the distance. A statue of Apollo stood nearby.

The tall one wore a white toga. Its head was marked with black stitch marks like scars. A seated dummy next to it had a tiny black pin head on a huge stuffed body.

Both were eyeless, seamed. Blank face, bobbin heads.

We are eyeless, heads stitched up but we see you, they said to her in flat singsong voices. *And we see her playing with the cards.*

Then the Muses sneered at her. "Thirteen poems in your last three months. Won't you do it, do it, do it?"

"You must be confusing me with someone else," A. said, and walked to the next stall. The marquee read ELECTROSHOW SHOW in flashing lights.

This was an exhibit of people getting shock treatment. The viewers were invited to apply the shocks themselves by the barker.

"Step right up and turn the handle! You'll only be helping them, not causing them pain!"

There was a pretty blonde woman on the table, strapped down.

28

A. pulled the lever and watched the blue lightning convulse the woman on the table, arching her back.

Was she better? The blonde was not moving now, and looked very pale. Was she alive?

A. ran from her, panicked. Ahead was a stand of bobbing, colored balloons. A man with a handlebar mustache handed her one for a dollar. He also gave her a long sharp pin, telling her, "If you pop the balloon, you win a prize."

She popped it. "What is my prize?"

The man laughed. "This," he said and handed her the limp shred of red balloon.

She put it in her pocket. Maybe the rides up ahead would make more sense.

She pushed her way through the crowd to the midway, toward the first ride—a lurching Tilt-a-Wheel.

The Moon and Yew Tree

A giant tree stood before her, towering almost as high as the Ferris wheel. Cars shaped like crescent moons swung out from its branches as it rotated, raising screaming children in the air. A. worried they would fall out, felt tears well up in her eyes. She decided to save her ticket for something else.

She walked down the path to a sign that said GAMES OF CHANCE.

"Spin the Wheel of Chance!" said the carnival barker. She stopped before it. It was red and black and divided into different sections. One read NURSE COMES HOME EARLY. Next to it was NEIGHBOR SMELLS GAS. Another read WIN STUFFED ANIMAL. The barker spun it. It whirled and whirled in a blur, but never stopped on anything. The pointer never settled.

It is so odd, A. thought and decided not to play. She walked away as the barker called after her, taunting "What are you so afraid of?" shaking his fist.

Bump–A–Car

This was an electrified platform on which small, realistic-looking automobiles whizzed, careening wildly into each other with loud thuds. It was surrounded by a deep lake. The goal was to not let your car be bumped off the platform into the lake.

As A. watched, she saw that some of the drivers thought the goal was to drive your car directly into the lake, because there were wrecked, half-submerged autos in the water with people clinging to their sides. They never called out for help, though, and there was no one on the shore to pull them out.

The Ariel Carousel

Here was a carousel kept immobile and silent by day. It had tiny multicolored lightbulbs circling its top and base; its horses were all black. They had no reins or handholds for their riders to grasp.

The sun had set, and the Carousel creaked to life, piping a fragile yet manic tune as it began to turn.

It speeded up with a shudder, but there was no carousel operator to halt it. A. saw that you couldn't get off because it was moving too fast. Its riders became colored blurs as the tempo picked up, one with the horses. The red light shaped like a giant eye above the riders flashed faster, pulsing redder as they accelerated.

The Carousel ran all night and stopped at dawn. It halted so abruptly, riders were thrown off, their sprawled, bruised bodies spewed to the ground.

As she left, she noticed the smell of rotten eggs, gagged and covered her nose. Where was it coming from? A. shuddered. She would never bring a child here.

The Zoo

THIS WAY TO THE WILD CREATURES EXHIBIT, the arrow ahead pointed.

Several iron cages with tall bars stood in a row. The first one had a crudely lettered note on it: PLEASE DON'T FEED THE TULIPS!

A bouquet of vicious, ravenous tulips snapped their red jaws at her, rattling and lunging their long stems between the bars as she gazed at them. Even though they looked safely caged, she stepped back. She felt their petals enveloping her throat, throttling her neck like a tourniquet, choking her. A. gasped, and hurried on.

The next cage was no better—a cluster of growling, vivid poppies whose black tooth-like pistils gnashed together, leaning eagerly forward to slurp at her, drooling.

She ran around the corner to the next exhibit. As she got closer, she heard a loud buzzing and saw the sign: HALL OF BEES.

A giant beehive with no fence or netting around it to protect viewers swarmed before her. Something sticky and molten fell from the canopy above her onto her head, dripping down her face to her mouth and sleeve. It was honey!

She tried to wipe it off but it was too late. The bees buzzed toward her in an angry swarm. She backed away, swatting at them in terror, but it was no use. Then a beekeeper in a white suit, high-sleeved-gloves and a shrouded helmet with a netted mask drew them away from her, saying "Beware the queen!" They followed behind him, a humming, wavering procession.

The Funhouse Mirrors

A. entered the Hall of Mirrors in the Funhouse. They were all different sizes and shapes. The first one was long and she saw herself elongated, stretched thin as taffy. In the next, a round mirror, she saw herself squat and stunted, a fat dwarf. Who would love her if she really looked like that? She wouldn't look English enough.

The diamond-shaped mirror that was next made her look much younger, first showing her as a child in Tel Aviv playing on the beach, then as a teenager dancing with the handsome British soldiers. A. walked to the last mirror, and saw herself aged, her hair grown gray. Then that image vanished and the mirror's center filled with a silver-scaled fish, expanding till it was no longer a fish but the glistening surface of a great lake that spilled over the frame engulfing her.

But strangely A. didn't drown. She was now on the shore of the lake. There were paddleboats on it, and she saw a tall man in one with a blonde woman. They looked familiar.

Though both were paddling, the blonde woman was sinking lower in the boat.

But he was not.

He kept paddling, not even turning his head as she disappeared into the water. Horrified by this, A. shouted for a lifeguard, but there was none.

She needed to get away from here, she needed an explanation, no matter where from, so A. followed the sign that said TO THE FORTUNETELLING TENT.

She found, then entered a canvas tent on the edge of the fairgrounds.

A. sat in the folding chair next to a table. The table held a flickering candle, an incense cone scripting acrid smoke overhead, and a small amethyst crystal ball. A hissing sound came from the tent's shadowed corners.

The reader was a tall gypsy woman with a British accent and big hands. She wore a spangled velvet scarf and a long tiered skirt.

"And what is your name, dear"?

A. couldn't remember. Was it Sylvia?

"Sylvia, I think," she said. Yes, it must be because she remembered sleeping in her bed.

"Funny, you don't look like one. But cut the cards, dear," the woman said, handing her the deck, and leaning back with a smile.

A. shuffled the cards, then split them into three piles. They felt sharp as she did so, and when she was done she had tiny red slits of paper cuts on her thumbs.

"Here is your fortune," said the woman laying down the cards. She turned them over slowly and fell silent, studying them. "Fixed stars govern your life," she said at last.

"These cards represent your past. I see you made a journey here from another land. Perhaps to escape confinement and evil."

"Yes, I'm originally from Germany" A. said. "Then I emigrated to Palestine to escape the war."

The Tarot reader turned over the cards.

The 8 of Swords. The Devil.

"I see you are involved with a poet—no, wait. She turned over two more cards. "Three poets."

"Well, my husband is one." It was amazing how accurate this reader was.

The cards on the table were The King of Cups, reversed. Next to it the Queen of Cups. Or did the card say The Cuck Quean?

"Now for your future cards," said the woman. "I see a couple entering your life. I see a woman."

The Tower, its turret struck by lightning, with bodies falling from it—she recognized that one. The Queen of Swords.

But the reader now turned over many more cards, ones she had never seen before, laid across the table.

The Queen of Ovens
The Two of Orphans
The Priestess of Pills
The Tower of Electroshocks
The Wheel of Misfortune
The King of Infidelity
The Six of Slashed Wrists
The Cups of Pills
The Page of Poetry
The Hierophant-Psychiatrist
The Nine of Overdoses
The Hanged Otherwoman
Bad Judgement
The Ten of Bees
The Lunatic Hospital

"The one you want? He will never marry you," the Tarot reader said, turning over the last card.

The card on the table now was the Magician. . . or did it say the Magic Man? And the Lovers Triangle, reversed. A picture of a woman and a man. Or was it two women and a man? A. rubbed her eyes. She was getting tired.

"But I'm already married," A. said, confused.

Just then, the woman's velvet scarf slipped off her neck and A. noticed her Adam's apple protruding underneath.

The fortune teller was not a woman! He was a man with big hands wearing a dark wig and a skirt. His deep voice was now evident as he lunged at her with a growl. A. pushed the flap to the tent open and stumbled outside, shouting "Imposter! Liar! Seducer! Help me!"

A. rushed outside toward the Ferris wheel in the distance. It seemed to dip down at her feet, beckoning her to mount it. An empty car pulled into place before her.

She handed her ticket to the uniformed ticket taker and climbed into the car. He latched the metal safety bar in place across her lap with a clink, locking her in.

A bell clanged, heavy as fate, in the distance.

A. saw that the front of her car was shaped like an oven, its white door open, and its seat was a mattress.

She thought, *Where is my little girl? I want her to ride with me. Have I lost her in the fairgrounds, is she looking for me, calling my name?* The child he wouldn't acknowledge.

As the Ferris wheel started to rise, she saw a child hanging by one hand from the car in front of her. *Oh, there she is! My little Shura!* Dangling from the car, trying to climb back in.

I don't want her to be without me. A. stood up, rocking her car precariously, and pulled her to safety beside her. "Mummy!" said the girl, hugging her.

She sealed the car, turned on its oven, laid down next to her child. *I'll give her the pills first.*

The mouth of the oven-car opened, hissing, released that smell of rotten eggs. The Ferris wheel operator below was laughing.

He looked up, his hands on the brakes. He could stop A. if he wanted to.

But she knew he wouldn't. *He wants me to go the same way,* she thought.

"I will never marry you!" he shouted up at her. She knew his name now—knew all of their names.

It is her world, the jealous, lucky bitch, but I can be like her this way. She breathed in the forgetting gas. *Now this will be my world.*

Looking down she thought, *Maybe Ted will miss me now too.*

I am Assia.

And I am dead.

When Only Bears Carry Arms, Only Weapons Will Be Born

~ Wendy N. Wagner

The bears walked through the streets with their long black rifles; we were powerless against them. They had the guns and we did not, and thus the world was theirs. At night we could hear them at target practice, the neighborhood cats screaming in fear and pain.

How the bears managed their weapons was a trivial mystery—how their flat brutal paws could grip the stock of a gun, their claws work a trigger, their black tongues slot bullets into the chambers. We did not care about such things. This was the time of the Big Snow, after all. There were plenty of other things to worry about. I lay in my bed worrying how I could keep my littlest sister from getting frostbite and also wondering, very quietly and only to myself, what I would do when I was no longer a girl.

Those nights were long and cold and lonely. Once we had kept a dog who liked to snuggle on my bed when the lights were off, but the bears had driven away all the dogs on that same gray day they rounded up the intellectuals and shut them beneath the bridges. The bears were dangerous, but not as dangerous as night felt after our dog disappeared. The guns were dangerous, but not as dangerous as the women hissing and growling behind the black bars of their bridge-prisons. The culverts diverting creeks and streams throughout the city boundaries echoed with their rage, and the train bridges, no longer used for travel, shook as if a thousand trolls hungered for billy goats.

Most of the mothers succumbed to fear and took in bear lodgers in exchange for food. Their daughters did not leave their houses to seek out the vegetables forgotten in abandoned gardens. Their yards filled up with snow, the ice packing between the neat little pickets of the fences and glowing blue when the sun played on it. My sisters and I beat paths between the yards of such girls and ignored their faces at the windows as we cut blocks of ice away from the sleeping earth. They never spoke or called to us, although one time I found a purple woolen scarf draped over an ice-sculptured birdbath and footprints leading back up to the porch.

I gave the scarf to Dora, the littlest of my sisters. She wrapped it around her shining blond head, giggling to herself as a little girl will do. She was young enough to still love presents, and this year, we had not been able to give her any on her birthday. The bears had taken all the childish things for themselves.

"Mind Elise, now." I shook my finger at her. "She'll know how to keep you safe in the woods."

She giggled again, and then Elise appeared on the front steps, carrying their collecting baskets. "Come and take your basket, Dora," she grumbled. Elise's temper, like her hair, was fiery.

Francine opened the door and waited patiently for Dora to take her basket and adjust her gloves and then beg me to fix her scarf, which had fallen over her eyes. "Are you sure you don't want to come with me, Gwendolyn?"

I spared her a smile. Of all of us, Francine was the kindest. Her black eyes always brightened when she could give Dora the biggest carrot or when she could sneak a little drawing under Mother's place setting before Mother sat down to breakfast. She cried for a month when the bears took our dog, and she always slept with a pillow over her head so as to muffle gunfire.

"You'll be all right, Franny. Mother asked me especially to check the river, and I can't let her down."

Francine tied her crackling black curls back with a scarf I once gave to Mother. "Please be careful." She hurried down the stairs to press a kiss on my cheek. "If you change your mind, you know where to find me."

I nodded. "If I get done soon enough." I doubted I would. The pond where Francine was headed to search out cattail roots sat on the other side of town, just past the empty field where the bears took their revolvers. The younger girls were too terrified of the empty casings to even skirt the edges of that place, but Francine feared nothing. That was why Mother sent me to the river. A little fear could keep a girl safe.

I would find more than cattails on the river banks, of course. When the tides changed, sometimes the river left us treasures of faraway places and times, and it was those things Mother wanted. The barely edible cattail roots were merely an excuse; she hungered for pieces of the past. The past my sisters and I could barely remember, despite the fact it lay just behind our shadows. The snow had buried that, too.

It took me most of an hour to make my way through the town and down to the river, avoiding the taverns where the bears growled over beers, and carefully skirting the rumbling bridges. The path wound and twisted through thickets and abandoned schools, but it felt safe, at least during the day. I don't think any of us would have taken it in the dark—not even Francine.

The river smelled of mud now, the tide drawing its waters down to the faded green weeds. Shards of ice clacked on the rocks, broken into music by the tug of the ocean. Somewhere out there the sea hunkered on its beach, winding up its nets of rivers and creeks, drawing all the world's loose bits into itself. I could picture her as something like my mother, a big brown woman with broad shoulders and tough, broad-knuckled hands. We used to drive to the beach in the summer. I could remember that: the warm sun, the shrieking gulls, the strong grip of my father's hand on mine.

I wiped the cold from my eyes and picked my way down to the rocks. Mother sometimes brought us fish from the river, but the bears had learned to watch her closely and take anything she found for themselves. They cared nothing for us girls, as long as we kept quiet and ignored their eyes on our legs and backs.

The wind played over the river, stirring its surface into white teeth. My fingers burned with the cold as I picked through the worthless things left in the mud. Plastic bits, unidentifiable and half-bleached of color, a cracked sand pail, a rubber squeegee or perhaps a windshield wiper. There had been cars once, I remembered. Perhaps the snow had buried them and made them worthless, or perhaps, like the trains, the bears had destroyed them. Boats and planes and bicycles were likewise gone, so now feet alone we had. The arms, of course, belonged to the bears.

A little whiteish box caught my attention, and I worked it out from between two rocks. "Needles," I read on the plastic label. I opened the box, expecting only rusty water, but found everything snug and dry inside, the needles winking sleepily in the light. A good find, then. We were all learning to sew.

I picked up a small handsome tin, thinking Mother might find a use for it in her workshop, and then I dug a few cattail roots. There in the reeds I caught a surprise flash of blue and snatched it up—a small ball of yarn, not even enough for a Dora-sized sock, but perhaps worth something when mixed with the other fragments we had around the house. I lined my basket with leaves and laid all my damp and muddy river finds on the neat green lining. The sun wouldn't stay in the sky much longer.

I hesitated there on the river bank. The winding path I had taken earlier would put me in the way of the bears as they left the taverns for target practice. I could avoid them if I took a few shortcuts around the old playground, but that would certainly mean getting home after dark.

Alternately, I could follow the old bike trail—sometimes I struggled to remember just what those words even meant—where it followed Tinker Creek under a bridge, the trail divided from the creek by a neat railing. It would be a quick, dry walk under the bridge into the heart of the town, and I could very likely beat my sisters home.

I turned to face the trail going under the bridge. The deck of the bridge stood ten or fifteen feet above it, allowing enough light for safety. No snow had found its way beneath the bridge, and no ice glinted on the path. But a few feet up the sloping sides of the bridge's embankments, heavy bars cut off the darkest hollows, creating the little space beneath the bridge where the intellectuals squatted in their half-life.

Goose bumps rose up on my arms. Even before the snow, people had warned us about the intellectuals. Some women had even cheered when the bears shut them away, and now no one besides my mother and sisters would speak of the prisoners. I drew my shawl more tightly around me and wished I had a coat that fit.

I took a small step forward and heard a tiny clink. There at the edge of the path lay a gold flip-top lighter, brighter than the sun. I snatched it up. This had not come out of the river. This could have only dropped out of the coat pocket of some patrolling bear. To be found with it would risk being used for target practice myself. But Mother would certainly want it. Whatever she built in her workshop, kept secret even from us girls, it could only be improved by something as dangerous as this.

I slid it under the top layer of leaves in my basket, my mind made up. With that lighter on me, I'd rather face a dozen trollish intellectuals than one patrolling bear.

So I hurried down the bike trail and under the bridge. The snow might not have found its way onto the path, but the cold had. Here where the sun never really intruded, the cold gathered itself in damp folds, the creek hissing quietly beneath its frozen skin. My boots skidded on the kind of ice that cannot be seen, invisible and nasty. I caught at the railing and felt the iron bite at the top layer of my skin. Not so safe after all, this path.

"Girl. Hey, girl!"

I wished I could pretend my footfalls covered up the voice, but despite its dry grate, I heard it well enough. Keeping my grip on the cold railing, I turned my head very slowly to the left. Four or five feet up the sloping embankment, black bars held back a deeper darkness that swallowed the underside of the bridge.

"Can you please help us?"

The face took shape between the bars, a pattern of gray patches in the black. My tongue swelled with fear.

An arm as pale and thin as a birch branch slid out into the fading sunlight. "Kid. Please." The fingers flickered, beseeching me.

Then I saw the filthy strands of red and yellow circling that wrist. Red and yellow string, like the bracelets we had bought at the beach long ago to give to our friends, like the yarn my mother knotted around her own wrist. Though the nails were black and jagged and dirt had sunk into the folds of this woman's dry-cracked skin, she was as ordinary as any girl who had slipped a ring onto her finger or a necklace over her head.

I crossed the bike trail. "Hello?"

The woman grabbed the cage bars in her fists and pulled herself against them. I could see the brand burned black on her forehead, a square with a slash cut through it, and stopped climbing the embankment. "You were a writer?"

She nodded and then turned her face into her shoulder, covering a long volley of coughing. She wiped the back of her hand across her mouth. "Like most of us under these bridges."

My sisters little enjoyed reading, and of course books were no longer allowed. Mother and I had hidden what we could save in our cellar, and we passed books between ourselves in the last hour of daylight, straining the words off the pages in the blue gloom. Bears like candles almost as little as they like books.

"What did you write?"

She was quiet for so long I thought maybe she hadn't heard me. "Poems," she finally whispered. "A novel, once. About a governess."

I crept a foot higher up the embankment. "Like Jane Eyre?"

"Very much."

"I always wanted to be a governess. Before—"

"Before the snow."

I squeezed the bars in my hands. I couldn't see a lock or any hinges. "I don't think these cages were made to be opened."

She slid down to the ground, hugging her knees to her chest. Her skin showed through the holes in her pants. "I don't think so, either."

Pants. I remembered pants. They were gone like books and bicycles these days.

I could hear rustling behind her, see moving patches in the dark. This close, I could smell terrible things, a stink of death and despair, the distilled aroma of every night since the snow had begun to fall. Fingers crawled along the bars, filthy, nasty. I took a step backward.

"Please!" the writer cried. "Don't go!"

But I certainly couldn't stay. Already the sun had crept down into the west hills. Any moment, the bears would emerge from their drinking and start prowling the streets. And the lighter ...

I climbed back up to the cage bars, trying not to flinch as fingers crept over my boots and skirt. "Here," I said, thrusting the lighter between the bars.

"What?" The writer pulled herself back up to her feet and closed her fingers around the thing. "What do you expect us to do with that? Burn down the bridge?"

I pulled the few small cattail roots out of the basket and held them out, too. "They're food. Not much food, but something."

"Better than rats."

I waited a moment, wondering if there was anything else I could give her, but the treasures I'd found by the river would have meant less than nothing to anyone without my mother's hunger for the past. The intellectuals' real hunger felt vast and pressing.

"Did your governess have adventures?"

Her teeth showed in something like a smile. "Ever so many."

"Maybe when I come again you'll tell me about them?" I smiled back at her. It felt dangerous. It felt wonderful.

She pressed her forehead to the bars. "You really mean that?"

I glanced behind me. I had to go. "Yes."

"Then wait a second." She stuck her hand out between the bars, her fingers pale versions of the bears' claws as she flattened out her palm. "Take this, little sister."

The sunset drained the colors from her makeshift bracelet, but I could almost feel them, an odd warmth against my fingertips. "Thank you. Thank you very much."

"You better get moving," she called, but I had already jumped down to the bike path, my basket swinging on my arm as I ran.

I could hear the bears singing about the bottles of beer in their bellies. Their growls, barely musical, rumbled like freight trains hurrying down the abandoned railways of the world, shaking my arms and legs as I pumped them, faster and faster. I streaked through the twilight, and as I ran I felt myself changing, a transformation uncertain but no less mysterious than the metamorphosis of bears into marksmen and writers into trolls.

Elise stopped me at the back door. "There's a bear in the house," she breathed.

I doubled over, sucking at the cold air as if it could put out the fire in my lungs. I had run all the way from the bridge. The insides of my ears wobbled to my pulse.

"A bear?" I gasped. "Are you sure?"

Elise nodded and pushed her face close to mine. I could smell the pond water evaporating off her skirts. "It just showed up. Francine is making soup while Mother tries to keep it out of her workshop."

I remembered the basket in my hand. The bears had never forbidden our gathering, but we all knew there was risk in it. We did not want to be stalked as our Mother had been stalked. "I can't bring this inside."

"And you can't leave it outside, either." She nodded to the street, where two bears leaned languidly against the burned-out lamp post, smoking cigarillos. "If they think you're hiding anything worthwhile, they'll come after it."

The strings on my wrist went warm, almost as if they were burning a message into my skin. I pulled back the leaves and felt for the prizes I had gathered by the river. Just garbage really, and yet enough to get us all in trouble. I opened my mouth and put the box of needles inside.

Elise nodded, understanding just what I was doing. "Give me the yarn," she ordered, and as soon as it was in her hand, she tucked it inside her cheek. It made her face strangely lopsided, like the time Mother's tooth got infected and I had to draw it out with a pair of hot pliers.

There was no place for the little tin except in my sleeve. I hoped that would be safe enough.

Dora threw open the door. "Hurry up. The bear wants dinner."

We darted inside. My mother sat at the foot of the table, her best shawl wrapped around her shoulders. She gave me a strained smile, then turned her attention back to the beast across from her. The hot stink of cigar smoke rolled off its fur in clouds. I hadn't seen a bear up close since the snow began to fall. I had forgotten the way their eyes glinted and their claws clicked as they gesticulated around their harsh words.

Dora rushed to set spoons on the table. I moved to Francine's side as she knelt beside the fireplace. Wordlessly, the box of needles pinning my tongue flat, I slipped the tin—too fine to risk to the bears, no matter how worthless it seemed to be—out of my sleeve and passed it to her. She gave a quick glance over her shoulder at the bear and then dropped the thing into the cauldron of soup.

"Stir carefully, Franny!" My mother gave a strained laugh. "We mustn't waste a sip when we have an extra mouth to feed."

Francine ladled the watery broth into our largest bowl, and I took it with wavering hands. I walked very slowly, careful not to spill a single peppery drop, and placed it on the table in front of the bear.

As I turned back to the fireplace, a massive blow struck between my shoulder blades, and I staggered, nearly falling. The box of needles slid down my throat. It should have hurt, should have gouge and scraped, but somehow it was only like swallowing an overcooked cattail root.

"You call this soup?" the bear roared. Dust shook from the rafters, and the bowls beside the fireplace rattled. "Where is the meat?"

Elise darted forward and dropped the ball of blue yarn into the bear's bowl. "Here," she called. "Silly Gwendolyn forgot your meatball."

The bear settled back into its chair, eyeing the soup. "It's an odd sort of meatball."

Its voice rumbled through its sharp teeth, darker and smokier than before. The box of needles turned a slow circle in my belly. The transformation that had begun on my run home seemed to be continuing inside me.

"It's special, with blue cheese," Francine squeaked. She covered her mouth, her eyes wide. There hadn't been any cheese even before the bears arrived.

But the bear didn't seem to notice the lie. It popped the ball of yarn into its mouth and then swallowed. "It's good," the beast admitted. "Strange, but good."

Francine sagged with relief. But deep in my gut the box of needles twitched and danced. I clutched my stomach in hot pain.

"More!" the bear roared. "More meatballs!"

"That was the only one," Elise said. Her freckles stood out on her nose, a sure sign she was angry.

"Maybe we can find something else," Mother offered, but the bear had already leaped from its seat.

Its paw flashed out. "Meat!"

Dora hung suspended in the bear's grasp for a long, frozen moment. The light outlined each of us like something out of the movies I had watched as a little girl: angry Elise, sweet-faced Francine, Mother with her red-and-yellow string bracelet, Dora as tiny as a spark, the bear as big and black as the night, and each of them stood in for something else, like fire or hope, and for a moment, I was lost in the thought that we were all symbols in some dark story directed by another hand.

The fire in my belly went out, and time once again fell like snowflakes.

Dora managed only the tiniest of screams before she slid down the bear's red gullet.

Elise gave a shout of rage. Francine grabbed for the soup ladle. Mother leaped from her chair and ran to her illegal workshop. But I was already reaching down my throat.

No longer were the needles merely needles. Like me, the ordinary needles I'd found in the mud had transformed into something far greater than they had ever meant to be. The hilt of a sword rose up between my teeth, and my fingers closed fast around it.

I had never used a blade bigger than a chef's knife, but the stories I'd read about them ran power through my arm. Before the bear could grab its pistol, the sword flashed. Blood sizzled as it spattered the floor. The bear dropped like a meatball.

"Gwendolyn!" Mother collapsed in the doorway of the workshop, staring at me in wonder or fear or maybe both.

Elise and Francine grabbed the bear's death-flailing arms. I had cut it open from snarling mouth to jiggling thighs, and all the things it had ever swallowed lay exposed before me: the bleached human skeleton, a dozen beer bottles, the twisted frame of a lawn chair, the square shape of something I thought might have been called a computer. I reached down into the muck, shifting rubbish and men's shoes and ruptured innards. And then a small hand caught mine.

"Dora!"

She burst free, gasping and choking and wrapped head to toe in blue yarn. Only her face and her hands showed, a little scratched by the bear's rough teeth. I pulled her into my arms, and my sisters collapsed around me, crying and hugging and holding each other tight.

"I'm fine," Dora said. "This yarn is like armor."

A cramp rippled in my gut, and I straightened up. It seemed my innards weren't done with the box of needles.

Off in the distance, something rumbled and then boomed. Francine ran to the window. "Something's on fire," she announced. "I think it's the Tinker Creek bridge."

Mother jumped to her feet. "It's starting!" She ran back into the workshop.

My gut contracted again, and I drew another sword out of my mouth. Elise grabbed it, her eyes gleaming and her freckles nearly glowing.

I was already producing another, and another, until we each had our own sword balanced in our small girl-fists. We picked our way through the remains of the bear and found Mother working beneath the great and mysterious structure she'd been building since the first night our dog had gone missing. I could see the seams between the bits of river-flung trash, but now I could also see the shape of the thing, and although the snow had stolen my memory of what people had once called it, I knew it for the war machine it was.

She rolled herself out from beneath the thing and wiped a streak of oil off her forehead. It took with it the brown powder she used to cover the brand on her forehead. "It's ready, I think, but I don't know what it will run on."

Once, in the time of fathers and trains and warm breezes, the world had run on the blood of extinct creatures, a prosaic substance that couldn't survive the arrival of magic. I could see Mother wondering where she could find such a thing, and I knew she had spent too long hungering for the past. Now it was the time of the Big Snow. It was time for a new way of thinking, a way that could stand up to the power of magic.

I looked at Francine, and she nodded back at me, knowing just what symbol was missing from our transformation into a war party. She shoved her sword into the gripping mass of her hair and stalked to the fireplace where the cattail soup still simmered. Somewhere inside it was the mysterious tin I'd found by the river. Whatever it was no longer mattered: it had been immersed in magic and become something useful.

The door groaned open, and the writer from the bridge strode into our house as if she had always belonged there. She came to my side as my mother filled the fuel tank of her war machine with a liquid far more fiery than peppered roots and snow melt. The smell of smoke and burnt bear fur clung to the writer, and I knew the lighter I had given her had lit something more than just a cooking fire beneath that bridge.

She looked me up and down as if she could see the changes that had been wrought over this strange dinner. "So, girl. Do you still want to be a governess?"

The engine of the war machine growled like an angry cat, like a furious dog, like a bear that has never come out of the forest to taste words or beer. My sisters waved their swords and made their war whoops. There was a whole world out there full of symbols and magic, ready for us to nibble into weaponry and spin into an army. The bears didn't know what was coming for them.

I smiled with the white sharp teeth of the wind-whipped river. "I think I'm becoming something else. Something no girl has ever had a chance to be."

She put her arm around me. "Someday I'll write about you, then."

And the brand on her forehead dripped like ink down her snow-stained cheeks, spelling out power, spelling out change, spelling out the future.

Rewind

~ Josh Rountree

MONDAY

The dust biker comes into the video store that afternoon looking for slasher flicks. He heads straight to the horror section, not bothering to remove his breathing apparatus, and pulls a couple of classics from the shelf. *Friday the 13th Part III* and the original *Halloween.*

"You like this kind of stuff?" I ask when he hands the tapes to me for checkout.

"Yeah, so?" His voice is a mechanical whine and the desert winds have rendered his gray body suit smooth and practically transparent. I can't see his eyes through the scored surface of his goggles, but I can feel the edge in the way he's staring at me.

"I like them too," I say. "I've seen hundreds of them. Slasher flicks, I mean."

"Yeah, so what's the best one?"

I don't even have to think about it. "You ever seen *Sleepaway Camp?*"

His neck makes a stretching, leathery sound as he shakes his head side to side. "No."

I sprint to the back of the store, pull the sun faded VHS box from the shelf, and add it to his pile. "On the house. Just let me know what you think when you drop it off."

"You aren't charging me?"

"No, just a favor from one fan to another."

He might be smiling but I can't see through the grill of his mask. He looms there like Jason Voorhees, silent and unreadable. Dust rides the creases of his suit and he reeks of illegal petroleum. He's a seven-foot shadow come to life, an abstract artist's rendering of torn metal and melted rubber pooling along an endless broken highway. He exhales heavily and it sounds like the rattle of failing pistons.

"Do you have a bag?"

I bag up his tapes and he grunts his thanks on the way out the door. The front wall of the store is made of glass and I watch as he starts his bike and speeds away toward the shimmering red horizon.

I hope he likes the movie.

TUESDAY

Gandy catches me goofing off again.

We have a small television and VCR set up in the store that constantly runs movies, and I'm planted in front of it in one of those old style director's chairs, watching *Raising Arizona* for roughly the ten thousandth time, so I don't notice his approach from the back office until he's standing over me, his pen tapping against a clipboard.

"Jeff, what are you doing?" he asks.

"Sorry, just taking a quick break. I straightened all the boxes on the shelves and checked in the returns."

Gandy heaves a sigh that could reach from one end of the store to the other. He's a late middle-aged guy with a thin moustache and not much hair. A *Reverb Video* nametag is pinned to the chest of his purple oxford, and GANDY is spelled out in big block letters. I don't know if Gandy is his first name or his last name, but I've been working here too long now to ask.

"You're not getting paid to watch movies," he says. "The store's not in good financial shape. We need to be working hard to keep it afloat."

I think about telling him that we haven't had a customer all day and nothing I do in the store will help attract them, but I don't want to lose my job. Gandy likes to fret about the store being in trouble, but he hates when anyone else acknowledges it. This place is his life. Literally. The guy has a cot and a hot plate in the back office and he never leaves. I think he bathes in the sink.

Wind pushes against the front windows and the glass squeals like it wants to break. Gray smoke boils outside like it's being heated in a pot and it's so thick you can't see more than a few inches through it. Silvery shapes dart in and out of the murk, and I'm pretty sure I saw a nest of tentacles lash against the glass a few hours ago but I'm not telling Gandy that. His eyes are fixed on the front windows now and I can smell the sweat coming off him.

"I can run the vacuum again?" I say. "Gandy?"

"Yeah, thanks Jeff. That would be great."

Gandy returns to the sanctuary of his office and the rattle of an adding machine confirms that he's back to business. I vacuum the cheery lime green carpet for the second time today, then drop back into the director's chair and press play on the remote.

WEDNESDAY

I've barely flipped the CLOSED sign to OPEN when the first customer of the day walks in, slips off her protective body sheath and floppy hat, and dumps them in the corner where they sizzle for a few seconds before going quiet. The woman underneath is wrapped in layers of rough leather and her boots leave blackened prints in the carpet as she walks deliberately to the Musicals section.

"Anything I can help you find?" I ask.

"There's a musical I saw once that I liked but can't remember what it's called." She turns and I see the scar bisecting her face.

"Is it the movie starring that guy who was in that other movie with that one girl?" I ask.

She smiles, and her teeth are crooked in just the right way. "Might be."

I help her dig through the shelves, rattling off suggestions, but she keeps shaking her head. An oiled machete hangs from her left hip, and a one-handed chainsaw is strapped to her back, bits of unknown viscera still caught in its teeth. She plucks box after box off the shelf with torn and bruised fingers.

"Are you a hunter?" I ask.

"Most days," she says. "But even the stuff I kill doesn't like going out in this kind of weather."

The sky outside is green and twisty, and acid rain falls in sheets.

"What do you hunt?"

"Whatever they pay me to," she says. "Apelings and the undead mostly. But I'm certified for bigger game if needed."

"You need a partner?" I ask.

"I work alone," she says.

"No, I was just kidding. I like it here. Hey, you know this one, right?" I put *Singing in the Rain* in her hand.

"I've heard of it, but I haven't seen it."

"Well, since we can't find what you came in for, this would make a good alternative. Classic Hollywood. Hard to beat Debbie Reynolds."

"Sure, okay."

"Hey, so . . . if you want you can just watch this here? We have a TV. We can watch it together. Maybe the rain will pass by the time it's over."

The rain roars against the roof, and the stench of it sneaks in through the building's crevices, making the place smell like a high school chemistry class. The hunter's fingers tap against her machete blade and she studies my face with cold, unreadable eyes.

"I'm not looking for a date," she says.

"I wasn't asking for one. Just saying you could watch it here. Sometimes it gets old watching movies by myself."

"Okay, well that's not the worst idea then."

I offer her the director's chair and sit beside her, cross-legged on the floor. We consume the rest of the day with a procession of musicals and while she loves *Singing in the Rain,* we get lucky and realize that *The Music Man* is the movie she'd originally been hunting. She hasn't seen it in years but remembers the words to some of the songs and we sing together about River City and pool and brass band parades. Gandy pokes his head out from the back office a couple of times but he either no longer cares that I'm goofing off or doesn't want to come down on me in front of a customer.

When night arrives, it chases away the rain. The hunter, who by now I've learned is named Cutter, and who once upon a time wanted to be either a veterinarian or a social worker, stands up and checks her weapons. She studies the empty sky, and then dons her protective sheath and hat just in case. The smile she's worn for hours flattens and her face hardens like clay in a kiln.

"Thanks, Jeff," she says. "That was fun."

"Come back sometime. We'll watch *Paint Your Wagon*."

Cutter nods, pauses for a few seconds with her hand on the door. It's past closing time, but I don't mind.

She can stand there as long as she needs.

THURSDAY

Bryce comes into the store to show off his latest exoskeleton. "So what do you think?"

I'm sure it's the newest and coolest and most amazing exoskeleton that money can buy but it's still just a shiny metal suit that makes him walk like he can't quite bend his legs in the right places, and if I told him he reminded me of Robocop he'd probably start to sulk so instead I just say, "It's pretty cool," and try to sound like I mean it.

"Bro, pretty cool?" he says. "It's better than that. Check this out."

He holds up what looks like an unlabeled soda can, gives it a gentle squeeze, and his suit deconstructs into a swarm of nanomites. They make a few laps around the store, knocking a couple of VHS boxes off the shelf and then squash their way into Bryce's tin can which seals itself with a satisfying click.

I have to admit, that part was more than pretty cool.

"It's a Trimm-Henderson 42LX Klingwrap. You can't even buy one of these babies yet. Company has me testing it out. Nothing gets through this thing. Dino claws, bullets. A trash scavenger took a pot shot at me yesterday and it didn't event tickle. Supposedly it will stand up to gamma cannons too, which I guess I'll get to test out soon enough because the extraterrestrials are forming up on the south side of the vapor waste again and the company can't sit by and let them get a foothold. Bad for business, you know? Why don't you come with me? The company pays way better than this dump and you know you want one of these suits."

I'm running a pair of tape rewinders that hum pleasantly, thinking that maybe we need to get more of those stickers that read BE KIND, REWIND and wondering what the dirt biker thought of *Sleepaway Camp*.

"I like working here."

"What for? Jeff, bro, we've been friends since we were kids, but the difference is I grew up. Hey, I like movies too. I've seen *Armageddon* like five times. But you need to start living in the real world."

"I met a girl," I say.

"You went on a date?"

"Not really a date. We just watched some movies together."

"What's her name?" he asks.

"Cutter," I say.

"That her first name or last name?"

"I forgot to ask."

"Well I guess it's a start," he says, "but working here is still a dead end, Jeff."

Bryce's tin can makes a clattering noise. The lid pops open and within seconds the nanomites form an exoskeleton around him again. He snaps his head to the side and watches a blue shaft of light tear though the gloom, coming to ground somewhere in the distance, beyond the hills. "Green freaks are beaming down a team already. Look, Jeff, I have to go. To be continued, yeah? Time to seize the day buddy."

"Sure."

"Hey, can you put back a copy of *Red Dawn* for me? I'll swing by later and pick it up."

"Will do."

"And pack a coat this weekend. The company scientists are predicting ice. No telling what that means."

"Coat. Check."

"Later, bro."

Bryce lumbers though the exit and is lifted up by a squadron of hovering drones that carry him away, presumably to defend the profits of innocent shareholders.

I finish rewinding the tapes and then settle into the director's chair for a screening of *Close Encounters of the Third Kind*. I've seen it a bunch of times, but it's still a really good movie.

○

FRIDAY

When the lizard man comes into the store the air turns as hot as a tropical jungle. Squat leafy trees erupt from the carpet behind him and slinky vines drop from the ceiling like streamers at a middle school dance. Fireballs fall in lazy arcs outside, like rocks hurled by angry volcano gods. The lizard man's tongue licks in and out, tasting the stale air-conditioned air and turning up the heat even more in protest.

I know better than to offer my assistance. Lizard men are singled-minded, and he wouldn't have come if he didn't know what he wanted already.

Turns out his movie of choice is *The Great Escape*. He places it on the counter and pushes a pile of gemstones toward me with a three fingered claw.

"This is one of the best movies ever made," I say.

The Lizard man presses his thoughts into my mind and makes me aware that he's a huge Steve McQueen fan and that he's pleased that I agree the car chase in *Bullitt* is the best ever filmed otherwise he would be forced to take exception with me, and that would lead to the likelihood of a gruesome death by beheading or vivisection. He also makes me aware than his name is Alvarado, and that is neither his first name nor his last name, but simply his name.

Gandy comes to the front of the store with his clipboard, notices the vines dangling from the ceiling and casts a nervous look around the store like he's expecting Tarzan to come swinging in. Alvarado looks at him and Gandy freezes like he's been spotted by Medusa. Something passes between the two of them. One tear streaks down Gandy's face and lingers on his chin. A lot of people have problems with the fact that lizard men can project their thoughts, read minds, and alter the surface of reality, but I can take it in stride. Gandy isn't as easy going as I am. He makes a military about face and hustles back into the office, slamming the door in his wake. A worn poster for *Lethal Weapon 2* hangs on our side of the door, one corner unpinned and drooping forward.

"You've seen *The Getaway*, right?" I'm digging though his pile of gemstones, trying to find one that I can accept to cover the rental fee.

Alvarado makes certain that I'm flooded with embarrassment because of course he's seen *The Getaway*. How could he call himself a Steve McQueen fan if hadn't seen that one? My fingers clench around a handful of jewels and I lean forward on the counter to support myself against the onslaught of emotion that he forces at me. Eventually he senses my regret and he relents.

"Hey, so these jewels are probably worth millions and your rental fee is $4.32. I can't make change for that."

He gives me another mental push and makes it known that he doesn't require any change, that material things have no value to lizard men and these are only baubles to dangle in front of humans so they will dance and caper like the uplifted monkeys that they are. I may keep the entire stash and what's more, if the fear radiating off of my master is any indication they are sorely needed because *Rewind Video* has a limited life span, like a wolfman with its head caught tight in the maw of a hungry pterosaur. Furthermore, he informs me that his videocassette player is on the fritz and he will require one of those as well, if we have them for rental.

"Sure, VHS or BETA?"

Instead of invading my mind, he gives me an exhausted look and flicks his tongue.

"Kidding," I say. "We don't rent too many BETA tapes."

Our transaction concluded, Alvarado leaves clutching the VCR and his copy of *The Great Escape*. The temperature begins to cool and the vegetation becomes momentarily spectral before disappearing altogether. As sometimes happens, the lizard man left some of himself in my thoughts, and for the rest of the day I have the power to turn the lights on and off without touching the switch, and to float VHS boxes from one side of the store to the other like a flock of birds. I'm not sure if it's really happening or if my brain just tells me it is, but it's a lot of fun either way.

SATURDAY

Bryce was right about the weather. The ice comes in the afternoon, dropping huge chunks so that it feels like being in an air raid, and within minutes the parking lot is a solid shimmering mass. I remember the jacket I left at home as I turn the thermostat from AC to heat.

The stuff is two feet deep in some places by the time the woman and her children arrive, and I have to chip away at the frozen bits around the door in order for them to make it inside.

"We have five minutes," she says, "so pick something quick. We still have to go to the grocery store and get Lydia's chamber recalibrated before we go home. Don't dawdle Junie."

Junie is a hyperactive little girl who runs for the Children's section like goblins are at her heels. There she commences to yank down box after box and toss them to the floor, screaming that all she wants to see is *The Little Mermaid* and how this is a terrible place because we never have a copy. The woman's second child, presumably Lydia, is encased in an iron chamber shaped like an egg. The chamber skitters around maniacally on spider-like legs, knocking over the director's chair and nearly toppling the TV along with it. When it approaches I can see the baby inside. A hairless kid with too many eyes and not enough noses. I'm stuck wondering what's worse, sheets of ice or the mutative effects of radiation when Gandy walks up and puts the store keys in my hand.

"I'm leaving," he says. "Lock up or don't."

"Where are you going?"

"Do you have a copy of *The Little Mermaid*?" The mother sidesteps Lydia's chamber as it attempts to climb the check out counter. "We can't find it on the shelf."

The only thing remaining on the shelves in the Children's section is Junie, who hangs from the highest one like she's trying to rip it off the wall.

"It's checked out," I say. "I can put you on the waiting list."

"Are you serious?" She looks mildly terrified.

"Yeah, sorry," I say.

"Store is going to have to close," says Gandy. "You were a pretty good employee, all things considered. You'll be fine. Me, I don't have any other options, so I guess that's that." He slips a tan windbreaker over his shoulders and tosses his GANDY nametag on the counter. I don't understand at first what's happening as he heads toward the front door. The prospect of Gandy leaving the building is something I've never considered. Junie finally breaks the shelf and tumbles to the ground screaming. A red light starts flashing on Lydia's chamber and it's accompanied by a siren that's just a few decibels shy of a departing jumbo jet. The mother and her children spin around me in a vortex of chaos, and I stand frozen in the middle as Gandy climbs out onto the ice and begins walking in no particular direction. I realize that for Gandy, this is a form of suicide. He might have hung himself in the office with his bed sheet or guzzled down a gallon of the cheap blue toilet cleaner we keep in the back, but instead he's chosen life beyond these walls, whatever that might be.

The woman and her children leave without a movie, and I trace their progress along with Gandy's as they navigate the surface of the ice. A wall of sleet pushes in and clatters against the windows, causing me to lose sight of them all. It's only then that my brain settles down and I remember a couple of things.

We have two copies of *The Little Mermaid*.

Also, Alvarado's pile of jewels, which I estimate to be worth about eight million dollars, is still piled neatly on the counter by the cash register.

SUNDAY

The ice has melted and the trees are on fire again.

Customers rarely enter the store on Sundays. Instead they drop their tapes in the return slot like spies on a secret mission, eager not to get caught. I hear the clatter of tapes as they come into the receptacle, but when I look up to see who's dropping off, they're gone like ghosts.

In the morning's returns I find our other copy of *The Little Mermaid*, and all of the slasher movies the dust biker checked out. He's scribbled something in magic marker on the cover of *Sleepaway Camp*.

THIS WAS PRUTY GOOD. THK YOU.

I spend most of the afternoon in the director's chair watching *Groundhog Day* on repeat. I slip in and out of sleep, wondering if I have enough of the lizard man's mojo still inside me that I can warp reality. Maybe I could rewind to Monday, start the week again. Do it over and over and over, not so that I can get it right but so I can just keep living. I'm happy in this place. I'm not ready for it to end. I've always loved *Groundhog Day* and the quiet happy way it manages to be relentlessly melancholy.

I don't hear Cutter enter the store until she shakes my shoulder and says, "Hey, wake up."

"Cutter? You dropping off your movie?"

"I didn't rent a movie. Remember?"

"Oh yeah, right." I stand up, flatten my hair down with my hand and generally try to look like I wasn't asleep on a Sunday afternoon at work.

"So, Jeff. I came in to ask if you want to go do something. After you get off work."

"Like go on a date? You said you weren't looking for a date."

She's swapped her chainsaw for a sawed-off shotgun, and a leather strap loaded with shells crosses her chest like she just stepped out of a spaghetti western. She shakes her head and gives me a grin that seems to ask just how big of an idiot I can be. "All I'm saying is we could go to do something fun. Together. At the same time."

"I'd like that," I say.

"Great," she says. "So what do you want to do?"

"We could go to a movie," I say. "In a theater."

"Okay," she says. "It's a plan. What time do you get off?"

"I don't really have a boss anymore, so I guess now?"

"Then lock up," she says. "We can get something to eat first. My treat."

"I wanted to ask you something. Is Cutter your first name or your last name?"

"It's my last name," she says. "I just go by Cutter at work. My first name is Jennifer."

"Nice to meet you Jennifer."

I eject *Groundhog Day* and put it back on the shelf without rewinding it. I can pick up where I left off tomorrow.

Right now I'm looking forward to a movie I haven't seen before.

How Not to Come Undone

~ Richard Thomas

The family heard that the meteor shower would be visible from the cornfields of northern Illinois, just twenty minutes away from their sedentary suburban bliss, but Robert had been sleepless for weeks already, images flickering across his dreams—shadows and voices, a burning sensation running all the way to his core. They were mother and father, sister and brother—nothing special, rows of houses the same, but in blue, or yellow, or brick. But the boy—half of a set of twins, all the magic and wonder resting in his cells—the darkness and vengeance in his sister, Rebecca. So as they snuffed out the lights of the family sedan, hand in hand down a dirt path the boy had mapped out, trust so easy to come by in this family—the girl sparked danger in her squinting eyes, as the boy's ever widened to the stars, and possibility. Fresh cut grass lingered under buzzing power lines that disappeared as they stretched out to the horizon, a moist smell ripe with cleanliness and godliness—a hint of something sour underneath. The girl grinned as the rest held their noses, so eager she was to embrace death.

There was little talking, words so often failing them—the father full of muscle and pride, a quick arm around them all, a comforting presence on most days. The mother overflowing with worry, her long black hair often charged with static, as if thought and trembling nerves bubbled up to the surface of her pulsating skull. They did their best. And as the dry grasses and weeds rose up around them they held hands again, as the twins parted, spying each other, mother and father taking a breath together, searching for peace. They had spoken of meteors, talked about aliens, listed off planets—space so wide and unforgiving. Such potential, still, and yet, so much that was unknown, unimaginable. In each of them a different static, signals from far away mumbling welcome, whispering promise, giggling failure.

At the top of a hill they stopped, a blanket unfurled, some of them sighing, others grimacing in pain. The questions they would ask themselves on nights like this, and were in fact contemplating at this very moment, ran the gamut from inspired to self-destructive. Why me? Why *not* me? What does it all matter? Why are we *here*? On the darker nights when children lay healing, or feverish, or sick with disease, the father might pray a little—ask for the burden all to himself, willing to eat such pain with hardly a hesitation. On the darker nights the mother asked for forgiveness—somehow feeling that it must surely be her fault. Both asking quiet gods to pass over their twins, to find their sacrifice elsewhere. The boy might lie staring at his sister, the room black around them but for a singular bulb in the closet, her eyes as dark as coal, yet shimmering all the same.

"Becca, don't," he'd say.

"What?" she might reply.

"Any of it," he whispered, pausing. "All of it."

But he knew what she was, what she would become, and no matter his hope, his spark, there was little he could really do.

Or so he thought.

In the grass, on the hill, they scanned the sky for falling stars, for meteors, bits of fire and light and danger. The father fell asleep first, one last deep breath, searching his mind for the answer to so many questions, unable to quite figure it out before he went silent. It was like this on most nights—but then again, some evenings he solved many a riddle. The mother felt her husband go, and let it happen, the weight of it all just too much to carry, letting worry run off of her like rain on a slicker, giving in to weakness, expecting only the worst. But it rarely came. The girl had been waiting for this, the parents to slip away into slumber, for the darkness was calling to her, from every corner of the field.

"No, don't," the boy said.

"What?" she laughed.

"Any of it," he sighed. "All of it. Please. No. Let it be."

She batted her eyes, as if confused, and then lowered her gaze, incantations slipping over her lips, as the wind picked up, fireflies dancing on the breeze, a faint brush of lavender from the bushes back by the car.

But the boy was curious, and so he propped himself up on his elbows, the night full of so much curiosity—why not her? Maybe he was wrong. He could be wrong.

She found a stick and broke it into pieces, quickly stacking the twigs on a flat rock that sat exposed to the moonlight, forming the wooden splinters into a triangle, and then a pyramid, crossing one over the other, pulling a clover with four leaves from the grass, running a sharp thumbnail over her scarred palm, drops of crimson falling to the stone.

"No," Robert said, standing up, his parent oblivious, as if spellbound. "Not like that."

"This is the moment you always get queasy, brother," she whispered. "Not all that glitters is gold," she said, staring at the moon, baring her long, white neck as the boy took a step toward her.

"Must it always be death?" he asked.

"No," she said, bowing her head, as if that was the only trick she knew.

A flash of light overhead and his eyes shot toward the heavens, black felt dotted with pinpricks, slashes and sparks darting right to left, right to left, disappearing and fading over the hills and into the distance.

"So it begins," he said, embracing what she'd set in motion.

"I don't think that's me, brother," she laughed.

He spread his arms wide, as the stars fell around them, filling the sky, but so very far away. To the horizon it was as if they might land upon them, but no, that wouldn't happen. Couldn't happen.

If she had asked for death, then what had he asked for?

Evoking a crucifix he open his palms, and stardust fell upon them, as their eyes grew wide, a distant spark growing closer and closer until it lit up the field, the two of them trembling, his right hand catching something red.

He brought his hands together, the left hand over the right fist, a heat inside, bouncing and struggling, his hands glowing yellow beneath the flesh, orange seeping out, the girl coming closer, smiling wide, the boy trembling, skin gone pale, sick and uncertain.

What had he done?

"Open your hands," she asked

"No, I can't," he said.

"You must."

And so he did.

It glowed and pulsed, voices like underwater mumbling, a dark sphere spinning and rolling, spilling into itself, some sort of question being asked—forgiveness, perhaps, favor maybe, unable to breathe, his mouth open wide.

Without thinking he swallowed it down, hands to his mouth, as it burned and healed down this throat, burned and sealed as it descended, as it burrowed deeper, filling his body with light, rays pouring out of his mouth, his nostrils, his ears, leaking out of his eyes—arms wide, his sister stepping back in horror, his chest thrust out, neck bent back and then it was over.

Darkness again.

The boy collapsed.

The girl grinned.

And the parents woke up.

It was only the beginning.

After that, things were different.

The summer unspooled like a giant ball of twine, the boy glowing everywhere he went, his skin tan, eyes sparkling, his brown hair more blond every day. And the girl, just the opposite, pale to the point of translucence, her eyes two black orbs, her fingernails bitten to jagged daggers.

As long as they had been aware of each other, and possibly even before that, the twins had balanced each other out in so many different ways—yin and yang, dark and light, day and night. Things were more established now, nearly teens, the concrete nearly set, but it hadn't always been that way. The balance, it had been fluid. When Robert was joyful, Rebecca became angry. When the boy fell ill, the girl danced around the house, trying to cheer him, full of life. The best they could wish for was a rare neutral state where neither was happy or sad, just present—equal. And that was no way to live a life. Was it?

The family didn't talk about the meteors, the light show, what might have happened. It was a buried secret that no one ever brought up. Partly, the parents felt responsible, no surprise, and partly they didn't believe. But the twins knew, and their eyes lingered on each other, opening their mouths to speak, like baby birds eager for a worm, only to snap shut. Quiet. Uncertain.

More and more the boy would find himself sitting on the front porch of their house, Chicago brick, split with wooden frames, windows facing out in all directions, enough of a yard to run around. Rebecca would find him sitting with his legs crisscrossed, *applesauce*, eyes closed, open palms resting on his knees, a smile filling his face. Oh how she hated him then. The stories he told now, about what he could do. Had done.

And the she saw it with her own eyes—the boy so still, for so long, that a gimpy squirrel approached him, sniffing out the acorns he had placed in each open hand, its hind leg crooked, fur missing, a scar running across the mottled flesh. The little creature took first one acorn, and then the other, chewing at the shell, getting to the meat, finally resting in the boy's lap, against all odds—taking a well-deserved nap. The boy stroked the animal, gently, his hands resting on its hindquarters, his face rippling in pain as if he'd found a tack, and not soft fur. Her blood boiled. She opened the door, and shooed the creature away, its gait no longer hesitant or slow, bounding to the nearest tree, and up it in a flash.

When the boy opened his eyes and turned to her, she scowled.

"Did you see?" he asked.

"No," she growled.

"You did. I know it."

"There is nothing special about you," she whispered, her dark side of the scale dipping lower, as his face shone brightly in the sun.

It had come to this.

The rest of the summer would find strange cars parked in the driveway, bikes tossed to the grass, neighbors wandering over to return borrowed power tools, each of them pausing to say hello to the boy. They made it a point to shake his hand, slowly, to grasp them both, to hold them a little bit longer than necessary. He knew. And he smiled. Sometimes they gave him a hug, and he would hug them back, fearless, hands on their shoulders, sometimes moving lower to where a kidney might reside. Eventually he set a basket on the edge of the porch, so the giving would be less awkward, the words needed to explain, to thank, to rejoice now left on quivering lips—this would be their secret as well. The basket filled with candy and toys, with crumpled up dollar bills, jars of fruit preserves and plates of homemade cookies—whatever they had to offer.

Robert was not blind to Becca's descent, it had been up and down as long as he could remember, but there was so much darkness now, so much pain. He felt that he had driven her there with his joy, his love of life—and his gift.

He offered her a deal, but she refused. She hated him now. Perhaps it was too late. So he decided to trick her.

On the next full moon, when the parents were asleep, they went out to the back yard, behind the pile of wood for the winter, past the birdhouse swinging in the breeze from a rope tied to an ancient oak tree, past the pet cemetery down by the azaleas, to the makeshift altar the girl had built.

"What is it you want to see?" she'd said.

"Any of it," he whispered. "All of it."

She smiled in the darkness. She'd been building the shrine for days—the sticks, the feathers—the twine. There were acorn husks, a rotten apple, and a handful of writhing earthworms. There was paint in complicated hieroglyphics—stars, and circles, and lines. When she chewed at her ragged fingernail, pulling away a bit of keratin, blood blossomed to the surface, running down her finger, a single red coin landing on the rock below.

He acted quickly.

Robert took her hands, as she gasped and tried to escape, holding them tight, his own fingers now slick with her blood.

"You will not come undone," he said, anger flushing to the surface, a truth that danced across his skin, his eyes fading, his skin dulling. He pulled her close and held her tight. She struggled at first, and then realizing how strong he was, gave in. Her pain and suffering, it quieted for a moment, the voices dissipating, her tension unwinding into his frame. They met somewhere in the middle, brother and sister. A single cough, and the last of the glow escaped from his mouth, now a dancing firefly, heading out across the yard. As one lost its shine, the other filled with light, and as the moon overhead sat witness to it all, a shooting star ran across the sky, a spark of hope to all that saw it.

65

Diamondskin

~ Nicole Feldringer

The moles on my back form the constellation Cassiopeia. Sometimes when I dissolve between universes, I later discover the moles are skewed. Bunched on one side and stretched on the other, as though the perspective of the night sky is just slightly off. Other times the constellation isn't Cassiopeia at all. I wrap a towel around myself as I climb out of the bath, and, turning, catch my reflection in the mirror. I squint, wondering, is that how they were before? And: surely not. I hitch the towel higher.

Trauma branches me from one world to the next. Broken bone. *Branch.* Schoolyard bullying. *Branch.* Parental divorce. *Branch.* Car accident. *Branch.* Mugging. *Branch.* Trampled in a riot. *Branch.* Internet trolls. *Branch.* Gang violence victim (and perpetrator). *Branch (and branch).* Apocalypse.

Branching tears me from the previous version of myself, and that, in itself, is traumatic. I have been committed to mental institutions, sought solace in drugs, donned the delicious comfort of the martyr complex. I have leapt from airplanes and the highest flying machines a world has to offer, because why not.

I have committed suicide.

I am the glitch in the matrix. The one who retains memories against all logic. I have branched dozens of times, and in none of the worlds do I fit in.

Today is a whole new world.

I hang my towel on the rack shaped like a fish and painted mating-season red. The whole house is like that. Wood-paneled walls and chainsaw-carved bears, "gone fishing" and "gone hunting" signs. I find no computer, no phone, no technology more complicated than a coffee maker. I rummage in the kitchen, and my eyes widen at the thoroughness with which the pantry is stocked.

I help myself to a piece of jerky and pad into the great room. My bare feet, still wet from the shower, sink into a pelt that covers the floor from wall to wall. I swing open the front door and blink at the mountain vista spread before me.

Pristine, unsullied wilderness. Snow-capped peaks. The last rays of daylight are of purest silver. A floatplane bobs on a turquoise glacial lake. I consider that I might have to fly the plane back to civilization, but until I find a map, it's a death trap. A ticket to an empty fuel tank. Movement flickers at the edge of my vision, and I snap my head around.

A burly man—a real lumberjack cowboy mountain man—rolls shut a barn door. He crosses the yard with the easy stride of one who owns the dirt beneath his boots, and he grins at me. I feel my lips curve upwards in response. He mounts the porch steps and sweeps me into his embrace. My body, the traitor, melts.

My fingers flex against his flannel shirt, evidence of my internal war. Finally, I push him away. He backs up immediately, then steps off the porch so that he's looking up at me from the yard. "What's wrong, babe?"

Babe?

It would be convenient if the previous Leslie was secretly ambivalent about their relationship, but from the way my arms ache to lift, from the obvious hurt in his eyes, I doubt it. That Leslie had everything I want, but claiming her happiness is as unattainable as Mars. I don't even know if Mountain Man is my husband or lover. I want to fit in, desperately. But not as a sham. Not to be shoehorned into someone else's life. I don't even like beards.

I shrug helplessly.

"Come here, I want to show you something," he says.

I shove my feet in a pair of boots by the door and let him lead me around the back of the barn. I want to hug myself against the glacier wind, but he draws me forward, his calloused hand tugging mine.

He cracks open a shed door to the smell of wood smoke and wet dog. A pull chain *shnick-clicks*, then weak light pools around us.

I stand on a blue tarp. Tufts of hair surround my boots. The workbench by my elbow holds a collection of curved blades, and beneath it is a row of buckets. I peer into the first. Bloody rags. The second seems innocuous with salt, until I wonder what is packed *in* the salt. The next bucket has a lid. My hand moves as if of its own accord, freeing the edge to peek inside.

The lid falls from my fingers onto the dirt floor. "What," I say, my voice too loud in the confined space, "is that?"

He looks at me as though I have lost my mind and snaps the lid of the makeshift cooler back into place. Leslie wouldn't have asked that question. Normally I have more poise, but if this is to be my new normal, I am unprepared.

"A brain, for tanning the hide," he says mildly.

He's waiting for me to do or say something, and I peer into the shadows of the shed for clues. Against one wall is a massive frame. A skin stretches all the way across it, and I can tell by the way Mountain Man beams that I have found the prize.

I draw nearer, craning my neck up and up. The pelt is a grey-brown monstrosity. I cannot imagine the creature that must wear it. A giggle crawls up my throat because it's not like wearing a coat, and oh God what world have I wound up in, this world of monsters.

I walk out of the shed, a hand held to my mouth, the jerky sour in my stomach. "Leslie, it's not safe!" he calls, but I am running now, shoving tree boughs out of my way. I don't know where I'm going, I just know I need to get away from this strange man and his familiar hands.

The tears start to spill over, one by one. I don't hear him behind me. This version of myself must be more competent, more back-woodsy. Maybe I'm a bona fide Mountain Woman. I sniffle.

Between the black streaks of tree trunks, a pair of eyes gleam.

My stride breaks into an uneven trot, then a walk. The eyes disappear, then reappear as the animal blinks. Too high off the ground for a wolf or bear as I know them. I cannot help but think of the pelt stretched across the rack. The weapons left upon the work bench.

My boot snaps a twig and I freeze—even though the animal knows exactly where I am. It's stalking me. My location is not a secret to give away. I peer into the foliage anyway and call myself all kinds of idiot for not heeding Mountain Man's warning. I consider turning back towards the cabin, but I don't trust my route-finding abilities in the dark. Smarter to cut to the left. Once I reach the lake, I can follow the shoreline with starlight as my guide. But the eyes are also on my left.

Wild animals are more afraid of you than you are of them, I remind myself. Unconvinced by my own platitude, I steel myself to angle left. Not a hard left, but in that general direction.

A yowl sounds like a thunderclap. Too close. The hairs on my body stand to attention, and, irrationally, I break into a run.

If I can just reach the lake I'll be able to . . . Well, I don't know what I'll do. Hope the animal doesn't follow me into the open? Take a hypothermic swim? Better yet, hole up in the metal shell of the floatplane? I raise my arms to shield my face from whipping tree branches. The thunder of my own heart is deafening.

My toe catches a root and sends me sprawling. Ahead I can just make out the pebbled lakeshore. The stars are reflected in the lake like diamonds. I crawl toward the wash of moonlight. If I can just reach the lake, I will have space and options.

The lake laps just a few feet away, and I start to climb to my feet. Something stops me short.

I strain to move, but my leg is stuck fast. Slowly, so slowly, not really wanting to at all, I glance over my shoulder. The top of a broad head, darkly furred, blocks my view of my own leg.

My good leg crumples beneath me, and I land hard on my ass. From this new angle, I observe everything. Fangs poking gently into the skin of my leg, pinning me to the lakeshore. Gleaming eyes of a predator toying with its meal. Worse yet is the soft moist mouth enveloping my leg. It doesn't hurt—yet. I try to scoot backwards. A moan slips out when I fail.

The animal is so much more than its skin.

It mounts my prone form. It's not a bear or wolf or mountain lion or any creature I can identify from nature documentaries. The weight of its paw collapses my lungs. My mouth is open and I try, futilely, to draw in air. My body burns for breath. Warmth trickles down my leg, and the animal yowls again. A victory yowl. It fits its open mouth around my skull and chomps down.

I cannot scream, but I feel everything. Did Mountain Man know I was a goner the moment I fled? For the rest of his life will he carry the weight that his lover or wife was mauled to death by a wild animal? The thought that he'll remember me and not the previous Leslie makes me perversely happy.

Branch.

Traveling carries a certain grace. A traveler's place is not with the locals but with the other outsiders, the other travelers. The camaraderie is instant, and so what if it is fleeting, once strangers pass again beyond each other's spheres. My trouble is that there are no other travelers. No companions but the detritus left by the previous version of myself. Nothing would be so foolish as inhabiting the body of *that* Leslie and expecting her relationships to remain whole and intact.

After I branch from the mountain lakeshore, I find myself somewhere with olive trees and citrine light. Outside showers and bamboo-fiber towels. At first I mistake the commune for a yoga retreat, though they prefer "ecovillage," Sally reminds me.

I brace myself for an embrace. There are usually people, when I branch. Embracing or fighting or loving, and it is all too close and too fast. Vestiges of the previous Leslies remain like a haunting. I can find the bathroom at night, or get by at work. The right bit of music may even dredge up memories. But it's like watching a movie. The emotions I have to build for myself over and over and over.

Sally and Marisol don't push. We sit in the grass on a picnic blanket. I lay on my back watching the leaves rustle overhead. Sally is spinning yarn. Marisol is tinkering with some disassembled machinery. The smell of grease mingles with that of cheese and figs on a board. The figs leak juice onto the blanket, but no one seems to mind. It is peaceful in a way that no world has ever been, not even the one I was born into.

I rein in my thoughts. No good can come of lingering on the past. If I'm not careful, if my memories are not gentle with me, they will trigger another branch. The present is my solace. Ever forward I travel, and try to forget.

In this world, I am a park ranger, as I discover when I wake before dawn the next morning. I make coffee by rote and climb into a big green pickup with a California State Parks sign on the door. I do all of this on autopilot, and it's not until I'm shivering in the pickup that I wonder: *what next?*

I turn on the ignition to get some heat and draw my phone from my pocket. Leslie had her work address programmed into an app, and I let the phone direct me down winding lanes. Twenty minutes later, I roll into the gravel parking lot of a ranger station. I remind myself that, at worst, someone will ask if I'm feeling unwell. If I'm feeling quite myself. *I have been a bit under the weather*, I will say, *Maybe I should go home?*

Inside I make small talk and guzzle yet more coffee till my hands tremble and someone tells me I better go check on trail conditions out at Hatfield Ranch. I'm halfway out the door before one of the other rangers chides me for forgetting my firearm. I follow their glances to a locker. I try not to grimace as I fumble on my holster.

As soon as I step out of my pickup at the trailhead, I realize my mistake. These are different, drier mountains. More sunbaked. Definitely less remote, considering all the parked cars. But I flash back to the pressure of teeth penetrating my skin, and not even the gun makes me feel safe. I consider driving back to the ecovillage, but I don't know enough about my place in this world to throw away employment.

I lurk in the cab of my truck. Then, bored, I snoop. In the truck bed, I find the makings of an outreach station, so I set up a folding table in the parking lot. The display is dried plants and animal skulls. I bullshit to visitors about local flora and fauna, things I do not know. All of the skulls on the table are reassuringly small, and it makes me feel powerful to handle them. When the sun sets, I drive to Leslie's home. I tap the steering wheel as the chaparral blurs past the windows. How long will I be able to keep up this charade?

In the big farmhouse kitchen, Sally and Marisol prepare dinner. They refuse my offer of help, and I join Sally's son Justin in the family room. He wears a VR headset and haptic gloves, and I find it soothing to watch his hands dance in space, directing invisible armies.

Sally comes to call us to dinner and touches him gently on the elbow. Justin lets out a grunt. "Just a sec, lemme save my place." A moment later he pushes the headset off his face and sags back into the couch cushions.

"Hey Les, why didn't you join me?" Justin points at a spare headset on a shelf.

"Dinner was almost ready." I shrug, but I can't take my gaze off the headset.

After dinner: "It's like you've never played before." Justin's avatar laughs at me. "Follow my lead." As though that's not exactly what I've been trying to do.

The soundtrack fills my ears, the *whup whup whup* of air bubbles expelled as my avatar explores an underwater world of kelp forests and mer people. Justin warns me to watch out for tentacles. I almost laugh because this is the least scared I have been of monsters. Yet, the game has its own set of puzzles and challenges that make it as real and engaging as any other world. I should know.

I have no evidence that all the worlds I have visited are not in fact simulations, and the only thing that distinguishes me from the other inhabitants is self-awareness. In the game, though, the other players accept that it is a world within a world, and find it no less worthy a reality.

When we reach the end of yet another level, I push the headset off my face and check the clock. 3 A. M. I groan. "I have to work tomorrow. Don't you have school?"

Justin rolls his eyes and disappears to his room. I scurry to the toilet, then fall asleep on the couch.

Tomorrow is harder because I know what to expect. Headquarters. Gun. Trailhead. There was a frost last night, and I can't neglect my duties for a second day in a row. To top it off, I forgot to wash my uniform last night so I don my spare: shorts, not pants.

At the trailhead, I slam the door of my pickup and shiver in the morning chill. Goosebumps cover my bare legs as I blow into my hands.

As I hike, I listen to the thrum of my heart, evidence that my condition is not in fact purgatory. Late-season insects drone in the grass around my ankles, and one leaps across the trail and smacks into my leg. I remind myself to check for ice patches, and I consider my game plan if I encounter any off-leash dogs. I don't want to write anyone a ticket, but let it go and I risk getting this Leslie let go from her job. The last thing I want is to burden Sally with my freeloader ways. I like the people in this world; I want them to like me.

The trail cuts through a copse of trees, then opens up in a meadow. Ahead, a wiry man paces in circles. He is dressed in baggy athletic pants and a tatty sweatshirt with the sleeves ripped off. His head is shaved, excepting muttonchops.

At this early hour, I expect dedicated hikers. Khaki and fleece. Brightly colored packs. This man doesn't look like a hiker at all. His voice, when he screams at me, is surprisingly deep for his stature, with a smoker's rasp.

He wants his car. He wants Billy and his car. With a fist, he hits his thigh over and over again as he explains this to me.

I halt. I call across the gap separating us, "Did you park at the trailhead?" Stupidly, I jerk my thumb back the way I came. "It's back that way."

He takes fast steps in my direction and I'm too startled to do anything. He peers at me, shakes his head, waves me off. "Billy and me were supposed to go hunting."

"You can't hunt here."

He spits in the grass, then his gaze latches on my uniform. Shorts just do not carry the same authority as pants, and I regret again not doing laundry, and that's when I notice it's not a hiking pole at all that he's carrying but a—

"Are you fucking kidding me?" I ask as the tweaker aims his rifle at my chest and pulls the trigger.

Branch.

I miss that world. As I drift on the edge of consciousness awaiting the stars to resolve into my new constellation, I think: *I loved that world.* Which is not to say the drugs in *this* world aren't excellent, because they are. Very advanced. Very trippy. I'm going to need all the numbing I can find to make it back to where I belong.

I have never visited the same world twice, treating my existence like a river that flows in one direction. I have never appreciated the advantages of my unbroken memory, feeling it only as a burden. Now I see a glimmer of a possibility. I want to return to that world so badly that trying to manipulate my own trajectory seems worth the almost certain failure.

If getting mauled by a wild animal made me a park ranger, and being shot by a tweaker made me an addict, then what will it take to return to the ecovillage?

If I make it back I will quit the park ranger job. I bet there's something I can do at the ecovillage. Make bread, milk a goat. I'll figure it out.

I've filled the bathtub so high the water sloshes over the edge as I sit. I sprinkle bath salts over my submerged legs.

I lean back in the tub, which is dirtier than I'm altogether comfortable with, but I don't intend to be here long. The razor is dull and flecked with rust.

Branch.

Leslie is on a ship. It's not Justin's game, but it's a step in the right direction. I aimed for ocean, and here it is.

I immediately set to finding something heavy—diving weights from the SCUBA equipment room—and secure them to myself. It's best if I don't give myself time to stop and think. I'm wearing so many weights that taking that final step into midair is like walking through molasses.

Despite myself, I hold my breath. In survival situations, bodies assert their dominance over the brain. Sooner rather than later, Leslie's unconscious desire not to inhale water will be overruled by its inevitability.

I sink.

When the underwater people appear, I am glad I didn't rush death. They wear suits of neoprene or a similar material but no respirators, no tanks, no masks. Their lower bodies are covered in a single sheath, and I can't tell if they have legs or a fused tail. One swims past, languidly corkscrewing. Gills flutter on the side of their neck. No one seems to mind me at all; perhaps my stunt is depressingly common.

Relative to my descent, the underwater people seem to be rising like bubbles all around me. I giggle; my own bubble of air escapes my lips. *Whup whup whup.* I glance once at my feet. The darkness below is incomparable. A darkness that makes the night sky look friendly in comparison. It is inconceivable that a kraken doesn't lurk, poised to drag me into the depths. I'm already doing its job for it.

Buildings rise past me, not sunken, but built for dwelling underwater. The lights in the windows glitter like diamonds. I am the elevator going down down down to the basement. I shudder with cold. The people around me grow stranger. I am curious if they are modded or if evolution unfolded differently in this world. Perhaps they are all round-off errors in a simulation. My vision spikes with stars. A great plume of bubbles erupts from my mouth, further obscuring my vision, and it doesn't matter because Sally and Marisol and Justin and all the others are waiting.

Branch.

I recognize Justin's avatar immediately, green-skinned because water absorbs red first. Will Leslie be pissed that I'm playing her turn?

I force myself to consider what it means to visit the same world twice. I don't know what happens to the previous Leslies when I branch. I didn't get an instruction manual. I suppose I will find out soon enough if Leslie claimed that she'd been possessed. But then I remember I was shot; the doctor probably chalked up any amnesia to trauma. I snort. All the Leslies are fused together like a mermaid tail, propelling me through the multiverse. And I can't rule out the possibility that this is in fact a whole new world, so similar to the previous one as to be indistinguishable—similar enough that Leslie was shot even without my intervention.

Justin strips off his headset, and I will my arms to lift, but nothing happens. I remain in the game.

Alone, the NPCs seem more menacing, the kelp forests and mer people grotesque mockeries of the real thing. I try to ignore the sharp-toothed leers as I huddle waiting for Justin's return, but I don't even know if he saw me in that moment of our overlap. How long am I willing to wait, stranded half-way home? When I can no longer bear it, I find a new way to run away. There is more to VR than Justin's game.

In the chat room, insulated from the branching probabilities, my avatar's back is smooth and unblemished. I consider this may be a tenable solution, the blank slate of the virtual world, but I soon realize the people here don't see me. They see themselves super-imposed on me, and all the myriad traumas and joys and indiffer-ences that led them to seek permanent residency here. I find I like it even less than contending with the ghosts of other Leslies. Perhaps I imagined the sense of belonging in the eco-village, but it is the only world that calls to me, and my stubbornness is no less real for being late found.

Alejandro is the worst of them, pestering me for my story, but I didn't sign up for group therapy. His glance lingers, a challenge. "So why are you here?"

The hum of conversation around us dies. The chatroom is a riot of styles as though the graphics team threw up their hands and agreed to disagree. Bean bag chairs and chaise lounges and kitschy throw pillows embroidered with 8-bit inspirational sayings. The room is doubly periodic, like Ms. Pac Man, so while it feels infinite, if I squint I can see in the distance Alejandro's avatar looming over my own.

Before me, he purses his lips. I hear a whistle through the speaker in my headset, and suddenly I am aware of soft foam cupping my ears. Sweat damping the nape of my neck. My breath catches—a spasm of lungs—at the sensation of being connected to a body.

I refocus on Alejandro. "How do I find my body?" I ask, tantalized that there is one to be found. That perhaps I am not out of options.

He looks at me with scorn. His chest rises and falls on a sigh. "How are you doing that?" I jab a finger at him. "Where is my body?"

"Did you sleep through orientation?" Alejandro says. The fight drains from him, at my cluelessness, I suppose, and the onlookers disperse. He leads me to a pair of bean bag chairs. "Haptic suits suffer from latency," he explains as he settles in, "unless you can afford a firehose network connection. Full vfx avatars are the other option, the only option for some of us, and they are smooth as butter." He runs his hands across his chest. His avatar has nary a glitch to be seen.

A terminal screen blinks into existence before me, and his fingers hover to type. "Well? If you want me to help you, you have to give me something to go on."

I tell him my name and that of the ecovillage. Before I know it, he's accessing my account at the local bank. I open my mouth to protest at the invasion of privacy, but what does it matter?

"Accident on the job?" he asks, scrolling.

"How do you know that?" My voice is strained, distracted, as I try to absorb any of the data flying past.

"Worker's compensation settlement." He slows his scrolling. "Looks like you're paying for in-house nursing services. You sure your body isn't at home?"

Home. I roll the word around in my mind. *Ever forward I travel, and try to forget.* For good reason, it turns out. I force myself to confront what I left behind, after the tweaker shot me. The financial trail indicates Leslie's body remains in a coma, waiting for me. What will it take to revive that branch—to graft my self here onto my body there?

Here there are no wild animals, no razors, no bodies of water. But I have yet to visit a world that doesn't have some way to accomplish crimes ranging from unsavory to heinous. The terminal screen is still open, but the solution to my problem is beyond an internet search. "Who do you contact to get jobs done in meatspace? Jobs that might not be entirely on the up and up?"

Alejandro shushes me, though no one is near enough to overhear. "Talk to a therapist," he says, and the terminal screen winks out. "A lot of people have trouble adjusting."

As a demonstration of goodwill—and because maybe it will help—I do make an appointment with the therapist. I have done this countless times in countless worlds, and I steer away from topics that will trigger unwanted scrutiny. Instead, I sink into memory, recounting the warmth and yeastiness of the kitchen at the ecovillage. How Sally only swears when she makes cinnamon rolls. Marisol's infectious laughter at the rare crudeness.

When I leave the therapist's office, my cheeks are wet. I have finally found a place where I can't branch, and all I can think of is leaving. The receptionist shifts at the waves of frustration emanating from me. "Can I make another appointment for you?" he says dubiously.

"A friend suggested I come, but the help I need isn't here."

"Who's your friend?"

"Alejandro."

"In that case, may I suggest new friends. Michael is very good." The receptionist passes me a business card. When my fingers brush it, a private screen blinks open with an agency contact information and a 24-hour self-destruct notice. I flinch as though my fingers are burned, then reach forward again before the receptionist changes his mind. I have stumbled my way into the black market.

From that point on, it is almost too easy to hire a hitman for myself. I don't know if Alejandro was aware he was helping me, or if Michael and company are merely opportunists stalking the watering hole for easy prey. I don't particularly care. I follow the instructions on the business card to a private chatroom where an avatar appears behind the chipped formica counter.

When I ask if he's Michael, he shrugs, which I take to mean he's the agent regardless of what name he goes by. My awareness that none of this is real is heightened by the anticipation of escape. "You don't have to like me, you just have to pay me," the agent says, a complete misreading of my emotional state. Seriously, who am I to judge? The agent glances up at me. "You *can* pay me?"

I nod, thinking of the worker's compensation settlement.

"What services do you require?"

I am reluctant to voice my intent. Even though the hoops and secrecy suggest I am in the right place, I'm a stranger here. I brace myself for the agent's reaction. "I need to kill myself," I say. Words I can't take back even if I wanted to.

"Any requests for the final condition of the body and/or scene? Do you require shipping?"

"I need the body intact," I said hurriedly. "I just want someone to unplug my life support."

His response is an amount, nonrefundable. I pay it. A week later, a private screen blinks into existence before me, and I sink onto the nearest bean bag chair. I am not sure if I am ready to resume this journey. To see where it ends. *If* it ends.

Video footage shows the inside of a home. The offscreen camera-person passes a farmhouse kitchen with its island counter and old-fashioned hearth. I suck in a breath. The footage continues down the hall, and I feel more disembodied than usual. A man's hand, fingers coarse with hair, turns a door knob and the camera dips, revealing sensible nursing shoes.

I swallow back tears. Even though I paid him to do just this, I am repelled by the presence of this strange man in my room. Nearing my vulnerable body. If I could scream, maybe Sally or Marisol or Justin would come. I am unaware of anyone visiting me, but someone must be keeping my nutritional fluid levels topped off. Fear for their safety stops me from calling out. I feel like the traveler that has come and gone, having failed to hold on to my place in their lives. *Bon voyage!*

Yet, here I stand once again on their doorstep.

On the screen, my body is laid face down, the webbing of the cradle cutting into my chest. Tubes carry liquids in and out of my body. I wish I could disengage from the headset, block out this evidence of my vulnerability, but that's the whole problem isn't it? I am unable to do it myself.

The man's hand reaches toward my prone form in the cradle. Crushing my headset in his fist.

No life is free of trauma. I float for a time. I am relieved I haven't branched and awoken elsewhere.

My pride is wounded, I hurt all over, but lying here won't accomplish anything. Floating is boring. Weakly, I call for help. My voice rasps in my throat, and I recall that the video showed an empty farmhouse. I took it as a blessing, that Sally and Marisol and the rest were away. Now I worry my criminal-for-hire may have done worse.

I rip the tubes from my body. The machines that maintained my health are toppled and smashed. Had I not been poised to reclaim this body, the destruction of medical equipment would have been a death sentence twice-over. I don't know if I would have survived indefinitely, bodiless, in VR. It's not something I care to find out. I lay back, exhausted. Tears leak from the corners of my eyes.

A machine next to my cradle emits a dying beep, and footsteps pound down the hall. Marisol enters my room. Her shirt is covered in grease; she must have been working in the garage.

"I'm so sorry," I say. My experiences are what distinguish me from the other Leslies, and them from me, but I don't have to fight her. I don't have to fight my own skin.

She rushes to my side and helps clear away the tubes. She smooths my hair back from my face. Her touch soothes. "What happened? Are you alright?" Her dirty fingerprints mar the white sheets. "We missed you so much."

Today is a whole new world.

It's Good To Be Here In Alaska

~ Todd Zack

The Irish tenor was alone on stage, performing. He wore a tuxedo, shiny black shoes. He had only just begun to sweat. It was a sold-out venue in St. Louis, 1100 people, all seated, formally. The audience was rapt, an ocean of eyes shining out there in the darkness. A band of seven pieces—four brass, two string, one drummer—played beneath him, in the orchestra pit, stashed out of view of the crowd. The Irish tenor twirled on his heels as he sang. He was light on his feet, agile—with moves for miles—but it was his vocal brawn, his signature tenor that really made the money fly. He reminded a large portion of his audience of a golden age gone by. He made them think of Armstrong, Sinatra, Bennett—the titans.

The Irish tenor understood this, and he played to his audience's nostalgia; as those who came before him had, as those who would come after him would too. Someday, *he* would be a nostalgic figure evoked by a more contemporary performer. This, the Irish tenor imagined, was written in the stars. Even as one generation passed and another stepped forward, there would always be a cadre of crooners, a spiritual bloodline of performers with the talent to evoke the past, that true golden age: mid twentieth-century jazz/swing.

As a performer in this genre, you had to defer something to the titans. You had to perform a few tried and trues, in sepia hues. The "Summer Wind"s. You had to. The audience expected them, and that was fine, far as the Irish tenor was concerned. He always had a few oldies placed strategically in his set—standards you might call them—all the while making sure to keep his own material up front. One thing was for sure: you never closed with a classic. That would be capitulation. No. You closed with your *own* material.

The Irish tenor winked at the crowd. He was on his third song already ("Buy You a Cookie," an uptempo number from his second album *Hearts in Spring*) and yet to crack a cover song. That first cover—the initial token dip into nostalgia—would have to wait for another several numbers. Then, just before intermission, the Irish tenor would give his audience a souped up "Volare." If that made some of the old-timers piss their Depends, well, they'd have fifteen minutes to change diapers before the show's second half began.

As for now, he was coming out of the bridge, ripping into the last chorus—one octave higher then the former—of his own hit tune, "Buy You a Cookie:"

> *Gonna buy you a cookie, baby*
> *buy you a piece of cake*
> *buy you anything at all, that*
> *the man at the bakery makes*
>
> *Gonna try on you, a sonata*
> *Pen you a song, to sing—*
> *Buy you a cookie, buy you a cake*
> *gonna buy you a diamond ring*

The audience was all smiles and shining teeth, like a horde of Cheshire cats gleaming out there in the dark. "Buy You a Cookie" was one of the Irish tenor's most jubilant songs, and he knew well enough to place it early in his opening set tonight. He was responding to the feeling of the room. The mood.

The Irish tenor changed his set regularly, depending on the vibes he got just before hitting the stage. Then he'd number the songs on a scrap of paper. A stagehand would slip the night's set list to the orchestra five minutes before show time. Mixing up the set; this was a performer's intuition at work. It kept it fresh, for him and the crowd, some of whom followed him from gig to gig. Whirlybirds they called themselves, these die hard fans who took their name from one of The Irish tenor's deep cut tracks, "Coo Coo Bird." *"Only a Coo Coo bird would tell me what to do/ only a Whirlybird would follow me around like you."*

The Irish tenor had been performing this kind of 'period' music since he was a kid, really, but he didn't hit the big time until he was almost forty. Long apprenticeship. Numerous years on the casino circuit led to an appearance at a Macy's Thanksgiving Day Parade; lip syncing aboard a Pixar float in a suit and tie, with a hot orange boa forced around his throat, at the last possible second, by some network affiliated clown. "Fuck you think you're doing, buddy?" But, it was too late. Live television. Next day, the Irish tenor was a celebrity. Funny how things work. In retrospect, it might have been the comical neon boa (an act of unplanned self-deprecation) that captured the hearts of America that chilly November morning—a reckless, last-second touch of genius courtesy of a complete stranger. He'd never know.

There were those in his orbit who thought that it would never happen for him: celebrity. But, to the Irish tenor, his late blooming made perfect sense. When you're a fresh faced kid singing this type of "period" music; you come across, to many, as a novelty act, or worse; a joke; even if you're good. No, especially if you're good! Once you age up, appear a little worn, battle weary and wise—now you remind your audience of the titan's in their prime. Pushing forty; finally, you're really *there*. You've lost someone in the summer wind and you can emote that particular sentiment from a place within yourself that is real. At last, you've graduated from the school of emulation. Now you're *sui generis*, a man of your own, fit for touching hearts.

The Irish tenor wanted to commune with his fans. That was his motivation from the beginning: moving people. The money was great, the fame was fine, but touching hearts? This was the province of true talent: to reach people in the depths of their being. It wasn't something you could teach. Either a performer could do it, or he couldn't. Touch hearts. Move people.

Sometimes the Irish tenor would go for the soul, really dig deep. You'd have to be careful though—sensitive territory. "Love is an Evil River" was about as deep and dark as the Irish tenor was likely ever to go. This song was what he would call one of his "soul" songs. It changed the evening's mood, brought everything down into a vulnerable, wounded space. Everyone's been there. Then you'd have to turn that experience around, show some sunlight, build the evening up again, getting, in the process, ever more frivolous and flirty, until you closed the first set off on a swooning note with your first cover of the evening: "Volare."

But for now—low time—the lights dimmed, and froze. With the stage bleakly aglow, shrunken and suffused with groggy shadows—the Irish tenor sang "Love is an Evil River:"

> *Love was once an arrow in my quiver,*
> *and Cupid kept me dancing 'cross the days*
> *Now love is just an evil river,*
> *and I'm alone, staring through the haze*
>
> *I went down to the river*
> *and what there did I find?*
> *One face staring back at me—*
> *that evil face was mine . . .*

The stage lights shifted to a violet hue and proceeded to swell with false hope, then darken once again, as "Love is an Evil River" approached its denouement. The Irish tenor could feel his audience following him down into a place of great despair. He had drawn them together, in one piece, like a shade, string in palm—silent, still, in gloom, bereavement, heartbreak, ruin—he had them with him, as always. Some nights were more sublime than others; but tonight, he *really* had them, way down low.

He sang, softly, slowly, in his lowest register, "I went down to the river, and what there did I find? One face staring back at me, that evil face was mine." Shatter of snare drum, a splash of ride cymbals, a mournful parade of slowly drowning horns. "That evil face was mine . . ."

Stage lights out. Darkness.

Silence.

Finally, as if the audience remembered, of one accord, that they were all still present in the flesh, still alive—an eruption of rapturous applause.

I've done it once again, thought the Irish tenor. *I took them to the river. Sinatra couldn't do that to them, Bennett, Martin—Sammy . . . he'd get close, at times, with 'Mr. Bojangles', the talented son of a bitch, but even he couldn't pull the shade all the way down; not like I can. I bring them right down to the bottom, and then I build them back up again. One day, they'll have to reconfigure the totem pole. Put me on top. One day . . . they will.*

Ever so slowly, the midnight purple lights at the foot of the stage began to rise, breaking apart the shadows. In response—in perfect equilibrium with the ascent of the lighting—the mountain of applause began to collapse into itself. The Irish tenor took three careful steps backwards, towards the velveteen curtains. It was important to move after a big number, relocate—let the audience understand that you were beginning afresh from a different space, a different mood. As the lights continued to gently rise, shifting through lighter tones, the Irish tenor found his new spot. At this point in the show, the orchestra would wait for him to introduce the next song to the crowd; perhaps say a few thank you's, even chit chat a bit. You had to let them know, things were going to be better now. There were still a few smatterings of clapping hands. The Irish tenor could well procrastinate this transition, knowing that his patience would only serve to thicken the atmosphere with anticipation. *I have them in my hand's tonight,* he thought. *Let them wait.*

Just then, he heard an awkward sound—off to his right, at the edge of the stage—something between a squeak and a scrape. Nonchalantly as possible, the Irish tenor moved his head, just slightly, towards the direction of the invasive noise.

There, before the corner exit, a table and two chairs were being positioned at the side of the stage by concert hall staff. They were moving quickly, surreptitiously—almost done—no, wait—the final flourish—two wine glasses, a bottle of red.

The Irish tenor understood the scenario unfolding before him. VIPs. Somebody had paid two grand for a stage-side seat and a bottle of wine.

Oh, here they were now: a man and a lady, taking their seats as the staff persons disappeared swiftly into the shadows. Assholes. Coming in halfway through the set. They could have shown some class by waiting until intermission, but, no, certainly not. They had to make a scene for themselves. A very-important-person scene. The woman was platinum blonde—long, straight, shiny hair to her elbows. She wore a dark blue dress with vertical strips of shining sequins, and had a string of pearls gleaming around her neck. The fellow wore a fine whiskey colored silk suit and a white tie. He was a bit older than his lady friend, thin at the wrists, beak-faced, and slickly haired. The Irish tenor was straining to stay in the moment, for the sake of his audience, but he also wanted a better look at this fashionably late VIP bastard. A self-professed "big fan," no doubt. Yeah, sure he was. Buying attention, more like it.

As the footlights began to peak, the Irish tenor got his "better look," and, taken quickly aback, almost dropped his microphone to the stage floor.

It was Freddy Fuccillo staring back at him. The one and only. Dropping down into his seat, staring back at him, grinning.

The Irish tenor knew that pasty sardonic grin. Freddy Fuccillo. They had history, he and Freddy. Bad history. They had had a war, long time ago. There was money involved, women, romantic intrigue, family ties, issues of treachery and honor—everything really, the whole damn soap opera. He and Freddy had a war. People died. There were casualties on both sides, but it would be fair to say that Freddy had won that war and a sort of belated truce had been called—not by the Irish tenor or by Freddy, by their "people." You could say that orders were handed down. Things couldn't go on. But it wasn't enough for Freddy. The Irish tenor knew it wouldn't be enough for Freddy, just to win. He'd have to rub it in, somehow, someday—Freddy never let bygones be bygones. Never. It had been a long time, but here Freddy was, sitting at the edge of his stage, mid show, with a glass of wine, grinning at him—that grin saying, "Look who won. Remember?" The Irish tenor knew what this was all about. Freddy Fuccillo had shown up in his life, one last time, when he'd least expect it (once he became truly, legitimately successful), just to humiliate him in front of his own audience. One last, final twisting of the blade.

The grin. That grin spoke volumes. That grin said, "You couldn't find me, after all this time, yet here I am, up on your stage with you. And there's *nothing* you can do about it. Stop the show? Is that what you're thinking? Go ahead. I've got a car waiting for me, right outside that door. You'll never get to me."

The grin said. "I've always been faster than you."

The grin said. "So, why don't you just suck it up and sing for me?"

The Irish tenor could hear Freddy now. He could hear him! "Sing for me, you goofy little leprechaun. You wanna-be. You phony. Sing for me."

The Irish tenor snapped himself free from Freddy's silent taunting, turned himself, by great effort, away from the face of his nemesis. He set his eyes, instead, on his audience. They were waiting for him. The orchestra was waiting for him. Everybody was waiting for him! He needed to take control of this situation. Now!

"Thank you, thank you," The Irish tenor said to the crowd, drawing his fingers down one side of his face. "Well, it's good to be here in Alaska!"

Scattered laughter from the audience.

"What? Did I just say that?" The Irish tenor moved the microphone to his left hand and raised his right arm, up and out, drawing a pointed hand in the general direction of the VIP table, yet taking great caution not to look there. Eyes on the crowd. "It's good to be here in Alaska!" The Irish tenor said once again. "Ha ha. No, that's an old troubadours' joke. Where am I tonight? Glad you got it—some of you anyway." He brought in his right arm, holding the microphone more intimately now, with both hands. "Of course I know where I am." The Irish tenor looked coyly at the crowd. "I'm in Saint Louis!"

Cheers from the audience.

"Saint Louis, Missouri!"

Cheers.

It shouldn't be long now. He just had to keep ad-libbing.

"Honestly, folks, Saint Louis? Let me tell you something about Saint Louis, and I mean this from my heart. Saint Louis is one of my favorite cities in the whole—"

Two gunshots went off in quick succession, loud as cannon-fire in the large vaulted room. Freddy Fuccillo flipped over backward in his chair, bounced off a stage light and landed sprawled out on his back at right corner stage, splayed on the shiny black floor. His blonde lady friend, eyes shining like greased marbles, pushed away from the VIP table with a scream. Wine flew in a high arc. She fled, arms writhing above her head, and her heels clacked madly against the stairs as she disappeared from the side of the stage.

Already, the audience was streaming towards the exits. The orchestra musicians were climbing from their pit, dropping various instruments behind them in a series of atonal crashes, joining the flow of the retreating crowd.

Taking advantage of the chaos, the Irish tenor unplugged his microphone and tossed it into the orchestra pit. He turned and made haste to where his inveterate enemy lay bleeding out on the stage floor. The Irish tenor dropped to his knees beside Freddy Fuccillo and grinned into the dying man's face; a face frozen in a pale blood-drained mask of astonishment and horror.

"It's great to see you again, Freddy," The Irish tenor said, calmly. He leaned closer to the stricken man, contriving a shared conspiratorial space for any observing eyes. "You've been shot in the lungs, Freddy. Both lungs. You'll live another minute or two—so stay with me." The Irish tenor turned his cheek and called out to no one specific. "THIS MAN'S BEEN SHOT! CALL AN AMBULANCE!"

He returned his attention to Freddy, staring deeply into the dying man's eyes. "I knew I'd see you again, Freddy. I know the way your mind works. I knew you'd come to one of my shows someday. You'd sit up front, where I could see you with your shit eating grin, and you'd rub it in—what you did to me—all that money, all that bullshit and bloodshed. AMBULANCE, PLEASE! HURRY UP!"

Freddy Fuccillo wheezed, spraying dark flecks of blood from his mouth.

"And then," the Irish tenor continued, "having stuck it to me one last time, you'd slither out, before the show ended, before I could get to you. Gone forever. AMBULANCE! HELP!" Through the curtain at his back, the Irish tenor could hear sounds approaching from backstage, a fall of rushing feet. Security was heading for the stage. His time with Freddy was getting short.

"Look up there, Freddy, in the rafters, behind the upper box seats." The Irish tenor motioned with his eyebrows. As ordered by the Irish tenor, Freddy moved his eyes, slightly, towards the perimeter of the room. "There's my man," the Irish tenor said. "Hiding up there— every show—for the last twenty years. Every show, all over the world, he's with me, waiting for my code words. Waiting for you." The Irish tenor showed his teeth and a random stage light caught his eyes, turning the pupils gold. "It's good to be here in Alaska, Freddy." He slapped Freddy's cheek playfully with one hand, and with this last insult, the dying man's face began to slacken and sour. "It's good to be here in Alaska," The Irish tenor whispered.

A gauntlet of security personnel stormed onto the stage and collected the Irish tenor from his knees. Briskly, they carried him off—through curtains, down a hallway, throwing open the double doors of an emergency exit, pushing him out, safely, securely, delivering him into the night. Off in the distance, the rising wail of police sirens.

As the small army of protective hands fell from his shoulders, the Irish tenor felt the cold winter wind rushing over him. The skin of his cheeks prickled. He looked up at the benighted sky and sighed.

It was snowing.

Unschooled

~ Christi Nogle

I'm twenty years old before I finally get up the nerve to run away. I just walk like I'm going to the high school in a pair of Mom's big jeans because that's all I can fit around my baby belly. Big hoodie and a heavy backpack. I pass the school and no one stops me, and I'm surprised. Walking out past the parks and the courthouses, past the fancy Victorian houses and onto the old highway, I keep thinking someone will take me for a kid and ask why I'm not in school, get up in my face, see how I'm not right, scream maybe. They don't.

I walk about five miles, all told, past the reservoir and up a steep hill and down again. I walk a bicycle trail between the highway and the burbling river. As I go, the rich people yell "on your left" and shoot past, or they come at me from the front and look at something else. I'm seen but not seen.

I sit on a bench by the bridge drinking the last of the water in my canteen. I think about food, decide to leave the granola bars for later, fill up the canteen with river water, think about catching a fish.

A rich-looking a subdivision lies east just across the old bridge. *Canyon Village* says the sign, hot white light glinting off of a little fountain. The houses are low and painted dull shades of green and fawn and gray to match the high desert and foothills surrounding them. West, there's just some dry land that used to be irrigated pasture and a couple of struggling trees. I sight something dark between the trees, and when it's safe, I cross the highway and see it's a roofline. I pull up a string of barbwire, heave me and my belly under the fence and head that way. Up a steep driveway and down again, I come to an abandoned house. Nothing special, just a little two-bedroom with a burned-out kitchen that's never been repaired.

The front door's locked, but the back door glass is gone and the door unlatched. There isn't much inside, but there's some old clothes I can use for bedding. Just the place to have my pups.

I gather a load of the tee-shirts and socks and things and make a pile of clothes in the floor of a walk-in closet. I press into the clothes in each direction to make a sort of a nest. Thinking how warm I'll be tonight, I unpack my backpack and arrange my things on the top of a little particle-board dresser. I put my clothes in the drawers. A mouse pops out of the first drawer I try, and I run it out back and then just sit in the nest for a while, thinking to doze but I can't.

After a while, I take off the jeans and hoodie. I hate seeing myself naked anytime except a moon night, but it's especially bad now with the belly and all the teats swelling out. I'm not right. Long, long feet and I go up on my toes. My thighs are short little things that look like part of the hips, my arms and legs skinny like a wolf's. All I can do is sigh, put on a sweatsuit. I'm good about not thinking of it once I'm dressed.

Before we moved to town, I'd go shirtless with my cousins, catching fish in the lake and running around the forest, nobody around but wolf-folk and all us pups. I had no teats then, just little buttons, but ten of them. Most folk just have six or eight. New people would always say something about that because there wasn't much else about me they could praise.

If they were family, though, they'd know to talk about how smart I was. How I remembered my Dad and his brother Aaron even though I'd been just a few weeks old when Aaron left and not more than six months by the time Dad followed. They'd tell how I climbed out of my crib at night to build things until Mom locked bars on the top. I couldn't get at anything to play with then, so I'd lay there making up stories and songs, talking all through the night.

I remember doing that, too, and I wasn't any more than a year, year and a half. Yeah, I was smart as a kid.

And everybody loved me. We had uncles and aunts and all sorts of cousins came over back then. They'd hold me on their laps, rub my belly and behind my ears while we watched T.V. They'd tell me how they had an old uncle or aunt back in the day or a friend of a friend—they'd all known somebody like me who got along all right. They didn't mention how times had changed since then.

Somebody was always home with me in the day, Grandma and Grandpa if no one else. Somebody always teaching me out of a book or showing me how to cook or fix something, feeding me things that I liked. I was happy, and I never felt *that* different, you know? Of course it was always, "Mary can't come into the store" or "Mary, you go to your room for a minute. Somebody's coming down the driveway," but nothing like how bad it was after the move.

I couldn't go outside when we moved to town, not at all.

Mom had got a promotion and a transfer and had to dress up every morning. She'd shave and dry herself, powder herself with talc from the Bon Marche's perfume counter. She'd exhale and suck everything in to inch into a high-compression bodysuit, slip in the expensive falsies that looked like cuts of fresh chicken. Thick department-store makeup in neutral colors, tight gold hoops. She'd dress in a long narrow skirt and high heels. I'd watch her sometimes, tell her how pretty she looked.

And wait the ten or twelve hours until she came home, nothing but the TV for company.

She'd cry sometimes. She talked about going back home, but then she met a woman at work who wanted to go around on the weekends, and then she met Gary, and a few months later, we drove back home but only to have a wedding.

First time I thought about leaving, I was twelve. We'd been in town a couple of years. My cousin Bart had moved in, and he was fascinating. At home he wore eyeliner, a half shirt showing off the pierced nipples on his belly. His girl was nothing but wild hair and perfect legs, and they were always making out in his room with the door open 'cause Mom wouldn't let them close the door.

He'd crack up Mom and Gary and anybody who was over. He'd throw on a hoodie and go out and bullshit with the neighbor boys, take out the trash. Always had funny stories about the people at school. I never could go to school, of course.

I thought how much happier Mom and Gary would be with him for a kid. I could go into the circus, be an actor, something. I'd gone stupid by that time. Living in town will do that to you.

That girl of Bart's, Melanie, she changed my life, I guess. She'd sit and color with me or play with dolls—whatever I wanted—and never say it was stupid or too young for me. That's just how she was.

She'd cook and talk with Mom, too. Just a sweet girl. She felt so bad for me she started bringing around people closer to my age, her sister and cousins. Up to then, I'd gone out on moon nights with Mom and folk like that, but soon I was running with the younger ones.

I'd find myself sneaking out when it wasn't moon night to party in some garage or basement. That's how I found myself in trouble that first time, running with wolves that Melanie knew.

The first night in the abandoned house, I open the front door and sit watching for lights to turn up the road, but no one turns. Around two or three in the morning, I think about the granola bars. Instead, I go on back to the river to fill the canteen. There's a trashcan by the bench and at the top of it, a half bottle of Gatorade and half of a cheese and cracker snack pack. It's all I need for dinner, but a scent catches me. I dig a little further and find a couple of bites of sushi from the grocery store up the road. I'll eat it and not get sick, most likely. Never had a weak stomach.

I watch the river for a while and start to get scared because anyone could drive down the highway, late as it is. Mom and Gary are already looking. Aunts and uncles, cousins, other folk—they could be rolling into town any time. They'd take the old highway in--didn't *we* always do that? I slink on back to the house and close myself in as best I can, old chair blocking the door and all.

I can feel the pups moving, how many I don't know. Up to ten, I suppose.

Melanie quit coming around not long after her and Bart's wedding. I never saw her belly or heard why she was gone, but she showed up at a cookout at Grandma and Grandpa's with a sweet little baby just like on a box of diapers. Melanie had always been so good to me, but that time she passed the baby around to all the relatives but me. When Mom asked, she said I might scratch it by accident, and everyone was quiet. Mom wasn't too pleased.

I wonder now how many pups there were and what happened to them. What all did Melanie go through? Why didn't she help me, later, when I had my pups? And why can't she be with me now, or Mom, someone? I'm miserable that first night in the nest, warm and safe and miserable.

○

The days go by. I lie low in the yard and watch people go by on the bicycle path, mostly cyclists during the day but sometimes walkers in the afternoon. Women go by in pairs wearing tight exercise clothes. A man comes by a couple of times with a Samoyed puppy that looks up at him the whole time. He talks to it, makes it sit down and lay down. He goes in his fanny-pack for treats, and their scent comes meaty and velvety-rich.

The moon gets fuller. There's something in the garbage can most nights, and after a week I get brazen enough to strip and get down in the river. I catch a couple of fish and get my bath in the morning sunlight. The bicyclists don't slow or even look my way.

I wish I had a TV. I stole Mom's e-reader. It's packed, but with like *Middlemarch* and *Jane Eyre* and modern romance novels that make me feel weird, like I want to party and run with the young people again, even though I swore all that off.

I wish the full moon would come before these pups, but I'm starting to doubt it will.

Someone rode a quad around the house, and I just about shit my pants. They revved and rode around a long time before they left. I'd been in the kitchen about to finally break into those granola bars, and then I hid and tried not to make any noise, and then the pups started to get ready to come. I was calm and slow. I breathed and waited.

It took me all back. I was sixteen. "Ought to have known better," Gary said, and Mom was mad as hell, but it smoothed out over the months in between so that we'd all started to talk about getting ready for the baby.

"Babies," I said. I could feel for certain more than one of them.

Mom said, "Maybe. It's possible, though I don't think. . ."

Gary said, "Wolf babies don't ever come in multiples."

Like I didn't remember my own dad's twin brother. But things were weird just then and had been weird, and I didn't talk back to them or ask any questions.

I guess I trusted them to help me through the birth and whatever happened after that, but they were out for a drive when I felt the pups coming—they hadn't expected that to be the night.

I'm alone this time, too. I ease myself down into the T-shirt nest and pull the closet door shut. My skin starts to prickle with a rush of new fur.

When I lay on my bed that time, I shifted all the way into my beautiful self. I'd never done that at home, never except on moon night out in the forest. I remember feeling calm and slow, like now. I remember each of those beautiful pups coming out, the tiniest one first, and the next two quicker and cleaner.

I was licking them, then and now. The first time, all three of them, tiny but mewling, had latched onto me.

And this time they keep coming. Three, brown-furred and strong, four, five.

I've never felt such peace and love.

Six is lighter, larger than the rest, seven is dark and grayish, eight and nine are just like the first ones. Ten didn't make it, but I lick her tiny body clean all the same. I'll bury her out by one of those struggling trees and bring it water and hope it will grow.

I lick at the pups until it seems I've never done anything else, until we're all clean. They're latched onto me, then sleeping. My own sleep comes without permission.

When I wake I've shifted back into what I am, and they're all still puppies. Our nest is matted with clumps of my shed fur, and I rub the rest of it off as quick as I can. I'm starving, but I can't get up. They're waking slowly, coming to nurse again, not like those first three who never woke.

That day's when I start eating the granola bars. That's when I start to wonder what's next.

By the time I shift again, the moon night, they're all starting to have baby faces, all but the lighter one. You can tell she's going to be all wolf. Her teeth are too much for me to stand already. The gray one, I can't say. Sometimes I think he is starting to change, sometimes not.

It's crisp and clear that moon night. The moon seems to fill half the sky, and everything's blue and bronze and pewter. I run over just-damp hills. I have to run miles and miles for a deer. There are sheep closer, but I don't dare.

All full and lumbering home, I'm lonely. I'm howling before I can stop myself, and that's when I think I've made the fatal mistake, but still, no one comes, not on moon night and not at dawn when I wash off all the blood and fur in the river. Great clouds of buff-and-sable fur float away on the current, and I think how Mom and Gary and Bart and all the rest never have to shed on moon nights. They're beautiful wolves and suddenly they're beautiful women and men, or almost beautiful. Normal. It's like what happens to them is some fantasy, some metaphor. Only for me is it a real and physical thing.

I am myself again now, cold river water stinging at bare skin. So overfull I feel about to puke, but wide awake. An early-morning cyclist flashes by without looking. For the dozenth time maybe, I cross the highway and go up and down the hill to the house in daylight. It's too risky, this walk. I'm naked this time. Hard as I am on myself, I know I don't exactly pass for a house-dog.

When I get back, the pups are wandering around the bedroom, but they come straight at me. They all want at my mouth. They won't leave it, and before I can think, I'm puking up deer and they're licking it off of the floor. I think what Mom would say if she saw this. I'm ashamed, but not ashamed enough to stop doing the trick for them. They want at it so bad.

Not too long later, they want milk, all but the lighter one and the gray one. They don't wake, and I grab them and put them on me. They suck for a minute and go off to sleep again. That's when I count: light, gray, three, four, five, six, seven, eight.

Light and gray, it's not like they're full. It's like they're stunned. Light, when I look close at her mouth, she has something dark in her fur.

And nine didn't make it. I crouch in the kitchen, run my hands over his blood-matted fur. I want to think something got in here, a fox or a dog, but I'd have smelled it. Something happened between the pups while I was gone. It was the light one, had to be. Those sharp teeth.

Gary's words come back distorted: "This is *why* wolves don't ever have multiples."

Or why they're not allowed to keep them, or why there was only ever one like me around. I feel I am about to understand something. To keep thinking of it right now, though, will make my head hurt.

Instead, I think how I'm not leaving the pups again, and I think how I can handle things, but next morning I lay low in the yard when I see Melanie's big blue truck parked by the entry to Canyon Village, just a few feet from my garbage can and my bench. She just sits there and finally moves onto the highway.

So she has found me. Probably somebody saw me or heard me and posted something about it online. It'll be days at most until Melanie tells Bart or Mom, if she hasn't already. Me and the pups have got to leave this place, but I can't think where to go or how.

What has it been, three weeks? Twice that? I take the pups outside to get warm, to see them clear. Their faces are all smooth now, all except for the light one, but fur still grows down their backs to their little tails. Not a one of them is going to be a diaper box baby like Melanie's. They're all going to be like me.

It's then I know for sure that those other babies didn't just die there on my chest in the night but that someone—Mom, Gary, even Bart—someone must have come in and pinched off their air. It must have been something like that. A mercy, they probably thought.

Watching the pups now, out in the sunlight, I know something else: babies like Melanie's are not the best ones. Folk think they're pruning off the weak ones, but what they're really doing is saving the weak ones and sacrificing the strong ones, the smart ones. I start to cry out of self-pity thinking how strong and smart I was when I was new like them, before I got trained to be different.

There is a man who bicycles along the river sometimes who's not like the others. He stops and sits on the bench by the river and reads from a thick book before he crosses the bridge and turns into Canyon Village. Glasses and a tight little beard. He could be a professor or something, maybe a scientist. I go into daydreams about the life my babies could have in a house like his. I think of leaving some of them there with a note to tell him all the potential they have. He'll teach them and they'll grow up to be some sort of superheroes, some great ambassadors of the folk.

And the light one, what could she be, somebody's house-dog? She'd murder them all in their sleep and slink off into the night. I smile an ashamed smile thinking of it, stroke her thick coat.

If there's one thing I was taught, it's that you can't trust people. I'd just as soon hide the pups in a hole as trust a person with any one of them.

Folks are coming, soon, and they're going to . . . I don't know. They're going to murder these children? Could they do that, at the age they are now, with their beautiful faces? They couldn't take so many and hide them away like they did with me. Maybe send them off to a half-dozen different relatives to hide? That's the best I can think of, but still it makes me cry.

The babies claw around in the dirt smelling everything. After ten minutes exploring, they doze, but there's such wisdom in their faces even then. I pick up a little pink hand and stroke the fur on the back of it. The hand squeezes my finger like it's made to do.

They don't have people names, but they're all individuals. Sleepy and Crabby, Toughie and Tootie, Runt and the Piggy, and of course Light and Gray. Gray's face changed later than the others, but now he looks a lot like Dad.

They're all growing so fast, but Light especially is older than she has any right to be. I've never seen anything like her. She rolls in the dirt and gets up sneezing. She tussles with the gray-furred baby and comes in to where the others doze around my legs. Right in front of me she starts to gnaw at Tootie's shoulder, makes her wake up with a shriek and there's a little bead of blood. I stroke the hurt baby with one hand and with the other pick the light puppy up and hold her to my chest, sink my nose into her beautiful fur.

I'm just so tired.

I can't take them home. I think of walking them to the woods, but how far would that be? I think about leaving them here and going for—what? Help? No one can help us.

But you can't just give up, can you? I pack the bottom of the backpack with parts of our nest, and I put on a clean-ish pair of pants, put on the hoodie. Seven pups go in the backpack, and I'll have to hope they don't smother each other. The light pup I'll carry to keep the others safe from her.

I walk out into the front yard and there, by the side of the highway, Melanie's sparkly blue truck is pulling over. Another will pull in, and another, and my people will rush up here to take care of family business, but as I'm frozen there, Melanie gets out and helps her little daughter out the driver side. They go to the back of the truck and take out a big bike and a little bike. Melanie puts a helmet on the little girl, and they ride away.

They look like the people who come here every day, clothes a little brighter, maybe, but otherwise the same. There's something strong-smelling in the truck, and I know that she's left it for me. She couldn't bring it up to the house because she had the girl with her.

When I can't see them anymore, I start down to the truck. The backpack's impossibly heavy and shifts with their weight, and the angry noises they make. I know I'm defeated. This walk down to the highway is the worst one of all, as I think of cars coming in from every angle and live a hundred different horrible outcomes, but mostly it's the dread of someone loved and trusted coming in--Gary or Mom or Bart or even one of those laughing uncles—someone coming in and taking away the last of my illusions about what folk are.

The bright day, dead grass, and dread, dread, dread with every step, but at the same time, the smell is clearer. Deer jerky, a lot of it. The light pup smells it too, and she's fighting to jump out of my arms.

I lean in the truck window toward the box full of wrapped jerky. I am going to just eat it, just let the pups in it as well, and we'll just sit here like caught mice until someone comes along. It could be folk from home or the police, or the subdivision people, Melanie— it doesn't matter—except I see the keys with their little rabbit foot keychain just hanging there in the ignition, and on the car seat a brand new phone, and in the extra cab are two plastic carry boxes with holes in the sides and locked gridded doors. I've still got Light against my chest, and she's screaming, and I'm taking the rest of pups out of the bag and getting them in those cages, rushing, rushing. I'm in the driver's seat and trying to remember a time five or six years ago when Melanie tried to teach me to drive out on the forest roads around Grandma's.

Oh God, Melanie. Why did you think I could still do it? The pups are all screaming. They've never been caged before. The truck's hot inside, the jerky so thick in the air, and I finally have the thing on. It lurches forward, and I find the brake. I calm myself. Slow and calm. A glance at the phone. There's a message on it: *You don't have much time. They're coming I just got here first.*

A bicyclist is approaching, and he does have his head turned toward me this time. Maybe it's because the truck's so blue. He's taking in how wrong I am, and I can count on one hand the number of times a person's seen me so clear. I give him a smile as he comes close, and he loses balance. Maybe he rides into the bench, maybe into the river. I don't see. I am easing onto an empty highway, hands at ten and two, and I do remember. I am moving faster, and the pups—because I'm calming, because of the stress they've just had— they're quieting. I relax my hold on the light one, and she lays by the side of my leg.

We move past Melanie and her pretty baby still riding their bikes. I don't wave. If she does, I don't see. I don't think we can go to Grandma's. It won't be safe. I don't know where we're going, not at all, but I do know I'm finally getting the fuck out of town.

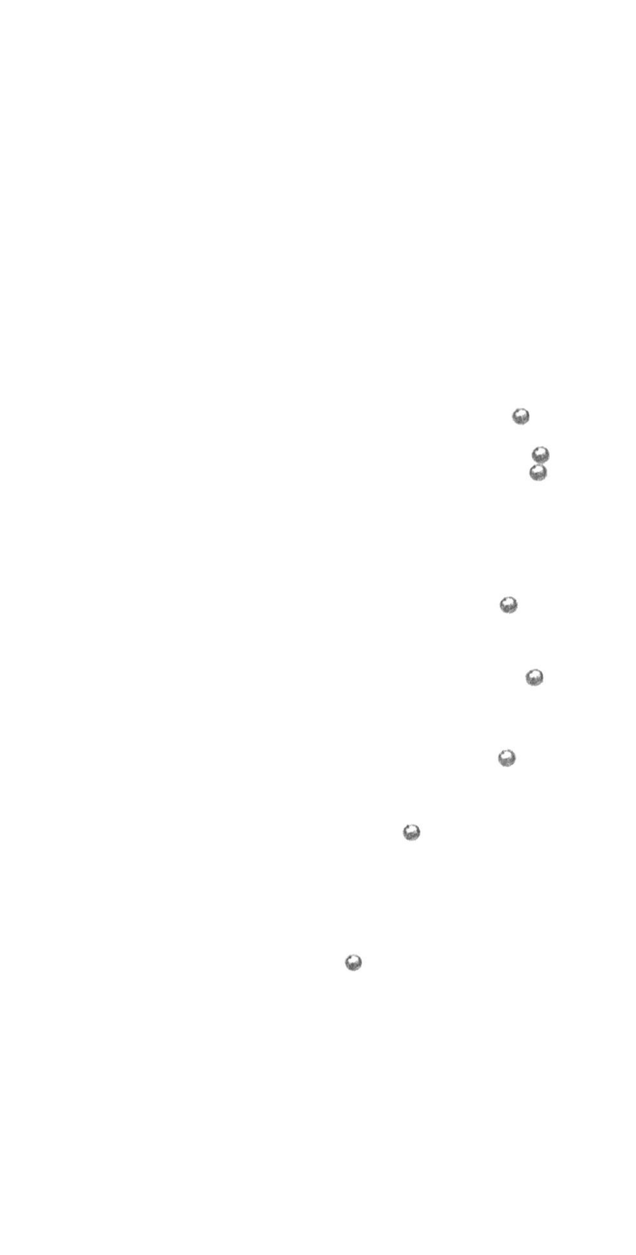

Old Gar

~ J. Dee Stanley

I met Jimmy in detention. Must've been twenty years ago, give or take. The river of life is long and winding.

Back then, Jimmy looked three years too-old for junior high school. His long, greasy black hair hung down to his knuckles. We didn't share any classes, but I'd seen him around.

A long time ago, my dad used to work for his dad. It was a small town. Even smaller school.

When the teacher left the room, Jimmy turned to me. He had a wild flame in his eyes. Like he knew something I didn't.

That irritated the hell out of me.

"So what'd you do?" Jimmy asked.

"I beat up Drew Hollander," I said.

"What for?" Jimmy asked.

"Talking to me."

"That's it?"

"Talking shit about my dad. How 'bout you?"

"I put a' alligator in the girl's toilet."

Jimmy said it nonchalantly. Like it was no big deal. And he didn't say, "an" alligator. He said "a" alligator, with a full stop.

Also, I hate alligators. Always have. Not just alligators—really, I hate all reptoids. They're cowards. They wait until you're weak and full of love. They take advantage.

So that pissed me off even more.

"Bullshit," I said.

I turned back to my homework. He sat there wriggling in his seat, waiting for me to ask how he did it. But I didn't give him the satisfaction.

Now there's something you don't know, I thought. *You don't know me.*

I didn't say another word all detention period.

As the week wore on, word about Jimmy's prank spread all over school. He wasn't lying about the alligator in the toilet, although it was only a baby.

Honestly, the alligator didn't surprise me. Jimmy's father, Big Jim Sr., owned an alligator farm by the Mississippi border. That's where my dad used to work.

A month later, Jimmy pulled the same stunt again. Another baby alligator in the girl's toilet. The second one nearly bit Barbara Hollander on the butt. I had ongoing quarrels with her brother Drew Hollander, so that was all right with me.

Normally, I never caught wind of any gossip. But these rumors were unavoidable.

First, I heard about Jimmy's momma. She took off some years back, and Big Jim Sr. raised Jimmy up alone, just like Momma raised me. I've only met my dad a couple of times—he's been in jail for a while.

But of course, Jimmy's momma didn't necessarily go anywhere when she "took off." More like, "went missing." Back then, people got lost in the swamp all the time. They still do every now and again. It's easier than you'd think. There's a lot of land and water. All of it mixed together. All of it unlivable—a reptoid wasteland.

Not long after that first time, I got another detention. Don't remember what for. Sure enough, Jimmy was there too. This time, I couldn't ignore him.

"Did your dad really feed your momma to the gators?" I asked.

"Get the fuck outta here," he said.

"That's just what I heard."

"That's all lies."

Jimmy's tone was defensive but not wounded. He seemed relieved someone finally asked.

"So what happened?" I asked.

Jimmy looked both ways, even though we were alone in the class-room. The gesture worked some kind of magic. I tried to resist, but excitement rose up to form a knot in my throat. Like a roller coaster or an action movie or church when somebody gets the spirit.

"You know how reptoids control the media, right?" He asked.

"Momma says liberals control the media," I said.

"Right, but the liberals are also reptoids."

"Like frogs?"

"No, dummy, frogs are amphibians."

I never could remember which was which. Plus I wasn't sure if there was a difference between reptoids and reptiles. It could've been another one of Jimmy's tics, like "'a' alligator."

Also, I didn't like being called 'dummy.'

"What's that got to do with your momma running off?" I asked.

"They turned her into one of them," Jimmy said.

"The media?"

"The reptoids!"

"Oh, the reptoids who control the—"

"But they're people, too—shapeshifters, right? And they don't just control the media. They control the government and the economy and everything."

"Okay. Which reptoid did it?" I asked, still testing him.

"Doesn't matter. They're telepathically connected. Could be Old Gar for all I know," Jimmy said.

I laughed. Only little kids believed the stories about Old Gar. Old Gar was a fat, ancient alligator that had lived on the same sandy riverbank for years. Most days he sat motionless on a rock with his mouth open trying to catch a breeze. He was too slow to hurt anybody.

Regardless, for generations the kids in town tucked flashlights under their chins at slumber parties and told stories about Old Gar's supernatural powers. Their parents tolerated this pastime because the resulting nightmares ultimately kept the kids away from the river, which was plenty dangerous without the need for magic. But after a certain age, you realized you couldn't believe anymore.

Kinda sad, if you ask me.

"That old suitcase?" I said. But Jimmy didn't find it funny.

"Think about it. Who would ever suspect?"

The thought had never occurred to me. Suddenly, I didn't find it funny either. I felt like I'd spent my whole life missing the forest for the trees.

I felt stupid, gullible, unexceptional—but only at first. Once this new knowledge took hold, my feelings changed. I felt righteous—justified.

I felt my consciousness press out against the inside of my skull. Like it was trying to take in vast machinations of power and capital that didn't make sense. But at the same time, and for the first time, everything made sense.

From the moment I was born until that moment in detention, I'd been spoon-fed lies. Me and everybody else I knew. Most people didn't even realize they were lies. But they fed us nonetheless, over and over, all day every day. What Jimmy and I would later call a "disinformation campaign."

This was sponsored by forces more powerful than I could ever hope to be in my tiny corner of the world, with nobody but Jimmy on my side.

How could anyone be expected to know anything?

After detention we drove to the sandy beach where Old Gar lived and shot him with paintballs. Mostly out of spite. Jimmy got held back a couple grades, so he had a car too—an 82' Firebird, straight out of a hair metal music video.

When we arrived, Jimmy took his shirt off and got in the water. I stayed on the bank, afraid of the gator and of taking my clothes off in front of everybody.

Old Gar slid silently into the water after Jimmy. He must've heard the dinner bell ring. They both disappeared beneath the green-black surface.

I stood alone on the shore. Seconds passed. It felt like hours. I didn't know what to expect.

"Jimmy?" I asked.

Stillness.

Silence.

Old Gar broke the surface first. I saw his scarred hide splattered with fresh neon paint. Then his gleaming, smiling teeth. But Old Gar didn't stop rising. Soon his entire body was lifted up, floating in air like a balloon. That's when I saw Jimmy.

The alligator's jaws rested oblivious on the top of his head. Jimmy had gotten underneath Old Gar and planted his feet on the bottom.

He clasped his hands around Old Gar's mouth and led him back to the shore. The alligator bucked and fought with minimal effort, and Jimmy easily subdued it. It didn't even try to bite his ankles.

After a while, we got bored with Old Gar. Momma and Big Jim Sr. both worked until the evening. Jimmy knew a place we could get some beer.

So we embarked on our first trip to Bud's.

Bud's was a truck stop watering hole up on West Ridge, way on the outskirts of town. The roads there were so narrow and winding, there was no room for any other buildings. So Bud's sat alone for miles on either side, lurching down the bluff to the river. Out back there was a dock and a ladder for swimming, but it hadn't been used in decades. To get there, you had to take a steep trail through about a mile of thicket.

Bud's was just across the border from a dry county, so most of the locals did their drinking there. Big Jim Sr. used to drink at Bud's, but Bud kicked him out. Years later, Big Jim Sr. would tell me that Bud was a "no good reptoid son of a bitch."

Half of Bud's was a gas station convenience store, the other half was a trucker bar. Bud worked the bar and the register by himself. That night, there were enough thirsty patrons to keep him busy. He didn't see us slip the beer out under our jackets.

We walked behind the lonesome truck stop to a trail leading down to the river. The trail was so overgrown, the naked eye might've missed it. But Jimmy knew the way.

The trail lead us to an old waterlogged dock stained green with mildew. A plywood shack covered in kudzu ivy stood further up the shore. At first glance, it looked abandoned. But inside we found several fishing poles, some old PENTHOUSE magazines, and a tackle box—Bud's emergency stockpile.

I cracked open the beer. Jimmy pulled out a pack of bologna for bait. I hadn't even noticed him stealing it. He always managed to surprise me.

We drank and fished until the sun set behind the ridge. Jimmy taught me more about reptoids and how they control the media. He laid out the argument clearly and succinctly over the course of three or four hours.

I listened.

We didn't catch any fish, so Jimmy invited me back to his house for dinner. Jimmy's house sat on the edge of the swampy flood plain, several miles south from Bud's. Big Jim Sr.'s gator farm was on the other side of the road. I could see beady red eyes glowing in Jimmy's headlights as we rolled down the driveway in neutral. The moon was full by the time we arrived.

The house looked empty—not a single light turned on except the back porch. We sat on the couch and drank our last beers in front of the TV. Halfway through Family Feud, the back door opened.

Orange light from the porch shone onto the fake wood paneling and got swallowed by the brown shag carpet. A silhouette stood in the doorway. It looked like an alligator climbing up a tree.

"Who's that?" Big Jim Sr. asked.

Jimmy shot to attention.

"Daddy, this is my friend. I invited him over," Jimmy said.

"What's your name son?" Big Jim Sr. asked me.

"Darryl," I said, "Darryl Martin."

"Sherri Martin's boy?" He asked.

"Yessir," I said.

Big Jim Sr. relaxed. I didn't like seeing him do that. I'd seen men do that before around Momma.

"Your daddy's a good Christian man," he said.

My dad had been working on Big Jim Sr.'s alligator farm the day he got arrested. Momma always told me she blamed the alligators, but looking back, I'm not sure that's what she really meant.

Regardless, and despite my better judgment, I swelled with pride. No one ever said anything good about my dad.

We ate baked beans and hot dogs slathered in mustard. Big Jim Sr. talked a lot. About the work he'd been doing in the bunker out back. About the liberals and the government and the media. And the others who conspired against us.

"Reptoids each and every one," he said.

We listened and understood.

Big Jim Sr. had a perfect setup for when the reptoid cavalry finally invaded from outer space. It could be any day now. He had enough canned food and ammo to last years. I was welcome to join them, but I had to pull my weight.

"No freeloaders in this house," Big Jim Sr. said. "I can't wait to see the looks on their faces."

"Like Bud?" Jimmy asked.

"Like Old Gar?" I asked.

Big Jim Sr. let out a snort.

"All of 'em. You boys stay away from there. Don't want you getting bit. That gator is meaner than he looks."

Jimmy laughed, but I wasn't sure if Big Jim Sr. meant Bud or Old Gar or both.

After dinner, Big Jim Sr. got to drinking and hollering. He said some unkind things about his missing ex-wife, Jimmy's mother. Jimmy offered to take me home.

"You come back now, Darryl. Your daddy's a good white man," Big Jim Sr. slurred as we drove away. I didn't say anything about it to Jimmy. It would've been impolite to say something about it.

Jimmy didn't have time to come in and visit. He didn't say a word the whole drive back, either. Momma stumbled out the screen door wrapped in her bathrobe as Jimmy's Firebird roared off into the night. She must've gotten off work early.

"Where you been?" Momma asked.

"Out with friends," I said, keeping my eyes down.

"Oh yeah?" she said.

"Yeah," I said.

"Was that the alligator boy?" she asked.

"His name's Jimmy," I said.

Momma took a drag on her long cigarette and blew smoke over her shoulder. She shivered even though it wasn't cold.

"I know his name. Get in the god damn house," she said. I don't think she ever liked Jimmy much.

Shit, nobody did.

After that, Jimmy and me were inseparable. With few other options, we hung out at Bud's or Old Gar's watering hole pretty much every day for the next twenty years. Time flies, I guess.

Of course, we had good days and bad. And we got into all kinds of trouble. I could go into more detail, but who am I kidding? None of that matters to anyone but me. All that matters to anybody happened last week.

It was the first day all year that it really felt like summer. So hot the steering wheel stuck to my hands, and my sunglasses kept slipping down my nose. But somehow the river was still cold.

We were down by the river behind Bud's, celebrating our day off work. Jimmy had one of his girlfriends with him, Mary Ellen, from Mobile. I never had much interest in women, but Jimmy always had a girlfriend or two. Mary Ellen tried to talk Jimmy into swimming off the dock.

"Hell no," he said, "you want my balls to shrivel up?"

"What balls?" she said.

We all laughed.

"C'mere," Jimmy said and picked up Mary Ellen. One second she was in his arms, kicking and punching, the next she was splashing around in the muddy water, hair plastered to her face.

"It's cold you jerk," she said.

"I told you," Jimmy said.

She climbed up the ladder and wrung her long hair out over the side. Then without warning she tackled Jimmy, and they fell into the river together. I liked Mary Ellen.

A log slid down the sand into the water on the opposite shore. But it wasn't a log. It was a gator—a big one. I couldn't tell from that distance, maybe twelve feet.

I tried to warn them, but it was too late. They were already out of the water. The moment of danger came and went like driftwood passing along in the river.

Jimmy gave Mary Ellen his shirt to dry off with, and we shotgunned our last two beers. The gator lost interest when we stopped splashing. It returned to its sunny spot on the bank. It sat so still I could barely see it.

Jimmy looked out at the water as the sun set.

"You know," he said, "when they finally come to take us in their spaceship, I wonder if there'll be anything this beautiful on their planet."

"Oh God, again with the reptoids," Mary Ellen said.

We'd had this conversation before. Obviously, she didn't get it. But whatever.

"Their whole planet is probably like this," I said trying to reassure Jimmy.

We never did reach consensus on why the reptoids wanted to invade us. The reason almost didn't matter.

I didn't have much else to say. Thankfully, neither did Jimmy. We always felt at ease being quiet with one another, so Jimmy kept looking at the sunset, and I tried to find the gator on the opposite bank.

Mary Ellen did research on her phone in attempt to find some evidence that might dissuade us. It was no use. Our minds were made up.

After the sun set, Jimmy and Mary Ellen said they were going to stay behind at the dock for a little while. Get some privacy. I sighed and started walking.

I sat down at the bar by myself. The place was empty. Finally after two songs on the jukebox, Bud came out of the back room, drying his hands on a towel.

That struck me odd. Bud always kept his eye on you. He never left the bar unattended. *What are you up to?* I wondered.

I pulled a wrinkled five dollar bill from my jeans pocket.

"Keep it," I said, "I'm gonna have another."

I cleared half the beer in one gulp. Bud watched me drink. Sweat pooled in his furry eyebrows and rolled down his gray, chubby cheeks.

"Where's your friend?" Bud asked.

"Jimmy's still fishing."

I lied to see if he'd catch me. Was he spying on us? Was he down by the water? Bud didn't seem to notice.

"I dunno why he tries," Bud said, "ain't nothing but minnows and moccasins down there."

"I saw a gator just a minute ago," I said.

"Yeah, I seen a couple gators come and go. Good luck catching one. Might end up catching you," Bud said.

I drank the rest of my beer and gestured for another. Bud refilled my dirty glass. Cheap bastard. The whole time I felt like he was looking over my shoulder at the door.

"You ever hear what happened to that boy's momma?" Bud asked.

"They never found her."

"His daddy's a nut," Bud said, changing the subject, "One of those tin foil hat kooks. Thinks aliens control the government. Alien shape-shifting reptiles or something."

"I've heard crazier," I said.

"Don't tell me you buy into that nonsense," Bud said.

"There's a lot of interesting coincidences," I said.

"His daddy thinks I'm an alien. He ever tell you that?"

"Never mentioned it," I lied.

"Said he'd shoot me dead if he thought it'd do any good. But that wouldn't stop the invasion. Oh well."

Bud leaned back to laugh. The laugh went on too long and turned into a hacking cough. He regained composure.

"I said, 'Appreciate you not shooting me, now get the fuck out of my bar and never come back.'"

I nodded and sipped my beer. I had a half buzz. Foam dripped down my lip onto my beard. It smelled like wet skin and rot. I wondered what Bud said about me and my dad when I wasn't around.

Jimmy and Mary Ellen stumbled into the bar, giggling and hugging on each other. Bud snorted at them.

"Where's your tacklebox?" Bud asked.

"Huh?"

"Your buddy here said you weren't leaving till you reeled in a catfish for dinner."

Jimmy shot me a dirty look. Immediately, my cheeks flushed with shame. I should've never said a word to Bud about anything.

"Guess I'll just have to go to Captain D's like everybody else."

Jimmy laughed. Bud stared.

"I hope you don't expect to buy no beer."

"Aw, c'mon Bud," Jimmy pleaded, his eyes big and wide like a hound dog, "I ain't had that much."

"Can't serve you in good conscience."

Jimmy shrugged and pulled Mary Ellen into the convenience store for a twelve-pack. Bud followed. Jimmy grabbed what he wanted quickly and passed it off to Mary Ellen.

I took the opportunity to grab a ten dollar bill out of Bud's tip jar and refill my beer from the tap.

Eventually, Mary Ellen paid for the beer.

"You been drinking tonight, young lady?" Bud asked her.

"No sir, I'm the designated driver," she said.

"You know, Bud, the kind of money you're rolling in—I'm surprised you don't have better selection," Jimmy said.

"What money is that? If I rolled over on some money, let me know."

Bud trying to make a joke was like a dog shaking hands. Like he really didn't understand what he was doing.

"Oh I know more than you think . . ." Jimmy said.

It didn't sound like much to me, just teasing. But Bud was slack jawed, incredulous. All of a sudden, Bud was angry.

"Of all the nerve. Get outta my store! Go on, get!" Bud said.

Bud's red eyes bulged. His chest puffed out. But Jimmy was too cool to fight back. Now wasn't the time.

"We'll be in the car," Jimmy said to me. Mary Ellen looked ready to leave. I couldn't blame her.

"And stay out," Bud hollered to the already-shut door. He hunched over and limped back to his stoop at the bar.

"You too, out," he said.

"Let me finish?" I asked.

Bud shrugged.

"That boy is just as crazy as his daddy," Bud said.

By then I'd had many suppers with Big Jim Sr. He wasn't a bad man. Odd and drunk maybe, but he didn't act like any crazy person I ever saw.

He was kind to me. More than I could say for Bud. Big Jim Sr. gave me a job at the alligator farm. And Jimmy was my best friend.

"Don't say that about Jimmy or his daddy," I said.

"The man said he'd kill me. That's not crazy enough for you?"

"But what if it's true? What's that make you?" I asked.

"I guess that makes me an alien then, doesn't it?" Bud said.

"Guess so," I said.

"I'd rather be an alien than a murderer," Bud said.

I put the ten dollar bill back in the tip jar. Bud looked perplexed. That was always his first reaction. I don't think he'd ever seen me tip before.

By the time I made it to the door, he figured it out. There wasn't nothing else in the tip jar to begin with. I bet he took it out of the cash register and put it there himself.

"Hey," he called out, "Come back here!"

But I was long gone. Jimmy revved the Firebird's engine, and we peeled off into the night. Mary Ellen laid out on the back seat. I sat shotgun and fiddled with the radio until I found a good enough station to let it ride.

◯

I wish that was how the evening ended. I wish we'd gone back to Jimmy's and watched TV until we all passed out. I could've slept on the couch.

Instead we cruised around in the Firebird. Mary Ellen called up her friend Susanne. We all got drunk.

Mary Ellen and Susanne had both just started back at college. They were talking about scholarships and internships. Jimmy and me were talking about work. But eventually we got on the topic of the reptoids.

"What's a reptoid?" asked Susanne.

"It's like...complicated," Jimmy said. He was pretty drunk.

"Yeah," I said, "they control the media."

"I'm a Marine Bio major, and I've never heard of any reptile that could turn on a TV, much less control the media," Mary Ellen said.

"Typical liberal denial," Jimmy said.

"I'm not even a liberal," Mary Ellen said.

"Me neither, my folks watch Fox News," Susanne said.

"Nah, they're all the same," Jimmy said, "CNN, FOX, MSNBC— they're all controlled by the same corporations. You can't trust any of 'em."

Mary Ellen gave up. Maybe it was the soft scolding in his tone that pissed her off. Maybe she knew he would never understand her—like they were speaking different languages.

I think she probably would've gotten tired of Jimmy if things had turned out different. Sooner or later.

When Bud's closed for the night, we went back to the secret dock. I don't remember why. We were all pretty drunk by that point.

It took a while stumbling through the dark, but once we got to the river, Jimmy wanted to go skinny-dipping. He didn't seem concerned about the cold water anymore. I turned my back to them, hoping they'd leave me alone and not try to make me join.

No one got naked except Jimmy. Susanne stayed near the trail trying to get reception on her phone. Mary Ellen stood on the edge of the dock, looking down. She shined a flashlight at the water. I couldn't see what she saw, just the reflection of the light. I heard Jimmy make his way down the ladder off the other side of the dock.

"Don't!" Mary Ellen screamed.

"Huh?" Jimmy asked, already chest deep.

"Don't get in the water!"

But it was too late. Jimmy let out a dismissive laugh.

It was dark. He didn't see the gator next to him, jaws open, waiting. Only it didn't look like a gator at all. Its hide was grey, like a wolf. Like Bud's skin, like his hair.

I've seen gator attacks. They clamp down like a trap. They shake your muscles loose from your bones. Then they drag you down to the bottom. That's not what happened to Jimmy.

The trap snapped shut. Then it opened again. Then shut. Again and again.

"What's happening?" Susanne said as she ran down the trail in a panic.

No more words, just terrible screaming. I screamed. Mary Ellen screamed. Jimmy screamed until it got to his lungs.

I tried to jump in after him but Susanne held me back. Mary Ellen was on the edge of the dock, reaching out, clutching Jimmy's limp hand.

Jimmy grew up with gators. He worked with them. He knew how to swim with them. That wasn't no gator attack.

It ate him alive.

Beady red eyes stared back at me in the bug zapper light. Dozens of gators slid through the water to get a bite of my friend. The quickest, strongest, coolest guy I'd ever known. My only friend.

The worst part was that I knew this was just the beginning. They had horrible plans in store for Jimmy. Just like his momma.

The gators finished eating Jimmy, but that wasn't enough. Urged on by their reptoid leader, they started thrashing their tails and gnawing at the dock in a frenzy.

It wasn't long before everything collapsed.

A stray plank of rotten wood hit me in the face. I stumbled into Mary Ellen. The force sent her tumbling down into the water.

The soggy remains of the dock slid into the river with her. The river long and winding. Susanne rushed in to help her friend.

I found my feet and ran.

○

The funeral was this morning. Small graveside service. Big Jim Sr. was there with his girlfriend.

Jimmy never liked her. If he had any say, she wouldn't have been invited. Guess that's the problem with funerals.

Momma rode with me to the service. I didn't see Susanne there. Mary Ellen came out in a wheelchair.

She suffered shallow puncture wounds and a broken leg. I was glad she was okay. I waved but she wouldn't look at me. I couldn't blame her. I let her down. I let everybody down.

Everyone comforted Mary Ellen like she and Jimmy were married or something. It was probably because of the wheelchair. Jimmy barely knew her. Nobody comforted me.

I've heard gators will wait under trees for days, waiting for you to go to sleep in the branches above and fall. That's exactly how they run the government and the media too. How the whole world treats anybody who has love in their heart.

After the service, I had a long talk with Big Jim Sr. about everything.

Then I dropped Momma back off at home and headed out to kill that gator.

To kill a reptoid you have to think like a reptoid; you have to be patient and wait on it to be happy. Then strike that happiness away.

Soon the interstate rounded the bend, and I took my exit. I fiddled with a cartridge. Taking it out of my shirt pocket, twirling it around, putting it back with the others.

Five red ones and one green—the one Big Jim Sr. said would pierce bulletproof armor. Every time I reached into my pocket, I grabbed the green one.

I pulled into Bud's parking lot. No other cars, not this early. Good, that's how I wanted it.

I'll never forget the look on his face when I opened the door. First, he was perplexed. Then he was happy to see me. Relieved, just for a second, that he wasn't being robbed. I bet he wanted to talk about that $10 bill. Then his eyes went back to the shotgun. Jimmy would've laughed.

I didn't let Bud speak; and I sure as hell didn't have anything to say. So I started shooting.

I shot Bud in the face, the gut, the arm. He went out quickly and quietly, all things considered. Better than he deserved. I took the $10 bill out of the tip jar. Then I dragged his heavy corpse through the woods down to the dock.

I didn't see the grey gator. I didn't expect to. A new reptoid waited for me by the shore.

The new gator's hide was greasy black. Same color as Jimmy's hair. It had familiar, fiery eyes that looked like they knew something I didn't.

I pushed Bud's corpse off the dock and into the open mouth of the waiting river monster. It flipped Bud's body in the water. The other gators slid towards us. Who knows who they were?

Maybe one of those gators was famous. Clinton or Obama, maybe. Maybe they're the mainstream media. Maybe they're your neighbor, your pastor, your spouse. Maybe you're one of 'em, too, and you don't even know it.

I loaded the shotgun again. I only pumped it once. Any more than that, and I'd expel the cartridge in the chamber. There's lots of false information about guns in the media. That's intentional, to keep you stupid and liberal.

The media says alligator hide is like bulletproof armor. "Bulletproof" isn't exactly bulletproof from this close. But just in case, I used the green shell.

I waited for the monster, my friend, to roll. I waited for the white belly to show in the water. I waited for that stupid, weak love to show in its cold blood.

He would've wanted it this way. He'd rather die than be one of them. I fired.

The buckshot nearly split that gator in two, Bud's arm still dangling from its mouth. I couldn't think of it as "Jimmy." It wasn't Jimmy, it was a gator. A reptoid. I wanted to cry, but I couldn't.

I fired again. Not-Jimmy's front half bucked and frothed in the black water. The other gators were coming now. They would finish the job. Another thing about reptoids is they eat their own.

The walk back up the trail was longer than ever. I thought about Momma. I wondered what to expect in the parking lot—wondered what the river had in store for me next.

Turns out nothing. No one heard the shotgun blasts, or at least no one found them unusual. So I called the police myself. I had to wipe reptoid brains off Bud's old-fashioned rotary phone behind the bar.

"Hello, 911?" I said, "there's been a shooting at Bud's truck stop. Bud is dead. I'll wait on y'all."

Big Jim Sr. told me what to say. The next call I made was to the lawyer he recommended. Big Jim Sr. knew a few guys inside that would help me out, too. All in all, he said, prison wouldn't be hard for me. Plus my dad was there. And my dad was a "good white man," according to Big Jim Sr.

I waited by my car. And waited. And waited. Shit, it felt like forever. The cops sure took their sweet time.

It's pretty far away from everything out here, after all. And the only road runs along the river.

A Case of Mamma's Love

~ Tammie Painter

Mamma has always had a love for other people's possessions. One of my earliest memories was of Mamma, slim then with a tiny waist on an hourglass figure, talking to our frizzy-haired neighbor about how much she just adored Mr. Chantry's shirts. Shirts, mind you. I think that's why the memory stuck so hard. I might notice someone's shirt, but to "adore" a person's entire collection of tops?

Still, that's how it was then, small things, things people wouldn't normally pay much mind to. For example, we often got our produce, milk, and other perishables from the corner store run by Ms. Stafford who wore the most extravagant necklaces. I didn't know it then, but our Ms. Stafford was having an affair with the mayor from the big city that sits about twenty miles down the interstate, and those bits of neck candy were gifts from him.

I later learned these sordid facts of life from Mamma after Mamma's tastes got a bit more—well, let's just say they just got a bit more and leave it at that. Anyways, I was only nine then and even I was delighted by Ms. Stafford's jewelry. Dang, except for the town's holy rollers who saw such displays as sinful, everyone in town marveled at Ms. Stafford's glittering strands.

But not Mamma. Oh, don't get me wrong, Mamma said Ms. Stafford's baubles were pretty and sparkled nicely, but whenever we'd see Ms. Stafford, Mamma would later remark to me about how much she loved that woman's hair clips. Ms Stafford must have thought I was the oddest child since, every time I was in her store, I'd end up staring at her head trying to figure out what was so admirable about a couple pieces of tortoiseshell-patterned plastic held together by cheap metal.

I often worried about Mamma. Daddy had died when I was only two so I don't remember him, but everyone says it was when he went trotting off to the great beyond that Mamma started her quirky, I guess you'd call it, admiration for other folks' things. After watching an after school special on the TV about a girl who couldn't help but steal things I wondered if Mamma's love for our neighbors' doodads might not be a hint that she wanted to steal those doodads. At the time, thanks to regular appearances of Skeedaw County's bookmobile, I was convinced I was destined to be the next Nancy Drew, so I followed my hunch and searched Mamma's closet for any of our good townspeople's shirts, hair clips, socks, teaspoons, and what-have-you.

Even though I did want to test my skills of detection, I really wanted to find nothing more interesting than a dust bunny in that closet. I wanted my mamma to simply be a woman who admired interesting trinkets. But that ain't how it went.

On a lower shelf in the back of the closet sat a case, an old travel case with brown leather sides, a wooden handle, and two gleaming metal clasps on either side of the handle that I flipped up with my thumbs to open. What I saw inside sent my heart zipping right down to my gut. It wasn't a lot of stuff and if my recollection is right, it looked like she'd taken exactly one thing from each person. One shirt from Mr Chantry, one hair clip from Ms. Stafford, and the like. I was disappointed in Mamma, but I was quite proud of my junior detective skills.

Still, this was my mamma. I couldn't be a proper detective and rat her out to the sheriff. Mamma wasn't hurting anyone and who'd care if a teaspoon or pair of socks went missing. Happens all the time, right? So I just closed the lid, flipped the clasps to latch them, and slid the case back onto the shelf.

For a while after that not much changed. Not until a couple summers later when my understanding of the world got a workout. Our town wasn't exactly a tourist hotspot. We had no natural wonders out our backdoors—unless you consider a mosquito-breeding swamp a wonder to behold—we didn't have a claim to any major event in history, and George Washington most definitely did not sleep here. The majority of out-of-towners passed through on their way to the big city, missing my hometown by blinking too hard and rarely stopping by, except for one week in summer when we held our annual Festival Days.

To be honest, I have no idea what we were celebrating, but the town went all out with one of those ride things setting up shop, little booths selling everything we could think to make from home-made jam to hand knit baby slippers, a square dance competition, a variety of music acts and talent shows, and a kiddie rodeo with anyone younger than ten years old being strapped onto a baby cow and let loose. For some reason, this little fair drew a pretty good crowd each day and each year Mamma would sit and work a stall where she sold handmade journals she'd put together using the covers of old hardbacks and paper she made herself.

Keep in mind now we didn't have a hotel, motel, or even rooms above the tavern for these fine folks to stay in. They'd trundle in for the day, park wherever they could find a spot, and leave some-time after sunset with smiles on their faces and their pockets a little lighter.

One day during the fair that took place in the year I'd turned eleven (the first year I was thankfully not being tied onto a bovine's back), I was sitting with Mamma at her booth and reading a book about unicorns when I heard her say, "My, but I do love those buttons." My stomach jolted and I jerked my head up from my story to see an attractive blonde woman in a red-and-white plaid-checked shirt with a blue neckerchief tied around her neck. The shirt had these heart-shaped buttons that looked like rubies with the way they glinted in the light. All I could think was, "Please, Mamma, don't reach out and steal her buttons right off her shirt."

She didn't, and the woman bought six of Mamma's creations which meant Mamma gave me a couple dollars to buy some cotton candy. I loved cotton candy then and was sorely tempted by the offer, but I didn't want to leave Mamma. I wanted to keep an eye on her. But other than to use the port-a-loo an hour later—and believe me, I did not let her out of my sight when she did—Mamma didn't have any other encounter with the button woman.

The week after the fair, I did my monthly check of Mamma's closet. I did it when she made her monthly run to the Costco to stock us up on giant jars of jelly, vast tubs of peanut butter, and a mountain of toilet paper. Since that first time I checked her closet, I had sworn to myself if Mamma started taking anything more than just one little item from people, I'd tell the sheriff. I honestly didn't think they'd haul her in. It'd be like on the TV when the sheriff just has a good talking to a person and straightens them out. This month I expected to see a pair of Mrs. Dubber's garden gloves Mamma had remarked upon. They were there, pink with little white daisies, but sitting at the tip of one of the floral-patterned fingers was a single heart-shaped button that shone like a ruby.

I closed the case. I closed the closet door. I stepped away.

There was no possible way Mamma could have gotten that button and not just on account of my keeping an eagle eye on her. I'd seen, *seen* with my own eyes, that woman leave the fair in a Mustang the same color as her bright blue neckerchief no more than half an hour after buying Mamma's journals. Mamma had not left the booth in that time. I didn't think Nancy Drew had an answer for that one.

I stopped checking the closet after that day. I couldn't reconcile in my head how that button came to be there without waking up in the middle of the night with my legs all sweaty and my heart thumping.

By the time I was fifteen Mamma had stopped admiring little things and started expressing her love for items like bicycles and televisions, and her eye was finally caught by Ms. Stafford's jewelry. It was also about this time Mamma began to put on weight. She lost her waist—it just kind of swelled away, and she opted more often for stretchy pants than slacks.

And yes, these items that Mamma adored would disappear. Like Mamma's waist, one day they were there and the next time you'd bother to look for them, they'd be gone. I was as scared as a hound who's just realized he's being taken to the vet, but I had to check Mamma's closet. I was pretty sure of what I'd find, but I didn't know how in all of Skeedaw County she could have squeezed Mr. Tibbs's mountain bike or Mrs. Hamlin's flat screen TV into her closet. I put my thumbs to the case's clasps, my hands shaking like Ms. Stafford's Jell-O-esque booty when she waggled it down Main Street, and held my breath as I flipped the latches.

There they were. It made no sense, but there they were. In little zippy bags that we got by the hundreds from the Costco were minia-ture versions of the items Mamma had loved. I know what you're thinking. Okay, I know what I was thinking: These can't possibly be real, right? She just went to the hobby shop and picked up a replica like someone would buy for a dollhouse or train set. Well, just like me, if that's what you thought, you thought straight out wrong.

See, these items worked. The little TV turned on and I could even change channels. I checked our TV. We only had what we could get free over the antenna, but the little TV matched the programs from theme song to laugh track. The bike's pedals turned the gears that turned the wheels and I squeezed the little levers on the handlebars and watched as tiny brake pads slowed the wheels' spinning. As I flicked through other baggies in the case, I came across a metallic green Volkswagen Beetle. Tommy Cardinal had just such a car stolen three months ago. I remember when it happened, not only because Tommy and I were going steady, but because the day after the car was stolen, Mamma had to go out and buy new clothes because the old ones "must have shrunk in the wash."

After opening the Bug's door and seeing the grass-skirted hula girl on the dashboard that Tommy thought was the funniest thing in the world—honestly, I think he missed that hula girl more than he missed the car—I shut and latched the lid of the case, put it back in its spot on the shelf, and left Mamma's room to pour myself some lemonade and have a good think.

I couldn't turn Mamma in. I loved my mamma, and I told myself that was the main reason I couldn't call the cops on her and have her locked up, but in truth I worried I'd be the one who was locked up. They'd slap a straight jacket on me in half a heartbeat and throw me in a padded cell and probably zap my brain with electricity to burn away the parts that were making me a looney bird.

I knew those objects were real. I also knew no one would believe me. And what good would it do to turn Mamma in? After those heart-shaped buttons, I knew she didn't need to be up close to the object to get it. She'd just say she loved it and some time later it was hers.

For most of the rest of my sophomore and junior years, Mamma steadily put on some pounds. She had long been more potato than hourglass, but there were no sudden runs down to the Penney's to make up for the washing machine doing its supposed shrinking act on her garments. Then, one day in the winter of my senior year, Mamma and I were in Ms. Stafford's store and Kenny Swinton, a sophomore boy, helped us carry our purchases to the station wagon.

When the final bag was loaded, Mamma said she just loved a boy who knew his manners.

I'd been shifting the bags to keep them from tipping over on the ride home especially as we'd bought eggs and I didn't want any of them to break. But at Mamma's words, my grip faltered on the sack I was moving and eleven of a dozen eggs cracked and splattered onto the asphalt.

"Mamma," I said sharply, "don't you mean you *appreciate* someone with good manners?"

"Don't get sassy with me. Just because I only got through freshman year don't mean I don't know what words I want to use."

"Yes, Mamma," I muttered as Kenny dashed into the shop to grab us another dozen eggs.

Kenny vanished that night. He went home. He had his supper. He did his homework. He went to bed. The bed was empty the next morning when Mrs. Swinton went up to tease her son for over-sleeping. There was a search party. There were even bloodhounds. They found nothing.

And Mamma swelled once again. I was able to drive at this point and had to go to the Penney's to get Mamma a selection of muumuus because she'd already gone far past the biggest waist size the store carried. When I got home she took the receipt to add it into her bookkeeping folder. It was a new thing then for the Penney's to add the cashier's name at the bottom. As if in a small town we didn't know exactly who was ringing up our underpants and t-shirts. Mamma was just slipping the receipt into her folder and I was just heading into the kitchen to make a PB & J when Mamma said, "Kathy-Anne helped you? I do love how sweet she is. Did you ever know anyone so sweet?"

I said I didn't and passed through the kitchen. My desire for a sandwich completely gone.

Kathy-Anne vanished. Mr. Duncan vanished for being "such an honest man." Mrs. Radley vanished for being "so charming." Anyone who had a personality trait Mamma loved disappeared. Our town was dwindling, but Mamma certainly wasn't. Mamma couldn't fit through the door anymore. She couldn't leave the house, but she also couldn't climb the stairs to her room. Shoot, I don't even know if our stairs could have handled the weight of her going up them.

I didn't want to, but my curiosity was bubbling over. Knowing she was stuck downstairs and I wouldn't get caught, I checked Mamma's closet. In amongst the baggies I expected to find miniature Kennys, teeny Mr. Duncans, and itty-bitty Kathy-Annes. Relief walloped me like a cool breeze in summer when I didn't find shrunken humans trapped in baggies, but that's not to say Mamma's case didn't have some new treasures.

Instead of little people, I found orbs about the size of baseballs. They weren't solid but were like a tangled mesh that reminded me of this display of electronic fiber things I'd seen one time when I'd gone to the mall in the big city with Tommy Cardinal. Those fibers had glowed with randomly changing colors. The objects in Mamma's case were round, not plumed, but they pulsed just the same from red to pink to violet to green. I picked one up. I grit my teeth expecting to get an electrical shock, but it was only warm like a battery that's been in use recently.

There's no explaining how I knew or even if I was right, but holding those spheres of color brought the word "essence" front and center to the spot of my brain just behind my forehead. Mamma loved one aspect of a person and that one aspect had been their essence, their soul, if you will. Without that, the person didn't exist.

My throat had gone completely dry by this point and my stomach was about ready to turn itself inside out when Mamma called my name from downstairs and startled me so hard I dropped at least half a dozen of the orbs. I scrambled to pick them up when Mamma called out again.

"Clara, whatchyou doing? You in my closet again, you silly lark? You always were the curious one."

I threw down the orbs I'd collected and yelled at Mamma. For the first time ever in my life, I told her to shut right up.

Did she even know what she was doing? Did she understand her love of people's possessions brought those possessions to her, never to be seen again? I hurried down the stairs, nearly tripping over my own feet like a cow with four hind legs. I threw myself at Mamma, my hands stretched out to cover her mouth.

But she was too big. I couldn't reach across her massive lap in time to stop her words.

"I just love your curiosity. Now come give Mamma a hug."

I gave Mamma a hug. I knew I had the rest of the day. Everyone else had vanished in the night. I've spent the time thinking of Mamma, of whether it would have helped if I turned her in all those years ago. I don't think it would have, so I've written all this down in one of Mamma's handmade journals, one with a Nancy Drew cover, hoping someone can make sense of it.

Tomorrow would be my last day of high school. I'm curious to know how it would have gone.

Introduction to Immersive Memory-Crafting

~ Christopher East

FADE IN: Exterior, deck of cruise ship, night. Stark contrast, light and shadow in film-noir black and white. A steady breeze as the ship circles Manhattan. Clear night sky with a full moon, the towering cityscape lit up with a million brilliant windows of fiery light.

The ship's crowded with students in formal finery, tuxedoes for the men, a variety of colorful dresses for the women. It's the second of September, 1990, the last day of summer before fall semester. The jubilant swing of big band jazz pulses from the ship's central dance hall, where first-year students flirt, chatter, and dance with abandon, celebrating their last day of freedom before university study begins.

Enter Edward "Eddie" Dunn: eighteen, tall and thin, pale by the standards of his era (and even moreso by ours), slicked-back hair in a precise side-part. He steps onto the deck, fussing with the polished cufflinks on his perfectly pressed sleeves. With a deep breath, he takes in the city atmosphere. Then he sees her: his case officer.

He strides over to her where she leans against the railing, waiting. With her effortless composure, chic style, and air of experience she might have been in, oh, her mid-twenties—to him, an impossible future state. Short, blonde, pleasant smile, pointy nose, and eyes bluer than the sky. (The sky was much bluer back then.)

"Why are you looking at the ocean?" he says, the prearranged, identifying code phrase. "Rather than the city that's about to change your life?"

"Because the future's out there, too. You'll see that, in a few hundred years."

"I should be so lucky." That ends the exchange: she's his contact, all right. "Smoke?" he asks, unsnapping a silver cigarette case. Tobacco still grew back then, and people still smoked it.

"Don't mind if I do," she replies, withdrawing a slender, brown cylinder with a gloved hand. A Nat Sherman. "I'm Beth."

"Dunn, Edward Dunn." He pulls out his Zippo, registering the potent, oily fragrance of butane. "So it begins."

"So it does. Have you settled in?"

"Brittany Hall, tenth floor. Just clothes, books, and a computer, per the briefing."

"Specialized equipment will be provided as-needed," Beth says, smoke jetting from her nostrils. She wears a flirty smile, playing to surveillance. "The Plans are *somewhere* in this city. It's your mission to find them."

"What kind of a timetable are we looking at?"

Beth shrugs. "Unclear. Four years, if you're lucky. Possibly less. Depends on how long your cover holds."

"What role am I playing?"

"Aspiring writer and capable adult. Are you prepared? This will stretch you out of your comfort zone."

Eddie Dunn is not prepared. But he tries a confident face, lights his own cigarette, and grins. "I'll have those Plans in no time. Just you watch."

Well done, Kendra. Nice, polished rendering. Class, see how Kendra's applied 1940s filmmaking style to this 1990s setting. Imaginative flourishes like this can present as historical ineptitude, but you've pulled it off admirably.

As for your rendition of the Subject, I think he would have been amused to be portrayed as confident and suave. He was, of course, neither.

Historical note: in reality, he never did see Beth again. In fact, at the time this memory was mapped, he wasn't sure that was even her name. But that's the beauty of memory crafting. Taken out of sequence, fully immersed, the moments can suggest any number of futures. For all the Subject knew, this woman might have changed his life forever. (She didn't.)

Story's a bit thin on the ground, though. Curious to see where Rolando takes it next.

CUT TO: Interior, underground corridor of the New York subway, later that night. Stained concrete floors, chipped tile walls spray-painted with graffiti. Clinging stench of urine, sweat, and petroleum, permeating the atmosphere of this grimy subterranean world. Like the air, the crowds are thick and stifling. Color imagery, but the palette is muted, the edges of the visual frame blurry and distressed.

Hands jammed in pockets, Eddie follows his new classmates into the bowels of the city, nervous and sullen in his jeans, black T-shirt, and scuffed white high-tops. The cruise was awkward and miserable, despite the pleasant chat with his case officer whose name may or may not have been Beth. It was an "Orientation Cruise," but he felt disoriented. Everyone else so comfortable, so put together. Surely they've seen through his flimsy cover. He's out of his element. He has no element. He's been training to find the Plans all his life, but doesn't even know what they are.

The RA from his dorm, Craig or perhaps Greg, leads the group. He stops on a platform, stands before a group of students. "Listen up! The next train will take you back to 14th Street. But if anybody wants an adventure, follow me!"

About half the group goes with Craig-or-Greg. For some reason, Eddie—who *doesn't* want an adventure—joins them. Is it because that cute girl, What's-Her-Name, is going? Or is he just afraid of getting separated, left to his own devices on a strange train in a strange city surrounded by strangers? Both, neither, who knows? Beth's first assignment was to join this group, but he can't imagine he'll find the Plans down in this hellhole.

The party leaves the platform, heads up the stairs, then down a short side tunnel, which leads to another, darker tunnel. Caged light bulbs provide the only illumination. The peculiar city odor intensifies as they enter this unventilated space. No other commuters walk here, just the wily Craig-or-Greg and his gaggle of neophytes, plunging deeper into an urban underworld. Watching the girls flirt with Craig-or-Greg, Eddie feels queasy. He's last in the marching order, vulnerable to ambush from wandering monsters. He hesitates, considers turning back, but instead lights a Camel, his version of donning armor. The smoke both smells and tastes better than the tunnel air.

Up ahead, the party disappears around a corner, where a bulb flickers out, creating an abyss. Eddie watches his classmates vanish into darkness, until he's the only one left. When he catches up, he's suddenly all alone.

"What the fuck?" he says. The walls are no longer tile, but red brick, slimy with moisture and mold. He steps forward, turns a corner, then another. Soon he's in an Escherian labyrinth: stairs up, stairs down, switchbacks, warped curves, lights dim and flickering. The other students are gone, but there are people: homeless people, sleeping, sitting, begging, mumbling. His presence is an intrusion, so he walks, to remove himself from the scene. The others must be up ahead somewhere. He lights a new cigarette off the old one, holds it in front of him. Suddenly it's a dim, smoldering torch, lighting the way.

Then, out of nowhere, a cowboy appears.

The man wears a ten-gallon hat, a stiff, red bandana around his neck, a flannel shirt under a dirty army jacket. Brown hiking boots with spurs, blue jeans crusty with dirt.

Eddie's heart jumps in his chest. "Pardon me," he says, trying to move past.

The cowboy blocks his way, upright, arms crossed, an inscrutable expression on his face. "I'm going to ask you a question," he says in a monotone drawl. His breath smells like a dentist's drill, the blood-and-bone stench of oral surgery. "A man's attitude goes some ways to the way his life will be. Do you agree, or do you disagree?"

Eddie takes a drag on his torch. "I agree."

The cowboy blinks once, long and deliberate. "Is that what you truly believe, or what you think I wanted to hear?"

Perplexed, Eddie reconsiders. "Now that you mention it, the latter. I disagree."

"So attitude *doesn't* matter." The stony certitude of the cowboy's expression falters, a subtle downward turn to the lips. "Your behavior has no impact on your future. You're driftwood tossed by the waves, manipulated by forces beyond your control."

"Sure. Pretty much. More or less."

The cowboy nods. "You'll feel differently some day. If you live." He snaps his fingers.

Eddie feels a weight in his lungs, as if anvils have landed on them. He staggers into a wall, steadying himself on slick, oozing bricks. It's not exactly pain, just intense discomfort, a powerful internal clenching. His legs carry him forward of their own volition, and he wonders if the cowboy did this to him as well. Does he have volition?

He turns to ask, but the cowboy has vanished.

The clumsy walking goes on forever, through other tunnels, onto other platforms, past dark tracks where trains rocket past. Until finally the weight lifts, he looks up, and he's standing on a platform surrounded by other passengers. A train coasts to a halt, and he sees Craig-or-Greg squiring his charges aboard. Impossibly, he's found them.

Eddie boards. The train carries him where it will.

High marks for verisimilitude, Rolando, at least for the geography and psychology. This is the Subject as he truly was, actual memories refined and modified. You've also effectively merged sense memories: the bronchitis he experienced early in his freshman year, with this hazy remembrance of a disorienting walk through New York subway tunnels. In reality, they didn't happen concurrently, but this is a fictional arts class. Why not conflate them? Rolando mined the memories, took them in a dark direction, which is in keeping with the Subject's personality—such as it was—at this time in history. Very 1990, very Generation X.

That said, for a group assignment, you clearly weren't collaborating. Kendra gave us a confident, enthusiastic protagonist in the 1940s, Rolando an uneasy, reluctant one in the early nineties. Granted, the Subject was all these things, in all these times. But we're crafting memories, right? Might want to make the narrative more coherent.

Also, the cowboy? Stolen from Mulholland Drive. *I caught that, Rolando. Do acknowledge your sources, public domain or otherwise. A simple touchlink will suffice.*

○

CUT TO: Interior, Eddie's dorm, night. Nobody home, a dark rectangular space, three beds in three corners for three roommates. A gridded pane of glass looks down over Greenwich Village. The only illumination is light pollution, the only noise the drone of the city.

Brittany Hall is a converted hotel, and Eddie's room has that feel: a short entry corridor leading past a walk-in closet and a bathroom into the room proper. Two of the beds have desks beside them. Eddie's, near the window overlooking East 10th, does not; his space has the smallest footprint. You wouldn't even know he was here.

He lets himself in with a dusky brass key, still coughing and hacking from the cigarettes and subway air and bronchitis. He slams the door behind him and flips the lightswitch. Instead of an overhead light, though, a muted red-orange circle slowly climbs the largest wall, an incongruous natural sunrise dawning over the dormitory landscape.

In fact, as the light grows, the room becomes a fantastical microcosm of the Earth itself:

Miniature birds chirp, microscopic insects buzz, a cool breeze stirs in the space. The floor isn't carpet, but a rolling, grass-covered field, alive with wee animals: rabbits hopping, squirrels scampering, deer grazing. The bedposts are tree trunks, the blankets sloping fields of wind-carved grain. The desks are mountains and the bookshelves are cliffs. A waterfall tumbles from the wardrobe, feeding a river that curls and twists its way into the bathroom, draining into the sunken ocean of a bath tub. An oboe melody, Stravinsky, as the sun rises on this perfect, tiny ecosystem; nature in harmony, a beautiful environment worth treasuring.

Eddie strides into the room, trampling flowers while ungulates scatter for cover. The music turns martial and percussive. He removes his sneakers—chiseled, non-biodegradable Styrofoam fixed with rusty metal treads—and bombs them into a field, crushing an innocent bear. He strips off a plastic shirt and drapes it over the forest of his bed, strangling the air and trapping panicked eagles. Then he heads to the bathroom, where he lifts the lid of a lake, unzips his fly, and pisses toxic waste into the clear, sparkling water.

After despoiling the toilet-lake, he makes his way into the walk-in closet just inside the door. In the cramped space is a desk, a massive, ancient computer that looks like a coal-fired manufactory, an amplifier, a guitar, an ashtray: it's both an office and an industrial hellscape. Shelves over the desk are lined with books, smokestacks, magazines, silos, video cassettes. Shutting the door, Eddie ignores the pain in his lungs and lights another Merit. Then he sits in his chair, uses a small scoop to shovel coal into the furnace of his computer, and turns on every light and appliance in the room. Clockwork machinery rattles to life, creating first an electric buzz, then a clanking, deafening din. Finally, guitar in his lap, he retreats to his imagination. He types, he smokes, he noodles away on the guitar. He leans back, glancing dreamily ceilingward. He invents worlds and visits other realities, manipulating figments of his imagination for fun and release, and (perhaps some day) for fame and profit. Maybe he writes a semi-autobiographical story about his past, from the perspective of a deep future. Perhaps the work he does will *create* the Plans he seeks.

Meanwhile the carcinogenic byproducts of his obsessed labor seep out of the factory of his closet into the biosphere of his bedroom. Smoke fouls the air, effluent from the pipes oozes through the walls to pollute the tenth-floor soil. Tiny humanoid minions emerge from desk drawers, venturing out to exploit the room-world's raw materials and natural resources and bring them back for Eddie to heedlessly consume in his lust for escape. Alas, he's oblivious to the invisible infrastructure of his life, the collateral damage. He's lost in his head, dreaming pointless dreams, filling the void of his existence with desperate attempts at communication and analysis. As if he has anything to say.

Really, the guy's a fucking disgrace.

But his efforts yield fruit. A stretch of frantic typing, then he pauses, leans forward, squinting at the amber text on the black screen. Buried in the code: a lead.

Hmm.

Well, Mireille certainly has . . . infused her segment with commentary. She's used the Subject to illustrate our modern disgust with the dithering environmental idiocy of that era. And why shouldn't she? The Subject is fairly typical of his times. But remember, at that point Manhattan hadn't even started sinking. Temperatures were only just beginning to rise, and in the greater scheme of things, pollution was in its infancy. Many of us, in his shoes, may well have taken the comforts and conveniences of 1990 for granted. A different time.

Or perhaps I'm . . . overly sympathetic.

No no no, I'm not offended. I'm not him, remember?

Anyway. Very thought-provoking, and a nice shift into eyeball-kicky fabulism, now that I see what you're all doing: an exquisite corpse! Still incoherent, but interesting. I'll try to roll with it.

Let's move on . . . I want to see if he finds the (cleverly vague?) MacGuffin.

CUT TO: Exterior, off-Broadway theater [*STREET ON UPPER WEST SIDE?*], night. The city that never sleeps, not sleeping. Jazzy transition music suggests excitement, optimism, the recreational luxury of pre-collapse times.

Glamorous New Yorkers erupt from the glitzy, neon entryway of [*INSERT NAME OF OFF-BROADWAY THEATER HERE*], a red carpet in reverse as fashionable luminaries climb into luxurious, gleaming limos that glide up to the curb with clockwork precision. Rotating spotlights carve patterns in the foggy autumn air. It's late November, streets and sidewalks slick with rain. Real, clean rain, not the acidic bullshit we have these days.

Eddie steps out of the theater into the brisk Manhattan night, smiling and cheerful and, like, all photogenic. He's in a group, though: two other men and two women, and as they reach the pavement, they walk arm-in-arm in a line, smiling to cheesy montage music. You know, cheerful Big Apple adventure shit.

As they walk, Eddie assesses his companions, hacked from his imagination (*during that bonkers environmental dystopia writing scene—Jesus, Mireille, angry much?*) as potential sources for the Plans' secret location. He's comfortable, working his angle, confident they don't suspect him. They're just friends, out on the town, hanging out.

They reach the corner of [*EIGHTY-SOMETHINGTH AND*

CENTRAL PARK WEST?] "Which way's the subway, again?" asks Angelina Jolie, tossing her long, flowing hair as if advertising shampoo.

"Two blocks south," Philip Seymour Hoffman responds, brandishing a gold cigarette case from his overcoat. He taps loose a [*KENT? COULD THIS GUY SETTLE ON A BRAND, ALREADY?*] and hands it to Eddie.

"Thank you, sir," Eddie says, tucking it into the corner of his mouth. Hoffman is his prime suspect, because, I mean, come on: Philip Seymour Hoffman. "You know what? Why don't we walk."

"Say what?" Sarah Silverman exclaims. "You're out of your fucking gourd."

"Yeah, dude," Ethan Hawke says, leaning over to light Eddie's cigarette. "That's like seventy blocks."

Philip turns on them, exasperated. "What's with you people? Where's your sense of adventure? Yeah, the idea may be ludicrous, but imagine the creative fuel! Walking a gazillion blocks tonight might inspire Eddie's writing genius, fill his mind with brilliant dialogue we'll deliver in Oscar-winning performances some day! Ever think of that?"

The four young actors mused: yeah, maybe, sure.

"So who's with me?" Eddie said.

"Actually, I'm only with you in *spirit*," Philip said. "My dogs are killing me, I'm going to catch a cab."

In the end, only Ethan joins him, as the others abandon them at the nearest subway station. They set off with a spring in their step. The winds, the chill, the lights, the people. There's nothing like New York in 1990, a veritable factory of future stars of the silver screen. You can, like, buy coffee and chocolate *everywhere*. Pure luxury.

Eddie sizes up Ethan, who recently appeared in [*DEAD POET'S SOCIETY? WHITE FANG? CHECK THIS*] and, you know, seems to have his shit together. Maybe *Ethan* knows where the Plans are. "Hey, Ethan. You seem ahead of the game. What's your secret?"

"Dude, all the answers are on the fourteenth floor," Ethan says, conveniently advancing the plot. "Swear to you, get in there, unlock the loot chest, instant power-up. It will nerf the world. I was famous the next day. All my problems solved!"

"What room?"

"1412. But the security's fucking airtight. You either need to Barney Collier that shit, or Mata Hari it, know what I mean?"

Of course Eddie knows what that means. Not that it bodes well for him. "Thanks, man," he says, wondering how the hell he's going to get up there and infiltrate the meaning of life.

So here's our resident film buff, exploring his passion for Hollywood history. I think you may have uploaded a working draft, Stephen. Oh? Deliberate meta-commentary on the Subject's half-assed academic effort? Ha ha, nice try, very funny. Anyway, interesting fact: those celebrities did *attend NYU, during roughly the same time period. But the only one Eddie met was Ethan Hawke, who was in his freshman writer's comp class. He didn't even know Ethan was an actor. Typical Eddie, right?*

A picturesque effort, but not particularly artful with the plot, there. Several scenes in and Eddie's still a cipher, isn't he? Your metaphorical MacGuffin ought to raise the stakes a little more, too. Next semester, we'll tighten it up in post.

CUT TO: Interior dorm room, evening. Twenty-odd people crowd each other in the tiny space, drinking from bottles and plastic cups, getting blunted. Repetitive low-end music thumps away in a monotonous drone that inspires the kids to insane levels of ecstatic gyrating.

Months later. Eddie's made no progress on his mission. He's in the middle of the room, playing air bass with one hand while the other cradles a half-full cup of cheap whiskey and 7-Up. There are exactly three girls in the room he has a crush on (or thinks he does, he barely knows them, he barely knows himself), and two of them are in the drunken mosh pit, flirting mercilessly with everyone. With the confidence of a puppy with PTSD cringing from a rolled-up newspaper, he flirts back, his low-key, nearly imperceptible version of it. But it's a pose, an attempt to maintain cover. He's aimless, hoping liquid courage will get him laid, or a makeout session, or even just to feel like someone else, someone different, someone better, for a few bloody minutes. Fuck the Plans.

But as the night passes, his energy flags, his lungs start to ache, and the party breaks up as the girls choose their boys, or their girls, or nobody, and disappear, leaving him behind with a cluster of sad hangers-on.

The evening's hope evaporates. He bails, slouching into the corridor in a state of renewed, stupid-feeling sobriety, almost as bad as being sick-drunk. He is a hollow fraud, he thinks. The unwitting victim of a patriarchy he hasn't yet decoded. Deeply, miserably alone.

But as he reaches the elevator, prepared for a long night of huddling under blankets with self-hatred, he hears laughter. A girl lies on the floor near the stairwell, barefoot, wearing pajama bottoms and a T-shirt, clearly plastered. Eddie recognizes her from hours of hangout sessions in the basement lounge: Mai, a Japanese-American girl from Chicago, slim and slight. Sometimes she bums cigarettes off him, and he always feels guilty, because she doesn't look old enough to smoke. "Eddie!" she cries. "My hero!"

"Oh?" he says. "How's that?"

"I can't make it to the elevator. Help me."

Cluelessly, he goes to her side and helps her to her feet, but her balance is nonexistent. She droops and flails against him as they stagger toward the elevators. "What floor?" he asks, wondering how he ended up in this predicament.

"Fourteen."

"You bet." He stabs the Up button, losing his grip on her. She flops to the floor, laughing, as the elevator ascends.

"Sit with me," Mai says, slumped against the wall. Seriously drunk.

"I'm good here," Eddie says, feeling a lunge of nerves in his belly. Mai looks sexy down there on the floor, carefree and unselfconscious and relaxed, but also out of control, vulnerable. Even programmed as he is by the deplorable gender politics of his era, his excited reaction feels *wrong*. When they arrive at the fourteenth floor, Eddie helps her up, and they lurch into the hall. "Which room?"

"1412."

He remembers Ethan's intel. The nervous flutter is back.

The Plans.

They walk . . . ish. Halfway down the hall, Mai's legs give out again, and he's holding her up with all his liquored-up adrenaline. He feels like Leonard Nimoy in that episode of *Mission: Impossible* where Paris breaks into the vault with the brain-frying sonic security, a video sequence he remembers more vividly than his own freaking childhood, for some reason. Time slows, vision warps, walls twist and lurch. Suddenly he wonders if he's even more sloshed than Mai is, that maybe she's pranking him, or seducing him, or luring him into a trap.

With ten feet to go she collapses completely, giggling on the floor. "You'll have to drag me," she says, and because that's what she seems to want, he does so, by both arms, sliding her along the carpet. It's only when he reaches the door to 1412 that he notices her pajama bottoms have slid down to her ankles. She's laughing hysterically.

He lets go of her hands, helps her pull the pants back up, trying to avert his eyes and guiltily failing. "You have a key?"

"In my sock. You'll have to get it."

He does so, and fumbles the door open.

"Carry me."

Obediently, Eddie kneels down, slots his arms underneath her, and hoists her into an awkward carry. He turns sideways, carrying her across the threshold.

Or, rather, the *vault*, for that's what it is: a bank vault, walls lined with safety deposit boxes. Red safety lights provide dim illumination, lurid ambience. But wait, no, it *is* still a dorm: three beds, one in each corner, arranged just like his room. Empty beds. They're alone.

"Mine's over there," Mai says. Suddenly she's not drunk at all. "Take me."

He does so, lump in his throat, pulse racing. So close to the answers he seeks. The bed has four posts and a gauzy veil; an ornate, incongruous relic. She pulls back the curtain as he sets her down in the bed.

"I know why you're here," she says.

Eddie feels his face flush. "What?"

Mai pulls the covers up to her neck. "You're here for the Plans. I bet you can find them, if you look. Go ahead."

Because the idea of searching Mai's room for the Plans makes him less uncomfortable than Mai herself does, he stands back from the bed, scanning rows of identical, numbered boxes. Were the Plans in one of them? How could he know which one?

Numbers, numbers. He walks, studying digits, wracking his booze-addled brain for the key to the mystery. His investigation of this city, his classes, his interactions, surely something he's done on this vague, dispiriting deep-cover assignment will direct him. How did Ethan find it?

Then his eyes lock onto a box in the middle of the wall, slightly larger than the others, with red glowing text on it that reads THE PLANS.

Oh.

He approaches, heart hammering.

"I've got the key," Mai says.

He turns back to her, walks to the bed. Her pajamas and panties are lying on the floor beside it. Under the covers, Mai grins drunkenly at him, bare shoulders exposed.

"There's one condition," she says. "It's somewhere on my body. You have to find it."

Then she passes out.

Eddie hesitates. This doesn't seem right. It's too easy, it's too difficult. Haltingly, he reaches for the bedspread, then stops himself. He feels gross. He feels sick. This is his chance, he's been pursuing it so long. But none of this is right.

His nerve leaves him. His will is gone. "Good night," he says, and flees.

Wow. Huh. Uh, no, Maria. I mean . . . interesting. Moody. That's not what happened, though. I mean, it was all much more innocent than that. I think. But, you know, great job painting an unsettling picture of male sexual confusion in the twentieth century and all that, but . . . wow, yeah, no I wasn't that skeazy.

I mean, the Subject wasn't.

Did you think he was skeazy?

I'll have to collect my thoughts on that one. Let's move on . . .

CUT TO: Exterior, rooftop balcony, night. Sixteen floors up, atop the residence hall, just off the penthouse study. A small, square space with a chain-link fence around it, a cooped-up enclosure looking out over all the world's possibilities. Which is totally a metaphor.

Eddie stares across the myriad of windows, boxes of light and life, from Washington Square Park to Soho and beyond. Way off in the distance stands the World Trade Center. The towers can be seen from his bedroom window, majestic sentinels watching over him, but the view's even more spectacular from this vantage.

Beth emerges from the penthouse study room and crosses the balcony to stand behind him, wearing a trenchcoat, looking sultry. "Well, that's a year. No progress?"

Eddie looks at her. It's Beth, from the orientation cruise. It's also Beth Davenport from *The Rockford Files*, whom Eddie has a weird, persistent crush on. "Uh, no. Why, you pulling me off the mission?"

"That's your call, Agent Dunn." She extracts a pack of Marlboro Reds from her trenchcoat pocket, and offers him one.

"No way, gross," Eddie says.

"There's always next year."

"I suppose." Eddie hasn't figured out yet that this episode of his life is over. That it was all a failed experiment. The mission might go on, but with a completely different shape than he anticipated. "I thought things would be easier."

"Some feel similarly. Others don't. They're all right and they're all wrong. No big deal in the cosmic scheme of things."

"I don't even know what I'm doing here," Eddie says. "Why did I come here?"

"Two answers. One: no reason at all."

"What's the other?"

"To tell stories," Beth said.

"What's the point of that?"

"Because story is how we make sense of things. Without story, we're lost." She smiled. "But, you know, maybe you have to collect a few first. Live a few."

"What about the Plans?"

"Oh for fuck's sake, haven't you figured it out yet?" Beth sighs. "You will eventually. Maybe in the deep future, when you're an uploaded consciousness teaching the children of tomorrow how to craft memories in the global immersa."

Eddie sighs. "I'll never figure it out."

"Sometimes not figuring things out is the story."

Eddie looks at her. She's an amalgam of all the good, smart people he's ever known or ever would know: every mentor, every confidant, every meaningful encounter and moment of insight. She stands right next to him, forever out of reach.

"What's next, Eddie?"

"Go home? Figure shit out? Fail? Try again?"

Beth nodded, smiled. "Good answer."

Ah. I see what you did there. Who's teaching who, here? Very clever. Consider me schooled. The New York University of Hard Knocks. Wiseasses.

You'd think I'd have figured out these lessons by now. But I've always been a late bloomer. And my memory sucks.

I mean, Eddie's memory sucks. Not my memory. I mean, yeah, I was mapped from him, I'm not him, I'm just this software version of him who donated his brain to entertainment. Maybe I can't see him clearly, maybe I'm too close. I mean, if other versions of me had crafted these scenes, I'd have judged them pretty harshly. Self-indulgent, clumsy. But honest, I guess.

So. How do I measure up to your corporeal professors? Better? Worse? Weirder? I hope weirder, at least a little. Eighteen-year-old me never would have imagined this future.

The Plans. Heh, you got me: they don't exist. But we do still keep looking.

Might as well, right?

The Spread

~ Emma Johnson-Rivard

The cannibal bought her dinner at the best restaurant in town, which Clarabelle thought was either kind or horrifically ironic. The cannibal came dressed in fine French silk, diamond earrings glinting under her hair, and offered Clarabelle a gift upon sitting: a small box containing a single plain bracelet, wrapped carefully in tissue paper.

"For you," said the cannibal. "I do hope it's not too forward."

Not for the first time, Clarabelle thought about how much this felt like a morbid sort of prostitution or, perhaps, a well-staged death wish. The cannibal was, undeniably, a beautiful woman: dark haired, with a cutting chin and large, watchful eyes. She had a name, of course—something long and vaguely Latin sounding—but Clarabelle had decided only to refer to her as the cannibal, to stave off any delusions about what they were doing.

"No," Clarabelle said, "it's not too forward."

She put the bracelet on. It was gold with tiny, delicate stars etched into the surface.

The cannibal smiled. "Shall we order wine?"

"Not for me," Clarabelle said. She wanted to be clearheaded for this. "Though don't let me stop you."

"Nothing at all?" the cannibal wondered.

"Coffee, please. I would love a cup of coffee."

The waiter, dressed in a sharp black suit, took down her order. Coffee was produced. The wine was poured. A little while later he returned with cream and sugar on a little silver tray. It was all very civil.

Clarabelle took a moment to set her coffee right, measuring out cream and sugar in turn.

The cannibal sipped her wine–a deep, startling red–and gave her a polite smile. "I'll admit, I wasn't sure you'd come."

Clarabelle drank some coffee. The bracelet clicked against the mug. "I've always had a thing for older women."

The cannibal laughed. "Is that so?"

"Ever since I was a girl. I had a crush on my primary school teacher, Ms. Martin. She taught English. Nothing happened, of course, but I suppose that sort of thing gets wired in your head."

"I suppose it does," the cannibal agreed. It was expected. The two of them had met in the library, searching for some out-of-print book on abnormal psychology. "Still, that can't be the only reason you agreed. I'm not unaware of how this seems."

Clarabelle tipped her head to the side. "I was curious. You admitted it when I asked. And I've never met a cannibal before."

"Inevitably, there must be a first time."

Clarabelle nodded. It helped that the cannibal was a woman and that she was beautiful, in the distant sort of way the silent film actresses had been. It meant she could pretend this was safe, because who ever heard of women—especially the beautiful ones— ever becoming cannibals?

But, in truth, Clarabelle was bored. Nothing worthwhile had happened in her life and she had unfortunately become a romantic in response. She craved metaphor and if something deeper didn't come worrying up beneath the subtext of her life, Clarabelle feared the monotony of it all would kill her. It wasn't that she was unhappy, precisely; she had no reason to be. Nothing awful had ever been done to her and she had no business being anything but content with her life. She had a job that kept her comfortable, she was considered moderately attractive, and the disasters that had come crashing down on her colleagues—sudden deaths, cancers, a miscarriage—had passed her by without so much as a parting glance. There was no reason for her to be unhappy. Therefore, Clarabelle decided she was bored. And in her boredom, she had gone strange.

"The novelty intrigued me," Clarabelle said after a moment. "You were very honest."

"It's something I'm trying," the cannibal said. "Results have been mixed."

"Oh? Do I count as *mixed results*?"

The cannibal sipped her wine. "I haven't decided yet. Though I would never call you anything that crass."

Clarabelle thought that was fair. She turned her hand this way and that, admiring the bracelet. "Why stars?"

"We all come from stardust," said the cannibal. She spoke fondly, eyes wide and bright. "In time, everything will be stardust again. It appeals to me, the poetry of it all. I might be a romantic. It's a strange thing to realize, after all this time. But I suppose you know something about that."

Clarabelle smiled just a little. She added more cream to her coffee, mixing it with the silver spoon until it stopped changing colors and settled. "I read Shakespeare in high school, if that's what you meant."

"Not entirely. But you're here and that is worth far more than you know." The cannibal paused. "I have something to tell you, Clarabelle. You may not like hearing it, but sometimes we must face unpleasant things in the course of living an interesting life."

More than anything, Clarabelle wanted an interesting life. She put the coffee down. "Maybe I can guess it. It won't be so bad, if it's a game."

The cannibal blinked, looking surprised.

"I don't mean to make light of it," Clarabelle added. "I don't want to make light of anything. You're trusting me a lot right now."

She had considered going to the police in the beginning, had considered a whole mess of options when the rich woman from the library whispered a secret and turned forever into the cannibal in Clarabelle's mind. The cannibal had explained it was an occasional habit she indulged, at significant cost, but ultimately with no harm to anyone but the cadaver. She purchased specimens from the local anatomy school, where such things were allowed, if not exactly approved of, once certain sums of money had changed hands. Clarabelle had spent the better part of an evening clutching her cellphone and trying to compose her speech to the 911 operator. How she would lay everything out—if, indeed, there was anything to say. There wasn't any harm in it, not really. It was morbid and strange, leaving Clarabelle with anxious butterflies in her gut whenever she imagined the act of it. Yet there was a place within that strangeness, where the butterflies gathered and cooed, that beckoned to her.

In the end, Clarabelle had put her phone away. The next day, she went to dinner.

The cannibal hummed to herself. "I see. You learn something even if you guess incorrectly, is that right?"

Clarabelle nodded.

"I suppose there's no harm," the cannibal murmured. "Go on, then. Make your guess. But don't take too long. We ought to order soon. Unless you need more time to consider the menu?"

"I've never been here before. What would you recommend?"

The cannibal shrugged. "The special, I suppose. Their food is excellent. But that's not why we're here."

It seemed to Clarabelle that food, if not precisely this food, was entirely why they had come together. A beautiful woman was wining and dining her—or had at least offered the wine, even if Clarabelle had turned it down in favor of coffee. This sort of thing had a predictable ending. She watched the cannibal for a moment, thinking.

"You won't offend me," the cannibal assured her. "I think I'm beyond that now, being offended by what people think of me."

Clarabelle doubted that was true, but she nodded regardless. There wouldn't be much point if she'd come this far and didn't walk away with anything. "Three guesses."

"How traditional. Go on."

"Are you going to kill me?"

The cannibal shook her head. She didn't look surprised by the question. "Hardly. It crossed my mind, I'll admit that. A great many things cross my mind. It's best if no one knows them. But killing you is not my intention. Is that something that worries you?"

"It crossed my mind," said Clarabelle.

"As it should. We are logical people, after all, and it's a logical thing to consider. But that was a question, my dear, not a guess."

"I'm sorry," said Clarabelle. "I *guess* that you've never actually killed someone. But you've thought about it a lot."

The cannibal hummed to herself, gesturing to the waiter. "You're wrong about that, I'm afraid. I have killed someone, though not for the reasons you'd think."

The waiter returned. The cannibal ordered the house special, grilled salmon and a salad filled with nuts and dried oranges. Clarabelle ordered the same. There was a discussion about appetizers before they agreed to split an order of crab dumplings. The waiter collected their menus without a word and retreated.

The cannibal watched her for a long moment before speaking. "I was in the Army. It seems like a long time ago. I won't bore you with my reasons. They're hardly important now. But I rather liked the military. It was easy once you learned the rules. And then, one day, I found myself in some strange place you'll never know, on the edge of a conflict—it's all so polite when you call it a *conflict*—and, as it happens, I shot a man. He died rather quickly. I never knew his name. But I dream about it sometimes."

It was all said quite calmly. The cannibal sipped her wine, adorned in silk and diamonds like something out of a fever dream.

Clarabelle swallowed. Her throat had gone tight. "Did you want to kill him?"

"It seemed like the thing to do, at the time," said the cannibal. "Do you mind if I ask you a question? I don't want to interrupt."

"Go ahead," Clarabelle murmured. She tucked her hands under the table to hide their shaking and held onto her purse as tight as she dared.

"Thank you," said the cannibal. "You might have guessed, I'm quite well read on the subject of my own proclivities. Cannibalism appears in so many texts, some of them quite old. A subject of morbid fascination, I suppose. It's human nature to wonder about such things. Most of the old ones are quite fanciful, mind. They're all so wonderfully *colonial*; you can't believe half of what they claim. They're important from a historical standpoint, of course, but it's the newer works that intrigue me. Specifically, the fetish aspect. The sexual aspect of consuming and being consumed. It's all quite fascinating. Sometimes I regret not pursuing higher education; perhaps I could have been a doctor. But I'm getting off topic. This is my roundabout way of inquiring into *your* proclivities, Clarabelle. You're a curious girl. It's a boon, really, to be blessed with questions and a mind quick enough to answer them. But is it just curiosity that brought you here?"

The cannibal smiled. "I *guess* that it's something a touch more personal. Am I wrong?"

"No," Clarabelle said, "you're not wrong."

The butterflies returned to her gut. They gnawed at her, devouring her insides with their small and impossibly sharp teeth. It ached. All through her, it ached.

"Are you hungry?" the cannibal asked.

"That could mean so many things," Clarabelle replied. She twisted the strap of her purse between her fingers.

"It can, and indeed it does," said the cannibal. "Nonetheless, I ask."

Clarabelle looked away. She drank some more coffee.

"Yes," she murmured. "I'm very hungry."

The cannibal hummed to herself, looking pleased. "But hungry for what I do, or the thought I might consume you? Now there's the real question. Don't tell me yet. It's better if I don't know. I read a case study not so long ago you might be interested in, about a man who amputated his own arm and served it, unbeknownst to his lover, in a roast. It might have passed unnoticed if the wound had not become infected and the good doctor become suspicious about what had become of the missing limb. So it came out, in the end. By all accounts, it was quite messy. When asked, the man said it had always been his greatest and darkest desire to be utterly consumed. Indeed, he had vivid fantasies about a giant plucking him up off the ground and swallowing him whole. For him, the act of consumption meant that he was loved absolutely, that all parts of him—from the flaws right down to the small intestine—were desired and indeed useful. He claimed the severing of his arm was accidental, some mishap with heavy machinery. He was a construction worker, so there might have been some truth to that part. Regardless, he saw the flesh and bone, so recently a part of him, and became struck by the need to cook it and feed it to his lover, so they would never be separated. The lover didn't know any of this, of course. He ran for the hills the first chance he got. And the man, our dear construction worker, went to prison. He died there eventually."

"How sad," said Clarabelle.

"Yes," agreed the cannibal. "I suspect that man was very lonely."

They contemplated their drinks.

"It's odd that you'd bring that up," said Clarabelle, after the silence had stretched on for a while.

"Oh?"

"Because that was my second guess. That you're lonely."

The dumplings arrived before the cannibal could respond to that. They were sweet and surprisingly light, served with a small dish of ginger sauce. The two of them ate in silence for a while. More wine was offered. The cannibal accepted with a nod. It wasn't until her glass was full again and the waiter departed that she spoke.

"It's an odd thing to be lonely," said the cannibal. "And not for lack of company. I've known many people. I had siblings as a child. Yet for all that, I've never had anyone that truly understood the whole of me. And once I came to know myself I did, as you say, become terribly lonely."

"I'm sorry," Clarabelle said, for the second time. She almost said that she was lonely too, that she had been lonely and sad for a very long time despite wanting for nothing. She refrained and bit into a dumpling. The food was excellent. "Do you love me?"

The cannibal raised a delicate eyebrow. "No, Clarabelle."

It was said quite simply. It had no right to hurt as much as it did.

"I'm capable of love," the cannibal added. "In the Army, I loved another soldier quite dearly. She thought there was poetry in my name. I'm afraid she spoke little Spanish and conflated my name with another word. Marisol to *mariposa*. It means butterfly. My soldier thought that was lovely. I never had the heart to tell her that Marisol comes from *Maria de Soledad*. Maria of Solitude. Another word for the Virgin, you see. Poor, lonely Maria. Not nearly so pretty as a butterfly. But I loved her, so I lied to her."

Clarabelle swallowed another bite of dumpling. "What happened to her?"

"She died," said the cannibal. "As soldiers do. But I think you mistook my meaning, Clarabelle. I didn't intend to hurt your feelings. You see, it's quite easy to love someone without understanding them at all. I knew my soldier—I certainly knew her!—but did I understand her? Did I truly understand the means and methods of her life? No, of course not. Just as she never understood mine. You and I, we aim to understand each other. Quite the undertaking, no? And it's possible I might love you after that. But it will take time. Most things do. And I do find you fascinating, Clarabelle. Perhaps that can be enough for the night."

There was silence between them. The dumplings were gone.

Clarabelle wiped her mouth on a napkin. Her eyes were dry. She would not weep.

She said, "I'm hungry."

The cannibal gave her a gentle smile. "I know, my darling. Have patience. It won't be much longer."

The waiter arrived with their plates. The salmon was beautifully arranged and parted easily under her fork. Clarabelle ate and the cannibal ate. There was silence, for a time.

"You've told me three things tonight," Clarabelle said when she was done. The bracelet clicked against the forks. "That you don't want to kill me. That you've killed someone in the past. And that you're lonely."

"I did," the cannibal agreed, finishing her glass of wine.

"I have one final guess."

"You do," said the cannibal.

Clarabelle nodded. She reached for her purse and set it on her lap. Inside was a single thin blade. "My final guess is that one of those things is a lie."

The cannibal smiled at her. It was a soft, gentle sort of expression. "You're quite right, of course."

Tension gathered in Clarabelle's gut; the butterflies had returned. She welcomed the ache just as she welcomed the feel of the knife, cool and sure, tucked away in her purse. She was so hungry.

She smiled and the cannibal smiled and in that moment, the two lonely women drawn together by a singular urge, understood each other.

"We should have dessert," Clarabelle said. She held the knife under the table. It felt inevitable. "And after, we'll sleep together. And you'll love me because you'll know me."

"We should," the cannibal agreed. "And I might."

She gestured for the waiter. "Any requests, my dear?"

Clarabelle nodded. "Something sweet. Like a butterfly."

"How fitting," said the cannibal, and smiled.

The Taste of Things to Come

~ Ingrid Garcia

In the underground part of *Teotihuacán* known only to locals, in between a veritable jungle of stalactites and stalagmites, is Doña Juanita's Cantina. An unassuming eatery, where affable waiters and efficient waitresses serve subtropical dishes to a subterranean crowd. While the menu is a mix of Mesoamerican and Mediterranean, the wine list is cosmopolitan. Only a rare few regulars know how truly eclectic it is.

On November 2nd, an event so small, surreptitious and sacred takes place that only three people realise its true portent. A surprise wine tasting not listed on any menu or blackboard. Not for the faint of heart, as the tasting starts at breakfast and continues past dinner. The extremely select cadre consists of Dione Gaia, the seventh High Priestess of Adelphi; Michel de Nostradame, Duke of Oraculus; and Doña Juanita herself, her face and skin so white and brittle that the bones seem to shine through. They're seated at the round table in the far corner in an acoustic niche where barely any sound escapes.

The nine courses of fine wines and carefully selected, accompanying dishes (most restaurants have it backwards: a true sommelier selects food to fit the wine, not the other way around) provide, for these connoisseurs of the eccentric, the taste of things to come.

Instead of sensory characteristics, winery history and recommended food pairings, the back labels of these fine wines only feature a poem—in most cases, a haiku. The first wine is called

Triomphe de la Jeanne, a Chenin Blanc, served at a spry 7°C. The food pairing is either fluffy mushroom omelette on a perfectly baked baguette or an oven-fresh ham & cheese croissant. The haiku reads:

> *Contre le dédain*
> *Triomphe de la Jeanne gagne*
> *Victoire á Orleans*

As her long, light-blue gown matches the ethereal quality of her ashen hair, Dione Gaia reaches for the bottle containing a sparkling white wine just waiting to burst upon the scene. "See the mist form the *antichambre'd* bottle," she says, "descending like the myth of a maiden upon the expectant land." The cork pops like the (re-)birth of a nation, and Dione Gaia pours the *Triomphe* in a perfect arc, otherwise the subtle sparkling would become a frothing madness.

"A fresh fragrance of apricot, pear and apple of my eye cherishes my predawn nose," Dione says after smelling the wine several times. Then she takes a careful sip, swirls the spirit over her palate and swallows. "The tongue licks through an effervescent sea of brisk pineapple, cantaloupe and grapefruit to discover an invigorating mix of kiwi, mint and extra virgin olive oil," she notes, "the finish is short yet bright, with the promise of more, so much more . . ."

Her table companions nod in unison.

Ou la la! The next one wastes no time with making an impression. The explosion of bold lines, primary colours and shapeless shapes on the *étiquette* proclaim that *Rosé d'Enfant Terrible* isn't your average, run-of-the-mill wine. "Grolleau and Cabernet Franc," Michel de Nostradame reads from the front label in a hollow voice, "slightly carbonated." He raises one eyebrow and remarks: "This pink semi-bubbly is so ambitious it mistakes a *coup d'état* for a *coup de grâce* and so young it forgives a *faux pax* with *pâté au foie gras*."

He opens the cool bottle—recommended serving temperature 11-13°C—with some effort, not helped by the composite cork whose swirling, multihued materials provide precious little grip for the corkscrew. The side dishes are served—pickles smothered in white chocolate, peanut butter sandwich with Tabasco, *pâté au foie gras con ketchup Américain*—as he pours the *Rosé d'Enfant Terrible* in the three glasses.

"Initially, the nose is a welcoming waft of naïve pineapple, native grapefruit and naturalised coconut," he says, then makes a face, "until feints of plastic and oily tobacco come to the fore." His expression returns to normal as he takes a sip. "On the tongue, it has an even greater mix of spontaneity, candour and unorthodoxy: pomegranates in palm oil, saccharine cassis smothered in watery melon and assertive pumpkin in volatile mango."

He shakes his grey-bearded, long-haired head. "A bit ingenuous while trying too hard. The finish is oddly stimulating without leaving a lasting impression, like a dash of red pepper fading in a sea of mediocrity." He turns to read the back label.

> *Sacre blue, merde*
> *Rosé d'Enfant Terrible*
> *Est avant-garde*

"I rest my case." He says. His associates whisper their assent.

The sommelier places the next bottle near Doña Juanita, a *grande dame* of petite stature who—if rumours may be believed—is related to Catrina Calavera. The bottle's in the bucket, whose double wall is not wet with condensation, but ripe with frost. *Ønnøsköllön Víkìn* is a frozen Riesling in the truest sense of the word. Outwardly, it seems that the bottle is encapsulated by the ice in the bucket, but as Doña Juanita pulls it out, it makes a sound like a sword drawn from its scabbard. It is as it is, as the recommended serving temperature is a tad above freezing.

The tasting glasses are also frosted, and set upon cork coasters. She pours the wine in the iced glasses, a crisp wine like a cascading waterfall on a clear winter morning when conquering warriors set out to charge the world. Doña Juanita swirls the thick liquid, almost completely colourless with only the slightest hint of blue, in her glass. She smells deeply, then takes a bone-chilling sip. "Coy on the nose to the point of standoffishness," she says, "Yet, on the palate, it's a full-on attack on the senses. Peach, pear and the dried sweat of a petrified enemy. Slick tannins like slicing longboats, powerful papaya exploring dragon-spiced shores and avaricious avocados with pickled onions."

The matched food is served. Stockfish and—what looks like—raw red meat.

"Shouldn't it be cooked?" Dione Gaia wonders.

"Or slightly seared?" Michel de Nostradame asks. "Even if just a few milliseconds?"

"No," the sommelier says, "Raw. Red. Meat."

"The finish is short and exquisitely sharp, like an ice dagger through the heart." Doña Juanita says. "Ice wine at its iciest."

> *Neither foe nor friend*
> *Ønnøsköllön Víkìn's brand*
> *Will conquer the land*

The back label reads. The three tasting visionaries have nothing to add to that.

If anything, the next wine—*Syrah of Tomorrow*—is an aspiring one. Dione Gaia, her gown and hair bellowing out like great wisps of smoke, looks at the front label and sees a blurry face about to clarify into view. The back label is more explicit:

> *Deceptive grandeur*
> *The Syrah of Tomorrow's*
> *Visions of splendour*

In the glass, the wine's color is a bold red-black like a statement of intent. Its recommended serving temperature is 14-17°C. "A promising nose of cinnamon, caramel, liquorice and leather," Dione says, after taking a few careful smells. She takes a long sip, lets the wine roll over her tongue and swallows deeply. "On the palate, a teasing hodgepodge of spicy plums, tart blueberries and juicy forest fruits with a velvety richness of cacao, freshly cracked black pepper and gently developing tannins," she says, "A mix that's always one step short of perfection, getting there but never quite reaching it."

Her companions take a few bites from the truffle cheese, fried chicken with pine nuts and fuet that accompany the *Syrah of Tomorrow*. "The finish is middle-long; deep but not quite deep enough to fully satisfy, leaving an aftertaste for more," Dione Gaia says, the tiniest bit of disappointment reflecting in her eyes, "an audacious wine always on the brink, just short of perfection."

Her companies let out a minute sigh in rueful agreement.

Near the end of the afternoon, Michel de Nostradame swallows his trepidation and turns his attention to the next bottle. The front label depicts mountain flanks speckled with vineyards growing the specially cultivated Malbec grape. "*Castana Alta Chuevara*," he reads, "carefully grown on high altitude lots in the Cervandes mountain range, *Castana Alta Chuevara* mixes centuries old crafts-manship with pioneering approaches." As he swirls it in the glass, the purple wine lights up with striking blue hues.

He sticks his big nose in the even bigger glass. "A bouquet of violets and lavender pirouette in a storm of ripe red and black berries, barely held together by a contrivance of leather and lace," he says, then swallows deeply. The wine is served warm, at 21-24°C, and is accompanied by dinner-like dishes such as entrecôte from pampa-roaming cattle, black beans with rice and ceviche, polenta with chorizo and lentils.

"Swirling tactile tasting sensations are racing on the tongue like a flamenco dancer on acid," Michel de Nostradame says, "roasted chestnuts in a sulphur fire, forest fruits exploding with readiness and acidity, sweet tannins pierced with oregano, garlic and aniseed, topped off with blackcurrant, black velvet and black pepper."

A wine that refuses to play by the rules. "The finish is exquisitely long and wide open," he says in a contemplative tone, "earthy tones, tea and mocha resonate long after the wine is downed, suggesting that this subversive approach may, indeed, hold."

*Viva Catena
Alta Chuevara, a
La Revolución!*

The back label proclaims. Casting a weary eye, his companions do not disagree.

The moment the sommelier brings the *Origami Bonsaké* forward, the three tasting visionaries know it's oblique. It's not just the square bottle on its wooden plateau and the accompanying wooden drinking cups. It's not only the way both labels are not glued, but rather folded to the bottle in an indecipherable, labyrinthine manner. Neither the very specific serving temperature of 31.41592635 ± 0.000000001 °C, nor the exquisite side dishes of Kobé beef and torafugu. There's an aura around the wine that defies the common sense, Western approach.

As the bottle is opened, the rice wine is poured in its wooden cups and Doña Juanita takes her first smell, something happens to her. As if a powerful medium takes over, her eyes turn white and she recants with a hollow voice:

"On November 11th, the Day of Reckoning, as the Sun reflects in Edoistic perfection on the Mirror Lake atop Mount Fujitsu, the priestess—Reibai—signals the Shogun that the time is right. The Kamikaze Shogun gathers his daimyo, who then, as the Reibai rings the Gotemba Bell, fold a thousand orizuri. The Reibai launches the senbazuru from the temple's bonsai garden into the Rising Sun as the Shogun breaks the Kagami mochi. The Reibai lights the eternal flame of peace as the Shogun, using jujutsu, breaks the sacred *Origami Bonsaké* cask. With immaculate care, the Reibai pours the *Origami Bonsaké* in a thousand choko which the thousand samurai empty—*ad fundum*—in perfect synchronicity, after which they march, victoriously, into battle to end war forever."

Her companions look at her in baffled silence. "You wonder about *Origami Bonsaké*'s colour, fragrance, palate and finish?" Someone says in Doña Juanita's voice. "Obviously, after such impeccable preparations, it cannot possibly fail to impress."

It's habitual
Origami Bonsaké's
In the ritual

The haiku on the intricately folded back label declares with finality.

With a sigh of relief—after they survive the perfectly prepared tora-fugu and Doña Juanita returns to her, not-quite-normal, self—the three tasting visionaries move to the next wine, commencing the last trio of trios. It's definitely less singular than its predecessor, being a mix of Syrah, Cabernet Sauvignon, Tintilla de Rota, Petit Verdot and Merlot.

Dione Gaia inspects the front label. "*Finita Musica*," she reads, "a wine from the lost shores of Aquadir." The sommelier pours and a thick wine—served at 16°C—with an enduring ruby color fills the glasses. Dione closes her eyes as she inhales the wine's fragrance. "An ancient nose of dried fruits, mushy earth and roasted coffee beans," she says in approval.

"A verdant potpourri of grapes that seemingly clash at first, but surprisingly harmonize the longer they stay on the palate." Dione Gaia says, then takes a few quick bites from the highly aged blue cheese and txuleta steak that accompany the definitive wine before she takes another sip. "An intense taste of melancholic red berries and cherries grounded in acidic limestone and cloying clay, tinged with tannin overtones of loss and despair." She says with a wistful look in her eyes. "Subtle floral spices and almost musical, balsamic notes hint of the beauty of what was and what will never be."

For the longest of moments, she's silent. Then she concludes with: "An exquisitely long finish that keeps you longing and longing and longing."

Syrah/Cabernet
Of Finita Musica
Aren't here to stay

The back label's rhyme echoes with the transience of existence.

○

In the end, is a dessert really the end? Michel de Nostradame wonders. *Bay under Poincaré*'s dessert wine from the renowned Palomino grapes begs to differ. Outwardly, things seem normal. But the back label offers an early warning.

> *Ouroboros worms*
> *The Bay under Poincaré*
> *Twists, turns and transforms*

Somehow, though, the glasses don't shatter as the sommelier pours out the wine at the prescribed serving temperature of cosmic background radiation—or 4.2°K—and neither does the super-cooled wine burn a hole through Michel de Nostradame and his companions' palates as they taste it.

Possibly because they have been antichambered by the cold desserts served alongside it: Baked Alaska á la The Fat Lady Sings, The Farm Has Been Bought Celebration Cake, and Grand Finale Celestial Crème Brûlée. In an icy voice, Michel de Nostradame analyzes the near absolute zero wine.

"The deep mahogany color in the glass is so dark it reflects star-light." He says. "In the nose, walnuts, raisins, and balsamic orbit around old furniture in a magnificent, ungraspable four body inter-action." He takes an impossible sip and continues. "On the palate, a tongue-twisting topological transformation of laurel leaves, golden tobacco and noble wood through an ether of nuttiness: walnut, pistachio, pine, hazelnut and macadamia."

"The finish strikes the throat with the enduring finality of coffee, toffee and stuffy truffles and is exceptionally dry." He says. "A dessert wine so final it only fits the final dessert." His companions tend to agree, but then remember that there still is one more wine to come. . .

The sommelier starts with serving the side dishes. Melon with jamon or prosciutto, a fresh garden salad and gazpacho seem to announce a new beginning. Then he serves a bottle of wine not in a cooler, but on top of a stove. *Ashphoenixia*, the front label reads, depicting a dark, tapered mountain with a smouldering top. The wine is served a tad below boiling temperature, yet the scorching heat does not seem to faze Doña Juanita and her associates.

"A brutal, in-your-face wine from the fertile flanks of the Fat Man volcano, mixing Tempranillo, Graciano and Mazuelo." She says, looking at the red hot, almost living wine in her heat-strengthened glass. "An intense crimson colour with blobs of tawny hues rising and falling like the wax in a lava lamp."

The visible black fumes spiral into her nose as she takes a deep sniff. "A pungent mix of ashes, vanilla and quince punches on the nose," she says and takes a deep swallow. The simmering liquid doesn't seem to affect her. "The tongue is initially overwhelmed by overripe forest fruits, burning red peppers and desiccated prunes." Doña Juanita pauses a moment and casts a contemplative look into the far distance. "The patient palate is rewarded with a rise to the occasion of sludgy chocolate rich in minerals, spicy liquorice and a hint of hard cheeses."

"The finish is short at first—it seems dead on arrival—but resurrects after a lingering pause with a fierce intensity that burns all the way down." She says and her companions begin to nod as they eventually experience it, as well. "A wine that refuses to go gently into that good night."

The back label has the final word:

> *Fire, ashes and rain*
> *Ashphoenixia has died*
> *But will rise again*

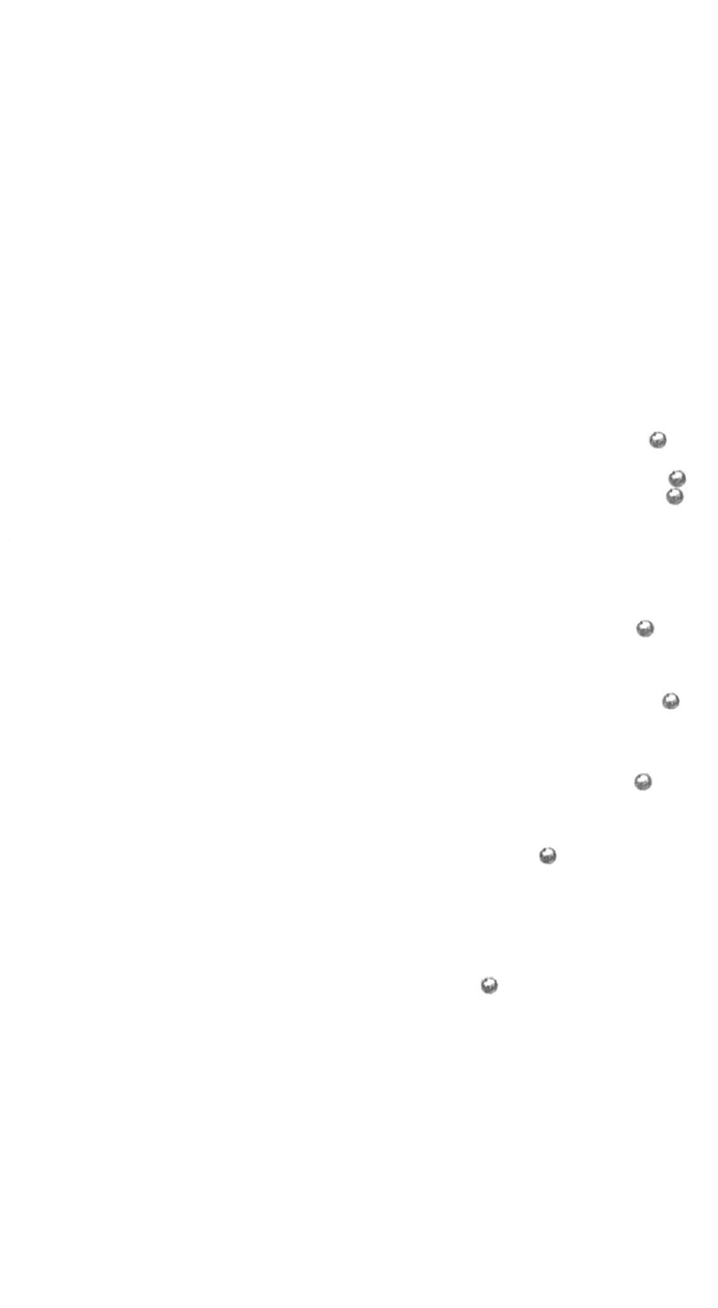

Snake Eyes

~ Mark Mills

He is a creature to be pitied, this one. You find him alone, deep in the forest, armless and legless, sprawled on his back, his slumber fills with visions of slashing teeth and children. Between the space where his legs once stretched, gaped a wound, still angry and red. When his dreams shine too vividly, he attempts to scream, only to reveal that his tongue has been ripped out at the root.

No man without limbs could have journeyed this deep into the forest. No man without limbs could hope to survive a night in this moonless wilderness. No man without limbs would have lain down on the mud and moss of his own free will.

He begins to stir and you want to quiet him, "Keep yourself still, you stump. Keep still, or the beasts will be upon you." But you can say nothing and he continues to thrash.

Undoubtedly, this is what draws the snakes.

They creep from fallen trees, creek beds, and warm basements; some thin and crimson, others huge and tawny. Their eyes show no emotions but they flick their tongues rapidly, lustfully--desire is thick in the night air.

Through the leaves, they reach his body, some crawling upon it, others slithering beneath it. They coil around him and for a moment you dare imagine that they've merely sought the warmth of his skin–then they open wide their fanged jaws and strike.

The first snake bites into the left stump on the man's hip; the next sinks its fangs into his shoulder; one squirms through his dry lips and strikes into his gums; another lashes into his unprotected groin. Two others join the fray, fangs dripping blood, they dig deep into his flesh.

The man convulses a bit but calms when the serpents begin to belch up blood into his wounds. They continue to regurgitate into his veins for what seems an eternity but just as the first rays of the sun appear, they quiver, the man groans, and suddenly he is whole. He stands and brushes off flecks of dirt, a pink worm pokes past his teeth then settles back as a tongue.

He could pass for human in a crowd but if you look carefully, you can spot the snake eyes at the base of his arms and legs, his member and tongue. The man wraps a cloak around him. No one will see.

He picks the farm well. Chickens and ducks, cows and cats. He licks the wind and smiles. They have a daughter.

"Have any work to be done?" the snake-man asks the farmer's wife. He knows very well that crops need tending, a fence has fallen in the far field, and two of the cows will soon drop their calves.

The woman studies the man. Old but not too old to work. Too gangly to be a good thief. "Three meals a day," she offers him. "You can sleep in the barn."

The little girl cries at night. Her father is far from sympathetic.

"It's past the first frost," he snaps. "No more snakes 'til spring."

She will not be put off until he agrees to light a candle near her bed. "Just the little ones. The ones we been saving to put on your birthday cake. Can't have anything bigger; you'd burn the house down."

He hates to be so gruff with her but times are hard. Doesn't like the hand his wife hired but can't find reason to fire the old fool. His chores get done. He works, they all work, but what is the matter? The animals are fed, sheltered, cared to, not a hint of disease but what can explain the dead fowl or why the calves are too weak to stand? At least, the cats–wherever they are hiding–are keeping away the rats.

He wonders if he should call the animal doctor in the village. Or a priest, he muses, but he soon dismisses the thought and gets ready for bed.

○

She knows she must be dreaming for snakes cannot speak.

This evening she had begged her parents to let her sleep in their room but they laughed and called her a baby. Now, as she dances on the bed, she is careful not to scream no matter what the snake says to her. "Don't make me come in there!" her father had thundered at her first peep and she decided there were worse things than dream snakes.

It all must be a dream. It will soon be over.

"Lie down and sleep, my dear," the snake whispers as it lashes at her ankle. "I can be gentle when I choose to be."

She does not stand still but the snake bites her solidly in the leg, flicking its tongue into droplets of blood, sucking up a mouthful.

"I could do much more," it tells her. "But you are far too sweet to eat all at once."

Another snake, about the same size as the first, emerges from the shadows to taste her blood. It looks at her hungrily before retreating with its brother to the darkness.

She does not sleep at night.

Her father grumbles that the cows are milkless. Never saw a cow go dry so soon after losing calves. Going to be a tough winter, that much for sure. No duck for Christmas, no eggs New Year's Day, probably nothing at all by February.

"You chopped the wood like I told you?" he asks the hired hand.

"Yes sir," he points to the stack of logs. "Just like you tell me."

Fast worker for an old fool, he thinks. "Well, it's getting dark. Call it a day."

This time the monster snakes glide from the darkness, just as she starts to nod off. One wraps around her arms, one around her throat. They feel like sacks of grain wrapped in leather. Their scales scratch her exposed flesh. She can't hold back the tears.

"Please stay quiet," the talking one tells her. "This will only be a minute."

She tries to scream when it plunges its fangs into her shoulder, tries again at the sight of it swelling in size like a tick, but the grip around her throat tightens and she can only gag. When the snake pulls its dripping jaws off her, it presses its teeth against her cheek, just enough to draw blood.

"If you do what we tell you, little beauty, it won't hurt. If you fight us, it will be horrible."

She doesn't want to sleep even after they are gone but she is too weak. Thankfully, the next morning she cannot remember her dreams.

He mends the chicken coop as quickly as a man half his age. Scraping and sawing, hammering in new wood to replace what's rotted, his arms do not ache, his legs are firm and stout. As he works, he listens for birds. They've all flown away; the trees are empty of song.

The farmer nods as he inspects the job. "Paint it as soon as the weather's willing," he finally acknowledges.

"I expect you'll be getting some new chickens," he says, careful not to reveal too much.

"Don't know. These are wearisome times."

He retires back to the loft. The hay is soft and still smells of rats and heavy beetles. He lies down and burrows in it until he reaches the soil underneath. Licking the rich earth, he tastes every living thing that walked, urinated, or died upon it. His mouth waters and where his saliva drips, no moss, mold, or life of any kind will ever grow.

Deep into the night, as the lights in the house go out, he crawls from the hay. His stomach is empty, his eyes are dull. He rolls on his back and, with grunts and twitches, releases his arms. Their eyes open wide, and, forked tongues flickering, they slither at first to the barn door but the cold air forces them back inside, coiled around the heat of his lantern.

The cows begin to rattle but he calms them with a glance. Each of the snakes licks at an udder before clamping onto a nipple, drawing first milk, and then, when the udder is spent, thick, hearty blood.

"It won't be long," he whispers to himself as his legs vomit up the fluids into his body. He stares across the yard at the candle in her window. The moon tells him that warm rain is coming soon. He can wait long between meals.

She has seen them from her window. The old man her mother hired—he's the one. Perhaps he keeps the snakes in that satchel he carries, or perhaps, as her worst fears tell her, it's something much, much worse.

At least two of the big ones–the little ones are too small to see at this distance–gather near the barn doors and, in the light of the old man's lantern, peer into the soft October rain. The old man walks into view and when she sees his splintered body, she knows the truth. She cannot keep from screaming.

Her father storms into the room, roaring and threatening violence. She knows the old man has heard her. She knows it will be soon.

When they crawl loose from his hips, his entire body feels violated. Even with his arms still attached, it is the loss of his legs that most frightens him. When his arms shed their skins and drop away, he barely notices. Mute and sexless, it is his limbless pelvis that drives him into the sleep of revulsion. *Where are my legs*, he asks himself, *where are my legs?*

They crawl in single-file, sliding across the yard to the back door, the servant's door, the door that the woman insists that he use. The snakes are happy to oblige her. One of the arm-serpents raises itself up and turns the knob with its mouth. Awkward, unnatural, but the door opens. They are inside.

Deaf and earless, they hear no moaning but they sense vibrations, their tongues lick the air for scent. They know the man is making busy with his wife, both will be even more preoccupied tonight than usual.

The moans excite the small red snakes and they wriggle up the stairs and slip under her door. Her candle is all but burnt out and she is huddled under the covers to her chin, shaking, whimpering.

Beautiful, mouth-watering, she is ripe enough for several more feastings but she has seen too much. This will be the last.

As the monster snakes push the door open, the red ones creep under her covers, wiggling towards her soft flesh, licking her legs, tugging at her gown.

A knife, cold and slick, lashes at the first one. It cries a final cackle and thrashes long after death. The other recoils but too is severed. In the barn, a tongueless throat vomits forth a scream.

The four huge snakes flail at her, mindless, feverish, like whips in the hands of blind demons. *You monster, you little monster. Go for her eyes, go for her throat, kill the little monster, kill it, kill it.* They tear into her body but knives flash in both hands. Blood, their blood, splashes against the wall. There is a shout and her father is at the doorway, a chair crashes upon the pythons, one of their brains is crushed into the floorboards.

For years when he tells unbelieving neighbors about the night, the farmer will swear that as he beat the snakes to the corner, to the window, anywhere away, that a human hand flew from the darkness, clawing at his face. He tells them how he would have fallen but his daughter—"And don't you dare call her Crazy Jenny"—hacked into it with her mother's good butcher knife. The hand vanished in the shadows, but before it went, he saw its eyes, hideous and cold, as out of place on a human hand as the snakes were in the bedroom.

Three snakes retreated into the darkness and there was quiet. They stayed vigilant all night, but the unholy serpents never returned. By morning, the pools of blood had dried and lay flaked upon the floor.

In the late mornings or early evening, you may see a beggar, struggling on stolen crutches, thick arms propelling his lanky body through the streets. He never talks, he never smiles, and when he relieves himself in the public park, right in front of policemen, he squats to make water.

You may allow yourself to gaze upon the old man and think, "What a bleak life he must have endured." You may even toss him a coin as he sits, his single leg bent and crooked before him, hamstrings severed years ago. You may even say a kind word to him, give him a coat or a warm meal. You may do all these things but I for one will show him no pity.

He still has two strong arms, long and muscled as his leg. And in the warm months, when scaly creatures live, he always looks well-fed. Believe me, you of a gentle heart, there are others more deserving of your kindness.

Gemini

~ Forrest Aguirre

"Through the thorny brambles we go," he said aloud, though alone, as if she was still with him. Eight years no, and he still felt her presence, as if she had been standing beside him, watching herself collapse through the liminal calm of the water's horizon, gazing with rapt curiosity as the flailing moil ceased and her saturated body tumbled along riverbottom, cartwheeling through the undertow, moving in two places at once, both alive and dead. Yes, this was how he spoke, as if she was still at his blindside, just out of earshot, still Felicity to his Felix.

Continuing up the lush green hill, he scanned its slopes as he approached the dark copse of trees ahead. The long grass rustled slightly in the breeze, as if the hill had momentarily awoken from its afternoon nap and was rolling over to go back to sleep. A flock of starlings burst out of the dark clump of trees and flew away over the hill, toward the high noon sun. The staccato scratch and click of their familial argument trailed behind them, faded, and was enveloped by the rush of wind through the leaves as Felix entered the blotch.

Inside, the sunlight became far more muted than interference alone would explain. He was plunged into darkness with only pinpoints of light showing through, as if the starlit blanket of the night sky had been suddenly thrown over the world by some cosmically-immense demon.

He stood still, allowing his eyes to adjust before moving. The faint green flow that limned the pitch shadow revealed what he had expected to see—a tangle of blackthorn and rowan—and something he had not expected: the inside junction of two rough-hewn stone walls. They were blackened with soot and Felix soon recognized that distinct odor of cold wood smoke that evinces a past conflagration.

"What do we have here, love?"

The corner intersection, wrapped in vine and ivy, loomed over him like an ancient standing stone. At the vertex, on the ground, the green glow that had provided him some little illumination was completely negated. Sharp, thorned branches were intertwined there, like the gnarled fingers of villagers protecting the last remaining child in the community from Viking raiders.

Desire tugged within him and he stooped down for a closer look. Beneath the barricade he could see . . . nothing. A hole, perhaps? Or just more charred remains of . . . what?

He found a stick nearby, two fingers thick, one arm long. Driving it in between the blackthorn branches, he levered backwards, pulling a few of them back enough to reveal what was, indeed, a hole in the ground fully three feet in diameter. Felix rammed the stick down, hoping to scare away any animals that might be inside, but nothing emerged.

The stick snapped as he pulled against the brambles once more, so he removed his shirt to wrap around his hands. The white fabric would be ruined, he knew, but why should he care? His father was away, as it always seemed, on business, and his mother was probably dallying with "handsome Mister Pentree, the solicitor," while her husband was, again, traveling. Felix could boldly dispose of the shirt, if needs be, procuring another from his mother by implied threat of revelation. He would sacrifice the shirt.

"Mother never was very fond of us, Sis," he said, layering the shirt over his palms and fingers.

Something tapped his shoulder and he turned suddenly, alarmed. But he saw only the dark womb of the trees around him. A falling branch, perhaps?

He turned back to the task at hand, tightening the cloth over his hands.

Despite the precaution, reaching in and pulling at the thorn-encrusted branches earned him spots and streaks of blood on his now-tattered shirt. But the deed was done, a way had been opened, and his curiosity drove him down, head-first, into the hole.

Vertigo instantly spun his consciousness around. He momentarily looked back up. Past his hip, into the trees. Then the dizziness seized him full-hold, and his brain seemed to tumble downward. He thought he recalled, in that last backward glance, seeing a glimpse of his twin sister, Felicity. Before he could look back again, darkness embraced, then smothered him.

Felix awoke with a sharp awareness brought on by a clawing hunger. He heard the creaking of wood beneath his prone body, felt in his neck and shoulders the ache and strain of having laid too long in an awkward position, smelled his soured breath mix with the odor of mothballs, sawdust, and old books. Dizziness came again, momentarily, as he swung his head around against the pain in his neck, then faded away as his vision caught up with the rest of his senses.

"What's this?" he groaned, sitting up. "Where are we?"

Sunlight shone from high up the walls of an old attic. The diagonal columns of light pushed down, juxtaposed with exposed wooden beams that reached up to form the peak of the room, as if mocking their stilled physicality with the promise of their own playful movement as the day progressed. The light lived on, while the wood which it had once fed was now dead, utterly inert, subject to the sunlight's ravages over time. Felix sat for a long time watching dust motes being carried about at the whim of the air, occasionally seeming to explode as they entered the radiant columns.

"When will it ever end?"

Hunger drove him to his feet. He looked about the room. Crates and boxes lined the walls. An old steamer trunk squatted in the far corner. Atop the steamer trunk sat a number of dolls, the sort that his sister would play with. There was a certain stern malevolence in their eyes, which made him uncomfortable. Their blank stares seemed to sweep the whole room at once, without movement, yet following his movements, which caused a shiver to skitter down his spine.

He searched for an exit, always keeping an eye out for the dolls, wary of their presence. There were no doors along the walls, only the high windows where the angle of the light became increasingly more shallow, indicating a setting sun. He looked along the floor, pacing its width, checking the dolls for any unnatural movement —for what could be more terrifying than the animation of simulacra? Then, moving down the wall, he would systematically pace the width of the floor again.

It was a few feet away that he discovered that a trapdoor—the only exit, lay underneath the old steamer trunk, mostly obscured by the trunk itself and completely within its shadow.

Resolve, tempered by fear, came to him quickly and furiously. He was unsure whether to be more afraid of the haunting presence of the dolls or the angry energy that welled up inside him as he struck out with his hands, sweeping them off the trunk, into a wall, and onto the floor. He was grateful that they all landed face down.

He pushed the trunk aside, crushing the dolls against the wall with a symphony of ceramic "cracks!" fully revealing the trapdoor. A hammered iron ring was embedded therein, surrounded by carved letters in gothic script:

Finis Opus Coronat

Pulling the iron ring activated a series of hidden (but noisome) gears that allowed a ladder to swing down from the hole to the floor below. Felix descended into gloom. The fading light from the trapdoor above gave the effect of the moon passing behind clouds: shadows deepened, the illusion of movement manifested as the dampened light rearranged itself. A growing sense of stillness and isolation overtook the room. He turned from the bottom of the ladder to face what he perceived (through dim eyesight and inference) to be a large desk. Atop the desk was a pair of large, dark candles; beside the candles, a matchbox.

"Is there such a thing as coincidence for us?"

He struck a match and lit the candles.

The flames flickered high. Felix was temporarily taken aback as the walls sparkled in response. They were a deep navy, painted to resemble marble, with veins of gold leaf shot throughout. While his focus was on the beauty of the walls, along with a mirrored ceiling that gave the illusion of a room much bigger than it was, he caught enough in his peripheral vision to know that this was a study or library of some sort.

He turned his attention to the furnishings—the immense mahogany writing table next to him, atop which was a globe of the moon, a silver ink tray etched with *art nouveau* floral motifs, quills, and sheaves of parchment; rows of glass-faced book cabinets; framed paintings and posters of sigils and strange scenes of angels, demons, and their robed supplicants making agreements and congress under such exalted symbols as the all-seeing eye, a golden hourglass, and crowned cherubim.

On the far side of the room, he found more candles, which he lit, more fully illuminating the space, allowing him to peruse the book spines, none of which bore a familiar title, though many of the titles were evocative and intriguing: *Obumbrafio Vitas, Stealing Passage Through the Gateways of Dream, Geminisque Sororibus Habeo Dilexit, Die Barriere durchbrechen, To Set the Hedge Aflame, The Rabbit Ruler, The Purified Essence of the Shadow of the Valley of Death, Labyrinthine Häxprocess.*

It was obvious that the tastes of whomever curated this collection leaned heavily to the antiquarian and the aesthetical. Some of the volumes were very old, but in good repair, where repair had been necessary. All of them spoke to a high level of craftsmanship, with barred bindings, foil impressions, tastefully-marbled end papers, and silk ribbons in abundance.

One volume in particular commanded his attention due to its contrasting condition. It was once a bright-yellow clothbound volume of large size. Its cover was embossed in black with a fine, flowing line drawing of Salomé holding up and kissing the decapitated head of John the Baptist, whose post-mortem glory was evident from the sweeping arcs of radiance that emanated from him like a crown despite the black tears of blood that flowed from under his closed eyelids. Salomé's expression was that of one mesmerized, whether by his glory or the audaciousness of her own request, it was unclear.

This tome was unlike the others in that it seemed that little effort had been made to keep the book in good repair. The yellow cover was faded in patches, as if it had sat neglected in sunlight too long and bleached a portion of its die pale. The corners were stubbed and dirty, and there was clearly wear at the places where one had opened and closed the cover repeatedly. The binding was collapsed in and the headbands frayed to the point that their original color could not be identified. They were now the color of lint dirtied by soot.

Felix retrieved this book from the case and hefted it to the writing desk, dropping it with a thud between the two candles. The sound echoed off the walls, then faded, as if the walls were murmuring from some unseen distance.

A black silk ribbon marked a page about a fifth of the way through the book. Felix turned to it, curious to know the reason that this page, among so many was marked.

The upper corner of the page (73 of 497, he found) had been dog-eared so many times that the wedge of paper above the crease had gone missing. Hand-scrawled marginalia littered the edges of the page, notes written in a careful hand, with spokes pointing inward like a wheel. The terminus beyond the arrowhead for each pointer was merely a spot of blank page within the confines of one thick-lined circle. The notes read, in counter-clockwise order, starting from the top:

α_1

Imminence is not eminence; your need to prove is only proof of your need to give yourself to the spiral dance, pirouette down into the labyrinth again.

ν_1

"The Appolyonic Protocols," the old man said, two fingers and thumb pointing skyward, "are not Law for the sake of Law. They are for the communal good, the individual's appetites cannibalized for the many."

α_2

The covenant is sufficient unto itself. One does not break the covenant, one breaks oneself against it!

β

Lawyers. Bankers. Politicians. Stay here you must. But carefully weave your way through the shadows. Someone must answer to the Shades who guard the way, but it need not be you. Entice another!

α₃
"That's the way we do it!"
"But Master Punch, it is not!"
"Right you are, my friend."
"You are not my friend, Master Punch."
"Oh, but you could be mine!
Be a dear and pick up that kerchief
I just dropped. WE will be friends,
Mister Belvedere. That's it.
Bend down to pick it up, please,
Good sir!"
[Punch stabs Belvedere in the back, mortally wounding him.]
"Friends forever, Master Belvedere,
Wouldn't you agree?"
[Punch puts a hand to his ear. Belvedere is still and bleeding.]
"Hearing no objections,
I declare it so!
Calay!
Calahoo!"

ι

tTl hiepb sl soi otdnoa fftnhie. e Imceosn ospup moe othhwo es.

ν₂
Liberty unbound, I am free to give or take away, justified saint or winner when and where I wish, a law unto myself!

ω

Death to the plunderers, life for the producers, and if they all call you "scoundrel," at least they all know your name. Use that reputation for good, dance for their pleasure!

○

He did not stop reading at the top of the page, but continued on, twice again, counterclockwise, compelled to weave the illogical chain until it started to make some sort of sense, as if it was a mantra being slowly revealed to him. His vision seemed to darken, the black circle, marginalia, and arrows inverting from black to white, as the background page and void within bled from white to black.

Felix looked up to the mirrored ceiling.

"My vision is faltering," he observed, rubbing his eyes.

But it was not.

Above him, he saw himself as if from outside his own body. The void, indeed, was a black pit surrounded by a chalk circle, with white arrows showing him the way ahead.

He fell, swiftly, upward and in.

Felicity sat surrounded by dolls in velvet and lace dresses. Their faces were, as a rule, more plump and less austere than her own, though their frozen looks of serenity gave off an aura of dread. She did not scowl, but her eyes and sallow cheeks showed a touch of world-weariness under the golden glory of her hair.

Felix stooped down, moving one of the larger dolls—a redhead with unblinking hazel eyes wearing a plaid print skirt of a distant cousin's clan—carefully to one side, so that he could face his twin unobstructed.

"Must we play this game?" he asked.

"We must," she said, "but only as prelude."

"To what?"

"The abandonment of these," she said, indicating the dolls with a sweeping gesture.

"Dolls? Toys? I don't understand."

"The abandonment of childish things. It is time for you to let them go. Only then will you begin to understand."

"I still . . . don't understand."

She smiled, knowingly, laughed and shook her head.

"You must let go."

"Of what?"

"Of me, of course."

Her body seemed to fold in on itself and was then swept away into darkness, as if by an invisible flood.

The dolls remained.

He saw something glint in the redheaded doll's eye. The reflection of a woman.

He turned.

Felix's mother reached down toward his neck. He flinched back.

"Come here, child!" she scolded him, "let me fix your tie."

Felix looked down at himself. He was wearing a black suit, white shirt - unsullied – and a black tie. His mother tightened the knot.

"Mustn't look untidy for the funeral. Everyone will be watching you."

"Because Felicity . . ." he started.

She cut him off.

"Because they will assess your composure, whether you are still a boy, or a young man."

He looked up at her through the black veil to her partially-obfuscated eyes. It was like looking through a dense clump of leaves. He could not make out her expression.

"It's time to be a man."

He looked down at his black, shiny shoes, then up again.

He was sitting in a coffin.

A spindly hag, head wracked by tremors, hands shaking, lowered a golden crown onto his head. Its asymmetrical spikes were ridiculous in their proportions, half again as tall as he, yet it seemed almost weightless as it settled above his brow.

The crone gave him her hand, helping him stand up in the coffin, then step out of it, onto the floor. She reached down to his neck, tightening the rough rope noose that was wrapped around it, pushing the knot into his adam's apple where it scratched his skin raw. She tugged at the rope, forcing him to follow her into a darkened tunnel.

"Once you are past this gate," he could hear her frail voice in the void ahead of him, "do not return, lest you are forever trapped as one who cannot become your greatest self. Die now, that your sister may live. If you turn back, you will deny the world the memory of your sister."

He ascended a set of unseen wooden steps behind her.

"If you deny the world the memory of your sister so you can keep her for your own selfish purposes, you choose to live forever in the maze of time, trapped. Within that labyrinth lies an eternally-gnawing regret, eventual madness, and a sharp passion for self-annihilation that can never be achieved. A final, everlasting itch that you cannot scratch."

A wooden creak sounded.

The floor dropped out from under him.

The noose jerked tight.

"Leave it be!"

He landed, hard, in the blackthorn grove. Ahead of him, a bare-backed youth was frantically wrapping his hands in a white shirt.

"Mother never was very fond of us, Sis," the shirtless one said.

Felix felt her growing absence, and with it, all the pent-up pain of years, pain that he had hidden from himself, but which burned slowly like acid within his soul, was fading fast, like a dream's last wisps in the morning light. He could feel her name being forgotten, slipping away, the sorrow almost gone.

Almost . . .

And yet, he reached.

Like Gold Upon Her Tongue

~ A. P. Howell

Olivia signed the paperwork on her clipboard. HIPPA disclosure, patient's bill of rights, all the things she'd signed before—that everyone had signed before—because it wasn't as though they were optional. As always, she winced a little to see her name, the big, round "O" a fat reflection of her flesh.

"You're here to see—?"

"Ryann," Olivia said. "Ryann Byford."

The receptionist frowned for a moment. Then the confusion slipped away and her brow smoothed. "Of course. Ryann. She's new."

Olivia offered her card for the co-pay, then settled down to wait. She slouched in her loose overalls. They disguised the specific contours of her body, but couldn't mask its inherent ugliness.

She told herself that she didn't have to look at the scale when the nurse weighed her in, but of course she couldn't *not* look, couldn't ignore the metal-on-metal sound as the counterweight slid into place. It echoed in her ears while she sat in an exam room, not quite distracting her from the way the nurse's lips tightened as she wrapped the blood pressure cuff around Olivia's arm.

There came the clicking of keys, a series of rote questions. "Okay," the nurse said, "in a few minutes you'll be seen by—" The slightest of pauses, then confusion visibly lifting. "—Ryann. She's new."

Olivia released a breath when the woman left. No eyes on her, for a blessed few minutes. She looked around the exam room, decorated with family photos and children's drawings and various diplomas. Veronica F. Bernstein's diplomas: she was apparently a D.O., not a nutritionist. Olivia had been in and out of enough multi-specialist practices that she wasn't surprised when the personal touches failed to match the practitioner she was scheduled to meet.

A quick knock at the door, and then a smiling woman entered. "Hello, Olivia. I'm Ryann."

Olivia immediately felt jealous of her slender form, her fluid movements. This was a woman who belonged in her own skin, whose flesh was not an imperfect, imperfectible prison. Worthy of jealousy, but also somehow transcending such petty feelings, because the world simply seemed a better place because she existed in it. Olivia forced a close-lipped smile, despite disliking the way the expression transformed her face, emphasizing fat cheeks.

"For this initial meeting, I'd like to get an idea of your daily habits," Ryann continued. "Typical exercise and food intake. All bodies are different—and all goals are different. No judgment: I'm here to help."

Olivia had heard similar words from doctors and personal trainers. She knew from experience that they were untrue, that disapproval would eventually seep into their interactions, that the advice would turn counterproductive. And yet . . . something made her trust Ryann.

Maybe it was just the hope that someone would understand. Pathetic—Olivia was an adult, she shouldn't feel such a powerful need for approval—but there were so many ways in which she was pathetic.

"I have a gym membership and I actually go. Sometimes I use a personal trainer." She hadn't known personal trainers could fire their clients. Maybe it was just her. "I try to eat a large breakfast, lots of protein, and a small dinner. Low carb, low fat. That sort of thing." She trailed off. Ryann was watching her closely, head cocked like a curious puppy. Seeing through her.

They all saw through her. But Ryann smiled, knowing and sympathetic.

"I can't get back under a hundred pounds," Olivia blurted. "I've tried so hard. I don't know if it's my metabolism or—" Or if she was eating too much, or waiting too long before bringing it back up. But there were some things you couldn't say in an exam room, not if you wanted help with a physical problem.

"You're not alone," Ryann said, and Olivia feared it was the opening of one of the standard speeches, that she was about to receive a referral to a psychologist. "I'd like you to try a pre-packaged dinner tonight. Eat it—and keep it down."

Olivia offered a wan smile. A nutritionist had been worth a shot.

"I know you've heard this advice before," Ryann continued. "You know the downsides of purging. But you are clearly strong-willed and you're not afraid to ask for help when you need it. So: let me help you. One meal. Come back tomorrow and tell me how it went. Deal?"

"Sure," Olivia said, stomach roiling at the thought of keeping a mass of food down, feeling it squeeze its way through her intestines.

The meal in question came in a cardboard box, about the size of a regular frozen dinner, with a stylized leaf logo in one corner.

The photograph was an idealized image of a plate heaped high with meats, vegetables, and potatoes slathered in butter and gleaming gold. All of it seemed to be golden, and even while the thought of having it in her stomach made Olivia nauseous, she did rather desperately want it in her mouth.

Olivia didn't know what language the text was written in; for that matter, she couldn't even identify the alphabet. (Arabic? Sanskrit? Tibetan? Elvish? One meal to rule them all?) Any promises made on the box had probably not been evaluated by the FDA.

She didn't find that intimidating. Sometimes she shopped in Chinatown and still occasionally used the tin of green dieters' tea, suggested by word-of-mouth and good for a couple pounds of water weight and a couple days of cramps.

The plastic tray contained the expected desiccated-looking food, though the colors were a little brighter than average. That was probably due to some chemical with forty-seven syllables. She punched the thin plastic sheet a few times with a fork and popped it into the microwave. Ryann hadn't mentioned cooking times and any instructions on the box were indecipherable, but it was a microwave meal, easy by design.

She hadn't expected the smell. Rich, textured, overwhelming—even while it was still heating, it filled the kitchen and living room. Olivia was drawn to the microwave, half an impatient eye on the countdown, most of her attention fixated on the rotating plastic tray. That smell couldn't possibly be real, it had to have been manufactured by chemists somewhere, it might cause cancer in laboratory rats, but she didn't care. She actually salivated for the food that smelled like that. Wanted to consume it, embrace it, make it part of her body.

The calories didn't matter. They weren't listed on the package in any decipherable chart. Maybe the box wasn't labeled for individual sale, or else it was really unregulated. She didn't care. Not about the legality, not about the origins, and not even about whether she might gain weight.

Olivia thrust the thought aside. It usually presaged overeating, higher than usual levels of shame, and binging voluminous quantities. Right now, she couldn't imagine *not* wanting to keep that food inside her.

The microwave beeped, a sound that resonated in Olivia like church bells for the holy. She ripped the plastic film off, reckless, ignoring the steam licking her fingers.

The food was beautiful. Almost like the photograph (food was never like the photograph) except better because it was *here*, it was *real*, and before she knew it she had a fork in her hand. She didn't even bother to bring it to the table before taking a delicate bite of potatoes.

If food could taste like gold, then the potatoes tasted like gold. Not the metal, but the *idea* of gold, a thing so precious that people would search for it and kill for it and work their electronic magic with it and weave it into story after story.

She swallowed, felt the warmth in her esophagus, imagined the potatoes in her stomach. (Surely she couldn't really feel it. Even now, that small and glorious bite was beset by acids, sullied by chemical reactions.) She licked the fork clean and tried the vegetables: the carrot symmetrical and practically neon, the broccoli mostly floret with just enough stem to provide a satisfying crunch. (How could it still crunch? No microwave meal had ever given her a satisfying tactile experience.) The meat parted like butter at the touch of her knife. Not at all rubbery when she chewed, tender and juicy, flavorful even aside from the sauce which complemented it perfectly. (Pork? It was probably pork. She didn't care; she had no dietary restrictions derived from any religion.)

And then, having sampled each component individually, Oliva swept her fork across the tray, scooping up a little of everything. If possible, it tasted even better. When she swallowed, the scent lingered in her mouth.

Olivia desperately wanted to savor each bite, but it was impossible to do the food justice. She ended up bolting it down, only barely refrained from licking the tray, and stared at the box for a little while, longing for another taste of gold.

She could feel the weight of the food, but it wasn't an alien impurity, not an unwelcome mass within her. This was the time when she should bring it back up, or feel increasingly guilty for not doing so. But there was no guilt, aside from an obscure echo, guilt for the absence of guilt.

"I'm here to see Ryann again."

"Ryann . . ."

"Byford," Olivia said. "The nutritionist."

"Of course." The receptionist took her credit card for the co-pay. "Ryann. She's new."

Ryann emerged, smiling. "Hello, Olivia." She turned and they went back to a different exam room. This one belong to another D.O., Geraldine Williams. Based on the calendar and pictures on the wall, she liked boats.

"So," Ryann said. "Did you follow the meal plan?"

"I'd like another box."

Ryann smiled. "So you liked it."

"It was the best thing I've ever eaten."

"Then let's get you another."

Olivia nearly swooned with relief. She knew something about behaviors deemed addictive, obsessive, or otherwise disordered and the way other people, including professionals, reacted to them. The food was amazing. Understanding and support was almost as good.

"I really think this might be a sustainable plan," Olivia said, belatedly realizing that she hadn't seen a nurse for a weigh-in. She hadn't weighed herself last night, either, or this morning. Hadn't been able to calculate calories. Hadn't weighed the microwave dinner. That was less-disordered, by the standards of the various doctors and trainers she'd worked with in the past, and surely that was a good thing. It was just surprising that it was so easy, that it was like a switch had been flipped in her brain. Her weight might have gone up—*must* have gone up—and she didn't care.

"Yesterday you were so skeptical," Ryann said with a smile that almost took the sting from the words. "You had so little faith that you almost threw it in the trash, didn't you? And today you want to embrace a plan."

"You're right, I had doubts." Could nutritionists fire clients as easily as trainers? Olivia felt the beginnings of fear. "But I did as you said, I gave it a try, and you were right."

"Have another dinner tonight, then breakfast and lunch tomorrow," Ryann said. "I'll see you before the end of the day for a weigh-in and resupply."

Olivia did some math. If she kept up like this, chained to the office for her food . . . well, twenty dollars for three meals wasn't bad. Three meals! She couldn't remember the last time she'd willingly eaten three meals a day.

Twenty dollars for *these* meals . . . was cheap beyond measure.

She lost a pound, per her bathroom scale. She didn't count it as confirmed, not yet, but she *felt* it. And this despite the fact that she was constipated, which usually made her feel like she was carrying more than a couple extra ounces in her bowels.

Olivia wasn't a fool; she knew different factors could affect body weight, make it fluctuate over the course of a day. She used to make that knowledge work for her, only weighing herself when she knew the number would be smallest, but knowing that she was cheating removed any joy she felt in seeing an artificially small number.

But this? It felt like a real loss, like times she'd successfully dieted and felt her bulk disappearing.

The scale at Ryann's office confirmed it. Olivia felt herself beaming—the number was still too big, but it was smaller and a data point that this new approach was working. Ryann, who did the weigh-in and took her vitals, offered a small smile.

Too small, maybe, to be encouraging? Was there a little condescension there? Olivia's joy was undercut, though still present.

Maybe she hadn't made as much progress as Ryann had anticipated, and of course a professional wouldn't come out and *say* that, not this early. Or maybe this really was just the start, and after induction the weight loss would be even more impressive.

Olivia ate the dinner with her now-normal gusto. But in the morning, staring at an unopened box, her doubts came rushing back. If she skipped breakfast, took in only two-thirds of her planned calories . . . Funny, how she couldn't imagine wanting to purge. It took an effort of will, but she slid the box back into the freezer.

Anticipation only made lunch taste more delicious. She wondered how strongly the FDA would disapprove of what she ate, and cared not one whit.

"I'm here to see Ryann," Olivia said. The name was barely out of her mouth before Ryann appeared, smiling.

Olivia's weight remained steady. She wasn't disappointed, even after skipping breakfast: there were quick results, and then there were impossible results, and she was in this for the long haul.

She didn't confess, and Ryann didn't ask any questions beyond whether she was still enjoying the food. Olivia clutched her new supply to her chest and headed home, already looking forward to dinner, as delicious as expected.

In the morning, she chose the breakfast she'd skipped the previous day. It didn't really matter—there were no legible sell-by, best-by, or expiration dates, but they were frozen meals—but she decided she'd eat them in the order received. The impulse might have been superstition, a holdover from eating fresh foods, or just a need to impose order. Olivia didn't really care about her own motivations. The photo of eggs, bacon, and potatoes looked fantastic.

When she opened the box, she knew something was wrong. She peeled off the plastic and reached into the tray. Dried leaves crackled and broke beneath her fingers.

Numbly, she put the tray in the microwave, and a few minutes later withdrew warmed leaves. She briefly wondered about their nutritional value and thought about her recent digestive complaints. Then she thought about the scale, the number inching downward.

Ryann had told her the schedule. It was her own fault for straying from the path. Her fault that this breakfast, and maybe all the breakfasts, was now spoiled. Olivia only hoped Ryann would still be in the office.

Maybe it should have seemed strange, a bizarre error at the food plant, something she should have reported to Ryann and remained vigilant about. But it was also subtly reassuring. Some things were too good to be true. Having confirmation about the ways in which they were too good meant the world still, somehow, worked the way it should. There were always tradeoffs and prices to pay. Penance to perform.

Olivia sat at her kitchen table and began to eat the leaves.

What Remains of the Great Alchemist (The Knight-Pile)

~ John Waterfall

I am writing this down for posterity. So that I may not be confused with the guilty party if the worst should happen. I am not the great alchemist, but I am his nephew and apprentice, my duties mostly confined to the making of porridge.

The alchemist is currently locked outside, banging his fists bloody against the bolted door. It was me who locked him out there. In the great scheme of my life this is perhaps my greatest sin, though he is unwell with the sickness he created.

He is a charlatan, my uncle. I'm realizing that now as I go through his things. Much of what he called alchemy was simply the thought-less combination of things he found in the forest or stole from castles. Anything expensive looking. He also may inadvertently be responsible for the end-times, if that messy pile of shambling knights is a sign of things to come. A fascinating thing to live next to, a snarling pile of snapping bones and squealing iron; flesh and armor and horse interlocked into a massive, bleeding lump the size of a small castle, undulating in the valley outside our tower where the pitched battle between the two great houses took place. All my uncle's doing of course. It was his love potion that helped one of the lords diddle the other lord's lady. It was that same lord who leapt from his horse onto the nearest pikeman and tore into his face, wrapping his limbs around the poor sod's torso. Then that pikeman bit another pikeman and wrapped him up and so on and so forth till the battle became a knot of strange dead. I do wonder what my uncle put in that potion. I've a note here that simply says, 'Lots of mushrooms. Some bones I found. Owl pellets. Powder, perfume, and place in something expensive looking.' Lords, Ladies: my uncle the alchemist.

The pile appears to be eating itself, or trying to. It's been seven days and the pile seems to only grow, capturing at first the cautious squires who sought to loot or disentangle their mentors and then the scavenging wolves. Not to mention the single overeager bard who sought to commemorate the pile with his lute despite my bellowed warnings. He ventured too close and was dragged in by the ankles, a fate my uncle nearly suffered during his efforts to study the pile, instead suffering only a nip on the shin. Although perhaps his fate is more alarming. The blood of the pile is inside him. He screams at me from outside, alternating between insisting that he is fine and cursing my mother, which is doing him no favors. He bangs at the oaken door to the tower, rubbing himself against it. But I am no fool, and have no interest in acquiring what he has got.

The night after his accident he ran feverish and wrong, moaning and laughing and gnashing his teeth against the cobbled floor of his study, shattering his teeth, contorting his limbs to their limits in a mix of rage and randy passion. He woke sedate the next morning with lidded eyes and slurred speech, a mere lull in preparation for his next fit. When next he left to study the pile I refused to let him back in. Outside he will stay till this is sorted out, or until what courses through his veins sorts him instead.

I've reached a detente with my brain-added uncle. I will occasionally throw loaves of bread down at him from the roof of the tower and he will cry a little bit softer at night. I've also agreed to be his proxy in developing a cure for the knight-pile, which is difficult as for most of the day and night he is a stark raving lunatic. In his brief hours of lucidity he yells various ingredients at me and I do my best to mix them together in his large cast iron chamber pot, ah, I mean alchemist pot. During his fits I do my best to improvise, using his various journals and recipe books, all of which are comprised mostly of nonsense. For instance, one book is filled entirely with the names of what I presume to be whores. At first I thought the names might be some sort of code; that was before I discovered the two Berthas, one qualified as 'Big Breasted.' Lords, Ladies: my uncle the alchemist.

So far none of our concoctions have proved successful. Most of what we throw into the pile produces only mild sizzling and is met by the excited, blood-curdling shrieks of the undead who seem to enjoy it. The most promising solution we have discovered so far is fire, although our dwindling supply of pitch restricts us to small localized bonfires rather than the cleansing inferno that is required. I've sent word by owl to the surrounding kingdoms to send trebuchets. To send sword and spear. To send anything to remove this monstrosity from my front door. I mean my uncle's front door. No. I mean mine.

After some consideration I've started to eat the owls. Their constant hooting is making it hard for me to focus on my recreational dissections, a passion I may indulge in full now that my uncle is no longer here to disapprove. Well he is still here, but outside. Screaming. He does that a lot now.

It seems that my uncle's perception of me was more nuanced than I realized. I long thought him to be a simple fool, which he is, but it seems that he has long held some deep-seated discomfort with me. After turning the aviary into my makeshift butchery, I took the liberty of going through his correspondences, where I discovered a series of letters between him and my father. I had assumed that they no longer spoke after my decision to leave home. It was a messy affair. The first and only time I ever saw my father weep. That poor violent man. I wonder if he's dead now. A tough bastard he was, possessing a certain brute genius as a blacksmith. But his dim mind provided him no outlet to his endless frustrations, asides from his fists, asides from his ruddy drunk's face. He hated my experiments. My ambitions. Every time I put a sick animal out of its misery, every time I searched its body for the source of its ills he'd fly into a rage, face turning red then purple. He was a stutterer, and his anger worked against him, robbed him of his words till he spoke them to me through my ribs. But he wept when I left, when my knave, purple-robed uncle sauntered into town, gold singing in his pocket, bright red alchemist's ring glittering on his little finger. How I coveted that ring! I always thought it strange that my father did not try to stop me. I was all he had.

These letters show me a different side of father. It seems he was a very sad man, that fatherhood hung heavy from his bones.

My uncle's condition is far deteriorated. He has taken to circling the pile at night, body hunched and coiled, fingers splayed to the point of breakage, his silver hair swept across his shoulders in a rangy mane. In a mere three days his body has vomited itself to gauntness and bone, his purple alchemist robes puddling around him as he stalks the valley, eyes black and bleeding, running like broken yolks. The image is nothing compared to the sound, the throaty cackling that escapes his liquified chest.

I met a shipwrecked man in a tavern once, who earned his drink on stories. He swore he'd been to a land where hermaphrodite dogs laughed in the darkness, eyes gleaming with firelight. They grinned he said, his eyes far away, they laughed and grinned like men. Then he imitated the sound and a certain tautness snapped in my mind. Something I'd felt loosen the first time I heard my father's knuckle crack against my jaw. It's hard to explain, but it felt like a rush of darkness, of mystery beyond the common brightness that surrounds us. What scarred that sailor, what had broken him, excited me.

I wonder where I'd be if I'd stayed with my father, instead of throwing in my lot with his knave brother, capable of little more than producing a copper from a child's ear. Would I be a blacksmith? Would I be a grave-robber? I suppose I could have been a doctor given my penchant for anatomy. But I was young, and seduced by the glamour of it all. The iron into gold. The promise of miracles. That glittering red ring. The dark, laughing dogs.

I suppose he is something of an Alchemist after all. He's managed to transform himself and half the kingdom into a monster. The pile is growing larger, fed by a steady diet of crows and cutpurses fooled by the promise of an easy bite or pilfered coin. And yes, I suppose I could be more helpful. I could warn the poor souls that the knight-pile has learned to lunge, to tumble its mass of screaming gore in the direction of its choice. I could. But I don't. It's all very interesting to watch. A dark miracle as great and majestic as any mountain in God's spine. Dead knotted so tightly as to be a single thing, crawling with fires that texture the writhing mass in shadow. Marvelous.

I do wonder what it is that my deranged uncle plans to do? He seems to be testing the pile, darting in and out of its range. Challenging it for dominance. Heaven above I hope he gets too close. It would be comforting to see him die this way, for once keeping the promises he sold to me: wonders outside of the dull mundanity of being a blacksmith's boy.

Soon it will all come to a head. Trees shake in the distance, swaying under the thunder of a thousand hooves. The king's army approaches. The great alchemist hears it too; he coughs his dog's laugh and scents the wind.

The king's army is a magnificent thing, a wall of gleaming riders bestride snorting chargers draped in color. Trebuchets and scorpions emerge from the tree-line like massive beasts, fanged and cruel. I count more than a hundred flags in the line, houses unified in the extermination of the knight-pile, every man and boy who can swing a sword. I wonder if my father is down there, if he is still able-bodied enough to fight, if he's watching me now from the midst of this vast, brutal assembly.

I have a great vantage from the top of the tower, the scene unfolding before me as if set for my amusement. I have taken the liberty of wearing my uncle's purple robes, of borrowing his foppish hat and drinking from his jeweled chalice. If only I could recover his ring. The king's army believes me to be the great alchemist, and I suppose I'll do nothing to dissuade them. I wave. They raise they swords to me in salute. Fools. I see how my uncle so easily lived off their backs.

Speaking of my uncle, all remnants of his former and might I add, false, dignity have deserted him. His is now wholly animal. A slavering, raving Grendel, visage marred by the rivulets of black blood that weep from his eyes and nose and mouth.

He stands between the king's army and the undead hillock, gesticulating at the gathered forces like a crazed ambassador for the dead, cackling between gouts of vomited ooze. For a moment all is silent, excepting the creaking armor and gasps that escape the knight-pile as it slumbers, near-dormant under the eye of the sun. Then an arrow looses and embeds itself in my uncle's face, crunching through the tip of his nose. The force snaps his head back, neck splintering with a crack but he does not fall. He stands, lolling, crudely gyrating and thrusting his hips towards the king's army, destroyed neck rolling his head along the back of his shoulders. The next arrow finds his groin, the next seven his chest and guts, and I watch his pincushion corpse explode under a sea of charging hooves.

Well, this is a disaster. My uncle has, of course, once again found a way to ruin everything for everybody. I don't think I'll ever be able to unsee the image of his ruddy, burst corpse tearing off the top of the king's skull, clawed fingers buried deep within the orbital cavity, making jelly of the eyes. My God. He just wrenched the top right off, crown and everything, leaving just a brain and bearded jaw peeking out from a tottering suit of armor. I've flayed and dismembered my share of cats and dogs but that was too much. After, the battle lost all appeal. If you could call it a battle. More of a strange consumption. After the amorphous-remnant-of-my-uncle half-decapitated the king he went about creating his own undead pile, his wet, skinned-self at the tight center of it. The two piles then proceeded to crawl over each other, like slugs fornicating, the still living squealing and exploding into geysers of lumpy gore as the tidal forces of limbs and steel crushed them into pulp. Well at least it wasn't boring.

Now my tower watches over a singular, massive, writhing plateau made from the fusion of every able-bodied man in the kingdom. There is no valley anymore, just a bedrock of the dead, screams and cackles muffled by density, tight enough to walk over, maybe even to build on. Perhaps I'll start my own little kingdom. Why not?

I've finished reading my father's correspondences. It seems I was the reason he led such a sad life. It seems I was widely thought of as a terror, that the villagers did not appreciate my interest in their cats and dogs. It seems that my father thought me deranged, thought that my uncle's pseudoscience might be an appropriate outlet for my proclivities. I did not leave. I was let go. Interesting. I'm sure he's dead. I know it. And I don't think he's in the pile. I think he died in his forge, drowning in his tears. Perhaps I am sad about this. Perhaps not. I've never been quite able to tell.

I've eaten all of the owls in the tower. All except one, should I need to contact the outside world. What's left of it that is. I feed him the remains of my experiments, my pickled cats and dogs and mice and frogs. The one unborn fetus I kept hidden at the bottom of my medicine chest, a rarity procured from the village headsman in exchange for an immortality brew of my own design. He was in the ground a week later. Dumb sod.

The world possesses a depth of silence I'd not thought possible now that it has been emptied. In my mind's-eye I see deserted castle hallways and market squares, dead leaves touched by the chilling fingers of autumn wind, the occasional whimper of a widow or orphan echoing from some deep recess, a queen weeping across a vacant throne. It is a beautiful silence, somehow deepened by the whispers of the glacial dead that swallow my spire. I hear my father's words, words I never heard him speak. They rise up from the letters of his last correspondence, misspelled in his idiot's script, 'Brother. Beware my son. Watch him. He is a dark hearted little boy.' Dark hearted? Dark hearted. Yes, I suppose. If this is evil, I can't say I'm not intrigued.

I walk up and down the spire in my luxurious robes, my purple silk, my foppish hat. The creak of the stairs, the groan of the stone, the titters of the knight-pile feel like sounds in my body: pops within my bones, blood rushing through my veins. It feels as if I have expanded to fill this space and now it is all me. I am the pile and the pile is me. It's my creation. My inheritance. Sure my uncle's carelessness started things off, but had I not tainted his porridge with the undead blood he would never have become such a wonderful catalyst. Whoops. Did I lie about that before? What did I write down? Something about a bite or something? No matter. I no longer have need to fear posterity. I poisoned him. I altered him. I put him into my alchemist's pot and watched the recipe unfold. Why? I don't know. I always thought about murdering him. It seemed like an interesting thing to do. And look how it escalated things!

Perhaps this is not so bad of a situation. For me that is. It seems pretty bad for everyone else. History is mine now. Not exactly how I planned my ascendance, but alchemy is an inexact science and everything and everyone is an ingredient.

From the roof of the tower I watch over the knight-pile, packed and near still, sleepy in its recent expansion. Yes, solid enough to walk on, I reckon. I hope.

What remains of the great alchemist catches my attention, an arm protruding in search of moonlight, red sigil ring gleaming darkly, ready to be pruned like a rose. I know what I'll do. It's not the ring I need. It's the finger.

This shall be my last scribbling for awhile, perhaps ever. If I survive perhaps I'll burn this record, save it for comfort on a dark winter's night, when the chilled wind carries the dim corpse chatter through the windows of my tower, the dark stone where I, the great necromancer, rule on the back of an undead tide.

The last owl is fed and ready to embark upon its plague flight, my message to the village tied to its leg and digesting within its belly: my uncle's virulent finger.

They will send me sacrifices. They will send me more owls. I must say I have developed a taste for them. They will see what it is that I can spread, what I can send their way should I be displeased. It doesn't matter if the threat is false. If the pile is stagnant and dull. People have no end to energy when it comes to feeding monsters. I'll tell them the truth. Even if it's a lie. The knight-pile is hungry, and that is a certainty.

I watch as the confused bird takes flight, a dark nimbus receding into a bruised dusk, its flight already wobbly and of ill rhythm, my plague spreading through its body. One day all will be the knight-pile, bodies to cover every inch of this world. I'll be waiting here in my tower, waiting for what bubbles forth. Me, a dark hearted blacksmith's boy.

A World Without You in It

~ Scott Edelman

So . . . this is what it feels like to starve to death, Marlon thought, during one of those rare moments he was coherent enough to think at all.

Drifting in and out of consciousness on a bed he hadn't the energy to leave for days, he stared at the ceiling, stared into the past, stared into his dreams.

He'd grown so weak he could no longer lift his head off the pillow, so lonely he almost regretted the decision which had delivered him to that loneliness, and so old he was finally ready to die.

The weakness . . . well, he'd at first foolishly thought avoidable, because, after all, *she* had been granted the power to avoid it.

The loneliness was a choice, a sacrifice he'd made because in his heart he knew not making it would have been even more painful for both of them.

And as for aging . . .

. . . there was a time he assumed he'd never have to. A time when the future seemed his.

Seemed theirs.

How long can this possibly last? he wondered, when his mind allowed him the energy to wonder, and how long it did last he didn't know. Eventually, though, a time came when he forced open his eyes once more and saw—not the ceiling, with spiderwebs drooping toward him—but *her.* She'd fluttered through the window, flown in a way he never had, never could, though she'd tried to lead the way, oh, how she'd tried, but it was a way he learned he could not follow, and so, once he fully realized what that meant . . . he fled.

"How did you find me?" he asked. "You weren't supposed to find me."

"How could I not find you?" said Juliette, looking no older than the day they'd met.

Or rather—no older than how she'd appeared a few weeks *after* the day they'd met . . . which was the day they'd both met *him*.

It had always been easy for Marlon to remember the exact date he'd first met Juliette, because it was also his first day working at PhoNicInn, the ill-conceived Vietnamese-Greek restaurant which only lasted six months after that before the owner burned through all his money.

He'd suspected the place would never last, but was willing to take a chance, because he thought it was a step up from the soulless chain restaurant he'd been cooking at until then, with its fake Italian decor and faker Italian food. And it *was* a step up, because even though the owner's hybrid cuisine never quite worked, at least it was well-intentioned. At least it was real.

And it brought Juliette into his life. Juliette, who was ending her then usual daytime shift as he showed up to begin his first evening one.

"Better get your resume ready," she said, as she stepped back from the burners and swept a sleeve across her face.

"But I just got here," he said. He pouted, only half-ironically. She laughed anyway, and there was something about the way she laughed . . .

And then she was gone.

That was pretty much all they saw of each other that first week, crossing paths for a few brief moments during the shift change, him showing up earlier than absolutely necessary (but not so early as to be *too* obvious) and making some small talk which he hoped made an impression without being nakedly flirtatious, her rolling her eyes as she left, him smiling even though he was still not quite sure what to make of it all.

Until the day he missed his bus and arrived later than usual to find her, not in the kitchen, but out back in the alley behind the restaurant smoking a cigarette while leaning against a dumpster. She was usually gone by then, and it struck him . . . had she waited . . . for him? He suspected she had, and wanted to say something about that, but knew himself too well, knew that if he tried, he'd only screw it up. So . . .

"I don't know anyone who smokes," he told her instead. "Not anymore. Not cigarettes anyway."

"You think I want to live forever?" she said.

"Well," he said, surprised at what he felt himself about to say, because he wasn't the sort of person who ever said such things, and before he'd arrived that night to find her lingering, he never imagined himself saying it. "Whether you want to or not, it would be a shame for there to be a world without you in it."

She surprised him then by gazing at him with an odd smile, as if seeing him for the first time. That, he later realized, was when he truly fell in love with her.

That was when he should have kissed her.

But because he waited until later, because he waited until after, neither of them could ever be entirely sure what was chosen and what was fated.

She then flicked her cigarette deeper into the alley, and walked off.

It would pain him during his years of hiding whenever he'd think of her out back asking him that question, because of what that question and the smile which followed did to him, how they made his heart reach for her, and the poignancy of his memory could be too much. But also because, yes, he *had* wanted to live forever—who wouldn't?—and look what became of that?

One night, as his second week at the restaurant neared its end, and he was starting to think the job might work out after all, he arrived and was surprised Juliette wasn't inside, or by the back door either, which puzzled him. He took a few steps deeper into the alley, thinking perhaps he'd find her puffing away again, but no, she wasn't there, and his heart sank at having missed her. He was about to take a step back and head into the kitchen, when in the shadows between the dumpster and the recycling bin (or so he would remember later, much later) he saw a man kneeling, hunched over, facing away from him, and beneath him, a brief flash of Juliette, before she became hidden once more.

Marlon ran toward them, reached for the man, determined to pull him the Hell away from her, when . . . he froze. Not out of fear. Not out of indecision. He had no idea why, actually . . . but he couldn't move.

The man turned round, his mouth bloody, his eyes equally as red, and the next thing Marlon knew . . . he was back inside the restaurant, sorry he'd missed Juliette that night, but remembering nothing from that moment of *not* having missed her.

Nothing of *him*.

So Marlon worked his shift glumly, went home crestfallen from her absence, and hoped the next day would be different.

He was woken the next morning by a call from PhoNicInn's owner. He wanted Marlon to come in and cover for Juliette—she'd called in sick for that day's shift—which seemed to worry only Marlon. So at the end of what turned out to be a double shift for him, he stopped by her apartment. It took several minutes of knocking before she came to the door.

He heard a moan at first, followed by the click of the lock. He waited a few moments for her to open the door, but nothing happened, so he pushed it open himself, and discovered that by the time he entered she had already collapsed on her bed.

"What's wrong?" he asked.

"I . . . I don't know," she said.

"Have you called a doctor?"

She smiled, the weakest of her smiles he'd ever seen.

"Do you think I want to live forever?" she asked, then smiled again, a smile which let him know their first meeting had mattered.

"At least let me stay with you tonight," he said. He quickly added, then felt foolish for having added it: "Just to make sure you're okay."

"I'm not sure that's such a good idea," she said. "I think I like you too much."

He thought he knew what she meant by that, but he wasn't to learn what she'd really meant until later.

He'd thought in that moment she was afraid something would happen between them which she wasn't ready to have happen. And in that he was right. But what he was wrong about . . . was the nature of that something.

He let her convince him to return to his own apartment, believed she believed what she'd said when she told him she was sure she'd be fine by the time they saw each other during the next shift change. But she wasn't.

Instead, he was woken by a call the following morning—not quite morning even, the sun was barely risen. This time it was Juliette, asking if he could cover for her again. And again, all she would tell him was—

"I'm just not feeling well, Marlon. I don't have any energy."

"Sure, I'll cover for you, but . . . Juliette, really, you need to see a doctor."

"No," she insisted. "No doctors. It'll pass, I'm sure. I'm just tired."

He should have pushed her harder, he knew—knew then anyway, for now he knew no doctor would have mattered—but he couldn't, both because he'd only known her for a few weeks, but also because he'd already learned, even in that brief period of time, she was hard to say no to—and she was even harder to say no to *after*. So he went in early to handle the lunch crowd, such as it was, and was surprised when, once night had fallen partway through his own shift, he stepped back from the stovetop and realized she was by his side.

Juliette had been so quiet he'd never even noticed when she'd arrived. She was just . . . there. She seemed pale, but still, at the same time, more herself again, managing to keep up with the orders. And more than keep up. Their moves as they cooked one beside the other was like a dance, a rhythmic duet throughout the kitchen, one he didn't want to end.

Only once it got later, and they'd turned a few tables, she seemed more confident, and told him to head home, that she'd cover for him the way he'd covered for her. And even though he didn't want to, even though regardless of how tired he was he wanted to stay by her side doing what he always wanted to do, he did what she told him to do (*how could anyone resist her*, he thought) and left.

It was only a day or two after that before she traded shifts with the other night cook and they began working side by side in the heat of the kitchen. And if you'd asked him, he would have told you—those times together was as good as it got.

Occasionally, if there was a lull, she'd sneak out for a smoke—she would pretend to him she was just going out for some fresh air, and he would pretend that he believed her—and he would keep up with the orders. Then one night he noticed . . . she hadn't come back.

Wondering what was taking Juliette so long, he set two plates by the pass-through for a server, then stepped outside, where he saw her.

After which he saw *him*.

And then he remembered.

This time, she wasn't on the ground, and this time, the man he'd thought of as her attacker, the man he'd thought of as a man, wasn't looming over her.

This time, they were standing side by side, Juliette's head tilted back, and she was offering her neck willingly. As willingly as one can offer a neck to one who would ask for such a thing.

And then Marlon and Juliette were back inside again, side by side by the burners, and everything that had been left behind them was again forgotten.

"You were gone a long time," he said. "So what were you out there doing? Smoking *two* cigarettes?"

She looked at him as if there was something she wanted to tell him. But then an unexpected party of eight arrived, with no reservation and with multiple food allergies, and there was no time for whatever she'd been about to tell him.

At the end of the shift, she looked at him again and sighed, then instead of telling him anything, she took his hand. They walked back to her apartment in silence. He knew better than to break that silence, knew what was to come, or thought he did anyway, not needing any words from her to tell him, and when what happened, happened, it was exactly as expected . . .

. . . except for that moment in the bed when she curled down over him from above and bit him on his neck, that moment when he both forgot who he was and remembered all which had gone on before.

And didn't mind in the slightest.

The next morning . . .

There was no next morning, for they slept through the day until it was night again.

When he eventually woke, his head still fuzzy, he found she'd been watching him. He turned to her, slowly, feeling as he did that he was almost too weak to do so. He thought nothing of that at first, and blamed it on the sex. He hadn't had a night like that in a long time—or ever actually, for there had never been anyone like Juliette—so such exhaustion was to be expected.

Then he remembered again what sleep had made him forget. And when it was the usual time he should have gotten out of bed and headed to the restaurant, he could feel that any rising was beyond him.

"Juliette, what—"

"Hush," she said. "Don't worry. It will pass. It passed for me."

"What happened to me? What happened to *us*? Who was that?"

"The giver of a gift. You and me, we're going to do it. We're going to live forever."

And then she was gone, and he was much too weak to follow that night. Or even the next.

He woke ravenous the second night after she'd brought him home, and dragged himself to the kitchen. He felt himself too weak to do what he needed to do, but then muscle memory took over, and he melted some butter in a pan, and pulled eggs and cheese from the refrigerator, and diced a tomato, and then a small onion, too, which smelled sharper and more pungent than any onion he'd ever smelled before, and fried up the omelette he'd thought would take his hunger away, only when he was done, and slid it onto a plate, and sat hungrily in Juliette's kitchen nook with fork in hand staring down at it . . . it might as well have been a wax replica.

He stabbed a portion of the omelette and brought it to his lips, but no matter how great his hunger, he could not bring himself to place it in his mouth. He dropped the fork to the plate, and sat there for how long he did not know until he felt Juliette's hand on a shoulder.

"That won't do for either of us any more," she said. "Come. Let us feed."

He followed her into a night which was as bright as daylight to him, uncertain whether it was because of the change the bite had made in him, or simply because she was by his side. And as they hunted, and as they fed, and as she moved beside him, it was just like when they moved together in the kitchen. The dance was the same.

They belonged together.

After, back in her apartment, again in bed, they fed, not on strangers, but off each other.

"Where should we go?" she asked.

"Go?" he asked, two voices in the darkness, two voices in the light. "Are we going somewhere?"

"We'll have to. At least someday. We can't stay here. Not forever."

"Why not?" he said, wrapping an arm around her. "I could stay here forever."

"Yes, well, *here*," she said, scratching at his chest with her fingernails. He was pleased to learn from her touch that he could still bleed. Though from what they'd just done, he already knew that. "I could stay *here* forever, too. Just not . . . here."

She nodded around the room.

"Our lives are going to have to change," she continued. "Because as the one who turned me told me, you and I, we're not going to. Because the rest of them, the ones who *do* continue to change, well, they're not going to like us."

She smiled.

"We're going to live forever, Marlon. We really are."

And they did.

So they lived and they loved and they fed and they moved on together when the time seemed right, and for awhile it looked as if they'd have forever together, until the fourth time they moved on—or was it the fifth?—he could no longer remember as he looked up at her in the bedroom to which she'd tracked him, without the strength to look away even if he'd want to look away—he'd noticed that though she hadn't aged . . . he had.

They'd fed that night in New Orleans, then returned to their bed to celebrate once more as they been celebrating when first she fed on him. She looked at him oddly, then reached to one side of his head and plucked out a single white hair, a hair he had never noticed before, because mirrors were useless to him after the change, and it had been years since he'd even attempted to look upon himself.

"What's this?" she asked. "When did this happen?"

"It must have always been there," he lied, knowing that he lied, knowing what that lie meant. "You just never noticed it before."

And she believed him, because she loved him, and belief is a gift one gives when one loves.

Until the changes became so great—a white hair followed by a wrinkle, a wrinkle followed by the hollowness of a cheek—even love could not believe the lie. He could see it in her eyes even as she pretended she still did. She knew. And so it was time.

She may have been immortal. And he may very well have been immortal, too. At least, he felt so. But he was continuing to age. And because he did not want her to see him that way, and because he did not want to see her pity, and because he did not want her to live with the daily reminder that he would one day leave her . . . he left her.

He ran.

Until he could run no more.

"Oh, Marlon," she said, and not in the way he'd thought she would say it if she were ever to have the chance to say it again. There was no pity there. No anger. No condescension. There was only love. And he knew he had been wrong. But it was too late for that knowledge to do either of them any good.

"I'm sorry," he said, not really sure which of the many things he'd done he was apologizing for. For aging? For running? For not changing exactly as she had? There were regrets enough to cover every mistake.

"You shouldn't have taken off like that."

"I know that. At least now I do. But I didn't want you to see me, not this way. We both knew this was coming."

"Marlon, we didn't know *what* was coming. We only knew our changes were . . . different. But I didn't think either of us expected . . . this."

She slid onto the bed beside him, stroked his hair, gone all white now.

"So will you just continue like this . . . forever? It's been . . . I don't know how long it's been. Long enough. Can't you . . . can't you die?"

He tried to shake his head, but no motion followed his thoughts. Yet he could tell she could tell that his answer was . . . no. No, he couldn't.

"Then you need me," she whispered. "Now more than ever. To finish what I started."

"I know," he said, then coughed. "Do you think I want to live forever?"

She smiled, and a red tear ran down her cheek.

"I tried," he said. "I tried not to need you. I tried not to burden you. I tried to die. But I couldn't. Nothing I did would end it. I'm getting older . . . but without you . . . no, I'll never die. I'm sorry, Juliette. I'd hoped to save you from this."

"Are you sure you have to? I don't want you to die. We were going to do it, really do it. Live forever. Together. You're the only one who knew me from before. The only one whose love I can trust."

"It's too late for that. It's time to free me. Just as you freed me from what I was before."

She slid her fingers from his scalp to his throat, and could find no pulse there. Wait. There it was, only weak, so weak.

"I wish we could have had more," she said.

She waited for an answer, but none came, and at first, she thought he was beyond answering.

Then he whispered, "We did have more, Juliette."

She bent then, and dug her teeth into his neck, and drank, drank deeply, until there was nothing more left to drink, doing what she had never done for anyone else.

And then she flew off, as he never could.

Following the Rules

~ Shannon Lawrence

When the dark comes, I have to lock my bedroom door. That's when my night parents come out. I have to follow the rules.

I've never met my night parents, but I've heard them. My day parents tell me to turn my music up, and to sleep with headphones on. Sometimes they're louder than the music. It's not my fault.

There was one night where I heard screaming. There was a lot of booming outside my door, and I heard it even when I kept turning my music up. I heard a lady crying. She said, "No, no. Please, no. No." It sounded like she was right outside my door, and I wanted to open it to see if she was okay. Maybe she was hurt. When I got a bee sting, I said "No." I cried, too.

But then there were growls. My door went *clang-clang, clang-clang, clang-clang.* I heard choking sounds and more growls.

I got in bed and put my pillow over my head. I did a little hum, too, and it felt tickly on my mouth.

My day parents say I'm never to look outside or open my door or windows. There are bars on my windows, so I don't understand why I can't open them. I don't understand why I can't open my door, either.

My door is very thick. When I knock on it, it goes *clang-clang.* It smells like pennies, but it's dark grey, not penny-colored. I guess that means it's metal, but not the same kind as my pennies. The lock is thick and slides all the way across the door and into the wall. I know it's locked when it goes *DONG* and vibrates in my hands for just a second.

Sometimes things hit the wall. One time, something *tap-tap-tapped* behind my bookshelf. It scared me so bad I peed my panties.

It was warm when it went down my legs, but then my feet and legs were cold and wet. It smelled icky, too. I took off my nightgown and wiped myself off with it. Then I put it on the floor where the wet spot was so it could clean it up. When my day mom came in the next morning, she didn't get mad. I thought she might, but she didn't. She just made a clicking sound with her tongue and helped me get cleaned up. We made my bed with "My Little Pony" sheets. Those are my favorite.

The rules are written in my bedroom and by the front door, so I don't forget:

Always be home by 5:00 PM for dinner.
Always be in your room by 7:00 PM. Lock the door.
Never get up before 8:00 AM.
Keep the music on from 7:00 PM to 8:00 AM.
Don't look outside.
Don't stick your fingers through any cracks.
Don't look under the door.
Never go in the basement.

I remember a lady a long time ago who used to stay in my room all night with me. These memories are fuzzy and blurry and weird sounding, like I'm listening through a seashell. Maybe I remember her voice, but maybe it's Mary Poppins' voice. They sound the same.

The lady was nice. She looked like grandmas look in books. Her hair was white, and she had dark, round glasses that made her eyes look double-big. She always had on a skirt and a sweater. The only difference between her and book grandmas was that her hair was long and flowy, like Rapunzel, and she never put it back in a round thing on her hair. I liked to touch it. Even though the looks and sounds are blurry, the softness of her hair isn't. Sometimes I close my eyes and touch my hair and pretend she's there with me. Especially when I'm the scaredest.

One day, the not-grandma lady opened the door. I told her that was on the list, but she said she needed to check, that she thought someone might be hurt. She told me to close the door and turn the music loud. I was listening to Disney songs. I closed the door and made the lock go *DONG*, and then I turned up the music. I kept turning "Supercalifragilisticexpialidocious" up more and more and more, because there were screams. Loud screams. Not like just bee sting screams.

Something hit my door. *Clang-clang.*

I put my blanket over my head and sang "Circle of Life" real loud with the music. I screamed it. I sang all the songs like that until my throat felt scratchy and my voice got whispery. Then I went to sleep.

The not-grandma lady wasn't there when I woke up. Or when I went to bed again.

Or when I woke up again.

No more pretty white hair or big glasses eyes.

My day mom said I was old enough to follow the rules on my own, so no more nanny.

I read to myself until I go to bed. There are lots of books in my room, and my day parents get new ones all the time. Sometimes I have a bedtime hot chocolate party with my dolls and stuffies. My day mom makes me special hot chocolate with a bowl of marshmallows, and she puts them on the table in the corner of my room. Then she kisses me on my head and tells me, "Remember the list."

It's right there on my wall. I would have to be stupid to forget it. Or a baby, and I'm not a baby. I'm a big girl. Six years old. I don't understand why she says that to me all the time. When she says it, her mouth is crinkly with a smile, but her eyes look scary and they don't crinkle.

My day dad says goodnight to me, too. Most nights. He comes in all stompy-fast and gives me a big hug. He says, "See you in the morning" and, "Listen to your mom." Then he walks away stompy-fast and pulls the door closed. I can hear him through the door, but his voice sounds funny.

"I want to hear it lock."

I lock it. *DONG.*

His feet go stompy-fast down the hall. Then down the steps. And it's music time.

One time, I asked them why I can't see my night parents.

"Don't they like me?" I asked.

"They don't really like anyone, Honey," my day mom said. "They're cranky and scary, so it's best you stay away from them."

"How come I have to lock my door?"

"It keeps you safe," said my day mom.

"Isn't our house safe?"

"It is during the day, but not at night."

"Can't my night parents keep me safe?"

"No more questions!" my day dad said. He sounded angry. His voice was barky. Mom smiled at me, and this time her eyes crinkled. I wish my eyes were pretty blue like hers, but they're not. They're green like grass. Like day daddy's.

A different day, I asked for a picture of my night parents, but my day mom said they don't like pictures, so they don't have any.

Maybe someday I can look under the door and see my night parents. Nobody will know I looked. The only reason I haven't yet is because I get real nervous when I think about it. And when I walk near the door.

The kids at my school only have one kind of parents. I asked my best friend if they were day parents or night parents. Her face got all frowny and confused, and she said, "They're the same both times."

That's weird.

I guess not everyone gets two kinds of parents.

The basement door is like my bedroom door. I like to knock on it when I walk by, because it's daytime, and it's less scary to make it go *clang-clang* during the day. At night, that sound is too loud, and it makes me feel afraid. It's too loud in my room, but in the open wide kitchen it doesn't sound so big.

The lock is just like mine, too, but it has a key lock in the middle of the handle. Sometimes I touch the handle, all cold in my hand, and I try to turn it. It feels slippery, and it makes my hand smell like pennies, too.

My day mom doesn't know, but sometimes I poke things under the basement door. Not my fingers. That's against the rules. But popsicle sticks are not against the rules. Wrappers are not against the rules. Leaves are not against the rules. I can stick lots of things through the cracks without breaking the rules.

A yucky smell comes under the door sometimes. It smells like the garbage can if my day dad doesn't take it outside for a lot of days, mixed up with the smell when someone hits an animal and it stays by the side of the road until it's all big and swelled up. When I ask my day mom about it, she lights a candle. Her favorite one smells like cookies. Spicy-sweet. Then she tells my day dad, "It's time to clean the basement." Her face is very serious and frowning when she says it. He puts big black plastic bags, paper towels, and a white spray bottle by the door, but he never goes down there when I'm home.

Today I went to my best friend's house. Laurie's basement had a great big TV set, with a shelf full of cartoon movies. We could watch whatever we wanted. She had toys down there, too. Lots of them. We played jump rope and checkers and dolls and dress-up. I wish I had a box full of neat dress-up clothes. She even had princess dresses. Mine was pink and shiny, and I kept it on even when we played jump rope. The crown fell off my head, but it didn't break.

Maybe my day parents don't want me to get to watch the big TV in our basement. I bet my night parents would let me. They don't tell me to read the rules. They don't yell at me or ground me.

I bet my day parents want me locked in my room because they're afraid I'll like my night parents better. My night mom is probably super beautiful. My day mom is pretty. Her hair is shiny black, and her skin is like milk. I like to touch it, because it's smooth and soft. She smells like flowers. But my night mom might be even prettier.

My night dad could be strong like Popeye. Or the Hulk. If he was all big muscles like that, he would carry me everywhere. He would build me a treehouse. My day dad has muscles, too, but they aren't as big as my night dad's might be.

Maybe when I hear them making noises at night, it's because they're playing fun games. Yes! I can't look because I'll see they're not scary, and I'll open the door. And my night parents will let me play with them. Then my day parents will be jealous, like my friend Beth was when I got the silver sparkly shoes. She got stompy just like my day dad does at bedtime.

Since my day parents won't tell me about my night parents, I have to open the door tonight. I want to play with my night parents and see what they look like.

First, I have to make a plan.

It's almost time to go upstairs for bed now. The tea kettle whistles. Tonight is a hot chocolate night. I can already taste it, sticky-sweet with marshmallows and chocolate. I bet my night mom would like a cup for her, too. I'll save her some.

My day mom gets the hot chocolate ready in a pot. She adds two big ice cubes. *Plop, plop.* I get the bag of marshmallows and put some in a little bowl. They're soft like sponges, and I squish one. Day mom isn't looking, so I pop it in my mouth and smush it between my teeth.

"You ready to go upstairs?" she asks me.

"Mm-hmm." I don't open my mouth.

She picks up the tray, and I follow her. The marshmallow is sugar-melty in my mouth, and I poke it with my tongue. It's still squishy, but it feels different.

In my room, she puts the tray on my table. We sit on my bed, and she brushes my hair. "What are you going to listen to tonight?" she asks.

"I don't know. I think maybe 'Road Trip Songs.' I feel like singing 'Clementine.'"

"That's a good one."

When she's all done, she puts the brush in its drawer and smooths my hair behind my ear so she can kiss me on the cheek. "I love you," she says.

"I love you, too."

"Remember the list."

"I do."

Then she gets up and moves to the door. Day dad comes in. *Stomp, stomp, stomp.*

He gives me a hug and says, "See you tomorrow morning."

"See you," I say.

Stomp, stomp, stomp goes day dad. *Smiley-smile* goes day mom. They pull the door closed.

Day dad's voice says, "Lock it."

DONG.

Stomp, stomp, stomp down the hall.

I turn on my music and play "Clementine" two times. I sing with it and twirl around. It's a sad song, so I put my hands together like I saw in a movie once, so I can look sad, too.

My hot chocolate is super chocolatey tonight. I float it around in my mouth before swallowing. It's so good I almost forget to save some for my night mom, but I pour it back into the pot before it's too late.

Now I've listened to ten songs. I bet my night parents are awake. It's time for my plan.

I turn off the music first, and sit down to read a book. If my day parents are still awake, they'll come yell at me, I bet. This is my test to see if they're awake. See, I'm not a stupid baby.

I read three picture books. No stomps or yells yet. My day parents are sleeping, I know they are.

There are no night parent sounds yet. I take my nightgown off and put it on my bed for later. Then I put on my sparkly purple shirt and long pants. It's a little bit cold, so I get my sweatshirt with a cat face on it, too, and I zip it up. My hot chocolate is still kind of warm. I pour it into the cup and drop a couple marshmallows in. They don't melt fast like they usually do. I put a flower next to the cup, so it's pretty for my night mom.

Then I walk up to the door. I put my ear on it, even though it's cold. No sounds. I knock, and my knuckles make a *clang-clang*.

I put my ear to the door again. The door goes *clang-clang*, and I feel it shake. At first I'm scared, and I run to my bed and hide under the covers. I'm shaky scared and my breath is hot under the blanket. It gets hard to breathe a little bit, so I take the covers off.

Clang-clang goes the door.

Something sniffs a lot at the bottom of the door.

I bet my night parents have a dog! No wonder my day parents didn't want me to meet them. I always ask for a dog, but my day parents tell me no. "A dog would not be happy in this house," my day mom says.

"I'd be nice to it. And I'd pet it and take it outside."

"No," my day dad says.

Fine.

But my night parents have one.

I run to the door and get on my hands and knees. There is a big crack at the bottom, and I stick my eye to it, so I can see the hall. The lights are off, but there's a night light out there, so I can see a little bit. At first, there's only the brown carpet. But then something moves by real fast, and I can't see what it is.

There's sniffs again, and then a nose. But it's not a black nose like my friend Melanie's dog's nose. It's creamish like mine. It twitches and sniffs. Then there's a mouth. It looks familiar, but weird.

I stand up and unlock the door. It's always a little bit hard to unlock it, and I have to turn super hard, but it comes loose with a big screech.

Clang-clang-clang on the other side.

The handle is cold in my hand. It's not smooth anymore. There's a rough spot on the very top. I put my other hand on the wall and I take a big, deep breath that makes my stomach get big. I twist the handle and pull the door open.

Nothing there.

It's dark. The night light isn't working. It was a minute ago. I turn on my big bedroom light and it makes the hall yellow-white bright, so I can step out of my room. I can't see anything to my left or to my right. Not inside the light.

A growl comes from my left, toward the stairs. I look that way and make my eyes squinty, but I can't see anything.

Something growls from my right, and I turn that way instead. What's that? I can see a shape, but I don't know what it is. It's near the floor.

"Doggy?"

It whines.

"It's okay, Doggy." I get down on my knees and hold my hand out. "Come here."

Pomp, pomp, pomp go the paws on the carpet.

And then it's there, but it's not a doggy.

Pomp, pomp, pomp behind me, too. I don't want to look. I don't want to see this anymore.

I back up toward my room speedy-fast, but my butt hits the wall. The door is next to me. They *pomp, pomp, pomp* toward me. My day dad and my day mom. They're crawling like dogs, and their mouths are long. They have claws and big teeth, and their arms and legs are different shaped, like they broke them. They both twitch their noses and sniff at the air. I've never seen them without their clothes on before, but they aren't wearing anything. Their skin is white and wrinkled.

My scary mom gets close to me. Her nose is moving when she sniffs. It puffs air on my face. She smells weird, like Melanie's dog when it gets wet. Drool slides out of her mouth and drips on my knee, warm and wet. Her eyes aren't blue anymore. Just black. I can see myself in them.

A squeaky sound comes from my throat, and I slap my hand over my mouth so I can't make noise again. My hands feel burned from the carpet like my knees get sometimes if I crawl on the floor.

My scary dad's mouth opens and he growls mean at me. His teeth are super big, and I'm so scared I can't breathe. He gets close to the ground and his back legs move. I've seen kitties do that before they jump.

I put my hands down and crawl until I'm all the way inside my room. Scary mom doesn't follow me. Scary dad keeps growling.

I stand up, and grab the door. My scary dad jumps, and I scream. But the scary mom jumps in front of him and knocks him down. She snarls like a wolf did once in a movie, all big teeth and frightening sounds, her lip curled up. Scary dad tries to run around her, and she bites him.

I slam the door with a big, loud *CLANG*.

DONG.

The door is locked, and I lean my ear against it. I hear whines and growls, scratching. All I can smell is pennies. I taste them, too.

I turn on "Clementine" as loud as it will go. It makes my ears shake inside. The music feels like my heartbeat, and I think maybe my heart is beating to the song now. I try to breathe slow, because my head feels black inside, and it's hard to breathe.

I climb into bed and pull the covers up over my head, but I leave a crack so fresh air can come in.

Tomorrow I will follow ALL the rules.

A Reckoning

~ Ben Gamblin

Miles, I can think of a hundred ways I could begin this letter.

After some consideration, I'll start by extending my heartfelt wishes for Elizabeth. Duane Whitehall and others tell me she's making excellent progress in her recovery. I've not been to see her personally. Frankly, I'm not sure if you or Elizabeth would welcome a visit from me. But I'm happy for you both all the same.

It's strange, sitting down to write a letter after so many years of emailing and texting. When I was a little girl, my mother made me write a thank-you note every time I received a present for Christmas or my birthday. It's important to learn how to write letters, she told me, you'll be writing them for the rest of your life. Seems quaint now.

Outdated they may be, letters are reliable. I've read too many stories lately about accounts getting hacked, sensitive information being leaked, people catching grief over messages they sent years ago. Given the nature of what I have to tell you today, I think my message is best suited for non-digital correspondence. Correspondence, I should add, that's also highly flammable.

As you've probably inferred by now, this letter concerns my brother. As of this morning, Justin has been missing for five weeks and four days. We officially suspended the investigation into his disappearance this week. Having served as a county deputy for eight years, I know this is standard protocol for any missing persons case with no evidence, no leads and no official suspects after more than a month. That Justin is my brother has no bearing on departmental policy.

I won't bother making excuses or justifications for my brother's behavior. He is—was—a complicated and, at times, deeply unlikable man. But there were things that might surprise you about him.

He was smart, for one, straight-A smart. Kids in school used to cheat off his tests. He charged them a dollar apiece and had a nice little nest-egg saved up by the time we reached high school. Sweet, too. When we were little he used to make me breakfast in bed when I was sick. I don't know any other boys who'd have done that for their little sisters.

Most people in this town don't remember much about Justin before he went to Afghanistan. He was a quiet kid who mostly stayed out of trouble and kept his own counsel. Much like our father, and myself to an extent. The war changed him, made him louder and more conspicuous. That's when everyone seemed to take notice of him. It wasn't a good first impression.

My parents and I tried to get Justin some professional help after he came home. It wouldn't take. I think feeling guilty helped him make sense of all the madness he'd seen firsthand and lived through. Once he started getting into serious trouble—the fights, the booze, the cocaine—there wasn't much more I could do for him, not with the deputy badge pinned to my jacket. I drove him home on nights when I was on duty and he couldn't drive himself, but that was the extent of our relationship near the end.

I guess what I'm saying is that I lost Justin long before he disappeared. I'll own that part of it. But in my experience, when someone sets out to destroy themselves, there's little that anyone—even a bossy older sister—can do to intervene. That's when God steps in. He tends to have the final say.

The last time I picked up Justin was the Saturday before Elizabeth's incident. Sheila, a bartender at the Marmot Lounge, called the station to report two boys scuffling over a game of nine-ball. Sheila's a kind soul and she didn't say Justin's name over the phone, but I assumed he was involved. My brother always seemed to be nearby whenever there was trouble in town, especially if the trouble was over games like nine-ball in places like the Marmot.

Sure as Sunday morning, I walked into the bar and found Justin cowering in a booth near the back. He reeked of beer, more so than usual. The other guy's girlfriend had tossed a pint of Rainier in Justin's face. The couple high-tailed after the fight broke up but Justin refused to leave, even when Sheila took away his whiskey and threatened to call the sheriff's office if he didn't skedaddle.

Justin was short on words with me at first, but then he started spilling and it was business as usual. The other guy shoved him. He'd only been defending himself. Sheila was lying because she didn't like him. I let him speak his piece, and when he was finished we got up from the booth and I followed him across the bar, out the door. We'd been through the same song-and-dance so many times that we both knew all the steps. On our way to the cruiser, we passed his Jeep parked on the street. He'd hitch a ride into town the next morning and pick it up then. He always did.

But Justin still found ways to surprise me from time to time. That night, for instance. He didn't utter so much as a peep for most of the ride, but once we hit Flatley Road a few miles from his trailer, he leaned forward and pressed his face against the mesh cage.

Dani, he said, *I want to see Dr. Sayer again.*

This was the therapist who'd seen him after his discharge. At the time Justin called the good doctor every name in the devil's dictionary, but I suppose time had softened his attitude about therapy. I couldn't be sure if Justin had an epiphany right then and there, or if these feelings had been building up for a while. Didn't matter as far as I was concerned. I told him I'd call Dr. Sayer's office first thing Monday morning to make an appointment for him. We reached his driveway, I opened the back door for him and he shuffled up to the porch without another word. No goodbye, no thank you, but none of the mean stuff, either, so we'll call it a wash.

Dr. Sayer's secretary remembered me when I called on Monday. We chatted for a few minutes while she wrote Justin's name in the appointment ledger. I rang my brother afterward to let him know but his phone went straight to voicemail. It occurred to me later, when he didn't return my call, that he might not have remembered our conversation during the ride home. Whiskey always made him forgetful. Or maybe he'd found an easier, less expensive way to score prescription drugs. Cynical, right? I try not to dwell on those thoughts but, quite frankly, they've rarely misled me. I don't know if that says more about the world we live in, or just me.

I meant to follow up with Justin later in the week, but you and I both know why I didn't. Duane phoned on Tuesday night, just as I was getting ready for bed, and told me what happened to Elizabeth. I threw on my jacket and drove to your house. Still took me more than half an hour on those choppy gravel roads. Don't know how you can stand them.

The ambulance had already taken Elizabeth away by the time I reached your place. Duane told me she'd called the station around ten to report a burglary at the house. She was lying injured on the bathroom floor when he arrived. There was no sign of her attacker, and the rest of the house was untouched.

Duane told me you were gone for the night, settling some family matter in town. Now, there's been speculation that you were considered a suspect early on, due to your absence. Let me put that notion to bed. We all know how much you loved Elizabeth then and still do, how you've cared for her over the years, and the thought of you causing her harm never crossed our minds. It was a lie, Miles, a damn cruel one. But you know how people can be when they don't have all the answers.

No, I knew from the start this was a different crime altogether. A few stray pills lying among the glass fragments on the bathroom floor confirmed my suspicions. See, in my experience, people who break into houses to steal drugs usually bring a large container, a plastic bag or a bucket of some kind. This way they can dump in all the pills at once to save time, plus they won't get caught holding prescription bottles with other people's names on them. But they still tend to drop a few pills in the process. Shaky hands and all.

The most bothersome aspect of the case was why they chose your house. Whoever broke in must have known about Elizabeth's illness. Why else would someone looking to score drugs drive all the way out to your property unless they knew she had a medicine cabinet full of painkillers? That's no judgment on her, by the way. Those pills are made for people with conditions like hers. It's the junkies who give them a bad name.

It must be cold comfort to know the intruder probably never intended to harm Elizabeth. In the depths of addiction people turn into animals—trust me, I've seen it firsthand. My best guess is that she confronted him in the bathroom after making the call. Maybe she thought she could reason with him, or that surrendering might be safer than letting him find her in the closet. He most likely panicked and reached for the first thing in sight. Which, as we've determined, was a glass vase on the counter.

If you'll recall—and you may not, all things given—you and I spoke over the phone that night. You told me you were planning to leave the city immediately and head straight to the hospital. I tried talking you into waiting until morning, what with the five-hour drive. You hung up. I'd have done the same.

None of your neighbors saw or heard anything. No surprise, considering the closest house is a quarter-mile way. Duane and I found fresh tracks in the driveway measuring thirty-two inches wide. Much too large for your short-cab pickup, and since Elizabeth doesn't have her own car we presumed the tracks belonged to the attacker's vehicle. We traced them back to the highway and lost them at the asphalt.

We figured they were long gone, but Duane and I wanted to be certain so we took out our flashlights and ventured into the woods behind your property. I never realized the spread you had back there, Miles. Eighteen acres, Duane told me. Those groves of hemlock and Doug Fir and Sitka spruce must stretch for miles, mostly old-growth from the look of them, and I spotted a large beaver dam at one of the creek crossings. It's hard to find untouched wilderness like that in the middle of logging country. You and Elizabeth are very blessed.

Duane and I spent a couple hours tromping around but we didn't find anything suspicious. The next morning—when we learned Elizabeth was in a coma—we shifted our investigation to town. Junkies are predictable. If they aren't spilling their guts to anyone who will listen, they're acting goofy in full view of the public. Duane and I figured somebody in town must have seen or heard something that night. We questioned every doctor, nurse and man of the cloth within the limits.

Then there were the bartenders. I won't lie, Miles. Since the night of the attack, my brother had been nagging at me like a raw mosquito bite. A few days earlier, he'd asked me to make an appointment with his old shrink, quite possibly to obtain medication, and three days later someone attacked Elizabeth and stole her pills. My brother knew as well as anyone in town that your wife had those painkillers on hand. So, whenever we set foot in one of the local watering holes, I made sure to ask if Justin had been there on Tuesday night. Took us four stops before I found the right dive.

Hoolihan's, if you know the place, though I don't imagine you've spent much time there.

The bartender at Hoolihan's told us Justin had a few drinks that night, lost at darts, settled up his tab and left at half past nine. She said he was a little wobbly but fine to drive as long as he went straight home. But what if he didn't go home? He could have sped out to your house, done the terrible deed and hustled back down the road before Duane came by. The timeline was tight, but not impossible.

After we left Hoolihan's, I told Duane I had an errand to run and drove straight to Justin's trailer. He must have heard me driving up because he was already on the front porch when I pulled into the driveway. We had one of our brother-sister staredowns—I won, as usual—and then I asked point-blank if he'd done it.

Did I do what? he asked.

Elizabeth Turner's place, I answered. *Tuesday night. You know what I mean.*

You think that was me?

Didn't say I thought it. Just asking.

Even then he refused to give an answer. I told him I wouldn't be able to bail him out, not this time, if what I feared was true. He stood on his porch, trying to look as angry and wounded as he could. An old trick he'd been using since grade school to make me and my folks feel sorry for him. Then he spat on the porch and went back inside, deadbolting the door behind him.

That was the last time I saw my brother. I didn't know it then, of course. Might have tempered my anger a bit more if I had. But on my way back to the cruiser, I got a good look at the tires on Justin's Jeep. The tread was about thirty inches wide, give or take a couple.

The next day we learned Elizabeth had awoken from her coma but was unable to speak or get out of bed. Duane and I stopped by the hospital later in the week. I remember that evening well. The coffee in the cafeteria tasted like cat piss and we all made faces when we sipped it. There was that woman and her son sitting at the next table, both crying their eyes out the whole time. I also remember your reply when I asked who, in your mind, would have done such a thing to Elizabeth. How you narrowed your eyes at me dug your elbows into the tabletop.

I don't know, Dani, you said. *Who do* you *think it could have been?*

I knew what you meant, all right. Word travels fast in a town like ours, especially when one of the local deputies starts asking folks what her no-good brother was up to on the night a violent crime took place. Half the town probably considered Justin a suspect. If I played dumb with you in that moment, I do apologize. I didn't know how to put my thoughts into words just then.

I called Justin when I got home from the hospital that night. Straight to his damn voicemail, as usual, but this time I left a long message. I apologized for jumping to conclusions and invited him to the office the next morning. We'd straighten everything out then. I don't know if Justin ever listened to the message or not, but he didn't stop by the office and he sure as hell never returned the call. Maybe he could tell I was bluffing.

That was Friday. More than five weeks later, I'm still trying to figure out what happened to my brother the following night. I know he went to the Marmot Lounge for a while. Sheila told me he walked in the front door around eight and apologized to her for fighting over the nine-ball game. Won't be any trouble from me anymore, he told her, I'm all better now. She kept an eye on him in case he was up to something, but he was good to his word. Nursed a beer, left a nice tip and strolled out of the place as sober as he'd ever been on a Saturday night.

Duane found the Jeep the next morning, parked beneath a "No Overnight Parking" sign near the bar. He checked the plate number to make sure it was Justin's, and then gave me a ring. At first I didn't think much of it. Most nights my brother tied one on, he at least had the good sense to stay out of the driver's seat. Only he wasn't at home either. I checked myself, even peeked through the trailer windows in case he was avoiding me.

Then, that afternoon, Noah Jarrett came to see me. Noah was working at the Pumpco station on Saturday night. Around half past nine he spotted my brother standing in the road, talking to somebody in a truck. *A smaller truck,* he said, but he didn't get a good look at the color or make. Didn't get a good look at anything, really, since the exchange didn't strike him as suspicious, but he was certain he'd seen Justin get into the passenger seat. The truck headed off from there. I asked which direction. Noah shrugged. *Off,* he said.

But when he heard through the town grapevine about my brother's disappearance, he thought he'd mention it to me. Noah's always been a busybody that way.

Duane and I kept an eye on Justin's trailer for about twelve hours before I opened a case file. Looking back I should have acted sooner. We lost half a day waiting for my brother to come home, but that's protocol for you.

I've never been a big believer in coincidences, especially when they start stacking up. It was a coincidence that Justin left Hoolihan's on that fateful Tuesday night, less than an hour before your wife was assaulted. It was a coincidence that his Jeep tires were large enough to make the tracks in your driveway. And now it was a coincidence that the main suspect in our investigation had gone missing, last seen by Noah Jarrett talking to someone in a smaller truck. A short-cab pickup, maybe. You know where I'm headed with this.

I drove back to the hospital that night. Truth be told, I wanted to rule you out as a suspect in Justin's disappearance as soon as the thought entered my mind. I knew you'd gone to visit Elizabeth every night, sometimes for hours. But I checked the sign-in sheet at the front desk. You weren't there on Saturday, Miles, not even for a few minutes. First day you'd missed since the attack. Coincidence, right?

I barely slept that night and drove out to your place first thing in the morning. Remember how I came alone? I didn't want Duane and the others to know, not just yet. You saw me coming. I could see you in the upstairs window, watching the cruiser when I pulled into the driveway. But you still made me ring the doorbell.

Morning Dani, you said. *What's this about?*

I didn't see any sense in wasting time on pleasantries.

Where were you on Saturday night? I asked.

I was here.

Anyone with you?

No.

I told you about Justin. How he'd been missing for two days. How he was last seen talking to someone in a vehicle matching the short cab's description. By that time I'd reasoned that whoever drove the truck must have had a piece. A .38 or a 9mm, something small they could point at another person from the driver's seat without drawing too much attention. But I didn't want to get into all that, so I simply asked if you had a gun.

I have my Heckler upstairs, you said, *and a valid permit. But I don't like that question.*

I didn't like it either, Miles. And I hated my next question even more.

Did something happen between you and my brother? I paused. *If it did, now's the time to tell me. Don't make me find out another way.*

I won't pretend to know how you felt at that moment. But in law enforcement training, we learn about something called aggressive stance, how someone looks right before they come at you. Clenched fists, bent knees, both shoulders pointing forward like bull horns. Color me crazy, but I believe you considered knocking me to the ground. Was it anger toward me over the accusation, or some sort of panic? A moot point, I suppose, since you slammed the door in my face without another word.

I returned the next morning with Duane, along with a few more deputies and two dogs on loan from state patrol. My word to yours, Miles, I didn't share my suspicions about you with any of the others. I simply suggested that we conduct another search in the woods behind your property. The boys took that to mean we were looking for evidence in Elizabeth's case with fresh eyes and didn't ask any further questions, which spared me the unpleasant task of lying to them.

We spent the whole day combing through those eighteen acres. My neck strained from checking the treetops, and by mid-afternoon my legs were heavy from trudging through those muddy, boot-sucking creek beds. We packed it in around dusk. You were waiting for us in the backyard, chopping firewood. I remember the look of relief that washed over you when I said we hadn't found anything. Then I told you I'd be back first thing in the morning to look some more. Should have seen your face then, Miles, because I sure as hell did. That's when I knew Justin was back there somewhere, in some form. Alive was the best I could hope for.

I returned the next day, and the day after that, and a few more times. I didn't know what I was looking for, maybe a cave nestled in the trees or a rock cropping that looked unnatural at second glance. Never did find any such things during my searches, but no matter how long I stomped around in your woods, you were always in the backyard when I called it a day. Mowing the grass, or fiddling around in your shed, or sometimes just sitting on your porch, watching me from a distance. How your hands would tremble when you asked how my search went that day, how your eyes would look away from mine. And I remember how that cheek-tugging smile would sneak across your face when you realized I'd come up empty.

Those were the visits you knew about. A few nights I came around late, when the lights were off. I'd park the cruiser down the road, so you couldn't hear me drive up, and then sit in that blind spot of your porch light for hours, listening to the owl hoots, waiting to see if you did something fishy like take a late-night stroll into the woods. Some nights I stayed put until daylight broke. Even then, you revealed nothing.

You'll probably be relieved to know that I won't be coming by your place to look for Justin anymore, day or night. Truthfully, I haven't felt right about it since Elizabeth was discharged from the hospital. That poor woman has been through enough for two lifetimes. She should be allowed to recover in peace.

But there's more to it than that, Miles, and this brings me to the other point of my letter. There's no easy way to tell you, so I'll just write it plainly. We got him, the son of a bitch who attacked Elizabeth.

I got the call yesterday morning. A trooper two counties over stopped a driver last night on suspicion of DUI. He searched the vehicle and found a stash of pills in a grocery bag. The driver wouldn't say who the pills belonged to but he couldn't produce a prescription either. His vehicle was a Dodge Extended Cab. Big old tires.

The trooper knew about Elizabeth's case and called our office first thing that morning. In a few hours, Duane will drive back from county lockup with a passenger cuffed in the backseat. Duane wanted to wait until the guy was in custody to tell you, but I wanted you to hear it from me first. Try to act surprised when he calls you tonight.

I can't give you the suspect's name yet but he isn't local, so I doubt you know him, and you'll learn his identity soon enough. So far, he's denied attacking Elizabeth and a public defender has been assigned.

He'll need a good lawyer. The trooper told me some of the pills in that grocery bag matched Elizabeth's prescriptions. We've also confirmed he was in town on the night of the attack. He swiped his debit card at Pumpco and a couple of bars on Tuesday night, and closed out his tab at the last place at twenty after nine. You probably won't believe it, but the place was Hoolihan's. Must have missed Justin by a few minutes. I know, coincidence.

I still don't have all the answers. I can't tell you why this man drove to your house that night, assuming you and Elizbeth don't know him. Let's say he overheard someone in town talking about her pills. That still doesn't explain how he knew your address, or even how to find your road. Not like it's easy. I can't tell you where he went afterwards either. Couldn't have been far since he was only picked up a couple hundred miles away. I hate to admit it, but if he'd kept pushing down the highway that night, it's likely we'd have never found him.

Here's what I think: this man set out on a path of destruction that night and, for reasons I've yet to understand, he ended up in your driveway. But his reasons don't matter. My promise to you is that we'll punish him. Won't take the jury more than an hour to find him guilty. Cold comfort, I know, but it's the best I can offer.

This is the reason why I won't be digging around your woods for my brother anymore. Duane and the other deputies are under the impression that I've been searching your property for evidence in Elizabeth's case. It wouldn't make much sense for me to keep looking now that we've caught the bastard. More to the point, I've come to terms with the fact that Justin is gone. God knows where you put him, but you found a good spot, alright. I bet I could spend the next ten years digging through all eighteen acres and I still wouldn't find my brother. You know that too. Your creeping smile gave you away too many times.

I've also come to terms with knowing my actions, in part, cost Justin his life. If only I'd kept quiet about him during the investigation. But that's where ifs are tricky. I was so certain my brother was guilty that keeping quiet would have gone against every instinct I had as an investigator. In my line of work, going against your instinct will get you killed. I thought I was doing the right thing, the just thing. I imagine you can relate now.

Five weeks and four days later, I can barely remember Justin's voice. For a while I called his cell phone to listen to his voicemail greeting. Then his line got disconnected, and now memories are all I've got. A lot of the memories are unpleasant, but my brother was a good man. A bad man's temperament, maybe, but a good man's heart. He'd have never hurt Elizabeth. I realize that now, and I chide myself for ever thinking otherwise. I hope this letter helps you reach the same conclusion. And I hope you'll think twice about assuming the worst in people from now on, no matter how hard-set you are against them.

You may wonder why I've gone to the trouble to write all this down. After spending half the night on it, I can't help but wonder the same. It's certainly risky to put so many of my lies, missteps and errors in judgment into writing, though I'm not worried you'll show anyone. You have much more to lose by revealing this letter than I do.

I guess I wanted to level with you, Miles. To tell you I understand why you killed my brother, but also to let you know that, while you may never face any charges, you didn't get away with anything. Not from where I'm sitting. My brother's case may be suspended, but it's most certainly *not closed*, and there's no statute of limitations for the crimes you've committed. Please remember that. And don't be surprised if I show up at your place unannounced one day. You'll know why. I expect you to come quietly.

Again, wishing you and Elizabeth all the best in the weeks and months to come. With her recovery and everything else. Please call if you need anything, though I won't be hurt if you call Duane instead. He's a good man. There aren't enough like him in this world.

Summer's End

~ E. E. King

Kate and Michael had come to the beach for the entire summer. Three months stretched out before them endless as the tide that painted white ribbons of foam on the sand. A diving pelican crashed into the waves as if someone had dropped a small rock out of the sky.

They stood hand-in-hand breathing shallowly, motionless, made temporarily mute and still by the glory before them, but only for a moment. Then they kicked off their shoes and socks, leaving them behind like the discarded skins of cicadas clinging to the tall, golden grass that lined the beach. Never looking back, they raced toward the crashing sea, laughing hearts beating in time with the tide and with all of creation on this perfect first day of summer. It was a summer that would last forever. They knew it by the way the sand crept in between their toes like the rough, adoring tongue of a family dog.

Somewhere, in a distant world, the townies stocked empty shelves with shiny packaged goods, filled their freezers with bags of ice and waited. Their parents prepared the Summer House, unpacking their suitcases, putting food in cupboards, ordering propane, and doing all the boring, unimportant things grownups did.

It was a strange beach, full of odd mounding stones that formed a wavy line right where the high tide washed against the shore, darkening each grain of sand. The mounds had once been sand themselves, hardened into rock by the centuries.

That very first day when they ran breathlessly down to the sea, daring the waves to catch them, Kate thought she saw first one, then two, then three, then dozens and dozens of boys, each standing in front of a stone mound, flickering in the mist that had risen from the meeting between sea and shore. But it had only been a trick of light, an illusion of the rising shimmering heat, of salt and surf and too much sun. Because when she blinked and rubbed her eyes, the mist and boys were gone, vanished into foaming surf.

"Did you see . . ." began Kate turning to Michael, but he was playing tag with the tide, screeching with laughter as the chill waters nipped his toes.

"This coast has history," Father had said. "It was home to an ancient people and you can still find artifacts on the shore and in the woods."

"Arrowheads? asked Kate. She loved searching for treasures, carved stones, odd rocks delicate seashells, and almost any kind of feather. Whatever she could find, which in the city wasn't much. Michael preferred books, magical lands that would not dirty his feet, scratch his thighs or make him itch, but only mark his imagination. He lived in a world apart from other boys, a place of gods and monsters, of dragons and enchantments. It made school difficult.

"There might be arrowheads, Father said, "Or small round stones that they used to place on the graves of their dead to make sure they didn't rise from the earth. They feared ghosts and worshipped a wild god of sea and woods, a kind of Pan."

"Pan?" asked Kate. "A frying pan?"

"No silly," said Michael. "Pan was a god with goat legs and horns who played a bamboo flute. No one could resist his music."

"It is said they stole children from other tribes, and buried them alive, under bridges and beneath crossroads as a sacrifice to their god. In exchange, he left them alone and kept their children safe."

"Are kids buried under our street?" asked Kate.

"Perhaps we should go out tonight with a shovel and see . . . Ah hahahaha . . ." Father's voice rose into a maniacal chuckle.

"Jonathan," Mother said. "Don't scare the children."

"I'm not scared," said Michael, but he shivered despite the heat.

Now they forgot ghosts and history, arrowheads and dead bodies. They played chase with the tide letting the cold waters tug at their toes, before running backwards screaming.

"Look," said Michael, poking his big toe into the damp sand, so that the grains dried, making a lightened circle around each foot. "It's as if each step I take turns the earth into diamonds."

Kate poked her toe in too. "We're rich," she cried. "I'm turning everything into diamonds!"

"It's how they will know that we are the King and Queen," Michael said. "All the people will follow the shining footsteps and crown us, Rulers of the Beach."

They marked solemnly down the shore, tucking big toes into sand, so caught up watching the creation of diamonds they didn't notice the boy standing in front of them until they saw ten naked toes wiggling at the edge of their circle of light.

The boy was four or five years older than Michael, his ragged cut-offs were frayed and faded. His bare chest had been tanned the same deep bronzed color as the wet sandstone dunes. Ocean breezes tousled his sun-whiten hair. And his light brown eyes were tawny, almost golden, flecked with tiny grains of darkness, like bugs in amber.

"I'm Tom," he said, holding out a salt-rough hand.

"I'm Kate and this is my brother Michael."

"Come play," Tom smiled. And in the way of children and young animals, that was the only introduction they needed. They raced down the shore looking for seashells and curious stones.

"Look," Michael pointed. "That moved."

Tom scooped it up. "It's a hermit crab," he said. "They don't even make their own shells, they just look for empty ones and use them. When they get too big they have to find a new home."

At night, their parents let them go to the beach.

"But just for an hour," Mother said. "And don't get wet."

At the shore's edge Tom waited. They wandered the strand, searching for small white sand dollars so fragile, a mean look could shatter them into a million pieces.

"Oh," Kate pointed at one sand dollar as big a flattened tennis ball.

Tom scooped it up and broke it.

"Why . . ." began Kate, until, like a conjurer, Tom extracted small bits of dove-shaped bones from the shell's fragments so perfect, it seemed they might fly away into the setting sun.

Tom showed them how the night water flashed when they moved their hands beneath the surface.

"It's magic!" cried Michael, making light trails in the water with his fingers.

But Kate knew it was not magic. She was the more skeptical of the two, less trusting, less willing to accept the welcoming invitation of an open door.

Tom studied them. "You're both right," he said. "Those light flashes are actually caused by little animals... or maybe they're plants, I forget which. But you can only see them at night, when the water is stirred up."

"Then how is he right?" Kate said. "I'm right. It's made by animals."

"Or plants," said Michael.

"Or plants," agree Kate. "And neither animals or plants are magic."

"They can make light," said Tom. "I mean—you can't make light—I can't make light, but they can—isn't that a kind of magic?"

Kate supposed Tom was just being nice, trying not to make Michael feel dumb. She liked him for it. Michael was usually not so lucky. All year long he'd been called a sissy, a girl, a moon-calf and a dreamer for preferring stories to baseballs, and magic kingdoms to soldiers.

"But I *can* make light," Michael cried. "Look! Everywhere I walk turns to diamonds!" He raced to where the tide had turned the sand dark and poked his toes in, pulling the grains upward.

"We are rich!" cried Tom. They raced down the shore together, laughing and jostling each other until Michael lost his balance and tumbled into the damp surf.

"Uh oh," said Michael

"Uh oh," said Kate. "You are going to be in trouble." She drew it out long, like it was two words: *troub-el*.

Michael shivered

"Just wash it off," said Tom, pulling him toward and under the beating waves. Michael struggled. Then he emerged, soaking and shivering, coughing up water as salty as tears.

Michael stumbled up and chased Tom out of the water. Tom, though half wet, didn't even seem cold, but Michael's skin was as bumpy as the plucked chicken Kate had once seen hanging from a butcher's window.

"Won't you get in trouble?" Asked Michael.

"Me?" Laughed Tom. "I'd like to see someone try. Besides, I'm not the one who's all wet."

"You are now," said Kate, pushing him backward into the lapping waves. He held onto her arm, dragging her with him. Soon all three were rolling in the sand and icy water, sputtering and laughing.

Kate and Michael got in trouble.

"Where does this Tom you talk so much about, live?" Asked Father. "Is he a townie, or are his people, summer people like us?"

Summer people. Kate liked the sound of that. As if they could spend their whole lives in summer, never returning to school, and winter, and the tormenting laughter of other children.

"I don't know," said Kate.

"Haven't you asked him?" Her father shook his head and sighed. "What do his parents do?"

Both children looked at him as if he were speaking a foreign language. They didn't care what Tom parents did, they only wanted to play in the waves, hunt for hermit crabs and sand dollars and make glowing trails of light in the night sea.

"Why don't you ask Tom to come for dinner," said their mother.

And Kate did, but Tom just shook his head.

"Can't," he said, disappearing into the darkening night. The children watched him go, fading into the flickering luminescence of sea and shore.

One night, at the end of summer, as they raced to meet Tom, Mother gave them a big bag of sunflower seeds.

"One – two - three - Crunch!" shouted Tom.

They cracked in unison, spitting the empty husks into the surf and chomping the small tender seeds like a chorus of frogs. Kate still remembers it as the happiest night of her life. Why was it so wonderful? So much fun? She still doesn't know, only that for a moment, they were all together, heart, soul, mouth, and teeth working as one.

Michael had been right after all, she thought. It had been magic. Magic, making the sea glow. Magic, letting them move through sand, surf and summer as though they belonged.

◯

The night after the sunflowers seeds, Kate, Michael and Tom played hide and seek. The obvious place to hide was behind a mound. So Kate lay in the tall golden grasses, barely breathing, but they scratched her bare arms and legs, and the sand fleas nipped her ankles. Cautiously she raised her head. No one was in sight. She sprang up, racing to crouch behind a dune. It must have been the perfect hiding place, because they never found her. She never found them either. She returned home after dark, tired and dirty.

"Where's Michael?" asked Mother.

"He's not home?" asked Kate.

"No."

"We were playing hide 'n seek with Tom and I lost them."

"Tom again," said Father. "I'd like to meet that young man and his parents."

They waited for three hours, but Michael didn't return.

The police were called. Mother and Father asked about Tom. But neither the police or the townies had seen, or heard of a ragged boy with golden eyes and beached hair. They grew silent when questioned, hastily changing the subject, organizing search parties, spending days and nights combing beach and woods.

"It just shows how good people can be," Mother wept. "All these neighbors we didn't even know we had. I always looked down on the townies . . . b-b-but now . . ."

"Don't worry," said Father. "We'll find him." He put an arm around Mother and patted Kate's arm awkwardly.

But Kate knew they would never find Michael. The night after he had not come home she had raced down to the shore, searching for Tom. She did not find him. Instead she saw a new mound. It looked like all the others, but slightly darker, slightly fresher as if it had only now changed from sand to stone.

And surely, thought Kate, *there must be a single moment when that happens?* When sand becomes stone, summer turns to fall, ancient gods return. and childhood ends.

She knew that Michael had joined the other children, the ghosts she had seen that very first night, flickering in the light between day and dusk, shimmering in the place between shore and sea.

Kate could imagine the scene.

"Why don't we bury each other?"

"Me first! Me first!" cried Michael. He lay down on the damp line where the water met the land.

"No," said Tom. "We have to dig a hole first, otherwise your toes will show. Lie here."

He carefully scooped out a hole just a little bit bigger than Michael's body. Throwing handfuls of wet sand back into the sea. The tide flattened them into beach and swept them away leaving no trace.

But Kate was wrong about two things, or perhaps she was both right and wrong. For she did see Michael one last time. It was not he, who was buried under the mound by the sea, or at least not yet.

It was five years after his disappearance. She'd been begging Mother and Father to return to the Summer House.

"I want to go in memory of Michael," she'd cried. Tears flowing down her face like rivers to the sea. "I want to return to the place of our last summer."

Mother shook her head, retreated to her room and bolted her door. The catch clicked in the silence, as final as endings.

"I will take you," said Father, his voice flat and toneless as a tideless ocean.

This trip was as different as from the last one as day from night, as life from death, as joy from sorrow. There was no joking talk of ghosts, or arrowheads. There was no talk at all.

Kate had to wait till Father was in the bathroom to race down to the beach. The sun was sinking into the ocean. A splinter of light lingered on the horizon and was gone. A tattered cloud, like a blood-spattered rag, swayed over the spot of its going. Then dusk crept over the sky, darkness crept over the sea, and all was as still as the last sunset at the end of eternity.

She remembered watching the sun sink into the waves from this very spot, hand in hand with Michael, not so long ago, but a lifetime away.

And then, in front of the newest mound of sand she saw two boys dashing madly through the surf, foam breaking against their legs as bubbly as laughter.

"Hey!" Kate called.

The boys froze. They turned toward her in the dying light. One was a stranger, but the other was Michael, her Michael! She tried to call to him but the words stuck in her throat.

For just a moment his face was illuminated by the fading light and she saw his eyes, no longer the clear blue of a cloudless sky, but tawny, almost golden, flecked with tiny grains of darkness, like bugs in amber. He stared at her like a stranger, like a townie, like an adversary, then pulled the unknown boy off into the sea and the sand and the night.

Sweet Water
~ Darin Bradley

Sweet Water found it, but that's not how we remember things.

We remember it the way you're supposed to. The tradition of men in the wilderness, finding themselves in Great Things. Joseph Smith and the Golden Plates, Buddha and the Banyan Tree. The burning bush. A man named Christophorus. Because, of course, finding is simply seeing things correctly.

What makes a Great Find, though, is confusion. Great Men don't find anything when they know exactly what's going on. I was confused. Sweet Water wasn't. Which was why we rarely let her decide anything.

I was a better choice.

It was in a woodland. Which made sense. We spent a lot of time hiding in woodlands then. Sometimes, they were aspens, with their jack-of-the-wood eyes, their black eyes, staring, staring. Or graying spruce. The sweating mimosa. Cyprus. Sycamore. Pine. Joshua trees and persimmon orchards. We knew ourselves by the trees around us, a different people every time. Trees became monuments, druidic things without explanations. They had only functions.

We did better there than we had on the grasslands, or in the bread-basket, or up the mountainsides. We moved and moved, a different species of tree per year, zodiacally. You can measure fortune by trees when you can't risk the open stars.

Sweet Water found it in a coastal woodland. And we were post oaks, and sawtooth elms, and magnolia trees. We'd been safe here throughout the fall. There were other groups around, not far, but by this point we were mostly done with trading murders—our old diplomacy, sacrifices that kept everyone feeling strong. The idea being we could kill everyone if we wanted to.

She found the salt spring in a depression, where Great Things usually are: belowground. In the underworld. The trees ringed the spring's ferrous-soiled lip, a gap of twenty yards between them and the waters. They would not go down the slope. Where the waterline rose and fell (down now), the soil looked volcanic—sharp and ashen and thick with the grays and whites of alkali mud.

The water was red, scabbed along the shore, where it tongued the bad soil. The water was dried on its own surface, because what choice had it but to lap at what was there?

A pond named Tantalus.

Sweet Water was standing in it, the bunched ropes of her hair like serpents down her back. The soft hair on her thighs fanned on the surface of the water, reddened.

Of course, this is why I had wandered. I was looking for Sweet Water, not paradise. The truth of the whole thing is that I was never looking for anything else.

She looked like someone else standing there. The water had dyed her skin and her hair. She'd bathed, and it left her rouged. She looked candied, with the spring's salt glaze along the gaunt lines of her shoulders and upon her narrow fingertips, hanging.

I screed into the depression, could smell the burn on the air. It was hot here.

She was a blood-dried effigy, a daughter of the red mother liquor. I didn't know such names—what you called brinewater after its salt precipitated. But eventually, there were enough of us. Someone knew, so we knew. Someone knew something about everything.

I couldn't know then that she was play-acting the future. Looking bloody like that.

The hair beneath her belly winked with salt, in oxidized curls. A sculpture's hair. We no longer had a life for plucking and trimming, for taming a body's secrets.

And I didn't want them between us anyway.

"It's a brine spring, Salis," she said.

That wasn't my name. Not then.

"Can I come in?" I asked.

She turned her vinegar-fly gaze back onto the center of the spring. "You don't have a choice," she said.

Father was salt. He was not gray salt or red salt. He had no saltpeter chunks, no natron skins. He was pure—the carefully gathered, the refined, the heights salt could achieve. Fleur de sel, white-on-white, flos salis.

But his eyes were as red as the brine beneath his heels. Everything he looked upon, including me, was red. He could see that everyone should be red. His children, born of Mother Liquor's water.

People should be red, or they aren't "people." Instead, they are the peat salts—the northern, the Celtic, the bay salts. Anything but pure. They were the Civil War ashes, cutting salt to stretch it further. Which was a crime in the Confederacy, not far from this woodland. Back then.

Even I knew what was to be done with criminals. What had always been done. Even so long ago, before Everything changed. Before it all Happened.

"Paradise," we remember Father saying, "begins with power."

He gleamed in the open sun. A great, living figurine, like those carved straight from the salt mountain, so long ago, by dirty Cardona workers. He was Lithuanian Roguszys—a spirit in a pickle jar. He was Saint-Guénolé, God's own eye, peering down on Le Bourg de Batz. Watching the salt marshes—their workers, the paludiers. They remembered still, in that land, the language of Vercingetorix. Even up to the First World War.

We had to realize that Father had always been all things to all people.

"Power," Father continued, "is the control of resources."

Father was *flos salis*, whom even Roman Cato had known. A resource, its acquisition, and its control. The holy trinity behind every war. He was even menstruation, our women *en salaison*—curing in salt. Fermenting, as they thought so long before Everything Happened.

That meant He was Sweet Water.

That meant He was me. In a salted state. "Salax," back when Pliny and Cato were still doing the thinking.

That is to say, in love.

"Resources begin, of course, with food, water, and shelter."

Of course.

"Shelter includes control not only of weather and predation, but of one's enemies as well."

I stood in Mother Liquor, becoming red—washing from the feet up. Like a disciple of Christ and what he did to people, who were the salt of the earth. Always washing feet.

"I will give you everything you need," He said.

I took Sweet Water's hand. The two of us in the same spring silt, now of the same red mud. A man and a woman made of earth, sharing a rib. As the red earth became flesh and Father exhaled His living breath.

Father who gave us everything we needed. Who gave us paradise.

Even if we forget that He had to build it first.

I knew Sweet Water before Everything Happened. I was confused even then. I borrowed great sums of money, student loans, to map, exactly, along which academic lines my confusion lay. I knew everything about it—I was an instructor of the misunderstood, and I worked middling jobs teaching this in beautiful, mind-altering ways. I published papers on the topic, and attended conferences, where we could all misunderstand each other together. Where we could be only discourse, which is far better than trying to mean discourse.

My boyhood came from manicured lawns, and Little League teams. Church membership and foreign exchange programs. I started out white, even if Father couldn't see that.

I worked by semester, working by credit cards, and loan payments, and buying nothing for my efforts. I had come from a modest suburb, and I had become confused. Because what they don't tell you is that such benefits can expire. I had done what I was supposed to, learned what I was supposed to, taught what I was supposed to. I was tolerance, and equality, and enriching the zeitgeist with a new cultural self, so we could correct the very language, the very thoughts, that produced selves who could not see the imbalances between different types of people.

And so. And carrying those suburbs, I looked fleur de sel. I looked flos salis. I didn't realize that it was part of the problem.

I had known Sweet Water before, and she had been the wrong color also. Had borrowed the same money and written the same papers and taught the same lessons to the same students. She had degreed her way to cultural enlightenment, too.

But Sweet Water was not confused. Sweet Water did not teach confusion. Sweet Water knew what flos salis really meant, and she didn't care about salary, or tenure, or temporary contracts. She was going to find the correct color, and learn to see it everywhere.

She was an expert.

Which is why we remember that I found the spring, and not Sweet Water. We make saints and martyrs of the innocent. It's better that way.

We had been together, on the campus, teaching our great tracts of nothing in different buildings, in different disciplines, even if we really were talking about the same things.

I knew her. We shared functions. Dinner parties. Intelligent discussions in coffee houses and at receptions where we pretended to listen to other people. We went to the same weddings, and the same hospitals, and the same personal tragedies. We visited the same coworkers' homes, who had given birth to the same children. All of them the wrong color, I would only, much later, realize.

When Everything Happened, I ran through the same crowds, past the same news-feeds. I ignored the same university-sent emergency-situation text messages that climbed into phone after phone, their digital fingers slipping into ours.

Everything will be okay, the little texts said, and it is good not to be alone.

I found her, and we ran together. I found her because I wanted to panic together. I wanted to continue seeing what made her trompe l'oeil.

She had eyes like green opals.

"Sweet Water," I said then.

She had eyes like a willow tree, and we hid there first.

"Follow me," she said.

And I will make you fishers of men.

God, of course, had something to say about Father. And Ruby passed it along.

> *Hark, the sound of holy voices,*
> *Chanting at the crystal sea*
> *'Alleluia, Alleluia,*
> *Alleluia,' Lord, to Thee:*
> *Multitude, which none can number,*
> *Like the stars in glory stands,*
> *Clothed in white apparel, holding*
> *Palms of victory in their hands.*

It was one of the few books we had. A Baptist Hymnal from 1885. From not so long after the Confederates and their salt crimes. Not so long after the need to distinguish between "Southern" and "Not" Baptists. They'd disagreed over what color people should be. Or they weren't people. Father had known this. I had known this.

Only people are allowed. This is crucial to building paradise. To finding it. You can't think of non-people as people. It complicates things.

We found the hymnal in a church, which had been sacked by a rival congregation, according to the graffiti on the walls. This was very common. The old book had approached us carefully, afraid when we called and whistled and settled on our haunches— our hands, like plates, extended. Our palms appropriately up.

Ruby skipped ahead. There were gaps in the old book.

> *They have come from tribulation,*
> *And have washed their robes in blood,*

This was what God had to say about Father, only He couldn't say it Himself. He couldn't say it through prophets or burning bushes, or political action committees. He'd said it through song, which is the greatest vetting. All of the Greatest Things have been remembered in song.

Hymns were choose-your-own divine adventure. A series of do-it-yourself beatitudes, with notes to play by number, that all the sons of man could pick up and sing, could remember, when the time was right. Like now. God, of course, having been divine enough to mean all things in everything He said. Even in everything we said. The devil was in the details, where it was best not to go.

It was difficult to tell what Ruby did and didn't believe. He was the hymnal's keeper, to be sure. I think that's what was most important. I didn't know if he Believed or not, but there were others of us, and they cared more that he said these things (someone had to), so he was ordained to the task by default—our bearded planchette, playing Ouija with his few, decrepit books. Aside from a Bible, I wasn't certain exactly which other books he had.

He spent most of his time with pieces of burnt timber, charcoaling things out of the books, their pale bellies exposed in love or submission. He corrected them. Working out just the right divine message for dirty people chasing food in the trees.

We were back in the camp, Sweet Water and I. Not everyone understood what Father had meant, by being in that spring.

"Everything begins with salt," Sweet Water told them. "We can cure food."

This was important. Winter was coming.

"We can make salves," I added.

A wind soughed through the camp, lifting our scraps of tarpaulin from their deadwood frames. Opening and closing the wedges of darkness, which were our doorways in. Normally, only we opened and closed them—they did not do this by themselves.

We were in a hollow beneath the trunks of our sassafras copse. It was a sinkhole, one of us knew, softened and grown over these many years past.

That should have been our first clue.

We listened as the leaves rattled. When we were sassafras, we knew to freeze when the leaves rattled. They made good cover for other things, approaching things on the noisy woodland floor. We stared animal-distances, into nothing-places, listening the way herds do. When the first of us ran, the rest of us would, too.

We could smell ourselves in the sinkhole, on the wind. Nothing smelled out of order.

Ruby thought for a minute, the ropes of his fingers working the spine on his hymnal. "Other people will want the salt."

That was the thing.

Missy scratched at her side. I thought of Sweet Water, where Father had implanted that first rib.

We called her Miss. She was the youngest of us. She sometimes sat with Ruby, pointing where and where things should be crossed out of the books, with the charcoal. She behaved like a Believer, but there were parts, there were songs, she didn't like. Ruby's books were afraid of her, and they trembled to keep from running away.

She and Sweet Water were the strongest of us. She and Sweet Water were not confused. They knew how to find things.

Miss had dirty eyes, and a dirty gaze, and she looked at everything. Always.

She had killed the most. But she still listened to me, like they all did. Since those early days, when that life had still offered the luxury of ideas. Like democracy. When I was voted into power because I was like each of them, without being anything particular myself.

"That's the point, Ruby," Sweet Water said.

"That's part of the point," I said.

Miss folded her narrow arms across her narrow chest. "We want them to want it."

Ruby's caterpillar brows inched together. "Why?"

"Power is the control of resources," I said.

Sweet Water and Miss smelled like sassafras, when they looked at me then.

There were already a few of us when we found Miss on a stretch of the old Interstate 20, in Mississippi. Which is how we named her.

Sweet Water and I were first, the two of us moving, moving. It didn't take long to realize there were things we couldn't do ourselves. Ruby had come next.

People still had guns then, though they were running out of ammunition. The idea had been to hoard it. To rise to power on bullets alone, but that hadn't worked. There had been too many people to shoot at. Too many shooting back. Bullets had picked up minds of their own, and they ran in lemming-herds any direction they could.

You knew them by their gibbering, and they were difficult to understand, once they started their stampedes.

We still had gas then, though most vehicles were busted or burnt up. Pushed too hard, too long, by people who needed them to be more than machines. To get them away.

People had tried to hoard gas, too.

We had to stop because Miss had laid barbed wire across the highway. With the tires flayed, she killed the first of us by throwing a bottle of rags and gasoline through the back window. The person she hit did not have a name, we later taught ourselves.

We could have helped that person, but there was too much to risk. There was ourselves, who we couldn't let burn. If we had put her out, she wouldn't have burned.

Outside the van, when Miss tried to kill Ruby, he broke her nose against the asphalt. And her knives came spilling from her coat, and they were red. They blinked at us in that sunlight, squinting against our phosphene silhouettes where we were reflected on their surfaces. Clearly, Miss knew how to care for small things. For frightened things.

Those knives were just the color we were looking for. Red even then.

We talked to her while that other one burned.

Sweet Water and Miss left the camp. They came back, from that nearby town—what remained—with rakes and trowels, which were ready to do our work. Father's work.

The women said there weren't many people in the town, which was probably true. Those who could move on already had. Those who couldn't were simply branches on the forest floor. The bullets, in their great herds, had gone extinct, and enough of us had died that we didn't compete so much for what we needed.

We set the tools to work, scraping and raking—harvesting the salt from the spring. We gave the tools food and shelter in exchange for this work, but, of course, they weren't people. Soon, we wouldn't see them at all.

○

When we were Phoenicians, we figured this process out.

We left behind our precious coast, left behind its fish, like fish ourselves, testing our missing-link legs for the first time—going inland. Our city of Sfax was not so far from those reaching desert beds. From those sometimes-dry places and their great, salt plains.

But always we went back to the water, back to Sfax, dragging and gathering ourselves, just like the salt from its sands. And we waited again for fresh saltwater and the slow precipitation.

Others of us had waited before, in the same way around Lake Yuncheng, while others of us were still figuring out pyramids—even though we had, in those Egyptian sands, figured out how to drag and gather just the same. A world away, awakening to the same salt call. Listening to the same Salt Father, even if he carried other names then. Even if his name was wadi. Even though we called him Sebkha, and his breath of life, given in beds of golden dust, Natrun.

We learned to cut the mortal cord, then. To free our mummified rulers to eat in the afterlife. And we did this to the youngest of us. To the Living Image of Amun. To his dead throat with our holy knives. We learned to sleep in natron, to eat it, to become Salt Fathers ourselves, lying those seventy days in salt, our brains scooped away by priests' hooks. The best of us in tombs that had cost the lives of most of us.

We figured it out again, here, with our new tools. How to drag what we needed from the red water. We watched Mother Liquor, her floating algae scabs. We watched Her lap at Father's Salts while the magnolia winds blew.

Really, we didn't know what it was like for other people. We began running on principle, Sweet Water and I, because we had everything to get away from. We had the debts, and the all-but-aborted tenure tracks, and the meaningless bounce from thing to thing. Really, it had been a chance to get something going for once.

Mostly, people just went away. What we knew about the murders we heard from other people—those few we didn't flee from, simply because we didn't want to talk to them. Sweet Water and I were re-enacting faculty retreats and hiking trips. When we tried to pretend in groups that we could be something other than writers and researchers. Mostly, it worked.

Sweet Water and I were simply done with it all. As most others were. Really, I think that's what made Everything Happen. People just walked away. They stopped getting paid, and it didn't end with their jobs.

Bullet wranglers, and church-burners, and city-state builders were around, to be sure. But they had been around before. They just took up the new spaces left behind. It was hard in some places, like Mississippi, but where we were—that particular spot—had been hard before. We talked to Miss, convinced her to come along not because she could kill, but because she had the energy to. Which was hard to come by—for most people, those we saw, it was all they could do to read books on bean farming and generator repair. It was all others could do to repair dams and turn their homeowner's associations into something more serious.

There were other kinds of people. We were tree people, but there were mountain people, and lake people. There were highway people, who used roads like old rivers to open the veins of new business.

But most were gone, had run away, like Sweet Water and I.

There were no mutants. What gangs there were had existed before. I hadn't heard of any warlord kingmakers, or of any New Ethnic Empires. People killed each other, like we did, but, really, they'd done that before. Mostly, we stabbed on impulse when we surprised each other in the trees. Miss, I think, was never surprised, but it really didn't seem to matter if she killed a few people. We had rules, which I'd enacted, about killing others in our group. No one did that. We didn't have much need for other rules.

Really, we only started accepting others, Sweet Water and I, because we needed them. Not to bear arms in phalanx against other barbarians. Not to divide and conquer. We needed them because some things are difficult to do between only two people.

It was all right to be confused. I think it was the new spirit of the age. What the hell was the point? Where were we going? Sweet Water and Miss, they weren't confused, had never been, but that's because they were looking backward, at what came before. What they'd do with knowing it.

Sweet Water kept me from being alone. I didn't have loans anymore. I didn't worry about what it meant to come from where (from what). I didn't care anymore about balancing the representative discourse of the age. Because there was really only me. Sweet Water and everyone else being my own thoughts about them because, after all, you can't get someone in your brain. You can't know them. That was always something no one ever paid attention to, looking at me and having ideas about what it meant to be someone like me.

Sweet Water was the point. And that was nice, because she wasn't alone either.

But this isn't how we remember things.

Really, this isn't the way things were.

You have to remember, most of the others didn't come until later. Until after Father had built the paradise he promised. A modern-day Taghaza, a city built of salt, transplanted from the Western Sahara and straight into what remained, where we were, of the old U.S. Even Pliny had seen buildings made of salt in Old Egypt, and he and Father had talked often. It was not a new idea—building civilizations out of resources.

It wasn't long before Ruby decreed that we needed a Salt Chapel. We remembered that the miners, in Polish Wieliczka, had done so. Had carved one belowground. The underground omphalos, where faith and resources came together.

I didn't mind because, by this point, we'd expanded from simply caring for rakes and trowels. Now we had boilers and sifters, hammers and nails—tools upon tools for collecting Father's salt. And then there came the livestock, the needles, the beeswax and the lime. All the tools that wandered, apprehensively, back down our salt trails, back to the source. The first American roads were merely widened footpaths, traced from the routes animals wandered in their quests for salt. Before we paved them. So we could die more easily, at greater speeds, in traffic accidents. Of course, we had mirrors for looking backward. At what had come before. But they didn't help.

And we cared for all these wandering tools. Some of them got to be people, based on value. Ruby kept them busy. Kept them in place, so I didn't mind.

But some tools just aren't necessary for harvesting and trading salt. These we turned away, and they were becoming angry. Enemies. In India, before Gandhi had started his salt revolution, we'd solved this problem with a thorn hedge. A 2,500-mile customs line culti-vated from prickly pear and acacia and bamboo. It kept smugglers out. We used one to keep away the not-people.

We weren't tree people anymore. We were salt people. We had tamed fires, like sheep, to heat the boiler-pans, and because we knew so many trees, knew them so well, we domesticated them, too. We told them "stay," and they did, while the fire took hold, shyly, and burned them to boil the salts from their brine.

Everything had been Happening for a while. Before.

Sweet Water had paid someone at her salon to put beeswax in her hair. They created false dreadlocks, which she bound in an oversized ponytail against the back of her head with a band of cloth—some-thing stitched in Orissa. Fair trade. Organic hemp. Or something.

Like I said: for a while. Things didn't just Happen.

We had conversations like this:

"What do you think?"

One dread dangled free, by design, from the corner of her hair-line onto her shoulder. It looked like a finger.

She looked upward, thinking, still chewing. Fork suspended. "Pre or post?"

I'd made lamb tips over couscous. "Whichever. Both."

Now she had an answer. Hid it behind her gaze, planting it on the plate. "Well, it resists a normative paradigm. Post doesn't mean anything. It all happened before."

Acid jazz tinned softly from the mp3 dock in my living room. Cars sounded like come-and-go rain as they whispered down my suburban block. My front door window was a mosaic of leaded glass, so the passing lights were just glowing shivs, trapezoids and other sharp things, in my six-by-ten feet entryway. My foyer.

We were both experts.

"In Sweden, girls used to make porridge," I said. "They'd salt it and go to sleep, thirsty. The men who brought them water, in their dreams, was whom they'd marry."

"Yes," she said.

"But it's too early. To talk about that."

See?

○

Primarily, the reason the spring was red was because of the brine shrimp. The springs in this area were high in concentrations of Dunaliella salina, pink micro-algae. It's high in beta-carotene, which protects the algae from the bright, white light. The shrimp eat the algae. This is why flamingos are pink—because they eat the shrimp, unless they were zoo-raised, and then they were fed canthaxanthin, which was a pigment used in illegal tanning pills. Farm-raised salmon were fed the same thing. To be sure they were the correct color.

But Mother Liquor was red, too, for different reasons. After Father precipitated himself from the brine, to take form and speak, the fluid wasn't brine any longer. Then it was Mother Liquor, and she was still red, her shrimp and algae long since leached of their colors by the acquiescent trees, who accepted the tamed fires, to boil the fluid out of the brine. To reduce it—Mother for Father.

For a while, we kept boiling Mother away. It wasn't until Ruby blessed the spring, and we sent the pick-axes and sluices and back-packs down underground, into the salt veins themselves. It wasn't until then that we had any eucharist.

We didn't know why Mother remained red. But it didn't matter.

Ruby led us in a hymn that day. An old one, which he'd recon-structed from the crippled hymnal's moldering pages. He'd had to wash many of the pages with quicklime to kill the book lice, so there weren't many charcoal-line-edits anymore. He'd reset the splintered hymns, in their correct forms, from memory. The little book was proud and clean, and it responded well to strangers now.

There is pow'r, pow'r, wonder working pow'r in the blood
of the land

I wasn't sure what he was leaving out. None of the others seemed to care. Sweet Water didn't care. Neither did Miss, or any of the trowels we'd promoted to people. Or the hammers-and-nails. Or the knives.

*There is pow'r, pow'r,
wonder working pow'r
in the precious
blood of the land*

Ruby came at us with a tarnished chalice. It sloshed, full of Mother. Father had been filtered slowly out, by hand, and placed back into the spring.

Ruby's cheeks were already red as he came over. To me first.

"This is the blood of the covenant."

The little, clean Bible looked pleased, flapping in the shade with the hymnal, and some of the newer books.

"Do this in remembrance of me."

It didn't take long to become the correct color, ingesting Mother like that. Like eating brine shrimp. More importantly, it didn't take long to cease being the wrong color, which was how we thought about it.

Sweet Water wasn't being idle, either.

With enough trowels, you can carve almost anything from salt. Quickly. Miss was good at finding dynamite. With Ruby's help, she recruited the nitrates and chlorides and acids. He sent his ever-growing flock of white-washed Bibles and hymnals and prayer books with her. And, escorted by the flashing herds of Miss's knives, the flock reconciled the differences between the chemicals. Convinced them to play along. To learn to love woodmeal.

With enough dynamite, you can carve almost anything even faster. The dynamites had no hope of becoming people. There was just no way, given their necessarily apocalyptic worldview. They were eschatological, whether they liked it or not, and once we sent them down, they weren't allowed to leave the mines. They had their children there, had chemical sex and shared meals in saltbox rooms they carved in their off time.

So, not only had we carved a chapel, we had baths, too. I found Sweet Water there most days, pickling in the hot waters. Preserving herself en salaison. Her red skin perpetually smooth. I wondered if Sweet Water, so long in salt water, would begin to reproduce.

Parthenogenesis. Immaculate conception. It wasn't so long ago, on those ships overrun with rats and yersinia pestis, that we thought rats could reproduce without sex, simply by being in salt. Sweet Water was another vessel, too long at sea, too long in the salt. Likely to become more.

There had been moonlight on the lake that night, but not much else. We'd taken Sweet Water's vintage Yugo out. After watching an awful production of *Copenhagen* at the community theater. We supported such things, in the months between spring and fall semesters, by telling each other "For such a limited budget, it was an effective use of minimal light," and "The new director has potential." We'd finished half a terrible bottle of scuppernong wine, which we drank because Sweet Water had a sister in the Carolinas who sent it to her. We liked to support such awful things because we believed they had a place in an enlightened society. We believed they were a part of correcting normative discourse. Of deconstructing hegemony.

There wasn't anything on Sweet Water but moonlight either. Her clothes were in a pile next to mine on the shore.

Like I said, we were experts.

"Do you ever wonder about the point?" she asked.

"Of what?"

"Anything. Research. Articles. Conference papers. Cooking dinner."

It is difficult to converse while treading water.

"Sure. I guess."

"Sure."

She flashed her chest, not at me, but at the moonlight, back-bending. "Some days it just feels like killing time."

We hadn't been at the university long, then.

"Are we wasting time now?"

"It's too early," she said, "to talk about that."

But her skin had all become one tone. There was no distinction anymore, except by touch, between lips, nipples, or elbows. If anything, it was too late. She'd never been confused about any of this. About articles, research, or the lowest APR between three cards.

The demand for salt had increased, and now, there was need for purity. For difficult salt. For a luxury that others didn't have, which meant it had to be purified.

We knew this necessitated fluids—either blood or beer—to clarify the salt. But we didn't have much beer. Miss was meeting with the Blood Father tomorrow, to negotiate. We would need a lot.

Livestock was for eating, not for purifying salt, after all.

There were sassafras leaves steeping in the bath around us. Sweet Water had eyes like blue-green algae, and I hid there now.

This was all okay.

The Blood Father had a daughter, who'd been Aztec. Vixtociatl, banished to the salt water by those who loved fresh water. Every year after that, one of the Blood Father's Aztecs stood in for Vix, who'd taught the people to harvest salt. The stand-in danced for ten days before they killed her.

So it was okay then, and it was okay now. We paid the Blood Father in salt, which seemed rather circular.

Ruby led a responsive reading that day, as the blood was escorted underground, to its new quarters. He'd patched the reading together and taught it to his others, who were no longer books or pages, but Rubys in their own rights:

By terrible things thou wilt answer us in righteousness.
Which stilleth the tumult of the peoples.
Thou visitest the earth and saltest it.

The salt we produced, in the end, was pure. We named it *flos salis,* and we traded it to our non-red allies, like the blue men fishing silver from the mountains. They were strange. They worshipped the silver, ate it, even, and it turned them blue.

Ruby used the chapel to inter the leaders of our enemies in the walls. He mummified them with dirty salt, and sealed them, semi-transparently, into their vaults with buckets of rendered fat and gypsum. We looked after the conquered belowground. In the mine. They became blood.

What was odd, though, was that these leaders looked just like people, after they'd been interred.

Once, we had traded the salt to the Hanseatic League, to the Genoans, and Venetians.

After that mob of unbelievers assassinated Joseph Smith, Brigham Young led the Mormons to the Great Salt Lake. They became the salt of the earth.

This was all okay.

I hadn't seen Father in such a long time. But I saw Mother every day. We called her Sweet Water, for we took pains to remove Father. To precipitate the union.

Because I'd been elected back then, when we had time for luxuries like democracy, I am remembered for this. I am remembered for the inalienable rights we manifested for all people. For our democratic nation. Our people and religion. I am remembered for Miss's gentle hand, tending her flocks, for Ruby's painstaking transcriptions. Saving herds and herds of Holy Writ, one re-created line at a time. I am remembered as the one who spoke to Father.

We purify more salt now than anyone, and sometimes we get together in one another's homes to tell jokes. To play games, and to sleep in the soft, suburban shells of our homes. Once per week, we put on our finest clothes and gather to hear what Ruby has to say.

Every night, before bed, Sweet Water puts lotion on her hands. She applies balm to her lips, and she reads for a few minutes, no matter how tired she is. Some nights, we sleep without touching, and the pecan trees make noise like come-and-go rain, when the wind blows.

Once More With Soul

~ Jessie Kwak

The main thing about being a crossroads devil is the hours.

Nights are the best, of course—musicians and artists are night owls naturally, and slipping out to the crossroads to sell your soul for Robert Johnson's fingers and Maria Callas' voice and Einstein's vision is a thing more naturally done past midnight.

Only, every once in a while—every once in a *very great* while—a perfectly delectable soul comes by in the bright light of the afternoon. Or decides to get an early start on their day with a quick bargain. And then, as the saying goes, early devil gets the soul.

But for the most part, it's shift work. Moon comes up, crossroads devil sets up shop.

Everyone who comes to me is talented already. They're not here for their first guitar lesson, you don't sell your soul in order to pass your freshman algebra class. You sell your soul to go beyond what's humanly possible. You sell your soul because you've seen your limits—you've seen humanity's limits—and you covet whatever lies in the unknown lands beyond that border.

My job is to unlock the gate.

There's not a lot of individual prestige as a crossroads devil. Nobody knows your name. Nobody thanks you in the liner notes or from the stage when they're receiving a lifetime achievement award.

Doesn't matter.

I see their miraculous work and I lift a glass of scotch, and no matter where they are in the world, I feel them shiver. They know who they owe for their talent.

Tonight I'm set up and ready to go right on time. The moon is *glorious*, butter yellow and heavy as it climbs up the horizon. I'm picking out cords on my six string.

The guitar's a pretty traditional crossroads devil prop, but I dig it. And in the end it doesn't matter what I'm playing, or how well I play it. When a seeker comes, they'll find me doing whatever they most desire, and they'll only hear or see the most unearthly, haunting version of it.

Because of this, some crossroads devils phone it in. One of my colleagues spent most of the 90s playing nursery rhymes on a child's recorder. It was hellish. But she thought it was hilarious when a seeker would drop to their knees in front of her screeching recorder and tell her she was dancing the most passionate flamenco or painting the most awe-inspiring landscape they'd ever seen.

I stick with the guitar. I picked my first one up in the thirties after a visit from a particularly skilled blues player. This one, a Gibson Kalamazoo model KG-14, is a tribute to him.

All right, fine. It's *his*. I stole it when he died a few years back.

I of all people know a good guitar does not a musician make, but I figured it couldn't hurt in my quest to truly master an art of my own.

If I was the confessing type, I'd admit stealing the guitar didn't help one bit.

I can recognize good work, even if I don't have the skills to produce it. When one of them walks into the crossroads under the light of the moon and says, "I have never seen anyone play chess with such precision and magnificence," I know what they're seeing. I can see it, too. Even as I know I'm just sitting on a stump plunking out a blues lick on my six-string, I envision me dressed in a fine suit—I'm always dressed in a fine suit, of course, so that's real — bending thoughtfully over a chessboard, the pieces so unearthly white they're glowing and so purely black they drink in the light, as though they somehow embody the very soul of struggle and conflict and exquisite dramatic tension. The speed of my moves and the grace of my hand create a sense of anguished lust in the very soul of the seeker.

I see what they see, and I feel how strongly they desire it.

Shit. I wish I could play that good, too.

And each time, when I lay aside my guitar, it kindles an ache and a challenge. Whatever vision they're seeing, they want it to go on forever. They want to be the ones who are doing the work.

They want to best me.

The white king topples over, tumbling from the board and into the crossroads, coming to rest at the seeker's feet like a challenge.

That's when I smile, embers glowing in my eyes and the moonlight glinting off my teeth, and ask if they'd like to play.

They always want to play.

Oh, man, I love that moment.

Tonight, I'm working on a bear of a chord progression—when I first heard Eric Clapton play it, it felt like the whole world had slid off its foundation for a fraction of a breath before he knocked it all back with a smile. When he plays it, it feels like your lover's licking all the way down your spine from inside your abdomen.

When I play it, it sounds like shit. I've been practicing for three decades.

This chord progression is my nemesis—and, as a crossroads devil, it's about as much of a nemesis as I'll get. It's a perk of the job. Different departments, sure, you get angels messing with you right and left. But crossroads devils? Nobody messes with us. Heaven wouldn't ever admit it, but they're willing to lose a few souls here and there if it means the Sistine Chapel and Mozart's *Requiem* and Miles Davis and the Theory of Relativity.

I'm so into mastering this chord progression I barely notice when she steps into the moonlight in the crossroads.

She clears her throat and I look up, preparing to see the vision of what she's here for. Does she want the gift of a golden tongue, an orator's persuasion to bring nations crumbling to their knees? Does she want effortless lightness on her feet, a dancer's grace that will get her a seat at the dinner table of any king or queen? Does she want the vision to see past the edges of the known universe, to describe what's beyond in mathematical equations that won't be understood for another hundred years?

I keep plunking at the guitar, breathless, waiting to see whatever it is she sees.

"Have you tried swapping the position of your middle and ring fingers?" She holds up her left hand, demonstrating what she means. "It makes it a lot easier to get to the next chord."

I stare at her, open-mouthed.

"Here," she says. "I can show you."

"I know how to do it," I snap acidly. As a crossroads devil, it's not my finest opening line. But in my defense, this has never happened before. "What do you want?"

She holds up her hands like she's trying to calm me down. "Sorry, I know that was pretty rude of me. I just really like to help. I'm a guitar teacher."

I lift an eyebrow. Every once in a while I get educators, but I can't do anything for them. Sure, artists and geniuses will tell you that they're here to sell their souls because they want to leave a gift to the world, but they're really doing it for the glory. The few educators that have come to me say they want to change lives, help the world. And they're telling the truth. I can't take someone's soul in payment if the motives are selfless.

"I'm sorry, there's nothing I can do." I start to tell her the thing about educators, but she cuts me off.

"Oh, I'm not here for magical talents," she tells me. "I'm actually here to thank you."

I narrow my eyes at her, taking a good look. This woman is youngish, kinky black hair pulled back in a pair of short French braids. Dark skin, dark eyes, slender, calloused hands. She's dressed nicely, but most of them do dress nicely when they come to the crossroads. Sunday best and all.

There's something about her face that's familiar, but I can't quite put a finger on it. I know I haven't seen her before.

"You might have the wrong crossroads," I tell her. "I don't think you and I have ever—"

"Oh, no. You met my great-grandfather." She points. "That's his guitar."

Now that she says it, she's the spitting image of him. He'd been wearing his nicest suit that day, too, shoes worn in but shined so bright the moon was a pair of round discs on his toes. He'd had his guitar slung around his back, and when he'd played it for me I had known there wasn't actually anything I could do for him. His skill was already unearthly.

I lean the guitar against the stump and stand to face her.

This part is always uncomfortable. It happens sometimes, though, a lover or a descendant who finally figures out the truth and comes to confront me for their loved one's soul.

"Now listen," I say.

"Tessa," she says.

I blink, not expecting her to admit her name to me. It normally takes them forever to work up the courage, and the ones who return for their loved ones's souls never tell me. I mean, I obviously already know their names. I just need them to say it out loud for the whole shtick to work.

"Listen, Tessa." I shrug, hands wide like *what-can-I-do*. "What's done is done, that's the rules. I don't make the rules. If you want to know the truth, us crossroads devils are pretty low in the pecking order."

"Oh, I'm not here about his soul," Tessa says. "Gramps never wanted to take the agreement back or anything, he was pretty happy with how everything turned out."

I was pretty happy, too. I mean, seeing a scientist go on from my crossroads to create vaccines that eradicate an entire disease is pretty cool, but I'm a sucker for a really well executed guitar lick.

"Then why are you here?" I ask.

"Like I said, I wanted to say thank you," Tessa says. "Gramps made amazing music, he lived a good life, and he died a very happy man. He said he owed it all to you.

I grimace.

"I also wanted to thank you personally. Gramps taught me how to play, and it's my life now. I mean, I perform here and there but I'm not famous, I'm never gonna be like him. And I'm definitely not interested in your bargain. But I love teaching, and I love that I can make a living playing guitar all day. It's pretty wonderful."

People have told me thank you before. It's just normally while they are in the throes of recognizing their new power, so captivated by themselves they haven't really thought about what they just did. They'll thank me breathlessly as they leave, their fingers, their vocal cords, their minds shining like pure gold.

Her great-grandfather had thanked me, too. A polite tip of his hat as he slung his guitar back around his shoulder. He'd wished me well, which seemed like a strange turn of events. And in that moment I thought maybe I'd made a wrong decision. Maybe I should have actually taken his soul.

But I don't know what I would've given him in return—I certainly couldn't have improved on his natural talent.

Tessa is staring at me expectantly.

"You're welcome?"

She smiles brightly. "I always wondered where his guitar went," she says, but before I can vanish it out of her view, her smile becomes gentle. "He would have wanted you to have it."

I frown at her. "Thank you?"

"You're welcome."

Her lips purse. I can't figure out why she's still here.

"Hey," she says finally. "I know it's not my business, but? Can I just show you that chord progression?"

My nemesis.

As we've been talking I've been thinking about what she first said about switching my middle and ring finger. I've been eager for her to leave so I could try it, but it can't hurt to try it while she's still standing here in the moonlight. I pick up her great-grandfather's guitar and sit back on my stump, letting her move my fingers into position.

"Try it again."

My fingers fly through the chord progression like magic. It's been three decades since I first heard Eric play this, and I finally can do it too. I realize I'm grinning at her. It's not a becoming look on a crossroads devil, but I can't help it.

"Thank you."

"No problem."

She watches me play through the chord progression a few times, frowning slightly at my right hand. I stop. "What is it?"

"Has anyone shown you how to pick?" she asks.

"I'm self-taught," I say defensively.

"Sorry, I didn't mean to offend you, just . . ." She tilts her head, looking at me. "My great-grandfather taught me everything he knew about playing guitar. If you want, I can show you a couple things—I've got some time tonight."

The thing she showed me with the chord progression would have saved me thirty years of struggle. I'm suddenly desperate to find out what else she knows.

"That would be nice." I think it comes out sounding chill and relaxed.

"And I get down here to see my family every few months. So if you ever wanted another lesson . . ."

I'm grinning again, but whatever. The moon flashes off the polished face of the guitar as I hand it over.

"Show me."

CONTRIBUTORS

FORREST AGUIRRE
Forrest Aguirre's work has appeared in over fifty venues, most recently *Vastarien*, *Infra-Noir*, and *Synth*. He has also written several roleplaying game supplements including *Beyond the Silver Scream* and *Killer of Giants*. He is a World Fantasy Award-recipient for his editorial work on the *Leviathan 3* anthology. His novel, *Heraclix and Pomp*, is available from Underland Press.

He hosts the blog "Forrest for The Trees" at forrestaguirre.blogspot.com and can be found on Twitter (@ForrestAguirre). Forrest lives in Madison, Wisconsin.

DARIN BRADLEY
Darin is the bestselling author of three novels—*Noise*, *Chimpanzee*, and *Totem*—as well as *Light Both Foreign and Domestic*, a collection of short stories. He lives in Texas and dreams of empty spaces.

You can follow him on Twitter (@darinbradley).

CHRISTOPHER EAST
Christopher East is a writer, editor, reviewer, and avid consumer of SF, fantasy, and spy fiction. His stories have been published in *Asimov's*, *Cosmos*, *Interzone*, *Lightspeed*, *Talebones*, and elsewhere. An attendee of the Clarion and Taos Toolbox writing workshops, he served for several years as fiction editor for *Futurismic* and is currently a regular media reviewer for *Lightspeed*. He blogs extensively about writing, fiction, film, television, music, comics, and more at www.christopher-east.com. Currently he lives in Portland, Oregon, where he works for an occupational safety consultancy.

SCOTT EDELMAN
Scott Edelman has published nearly 100 short stories in magazines such as *Analog, PostScripts, The Twilight Zone,* and *Dark Discoveries,* and in anthologies such as *Why New Yorkers Smoke, MetaHorror, Crossroads: Southern Tales of the Fantastic, Once Upon a Galaxy, Moon Shots, Mars Probes,* and the recent Harlan Ellison tribute anthology *The Unquiet Dreamer.*

His collection of zombie fiction, *What Will Come After,* was published in 2010, and was a finalist for both the Stoker Award and the Shirley Jackson Memorial Award. His most recent collection, *Tell Me Like You Done Before (and Other Stories Written on the Shoulders of Giants),* was published in 2018. He has been a Bram Stoker Award finalist eight times, in the categories of Short Story and Long Fiction.

Additionally, Edelman worked for the Syfy Channel for more than thirteen years as editor of *Science Fiction Weekly, SCI FI Wire,* and *Blastr.* He was the founding editor of *Science Fiction Age,* which he edited during its entire eight-year run. He also edited *SCI FI* magazine, previously known as *Sci-Fi Entertainment,* as well as two other SF media magazines, *Sci-Fi Universe* and *Sci-Fi Flix.* He has also been a four-time Hugo Award finalist for Best Editor.

NICOLE FELDRINGER
Nicole Feldringer's short fiction has appeared in *GigaNotoSaurus, Cast of Wonders,* and the anthologies *Press Start to Play* and *Loosed Upon the World,* among other venues. She currently lives in Northern California where she is a climate scientist and Professor of Earth and Planetary Sciences.

BEN GAMBLIN
Ben Gamblin is a lifelong resident of the Pacific Northwest. He currently lives in Tacoma with his partner and several furry roommates.

Ben's work has appeared in *Ink Stains Anthology, The Dark City Mystery Magazine*, and the *Strange Stories Vol. 1* collection from Forty-Two Books.

Follow Ben on Instagram (@bengamblinofficial).

○

INGRID GARCIA

Ingrid Garcia help to sell local wines in a vintage wine shop in Cádiz, and writes speculative fiction in her spare time. For years, she was unpublished. But to her utter surprise—after years of receiving nothing but rejections—she's sold stories to *F&SF*, and the *Ride the Star Wind* and *Sword and Sonnet* anthologies, amongst others.

She can be found on Twitter (@ingridgarcia253) and is busy setting up a website.

○

A. P. HOWELL

A. P. Howell has worked as a data wrangler, archivist, ice cream scooper, and webmaster, not necessarily in that order. She lives in suburban Philadelphia with a delightful pair of kids, a sweet spouse, and a dog who loves people but hates canines and groundhogs. She does her part to make the sun rise as part of a Morris dance side.

Her website is aphowell.com, and she sometimes tweets into the void @APHowell.

○

EMMA JOHNSON-RIVARD

Emma Johnson-Rivard received her Masters in Creative Writing at Hamline University. She currently serves as the Poetry Editor and Assistant Fiction Editor for the *Macabre Museum*. Her work has appeared in *Tales to Terrify, Fearsome Critters*, and others.

E.E. King is a painter, performer, writer, and biologist. She'll do anything that won't pay the bills, especially if it involves animals. She's worked with children in Bosnia, crocodiles in Mexico, frogs in Puerto Rico, egrets in Bali, mushrooms in Montana, archaeologists in Spain, butterflies in South Central Los Angeles, lectured on island evolution and marine biology on cruise ships in the South Pacific and the Caribbean, painted murals in Los Angeles and Spain.

King was the founding Director of the Esperanza Community Housing's Art & Science Program, worked as an artist-in-residence in Los Angeles, San Francisco, Sarajevo, and the J. Paul Getty Museum's and Science Center's Arts & Science Development Program. Her landmark mural, *A Meeting of the Minds* (121' x 33') can be seen on Mercado La Paloma in Los Angeles. King has also painted murals in Cuenca, Spain and in Tuscany, Italy.

King has been published widely, and Ray Bradbury once called her stories "marvelously inventive, wildly funny and deeply thought-provoking."

Check out her paintings, writing, musings and books at www.elizabetheveking.com.

Jessie Kwak is a freelance writer and author living in Portland, Oregon. She writes character-driven sci-fi and fantasy with a liberal dose of explosions, gunfights, crime, and dinner parties. She likes to make her readers laugh. She is the author of supernatural thriller *From Earth and Bone*, the Durga System series of gangster sci-fi novels, and productivity guide *From Chaos to Creativity*. When she's not writing B2B marketing copy or scribbling away on her latest novel, you can find her riding her bike to the brewpub, road tripping with her husband, or juggling various sewing projects.

You can learn more about Jessie Kwak at www.jessiekwak.com, or follow her on Twitter (@jkwak).

SHANNON LAWRENCE

A fan of all things fantastical and frightening, Shannon Lawrence writes primarily horror and fantasy. Her stories can be found in over thirty anthologies and magazines, including *Space and Time Magazine* and Word Horde's *Fright Into Flight*. Her short story collection *Blue Sludge Blues & Other Abominations* is now available. When she's not writing, she's hiking through the wilds of Colorado and photographing her magnificent surroundings, where, coincidentally, there's always a place to hide a body or birth a monster.

You can find her online at www.thewarriormuse.com.

○

GERRI LEEN

Gerri Leen lives in Northern Virginia and originally hails from Seattle. In addition to being an avid reader, she's passionate about horse racing, tea, ASMR vids, and creating weird tacos. She has work appearing in *Nature, Galaxy's Edge, Escape Pod, Daily Science Fiction, Cast of Wonders*, and others. She's edited several anthologies for independent presses, is finishing some longer projects, and is a member of SFWA and HWA.

See more at gerrileen.com.

○

MARK MILLS

A Cincinnati resident, Mark Mills teaches composition, literature, film, philosophy, music appreciation, and basic Noa robotic. He has published work in *Tor.com, Grievous Angel, Necrotic Tissue, Short Story America*, and other publications. He worked on and appeared in several low budget films, including *Satanic Yuppies, Live Nude Shakespeare, Chickboxin' Underground, Zombie Cult Massacre*, and *Uberzombiefrau*. Having recently survived advanced stage cancer, he hopes to have his brain implanted in a robotic body and avoid any further health woes.

CHRISTI NOGLE

Christi Nogle's horror stories have appeared in publications such as *Pseudopod, Vastarien, Nightscript,* and *Tales to Terrify.* She teaches college composition and lives in Boise, Idaho with her partner Jim and their dogs and cat.

Follow her at christinogle.com or on Twitter (@christinogle).

○

TAMMIE PAINTER

Tammie Painter turns wickedly strong tea into imaginative fiction. She's the author of the historical fantasy novel *Domna,* as well as *The Osteria Chronicles* where myths come to life as you've never seen them before.

Learn more at TammiePainter.com

○

JOSH ROUNTREE

Josh Rountree writes fantasy, horror, science fiction, and a lot of weird nonsense. His short fiction has appeared in numerous magazines and anthologies, including *Beneath Ceaseless Skies, Realms of Fantasy, and A Punk Rock Future.* A collection of his strange rock and roll fiction, *Can't Buy Me Faded Love,* was published by Wheatland Press.

Josh worked at the video store featured in his story until it finally succumbed to the end times. Since then, he's wandered the post apocalyptic wilds of Texas, searching for a VHS copy of *Streets of Fire* and tweeting about movies, books, and guitars on Twitter (@ josh_rountree).

Learn more at www.joshrountree.com.

○

ERICA SAGE

Erica Sage is an English teacher and writer who lives in Washington State with her two sons. When not reading and writing, she loves to hike around Mount Rainier and travel whenever and wherever. She is the author of the young adult novel *Jacked Up.*

Follow her on Instagram and Twitter (@erica_sage).

○

LORRAINE SCHEIN

Lorraine Schein is a NY writer. Her work has appeared in *New Letters, Hotel Amerika, Strange Horizons, Witches & Pagans, Little Blue Marble,* and *VICE Terraform,* and in the anthologies *Tragedy Queens: Stories Inspired by Lana del Rey & Sylvia Plath, Spectral Lines,* and *Phantom Drift. The Futurist's Mistress,* her poetry book, is available from mayapplepress.com. "The blood jet is poetry."

○

J. DEE STANLEY

J. Dee Stanley, a weird person who writes weird stories about weird people, may appear vaguely familiar like something half-remembered from a dream. However, J. Dee Stanley is entirely fictitious and any resemblance to real persons, dead or alive, or other real-life entities, past or present, is purely coincidental. He studied Literature and Anthropology at Auburn University before escaping to the wild, and has been infrequently observed living in the American Southeast with his spouse, two cats, and seasonal allergies.

○

RICHARD THOMAS

Richard Thomas is the award-winning author of seven books—*Disintegration* and *Breaker* (Penguin Random House Alibi), *Transubstantiate, Herniated Roots, Staring into the Abyss, Tribulations* and *The Soul Standard* (Dzanc Books). He has been nominated for the Bram Stoker, Shirley Jackson, and Thriller awards. His over 150 stories in print include *The Best Horror of the*

Year (Volume Eleven), Behold!: Oddities, Curiosities and Undefinable Wonders (Bram Stoker winner), *Cemetery Dance* (twice), *PANK, storySouth, Gargoyle, Weird Fiction Review, Shallow Creek, The Seven Deadliest, Gutted: Beautiful Horror Stories, Qualia Nous, Chiral Mad* (numbers 2-4), *PRISMS,* and *Shivers VI.*

Visit www.whatdoesnotkillme.com for more information.

○

JOHN WATERFALL
John Waterfall is a writer living in Manhattan and a graduate of the New School's creative writing MFA program. He is the proud father of two cats and one baby girl. His work can be found in *Jersey Devil Press, Crack the Spine, The Colored Lens,* and others.

You can follow him on Twitter (@JohnCWaterfall).

○

WENDY N. WAGNER
Wendy N. Wagner is the author of the SF eco-thriller *An Oath of Dogs,* as well as two novels for the Pathfinder role-playing game. She has published more than forty short stories. She is the Managing/Senior Editor of both *Lightspeed* and *Nightmare* magazines, and served as the Guest Editor of Nightmare's *Queers Destroy Horror!* special issue. An avid gamer and gardener, she lives in Portland, Oregon, with her very understanding family.

○

TODD ZACK
Todd Zack is a social worker, writer, musician, living in southwest Florida. His alternative rock band, Tape Recorder 3, composes soundtracks for independent films and documentaries. His journalism and fiction pieces have appeared in *Thrasher Magazine, Red Fez, Crimson Streets, Terrors Unimagined* Anthology and several recent volumes of *The Literary Hatchet.* His novelette, "Food for the Moon," is in The Great Void's *Unreal Vol. 1.*

MARK TEPPO

Mark Teppo is the author of more than a dozen novels, scattered across many genres. He's a synthesist, trouble-maker, and cat herder. He is also the publisher of Underland Press. His favorite Tarot card is, in fact, the Moon.

Follow him on Twitter (@markteppo).